GWEN HUNTER

Somewhere in the darkness, a stranger has her daughter…

SHADOW VALLEY

The space opened up, offering a dramatic view, fog rising in spirals over the treetops. I hated it. Hated everything about it. This was where my baby had suffered at the hands of the man I should have shot to protect her. Fighting tears and the chill that suffused my bones as sweat from the climb dried, I looked over the camp.

I struggled with a breath that wanted to freeze in my lungs. When it came it was painful, ragged, tearing, a sound like rotten fabric ripping. I felt Caleb move closer, his hand on my shoulder, so hot it burned. Unable to accept the comfort of the small gesture, I stepped away and walked to the small sleeping space. The second breath, when it came, was harder, a coarse groan. I erupted, kicking into the pile of brush again and again, movement so vicious it sent leaves spiraling down the heights in a lazy windmill. There was no sound on the mountain but the frenzied rustle and my breathing. I kicked and kicked until every last leaf was gone, until the spot was clear of that first night Bella had spent with Dell Shirley.

But I didn't cry. Not one tear.

"So much for the cops doing a crime-scene workup of this place later on," Caleb muttered under his breath, half laughing. The laughter died and he was solemn when he spoke again. "Come on. I'll take you down again and Ruth can get you back to the ranger station."

Whirling, I speared the tracker with my eyes. "Over my dead body." My voice was raspy and pitted as old stone, carrying grief that vibrated in the air between us. Caleb's face didn't change, expression didn't waver. "Over my dead, putrefied and decaying body." I heaved a breath so deep it growled. "I came up here to look for a note. To find my daughter. And I'll do that or die trying."

GWEN HUNTER

SHADOW VALLEY

MIRA

ISBN 0-7783-2130-4

SHADOW VALLEY

Copyright © 2005 by Gwen Hunter.

www.MIRABooks.com

Printed in U.S.A.

CAST OF CHARACTERS

Main Characters

MacKenzie Morgan (Mac)—photographer

IsaBella Morgan—Mac's daughter

Marlow Morgan—estranged husband of Mac

Dell Shirley, aka Delano Alton Gregory—geologist, survivalist

Caleb Howell—North Carolina main tracker

Burgess Morgan—Marlow's brother

Rachael Morgan—former 1950s screen star; mother to
 Marlow and Burgess

Gianna Parker Smythe—snow bunny

Park Service and Search-And-Rescue (SAR)

Yolanda Perkins (Yo)—forest ranger

Joel Durkowitz—incident commander

Jedidiah Wilkins (Jed)—dog handler

Ed—Jed's dog

Big Bertha—Ed's mama

Buddin Hasty Team—Buddy Buddin, Ned Gorman,
 Raymond Hamilton

Chandler Dog Team

Perkins Backtrack Team

Rebart ATV Team

Nesbitt ATV Team

Lonnie Curbeam—Tennessee dog handler

Buggy (Bug Face)—Lonnie's dog

Adin Boone—Tennessee main tracker

Law Enforcement and Emergency Medical Technicians (EMTs)
Harman Harschell IV (Har Har)—sheriff
Ira Schwartz—sheriff's right-hand man
Robbie Wightman—sheriff department investigator
Evelyn Wightman—radio communications and Robbie's wife
Ruth Ferguson, Rick, Mason Bartholomew—EMTs
Maxine Kloninger, M.D.—forensic pathologist

Ranger Station
Oline
Pearl
Sherman, Sheridan and Shelby—brothers and retired cops
Silas Newton—life partner of Ira Schwartz
Otis Bumgardner—preacher

Other
Doc McElhaney—M.D. and photographer

Prologue

And Cain said to his brother, "Let us go out into the field." And when they were in the field, Cain rose up against Abel his brother and killed him.

—Genesis 4:8

I had a Sunday school teacher once, years ago when I was young, who told me that for each of us there existed a reason, an event, that could cause us to do violence. To take another life.

I never believed her. Until now.

Now I know.

Deep in the dark heart of each of us lies a primitive soul. A soul dedicated to blood and the taking of life. I killed to protect, to save. And if God is watching, perhaps that is my only absolution.

1

The green gloom and the angle of dawn sunlight were perfect, the new light and last night's shadows offering harsh contrast against the spring foliage. Pressing the shutter, I took half a dozen shots in little more than a second, using the flash to smooth out the austere neutrals and accentuate the color saturation.

Adjusting the aperture in quarter stops, I took twelve more from two different positions on the bank, one set from above the old cabin site, the final set from below, turning the camera for longer shots, twisting to get just the right angle of the pliant, mutable light. All the while, I murmured to the camera, to the stone and mortar, to the seventy-year-old trees I used as frames for some shots, my voice revealing the excitement building inside me. It was a tingle, an electric charge that always came on a shoot when suddenly everything fell into place and the light was perfect and I knew—just *knew*—that I was getting great shots.

Grinding my feet into the rough shale for balance, I steadied the camera. The rising sun cast feathery shadows against the fire-blackened stones of the old chimney

ACKNOWLEDGMENTS

My thanks to the National Park Service, who provided
answers to technical questions.
David and Ellen Jenkins, of Arrow Creek campground in
Gatlinburg, Tennessee.
Rock Hill, South Carolina, Police Canine Unit for
SAR techniques.
Ed Howe, for hunting, weapon and ATV info.

Phil Moody, photographer.
Terry Rouche, photographer.
Joy Robinson, for contacts and support.

Joyce Wright, for proofreading.
Peggy Pharr, for proofreading.
Pam and Mike Hege, for proofreading the horse info!

Jason Adams, M.D.
Isom Lowman, M.D.
J. Michael Glenn, M.D., in Florida
Susan Prater, O.R. Tech and sister-in-love, in South Carolina
Barry Benfield, R.N., in South Carolina
Susan B. Jacobs, R.N., in South Carolina
Randall Pruett, M.L.T. and R.N., in South Carolina

As always, for making this a stronger book:
Miranda Stecyk, my editor at MIRA Books, who outdid herself
this time! I've had a lot of editors over the years. This one is
"Pert Near Perfect," as they say in the mountains!
Jeff Gerecke, of JCA Literary Agency, Inc.
My writers group for all the help in making this novel work.
Thanks for bleeding all over its bits and pieces.
My husband, for answers to questions that pop up, for his
catching so much in the rewrites and for his endless patience.

Aline Prater
Who, at the time of this writing, is 98.
"Still kickin'. Just not so high."

and pricked brightly at rough, frost-limned blocks of the aged granite foundation. Lichen, ferns and decades of fallen leaves had obscured the outline of the old home. Mountain maple, scrub cedar, water oak and dogwood twined with vines grew along the exposed stone border, easing root and branch inside the foundation itself, moving in from the surrounding forest, taking over the clearing and cozying up to the chuckling creek only yards below.

The last shots on the roll I took from inside the foundation itself, going for close-ups of the stones and crumbling, yellowed mortar, the frost quickly melting in the spring sunshine. Checking the light meter constantly, I adjusted for the rising sun and shortening shadows, feeling an ecstasy swell and stretch, encompassing the whole clearing. As the light shifted, a glimmer caught my eye, the unexpected bonus of a dew-laden spiderweb transformed into a geometric rainbow, bright against deteriorating cement, quivering and shimmering beneath the spider's legs. I whirled away.

It took forty-five seconds to change film in the Nikon F4 camera, a process I completed as I slid down the bank to the creek, tossing the used roll into my sling bag and inserting a fresh one from the same brick of film. Wading out thigh deep, I quickly consulted the light meter and dropped it into my sweatshirt pocket, then planted my feet on the uneven creek bottom. The hip waders I had donned before dawn were no longer a hindrance as they had been on the hillside. Felt soles cushioned my feet and protected me from slipping and falling into the frigid stream. Rushing water pressed against the thick rubber; even through the ample layers of socks, I could feel the icy temperature of the creek leaching body warmth from my legs and feet. My toes threatened to cramp in the cold.

The stream chittered and gurgled, as if talking to the rising sun. The light was still green, as though it had absorbed some essence of the leaves it passed through, giving the world a delicate, subtle aspect. But it wouldn't last—it never did. Perhaps only minutes remained.

My heart sped up, its pounding a bit irregular. Several shots later I stepped deeper, maneuvering toward the curved line of the broken stone dam, my knees bent against the current. Careful to keep the remains of the cabin framed in the shot, I followed the pathway laid out the evening before, placing my feet carefully, choosing my shots with absolute abandon.

The sun was coming up fast now and I cut the flash, closing down the aperture half an f-stop to decrease the amount of light through the lens. *I wasn't going to make it. I wasn't going to get finished.* "No," I whispered, my fingers clumsy for an instant as I again changed rolls. "No, no, no no no no." I was almost sobbing.

I had been frozen, numb, emotionally paralyzed for so long, and now I was finally moving, working again. And the light wasn't going to hold.

Stepping back up onto the bank, I took shots of the ruptured dam, changing film and aperture settings midway through the sequence. Focusing on a solitary leaf floating on the fast-moving water, I followed it through the broken arms of the dam, the light glimmering greenly on the rippling surface. As the light continued to change, I moved downstream, framing the rough stone chutes at the sides of the creek, and the pump house foundations farther down. Mist rose from the sun-warmed water, softening the harsh edges as I took another roll of film of the old, abandoned fish hatchery, and then another.

I suddenly began to think I might make it, if the light lasted another two minutes. *Just two minutes…*

"Mom. Above you on the ledge!"

Whirling, I looked where Bella pointed, high up across the far meadow. Coming down the ridge was a man on horseback, a packhorse negotiating the path behind him. It was sheer serendipity, with the light catching the mist through the trees in long streams. The day had matured radically, according to the light meter. Without even thinking, I slipped on the lens shade and increased the shutter speed to 250 for the brighter shot. "Get me the telephoto," I shouted, taking quick shots on automatic, letting the camera do the work of changing the aperture for me.

"Right behind you," she said, a grin in her voice.

I turned and took the adjustable Nikon lens from her, releasing the standard 50 mm I had used all morning, and quickly replaced it with the heavier one. She took the lens, tossing her binoculars over her shoulder on their slender strap, and stepped away.

With the adjustable lens, I could go from 80 mm to 210 mm with a pull of the barrel. I shot it all the way out and aimed at the horseman.

His hat was old and brown, a western type with a band of sweat showing traces of white salt. His chin was clean-shaven, the only thing I could make out beneath the brim. Riding western style, he neck-reined the sure-footed roan, his butt settled so firmly against the high cantle of the saddle that he could have been part horse himself. He wore a faded flannel shirt of soft green plaid and a denim jacket over it. Denim-clad legs gripped the horse beneath him, and old boots, the heels worn into rounded half-moons were steady in the stirrups. A long-haired blond dog loped ahead of him scouting at point, a reddish one trotted closer to the packhorse, a half length behind and out of the way of careless hooves.

I bent into a squat, moving laterally across the low rise, and took a second roll of film as he descended. "Yes!" I said, snapping off the shots. "Oh, this is *wonderful*. Beautiful. Why don't you lift your face? Come on! Lift your face...." But he didn't, not once. I used thirty-six shots on his descent, changing rolls only after he disappeared into the mist behind the trees.

The light had faded to pale morning gray long before I finished the last rolls of film from the brick, but I had what I needed. I was filled with elation, the euphoria, the sheer bliss that comes with success. I had done it. I had done it all alone! My legs were quivering with exhaustion, my back a constant ache. I was shaking from sugar deprivation and my usual faint headache had started. But I had really done it. The light had lasted, and it had been green and glorious, and I had that spider and the horseman.... A dull nausea settled in my belly. I remembered finally to breathe. I had completed an entire shoot without Marlow and his careful planning and his absolute control. And dang it, the shots were good! I knew it!

Pulling off the hip waders, I laced up Timberland hiking boots, loosely tied them, and finger-combed my too-curly hair as I stored the telephoto lens and the light meter, and slipped the Nikon into its sturdy cloth carryall. Moving back toward our campsite, I put the exposed rolls of film in the bag and stacked the equipment in a pile by the bedrolls. Pulling off the damp sweatshirt, I buttoned a camp shirt over my long-sleeved purple undershirt, leaving the hem loose. Bella had breakfast on and coffee made on the little propane stove; the scents of bacon and biscuits and the divine aroma of coffee wafted on the dispersing mist.

I had taken nearly two bricks of film, thirty-eight rolls and almost fourteen hundred shots, in the last twenty-four hours. There were a few great shots that would go to *Field and Stream*, and hundreds of good ones that I would send to a stock agency in New York to be sold as needed for a one-time-use fee. My lab time would be extravagant. And I was *starved*.

Fitting the F4 into my backpack and pulling my older Nikon F3 to me, I inserted a roll of black-and-white film as my stomach grumbled and the nausea increased. I needed to eat, but this was for family. Well, for me, then, as Marlow no longer wanted to be family. For as long as Bella had been coming on professional photography shoots with Marlow and me, we had chronicled the experience afterward with a roll of black-and-white. For posterity. For memories. For family. And just because Marlow was an ass, living it up in Aspen with some ski instructor he'd met at his mother's deathbed vigil last winter, did not mean that all traditions should be broken. Lifting the camera, I took a half roll of Bella as she sat before the little stove, catching a pensive look as she stared into the small flame.

At the shutter clicks, she looked up, both amused and mildly annoyed. "So stop with the cameras already. I'm hungry and so are you." She scooped bacon and canned biscuits onto a tin plate and added a fork, packets of butter and jelly from a Hardees in Asheville, and a napkin. "Put it down and eat before your blood sugar plunges to twelve."

Shaking badly now, I dropped the camera on its thong around my neck and poured coffee from the little percolator—I refused to drink instant even while camping. I was not uncivilized. Adding creamer left over from the same fast-food place, and three packets of sugar, I drank it down as fast as the scalding temperature allowed before sitting down. Bella drank her coffee mostly white, looking far too pretty to be my own flesh and blood in her purple thermal undershirt and skintight jeans.

Sucking air to cool my burned tongue, I said, "I should

never have let you take that first-aid course with me. You've been way too bossy ever since. Don't you know you're not supposed to boss your mom until she's old and decrepit?"

"And did you put on sunscreen this morning, my old and decrepit mother?"

"See what I mean?" Forking open a biscuit, I added a mound of butter and crumbled a stick of blackened bacon into it. I never worried about fat or cholesterol on a shoot. My heart would have the next few weeks to recuperate.

"You get that cowboy and his horses?"

"Um-hmm." I nodded, taking a huge bite.

"He was riding a good-looking roan," she said. "You gonna use the shots?"

I swallowed. "I didn't get his face, but yeah, they'll make good stock shots—unless he happens to show up for breakfast and pose for a close-up or two. That I could use for *Field and Stream.*"

"You're in luck, then. I think that dog is his."

I glanced up and spotted a dog, part golden retriever, part mutt, on the far bank of the creek. Its tail wagged slowly as it evaluated us, nose in the air, ears pricked, tongue lolling. A moment later, a second dog trotted up, a reddish, smaller version of the first. After a hesitation, this one barked, coming up on its hind legs and pounding down on the earth with excitement. Bella laughed. A high-pitched whistle silenced the barking and both dogs turned back into the woods.

I didn't like being approached by anyone; Bella and I were not in an area of woods where camping was encouraged. We had hiked up more than five miles from the park ranger station to find the long-deserted fish hatchery. The woods were desolate and we were miles from the nearest campground.

Easing over to the bedrolls Bella had secured, I fished for the gun I kept there. I hated guns. But I hated even more the idea of being attacked by a rabid raccoon or being unable to frighten off an amorous stag or a pack of feral dogs on the hunt. Without Marlow, it was our best protection. I slipped the small .38 Smith and Wesson, which had belonged to my father, into my waistband, and pulled my camp shirt over the bulge.

Bella rolled her eyes. "Men who like dogs and who ride gorgeous horses are not dangerous. Besides, you hate that thing."

"Then it won't matter that it's under my shirt and not in my hand, will it?"

"Long as you don't shoot off your ass." Bella laughed when she spoke, tossing her heavy dark braid back over her shoulder. "I would hate to carry you down this mountain, bleeding and moaning and all. You may have lost a few pounds since Dad left, but you ain't skin and bones."

"Thank you so very much. And don't use unladylike language. *Ass* is not a nice word. The proper term is buttocks."

"You sound like a mother. All prissy."

"You say that like it's a bad thing. And so long as you get the film delivered, you can leave me," I said wryly. "Or maybe you could borrow the cowboy's horse and haul me down to the ranger station."

"Promise?" my daughter, the horse lover, begged me facetiously. "I could take it home with me!"

"Cute. You already have a horse. Don't get greedy."

The dogs appeared on the far bank again, and moments later I spotted the roan through the foliage, moving downstream. The wind was behind us, and unless the horseman was suffering with a head cold, he could surely smell the coffee and bacon. He moved easily in the saddle, as if he spent long hours on horseback. When he reached the creek, he whistled again, a different set of notes, and the two dogs drank. He let his horses nose forward as well, and they dropped their heads to suck in long drafts. As they slurped water, he studied us.

He had an easy smile and bright green eyes beneath the brown brim, an average face with light eyelashes and brows that caught the sun when he pushed back his hat. "I've been smelling that coffee for the last half mile," he called. He crossed an arm over the saddle horn and leaned against it. A bit of white undershirt peeked out from beneath his sleeves. "I hope you ladies intend to take pity on a tired man who ran out of instant coffee two days ago. I would be forever in your debt."

Bella looked at me, her brows raised. She had a good ear for accents and this fellow was definitely not from around here. I stood, holding my cup easily. "Charleston?" I asked.

He tipped his hat, like someone from an old western, and smiled. "You found my secret. Dell Shirley, formerly of the Citadel, the U.S. government, and currently of the University of South Carolina, on sabbatical. Geologist by profession, which is why I am up in 'them thar hills.' I have ID if it would help." There was laughter in his voice and amusement in his eyes, but his face held understanding and patience. He was in no hurry.

I suddenly felt foolish. If Marlow had been here, the horseman, Dell, would already be at the camp stove, plastic cup in hand. "Arabica beans suit you? They've been ground for three days, and might be a little stale," I said.

"Ma'am, if you offered the used grounds to me, I'd chew them up and swallow them, I'm that starved for coffee."

I laughed. "A man after my own heart. Come on over,

then." Softly, I added to my daughter, "We are hiking. Nothing more. We expect your father back before noon, should he ask."

"I remember the rules, Mom. But, jeez, he's a geologist, not Jason from *Friday the Thirteenth* or something. *And* he's good-looking, for an old guy." She slid a sidelong glance at me. Bella knew her daddy was happy, while I was lonely. Once she'd realized that Marlow wasn't coming back, she'd begun trying to fix my life. For weeks she had been pointing out eligible men to me with a calculated intensity and sly amusement at her new game.

"We also have a rule about matchmaking."

"You have the rule about matchmaking. I don't."

"Bella," I warned. "The divorce isn't even final. Don't."

"Yes, ma'am," she sighed. But she didn't look at all repentant. She had that familiar, speculative, mischievous—okay, downright dangerous—glint in her eye. The one that has caused early heart attacks in mothers for generations.

"Bella. Don't you dare," I begged, trying to sound stern, but fighting my own smile.

2

Dell waded his horses through the creek. The dogs tramped across the ruined dam, jumping the gaps where water rushed through, slipping on the wet stones and arriving just in front of their master. The reddish dog, a male, claimed my daughter with the rough swipe of a tongue across her jaw, and settled down beside her. His eyes stared at the crumbs remaining on her plate. The blond dog took up watch on the high point of the hill, near the chimney.

Dell dropped the reins to the ground, an indication of his mounts' training and disposition. They wandered to the grass at the pump house foundations and began to munch. Dell pulled off his denim jacket and squatted down near the cookstove as Bella poured him a cup of steaming coffee.

"Beautiful morning." Holding the double-walled camp mug to his nose, he breathed in long and sensuously, refused the offer of sugar and cream and drank the dark brew. "Ladies, you know the way to a man's heart, right here. It isn't stale at all, ma'am. It's really very good."

"Bella Morgan," Bella stated, cutting her eyes at me.

"Mac Morgan," I said.

Dell paused, blowing across his cup. "Mac?" Before I could respond with my usual, *"It's short for MacKenzie,"* he repeated, "Mac Morgan," as if testing it for familiarity. "Interesting name. But you two women shouldn't be up in the mountains alone like this. It can be dangerous." His eyes surveyed our camp as he spoke, taking in the bear bag hanging from the trees, the propane stove with its extra tank of fuel, the toilet tissue on a branch beside the shovel, and two bedrolls piled by the mesh backpacks of camera equipment and personal supplies. I could have kicked myself for not bringing along an extra bedroll.

"My husband will be joining us later on today. Kept over on business. You know how it is."

Dell looked at me, his eyes missing nothing, his face revealing less. His gaze dropped to my left hand, the band of white skin marking the spot where my ring had once been. A slight chill slithered up my neck, creeping across the hair on my nape. The reddish dog rose up from his place on the ground and sniffed at the air. Bella sat suddenly still, looking back and forth from me to Dell, alarm in her eyes. I knew she could sense my disquiet. I had always been an open book to my daughter.

"More coffee?" I asked, resisting the urge to close my right hand over my left.

"It would be a kindness. Ma'am. That's the *truth*." The accent on the word truth was subtle, but I couldn't have missed it. I held his eyes, saying nothing, my left hand out, waiting for his cup. Finally he smiled and passed me the mug for a refill. "That's Rufus there," he said, nodding to the red dog, who looked over in response. "And that's his mama up on the hill. Polly is bit skittish with strangers but she'll come around," he assured Bella.

I said nothing, and he sipped his coffee. "I found a gold nugget in a worked vein on the side of a hill about six miles upstream." A light brightened his eyes, making his face seem instantly younger. Carefree. "Have you ever seen raw gold?" Suddenly we were on safer ground, the look on his face like that of a schoolboy with a rock collection. "Prettiest thing in the world, gold in its natural setting, twisting its way through a line of white quartz."

Rufus sat back down, and I poured myself a second cup of coffee, this one with less sugar and more cream. "Only small nuggets, and never in the ground," I said. "I'll bet it's beautiful."

"These hills had gold in them once. Miners took what they wanted and moved on. A single man can still pan or mine enough gold to support himself if he doesn't plan to live too lavishly. Or mine silver. Used to be a rich place, the Appalachians. Now miners and geologists look for other riches here."

He grinned, exposing white teeth, the bottom row not quite even. "I dug out some of the gold from the vein. Want to see it? I have a few samples in my tote. And a bit of malachite, and what I'm pretty sure will prove to be a small sapphire once I polish it up. And a few Indian artifacts I picked up last week." His excitement was contagious, the animate energy of a professional talking about his love. He was stepping to his horses as he spoke, the plastic mug cradled in his hand. Polly trotted down the hill, following him, scouting with nose and ears. Dell sent her off in another direction with the flick of his finger.

"What was that all about?" Bella whispered, referring to the moment of disquiet.

"I don't know," I whispered back. "Mother's nerves? Just be careful. We'll give this another half hour and then we pack up and head back to the car."

"We can't. We told him we were waiting for Daddy."

"But we didn't say where—"

"More coffee?" she asked me in warning, and I knew that Dell was within earshot.

"Please," I said. "And another slice of bacon. Dell, would you like a biscuit? Bella makes a fine pan of canned Hungry Jack and bacon."

"That would be mighty generous," he said, tossing down two vinyl mats. "I ate rehydrated eggs about five-thirty, but they're long gone. Let's see what we have here," he grunted as he sat on one thin pad and placed a bag on the other. It was a heavy-duty canvas satchel with Velcro clasps, similar to the bags holding my camera equipment, but it was filled with small sealed pockets and scores of smaller plastic and cloth bags, each tied with a strip of rawhide.

Polly circled back and looked at Bella, mistrust in her gaze, her jaw held low, her tail down and unmoving.

"I don't think Polly likes me," Bella said.

"Don't mind her. She's just jealous. She'll become friendly soon enough. Polly likes young girls." He lifted out a handful of small drawstring sacks, setting them on the vinyl mat at his knees, putting the tin plate of bacon and biscuits Bella handed him to the side.

Rufus scratched his way into a different position, turning his attention to the new plate, but Dell ignored him. The dog whined low in his throat, and Bella soothed him with a careless stroke.

Dell opened four of the small bags, emptying the contents into Bella's hands. I had seen nuggets of gold before, the bright raw metal twined with white quartz, but these were large, one perhaps as big as my thumb, and mostly gold.

"Ooh. Look, Mom."

"I'm seeing," I said softly. It was beautiful. And somehow just a bit odd that he would share such valuables with us. But perhaps this was his way of making up for the moment of disquiet.

The second drawstring sack held the malachite, a greenish, rough stone. Then the sapphire appeared in the palm of Bella's hand, a dull rock more greenish than blue.

"This is a perfect white quartz arrowhead," he said, adding to the pile of pretty baubles. "And this—" he held up a thin column of rock "—is a bit of aquamarine I picked up in Brazil. See how it looks like the sky reflected on the water, even uncut and unpolished? Back at the cabin I have emeralds from South America, olivine—that's peridot—and topaz that I mined last year in these very hills. Girls like pretty things," he confided to me before turning back to his satchel.

The phrase startled me. *Girls like pretty things.* The feeling of dread I had banished only minutes before was back, crawling insistently at the base of my skull. I stood and finished off my coffee in one long scalding swallow that burned my tongue. "I have to wash up," I said, turning off the propane that had kept the coffee warm. Bella nodded to me without looking up from the pile of stones. Dell ignored me. The .38 was warm and secure against my belly, close to my hands, not in the back of my pants, as Bella had accused me. *Girls like pretty things....*

I cleaned up the dishes in the creek, packed the lightweight stove and eating utensils in the backpack Bella had hauled up the mountain. The mother dog, Polly, followed me with her eyes, alert and on guard. What was it Dell had said about the animal? *She likes young girls.* I wasn't sure I liked the sound of that.

As I worked on the packs, I kept my eyes on Bella, willing her to glance up so I could give her one of the "mother looks"—her phrase for a silent message that said several things on different levels. She only turned my way once, while laughing at something he said, and her glance was fleeting. I didn't have time to react. I didn't have time to give her the *Be careful, he's a man, we're alone, keep your wits about you*, look I had ready.

The F4 was in the bottom of the backpack I usually carried, and I divided the personal items evenly between our packs. But I couldn't concentrate on what I was doing. I tossed items into the packs with little regard for balance. Though I could usually load a backpack in my sleep, we would have to stop halfway down to rearrange these. The poor weight distribution would make them and us clumsy.

Polly came close and sat, her head cocked quizzically as she watched me work. For a dog who liked young girls, she showed remarkable disinterest in my daughter.

On one level, the two people by the stream looked perfectly fine, a man and a young girl—a young woman—sitting on the bank, looking at pretty stones and bits of ore, the man talking about hydrous copper aluminum phosphates and the minerals beryl and corundum, and the girl holding stones to the light. But something bothered me about it all. Something was just not quite right. I tossed in the toilet paper. Collapsed the handle and secured the shovel to the pack.

Girls like pretty things…. Back at the cabin I have… Girls like pretty things….

I stood up slowly.

He was courting her. Old-fashioned term, but it fit. *Courting* her. Nice-looking man in his thirties spending the semester looking for rocks, taking time off from the university. Had a cabin nearby probably rented from a local. Most likely chased coeds all the time as he taught. Bella looked a good five years older than her age. Relief washed through me, half comfort, half worry at this new development in my daughter's life—an older man chasing my baby girl.

I could have laughed at myself. Bella was beautiful and innocent and unaffected, and he was on sabbatical and lonely…. Of _course_ I would feel protective if an older man showed an interest in my teenage daughter. On that level, he _was_ a threat, especially now that Marlow had run off, embracing his midlife crisis and a snow bunny in some chalet. Bella was my responsibility.

So. What would I do when he asked to see her again? If he did? Explain that Bella might look twenty, but was only fifteen and far too young to date an older man? Cross my arms and ask if his intentions were honorable? Pull out my revolver and chase him off like a silly panicked female? I was a single parent now, or would be in a month when the divorce was final. I had to be strong and rational enough for two. I tamped down the worry, allowing only a small spark of watchfulness to keep me on guard as I paused and studied them. They looked so innocent, sitting on the mat, looking at rocks.

I moved several items in the top of my backpack, placing them with thoughts of the walk down, instead of my fears. I strapped the stove, now cool, in place. I didn't want anything shifting on the trek back to the Bronco.

3

Twenty minutes had passed. My fear had settled into a low hum of motherly concern, and the packs were ready to go. I only had to wash and store the percolator and the tin plate Dell was still using.

As always, I pulled my old camera to me and framed Bella, and incidentally Dell. The light was overhead, not the best for the shots, but thin, wispy clouds were moving in and the canopy of leaves helped diffuse the glare. I slowed the shutter, checked the camera's light meter—the hand-held meter was long packed away—closed the aperture a bit to adjust for the affect I wanted, and snapped a few shots.

Dell looked up at the sound of the shutter's single clicks. His bright green gaze focused on me. Something flared in his eyes, an intense reaction as some strange emotion crossed his features and was gone. I was certain I caught it on film.

"I'm not fond of pictures." His voice was quiet in the clearing, his tone icy with threat. Polly growled low in her throat. The dog was somewhere behind me. Hairs lifted on the back of my neck.

Slowly, I looked over the camera. "I was taking Bella," I lied, then softened it with the truth. "Marlow and I always take shots of her on…hikes." I had almost said shoots.

The strange emotion crossed Dell's face again, lingering. This time I identified it. Fury. Blatant, uncontrolled rage. He had heard the lie. Polly's growl deepened in pitch, low and feral sounding, off to the side now.

Something was wrong here. Very wrong. The .38 against my belly seemed to heat my skin. A sense of peril pulsed through me. I slid my wrist along the bulge of the gun for an instant. Should I pull it? What if I was wrong? I *hated* guns. Hated everything about them.

Time seemed to slow, stretch, hang suspended in one long instant, like taffy pulled. I backed up a step, one hand angling beneath my shirt for the .38, but encountering only cloth as I fumbled. Dell stood, uncoiling fast, like a cobra. The familiar feeling of paralysis that had frozen me since Marlow left closed its fist around my neck. Dell stepped forward, stopped.

Coffee boiled back up my throat. My left fingers stiffened on the Nikon in apprehension. Hidden beneath it and my shirt, my right fingers curled, grabbing at the gun. But he was so close to Bella. Too close. A wild shot…

Again, coffee-acid blistered my throat. A vision of my mama's death, a scene I had only read about in local papers, blossomed in my mind.

"Mom?"

I glanced at Bella. She was gathering herself to rise, confusion in her eyes. *Run*, I wanted to scream, but my throat clamped closed.

Dell stepped between us, standing in front of her, his face now impassive, hands at his sides. Only his eyes showed reaction. I couldn't identify the emotion there, but it was cooler than a moment ago, and I discovered I could breathe again. His lips relaxed, the capricious expression again gone. His eyes on my camera went placid, like a lake after a storm, his emotions changing fast as heartbeats. He offered a small smile, gestured as if confused at my stance. He was suddenly the geologist on sabbatical again. The harmless, inoffensive professor.

I did not pull the Smith and Wesson. Perhaps I had misread the situation and the man. But I did not comfort myself that things were all right here, and I kept a grip on the .38.

Girls like pretty things…. I'm not fond of pictures.

Whatever he was, he was too close to Bella for me to safely use the gun if needed. I had to entice him away from her, off to the side. She peeked from behind him, rising from the ground. *Move!* I commanded silently with a glance. Bella froze in panic, still on one knee. Dell's eyes locked on the F3.

With one finger I hit the rewind button, moving the film as fast as the drive could work. "You know, we just love to camp, have camped and hiked all our lives. We Morgans love the outdoors," I prated.

"Mom?" There was an odd tremulous warning in her voice. Dell's face was stone and ice once more, the smile gone. My fear ratcheted up a notch.

I had to get her away from him, away from the line of fire, and pull the weapon. I had to pull the gun, even if I was wrong. But what if he took it from me? What if I made things worse and he grabbed my baby…. Panic swelled and pulsed through me. Heat and freezing paralysis, and two thoughts only: *get Dell away from Bella. Pull the gun.*

Walking three steps to the left, up the hill, my hand hidden, I ejected the roll of film and pocketed it, talking, hoping he'd miss the fact that I was hiding the film. But if he followed, I could pull the gun. If he followed I would have a clear line of fire. *Always, always, always have a clear line of fire.* Daddy's voice from so long ago.

"Marlow and I have shots of Bella in the Urals, and in Siberia, and on deserts all over the world," I said breathlessly, talking to cover the sound of a new roll being put in and fed through the auto load, and the clicks as I took useless shots of the ground. "We have her entire life cataloged on film."

Face impassive now, Dell finally pursued me, his boots steady on the loam. And I knew. *I knew.* Dropping the camera on its thong, sending several rolls of film bouncing to the ground, my hand curled into a claw around the gun. *Just a step farther,* I willed the man. He lifted his foot.

"Mama?" I heard my daughter's rising tone of panic. *"Mama!"* Shale slipped from the bank as Bella rocketed from the mats toward me.

"Run, Bella!" I screamed as I pulled the .38, sliding my hand from beneath the camp shirt. "Run!"

Dell was right beside me, an arm drawn back. Before I could free the weapon, I stumbled. Hot metal on my fingers and palm. *Too late!*

A quick, hard blow shocked my ribs. I lost air. Doubled over. I scrabbled for the gun, suddenly clumsy. Lurched back. The Smith and Wesson fell from my fingers, hit my knee and flew. I saw it disappear in the bushes. Saw his fist pull back again. Felt a ringing pain in my head. Heard Bella, her scream abruptly cut off as blackness closed in on me. A moment of nothingness.

Time compressed, stretched. I was gagging, facedown on the ground, the shattered F3 beside me. Hot, foul breath in my face. A dog.

Sobbing in the distance. *Bella!*

Low growl, blurred fangs, heat on my cheek.

My arms were stretched behind me, elbows pulled together. Pain lanced through both shoulders. *I was being tied.* I jerked away, gagging again. The fangs lashed at me.

The dog landed on my back, claws digging in. I lost my breakfast in a single violent heave.

My feet were jerked together. Roughly lifted and dropped. *Bella…*

Clarity returned slowly. Small stones bit into my face, pressed up into my field of vision. Long strands of my hair hung loose or were plastered in curly snarls to my skin. A pine needle, long and slender…. I had seen no pine trees in the area.

The dog, Polly, stood on my back, her bared teeth against my nape, her breath hot and fetid, a low growl, barely audible, vibrating against my flesh.

Bella's voice, far off. Hysterical. Weeping. I turned my head. Pain stabbed, a lightning streak of darkness and agony. Bella was on the ground, tied hands lifted to cover her face. He had hit her. I tried to rise and saw that her ankles were lashed together. Polly nipped at my scalp, trying to force me down.

Footsteps sounded, booted feet in my field of vision. The dog jumped off and away. One boot pulled back and slammed into my right side. The breath left my lungs in a single agonized grunt as I rolled over, trying to absorb the blow. Bella screamed.

"That useless man of yours knows how dangerous it is in these hills. No real man would allow his women into the wilderness alone. I'm taking the girl because he isn't worthy of her, and because I never waste a good woman. You… Lying whore. You get left for the scavengers." The boots and the dog moved away, Polly's tail wagging. "Good dog," Dell said.

He bent over my pack, digging through it, tossing things everywhere, the tin eating utensils and pots clattering, clothes and personal items falling in small heaps. When he found the F4 camera and the cell phone, he slammed them both to the ground, grinding the small phone with the heel of his boot into atoms of plastic and scraps of aluminum.

Writhing slowly, I turned myself on the hard earth until I could see Bella sitting on the ground, her hands tied in front of her, her face tear-streaked, red and swollen, bruising where he had hit her. More than once. Polly stood guard in front of her, and I could hear the threatening growl from where I lay.

I worked at the bonds holding my wrists together. Shimmied my feet against the ties there. With each motion, rocks cut into my face. My side, where he'd kicked me, sent waves of tight hot pain squeezing my chest. I couldn't breathe. *Broken ribs?*

Dell added some of my things to his packs, looked up at Bella. "This yours?" He held up the pack she always carried. Frightened, she nodded. His face twisted. "I said, 'This yours?'"

She quivered, unable to respond.

"I ask you a question, you answer. With words. Understand?"

She licked her lips. "Yes." Her eyes darted to me, met my gaze. I nodded to show her I was all right. Tears coursed down her face.

Dell tossed the pack over the saddle horn on the roan and brought the pack animal close to my daughter. That was when I realized what he was doing, what he had said. He was taking Bella. And leaving me here, trussed up, unable to help her. I wrenched at my bonds, screaming, the sound so breathless it came out a groan.

Grabbing Bella beneath an arm, he pulled her to her feet and pushed her against the pack animal.

"I don't know how to ride," she said, tears dropping off her chin. She was thinking, anticipating, trying to delay him.

"Not a problem."

"I'm scared of horses." Pride welled inside me. My baby was fighting, using words as a shield.

But instead of answering, Dell picked her up and tossed her over the bay's back, belly down, face and feet hanging on opposite sides of the horse. "In ten miles I'll let you sit astride," he said.

"No. Please. I don't want to go. I want to stay with my mother."

"She's dead. You can grieve while you learn to ride." One-handed, Dell lashed her hands and feet together beneath the horse's belly. "You're mine now. And I don't like women who cry."

"Mama?" She was gasping, terrified.

"I'll be okay, IsaBella. I'll be fine. I'll find you. I promise, I'll find you!" I said.

With three quick steps, Dell turned and pulled back his leg for a kick. Bella screamed again. I didn't see it land, didn't feel this one, but darkness melted in from the sides like a telescope closing. An awful ringing filled the clearing, the sound inside my head. Then nothing.

Friday
0800 hours

When I woke, I was heavy. Weighted down with pain that thrummed and sang in my bones. I opened an eye onto a world gone gray, flecked with green. Whorls of no-color in a diminishing palette. When my eye focused I realized it was rock, fine grained and smooth. I was lying on my side, the rock in front of my face. Another was sitting on my neck. Others were piled over me. A single pinpoint of light touched my face, falling between the stones.

A memory returned, muzzy and deformed. He had kicked me. And with it came understanding; he had buried me in the stones. Built a cairn to leave me for dead. The smell of vomit was sour in my nostrils.

A dog whined at the spot of light. Snuffed at the small hole a moment.

"Polly," he called.

Polly.... Dell. His name was Dell. And he had Bella.

Beyond the small point of light, I saw Dell mount his roan and ride out of the clearing, pulling the packhorse. My daughter was with him, draped over its back. "Mama!" Bella wailed, the sound almost lost beneath the damage to my head. And then they were gone. I lay still, only my breathing and the pain radiating down my legs giving away that he hadn't broken my neck.

I was alone on the side of a mountain. Buried. And the darkness took me.

4

Later, slowly, my vision returned. Focused on the red, bright and wet, overlaying the rusty layer dried beneath. My blood on the earth. The sun was shadowed and dull. Birds called. I knew time had passed. The ringing in my head was gone, replaced by a pounding headache so fierce I could almost hear the pain.

I had passed out. Slept within the cairn while Bella was taken away. I should have pulled the gun. I should have killed him.

I tested my wrists. My hands had swelled while I slept. There would be no getting free with simple struggling. When I tried to move, agony lanced through me, red-hot and burning. Breathing was difficult beneath the weight of granite. Dust filtered down onto my skin. I angled my head a fraction of an inch.

There was a small space at my upper shoulder and I shrugged into it. Pain grated along my flesh, beat into my head like a tribal drum. I shoved up, screaming with rage and agony. Dell should be dead. I should have shot him with my first fear. I rammed myself into the stones. *Dell should be dead!*

A stone above me shifted. Light pierced in. I took a breath, shunted the pain aside and shoved hard, up at the light.

The rocks gave. Tumbled. Shredded and abraded my exposed skin. I slammed into the stones above me, screaming with the effort. Rolled again. My clothes tore with short ripping sounds.

I paused to breathe, and the effort was rewarded with stabbing pain in my head, side, shoulders, arms. I was still covered with boulders. Surrounded with the gray-green of lichen-colored local stone and shadow. I was crying, my vision wavering in the one eye that wasn't blind. I couldn't stop. If I did, I would die here and Bella... IsaBella!

I sniffed softly and forced the pain aside, down into some small space inside my soul. Down deep. Where I wouldn't see it or hear it or feel anything, ever again. I concentrated on the small breaths that came without pain. Concentrated on calm. And rose upward, pushing one shoulder against the stone. Again. And again, shoving, twisting, writhing with the motion. Whipped my neck against the weight and knocked a large rock away with my head. Screamed again, the sound echoing off the mountains. *"Bella!"*

My face was free. I fought for breath, shallow gasps of cool air. The weight of rocks cast tight bands of pain and compressed my chest. My shirt was caught in the stones, trapping me. Only my right eye opened. The left one was swollen shut. I forced it open a slit. I could see. The eye wasn't blind. Tears coursed down my face.

His boot had caught the side of my head. My nose and jaw and perhaps my neck would have been broken, had the kick landed accurately. I had jerked at the last instant and he'd caught only my cheek.

I shoved at the rocks, sending them tumbling. Using my

shoulders, I twisted, freeing the shirt in a single long rip, fighting until my upper body was free. Then my hips. Finally my legs worked up and down as I thrust the last of the stones off me, screaming for Bella with each mighty shove.

Rolling hard, I fell over the piled rocks onto flat earth. My boots gave way as I pushed against the ground. What was left of my breakfast boiled up and I vomited once more.

When I could move again, I scooted away, fighting the pain in my ribs as I sat up. I looked at my feet. My ankles were lashed together with rawhide. *Why had he tied me with rawhide instead of nylon?* And then I understood. He'd used the flimsy rawhide because I was dead to him. He'd never thought I might live, might fight free.

Moving as best I could, I slid on my buttocks to the creek, down the bank and into the water. The cold sent a painful breath deep into my lungs.

It was frigid. Fifty degrees this time of year. If I stayed in too long, if I passed out, I could die of hypothermia. But if I timed it right, the water would loosen the rawhide binding my feet and hands. Maybe I could get free. Maybe.

I edged deeper into the cold, careful not to crawl too far and get caught up in the current, which could send me tumbling. Maybe the cold would ease the pain in my side and cheek, decrease the swelling in my hands. And then I could go after them. Get my Bella back. Anything for Bella, I thought. Anything for Bella.

The water closed around me, so cold it burned at first, then stole my breath for long seconds. I dropped my face into the water and watched bubbles rise from my mouth and nose as I exhaled, the icy water taking with it both body heat and pain. I drew another breath and resubmerged, over and over, as crusted blood dissolved and dispersed, billowing downstream.

After long moments, I began working my feet back and forth against the strips holding them. One section of rawhide had caught the top of my left Timberland and I worked to pop it down. Water loosened the bindings and I fought against them. I came up for air again and again, my lungs burning. My feet were as numb as my hands.

When I was beyond cold, dangerously approaching hypothermia, I rolled through the creek to the far shore, where a small sandy bank gave me purchase, and squirmed into position with my feet above me on the bank. Slinging my hair out of my face, I hooked the rawhide around my left ankle onto a branch and pulled. The moistened leather stretched. Slowly.

Grunting with the effort, I switched position, eased the branch into the ankle cuff of the well-worn boot and twisted, hauling back against the old leather. I had tied them loosely, lazily, for comfort around camp, and hadn't retied them yet for the hike back down the mountain.

When the leather had stretched as far as it could, I rolled back to the creek and immersed myself again. I started shivering and knew I couldn't stay here long. The water had stolen too much warmth and energy. Lethargy dragged at me, the deceitful call for rest. The water didn't feel so cold now. Forcing myself to move, I rolled back to the bank.

Sand worked into my clothes, abraded my flesh. Teeth chattering, I realized I was cursing or begging, and turned my plea into prayer. I hadn't prayed in months, not since Marlow left, but I prayed now, prayed to pull off my boot. For God, for someone, anyone, to help my Bella.

I worked the boot back onto the branch and pulled once more. The pain in my side had been diminished by the cold water and I was able to tug harder.

Long minutes later, the boot eased off a fraction. Jerking my knees, I ignored the stitch in my ribs that returned with the motion. And the boot came half-off. With a final pull, I worked my foot free, rolling halfway back into the water as I separated my feet and kicked off the last strip of hide.

I got to my knees and then my feet, standing in the icy creek, legs palsied with exhaustion. Crossing the water back to camp, I slipped once and was pretty sure I cut the bottom of my foot, but I was so cold I didn't even bleed.

Shaking with reaction, stumbling, I fell near the emptied pack and sat, swiveling my legs in front of me, nudging with my toes through the piles of things Dell had left. The knives were gone. The camp stove. The bedrolls and equipment. He must have taken them when he ransacked the camp. There was nothing sharp. I struggled uselessly at the bonds holding my hands and elbows.

Spotting a jumbo-size Snickers bar that had been crushed beneath a heel, I rolled to one side, my shoulder pinning the candy, and tore the wrapper with my teeth, spitting paper until I could get a bite. I tasted nothing, but the darkness that hovered at the edges of my vision receded as I swallowed chocolate and nuts. Somehow, I kept the sugary stuff down.

As I chewed, I discovered two teeth that were loose, but seemed whole and weren't painful. I glanced at the cairn where I had been buried. It must not have taken long. He'd simply hauled me against the foundation of the manager's cabin and toppled the stones onto me, adding a few from the small clearing. The work of a quarter hour. Still trying to get my breath, I found the sun through the leaves overhead. It wasn't even nine o'clock. Not yet nine and my whole world had ruptured. Not yet nine.... They couldn't have gotten far.

Rolling again, I found a soft-soled sneaker in the pile

of clothes, slipped my left foot into it and stood, gasping at the pain in my side. I turned in the direction Dell and Bella had ridden, and sobbed. I couldn't get my hands free. It was pointless to go after them.

Dropping back to the ground, I used my knee to shovel through the shards of plastic and aluminum that had once been the cell phone. Twisting around, fingers clumsy, I managed to pick up a sharp aluminum fragment, my hands so numb I could barely feel when I held it. Trying to get the metal husk into position to saw into the leather, I forced myself back to my feet and started down the mountain on weary, trembling legs, away from the path where Dell had taken Bella.

Tears had been falling and fell harder now, making the path before me waver. Shivers gripped me in long running spates of jagged arrhythmia. I moved as fast as I could, my breath heaving in sync with the pain in my side. But the cold water had slowed the swelling and the pain wasn't unendurable.

Cutting with the sharp bit of metal, trying to free my trapped hands, I followed the little-used path down and up and around, careful to keep the markers in sight, stumbling and murmuring prayers as I moved. "God, please help my IsaBella. Don't let him hurt her." But I knew he would. I knew what he intended. What he had intended all along.

I was slicing the flesh over my wrist bones, but I had to get the tourniquetlike strips off. Shunting the pain aside, shoving it down with all the other agony into some dark place inside me, I carved on.

The mountainside fell away below me. Dropping to one knee, I half slid down the steep hill, taking the fall on my buttocks and thigh. I had walked a mile. Four to go.

Hacking with the small bit of metal, I moved steadily

on. Would he wait until tonight? Or would he stop early? Pull Bella off the horse and…

Instead of taking pictures when I'd had the first inkling of doubt, instead of hesitating, I should have pulled the .38 and shot him dead. Should have. Hated guns. Hated them. *Should have killed Dell.* "Kill him," I mumbled. My lips cracked when I spoke.

My wrists came apart in an eruption of pain, a backlash of misery that thundered and throbbed through my veins. But my elbows were still caught, the binding on them thicker and wider than that on my hands. Slinging my arms, pulling at the bands, my body lurched left and right. I'd never get myself free. I screamed with frustration and anger, my throat a spasm of heat and horror.

I was hysterical, not in my right mind. I realized it when the path was no longer clear or familiar before me. I stopped, surrounded by trees, loamy ground beneath my feet, a thicket of laurel on three sides, so dense not even a rabbit could have gotten through. The silence of the forest was absolute. I knew, suddenly, I was lost. And I had dropped the metal shard that had freed my hands. Somehow that seemed momentous, a colossal failure. A dry sob caught me, wracking my ribs.

I took a breath, as deep as I could manage, and turned. Slowly. Behind me, a blood trail led back up between close-set trees. I looked down. My left foot was bleeding through the sneaker, blood squishing over the cotton sides. A small amount of crimson had escaped with each step, coating leaves, bubbled on dry dirt, smeared on stones. Just enough. "Thank you. Thank you, God, that I cut my foot."

I laughed at the words, the sound raucous and perhaps a bit mad. Following my blood back the way I'd come, I moved uphill until I was sure I was on the path again. Though steep and narrow, the trail was well-kept by the park service. I turned and followed it down, veering to stay on the path. Fighting to stay alert this time. Insanity faded back. I had no right to give in to fear. I'd been hurt and survived before, and I would now. I would find the ranger station and get my baby help.

It seemed that hours passed, but Bella and I had only hiked about five miles yesterday. That was just a day ago, when we came on this mother-daughter trip that was supposed to give us both a chance to recuperate from the months of emotional torment we'd shared after Marlow left. Guilt welled up with fresh tears. I knew when I got my baby back, I'd…I'd… I stumbled and fell, banging my knee. The pain was an electric prod at ribs and hands, head and knee. All I wanted was to curl up and sleep, just for a moment. My vision darkened, a dizzy feeling pulling at me. But I couldn't faint. "No," I said. "No." My voice so soft it was a breath.

Aching, I crawled back to my feet. *Anything for Bella. Anything for Bella.*

My shivering had eased with motion, and the day's warmth was bringing back body heat. My hair was almost dry against my face and breezed out in riotous reddish arcs that I caught in my good eye's peripheral vision. My clothes were nearly dry, rank with sweat and creek water.

I saw a form move up ahead and froze on the path, alarm shooting through me. But he was whistling softly, bird calls. And he was wearing ranger brown. Relief flung away the fear.

I tried to call out, but my voice was gone, wasted in prayer and mumbling. God would have heard silent prayer if He was in the mood to listen. I didn't think He was.

I moved one foot in front of the other, licked my lips and finally managed a rasping croak of sound. The ranger glanced up.

It was a woman. I saw her reaction to the way I looked. Shock. Fear.

"Water," I managed to rasp. And the tears started falling again.

"Oh, crap," she said, running to me. I thought she might curse, but she pulled a water bottle from her belt and unscrewed it, held it out to me. I looked at the bottle.

"My God. You're tied up."

A metallic click. I lost awareness for an instant and came to myself only when pain lanced from my hands to my shoulders and into my spine as my bonds were released. Then I could see my arms again, dangling and purpled. Without knowing how I got there, I was on my knees, sobbing. The shakes hit hard and I bent over, face nearly to the ground.

The ranger steadied me on my knees, held my head and lifted the bottle to my mouth; I drank, the water warm and yet sweet against my tongue. She was talking, asking questions, but I had to get the water. Gagging, I pulled back, swallowing convulsively until I was sure I could keep the liquid down. Then, nodding that I could drink again, I lifted my head, unable to balance the bottle with hands that didn't obey. When the water was gone, most of it lost down my shirt, I thanked her and tried to take her hand. My arm lifted less than six inches, the muscles paralyzed.

"Are you MacKenzie Morgan?"

"He took Bella."

"He who? Who did this to you? Can you walk?"

"Yes. Dell. A geologist. A man on horseback, two dogs and a packhorse. He took Bella." I babbled on, useless, confused words.

She interrupted the deluge of panic. "Bella is your daughter? When?"

"Yes. Just after we broke camp at dawn. Maybe seven?" I croaked. The water was gone, absorbed into my dried-out body.

"Where were you camped?" Pulling out her radio, she looped an arm around my back beneath a shoulder, lifting me to my feet and guiding me, stumbling, toward the ranger station and the Ford Bronco I had left in the parking area, where campers abandoned civilization and modern conveniences.

"At the old fish hatchery."

"That's four miles from here."

I nodded as the ranger relayed my report to the station. Bending my arms, I lifted my hands, supporting each in the crook of the opposite elbow to stop their swelling. The pain was ratcheting up quickly, which I figured was a good thing. It meant blood was still able to make its way into the damaged tissues.

"Your husband called the ranger stations at three parks on both sides of the state line last night. Said you were overdue to check in. We found your Bronco in our parking lot."

I shook my head. "Not supposed to call until tonight. And he knew where we were, or was supposed to know." I wanted to correct her, add *soon-to-be ex-husband*, but couldn't. I was too dry. Marlow had trouble lately remembering when we were supposed to do anything. He'd missed Bella's birthday by three days, forgetting everything but his new life.

"Good thing he got the days mixed up then. You're bleeding." She nodded toward my foot, though her eyes were on my hands. "We'll get an ambulance up here and get you to a hospital. You—"

I stumbled again and she caught me, my face against her chest, her name badge beside my nose. Her name was Yolanda Perkins and she smelled like bug spray and coffee and safety. That was when I noted that the pocket holding the film of Dell was ripped and hanging. I remembered the sound of tearing cloth when I finally forced my way free of the burial cairn of stones.

"Yolanda, I'm not going to a hospital. I have to go back to the camp."

The ranger steadied me and pulled long woven strips from a pocket. They were army-green, and she fashioned a single sling for my arms, hooking it around my neck and sliding my forearms through it. "Call me Yo," she said as she worked. "And that's not likely. You can barely put one foot in front of the other."

"I got a shot of the man's face. Dropped the film when I forced my way out of the stones he buried me under. I can find it. Searchers may not." The last three sentences came out broken, separated by long moments when my throat was so dry I couldn't speak.

Satisfied with the sling, Yo pulled out another bottle of water, unscrewed the top and held it for me. This time when I drank there was no nausea. Just a surge of adrenaline and a cold pain where my heart used to beat.

5

As we walked, I listened to Yo talk into the radio, a man's voice answering back. Her first request was for an ambulance. I'd let them clean and bandage my foot and hands and whatever else needed attention. But I was going back to the campsite. I could do five more miles. Blood squished up in my shoe and my breathing was labored, but I'd make it. "Got any Tylenol?" I asked, lifting my head to loosen the crick that threatened to immobilize me.

Yo's green eyes looked me over. "When we get stopped. *If* the paramedics say okay. And ice packs for the swelling and whatever you need to get cleaned up. What kind of shots?"

"Thirty-five millimeter, black and white. I'm a photographer. I managed to get the pictures before he jumped me. I should have just shot him with the gun. I knew there was something wrong with him. I knew it." My tears spilled over, salty burns on my broken skin. "Bella was too close. I might have hit her. I didn't want to hit her."

"I'm sure you made the right decision."

"No. I should have shot the bastard. I wish I had."

Yolanda had nothing to say to that; instead she asked about Dell. I gave his description, and Bella's, and as much as I could remember of his story, though I assumed he hadn't told us the truth. Or maybe he had. It was possible he'd decided to kill me and take Bella the moment he saw her. I should have shot him as he rode into camp.

"His dogs answered to Polly and Rufus," I said, certain the dogs' names, at least, were correct. I described the dogs and horses, the way Dell's pack looked, the samples in his collection, dredging up any bit of information that might make a search for Bella easier. "He said he was a geologist. He had a satchel of minerals and rocks in his pack, and some gold he said he dug out of a hill yesterday. He took Bella." The words were a cudgel against my mind. "He took Bella," I whispered.

"Your daughter?" Her tone said she had heard me the first time I'd answered that question, but was asking for verification.

"Yes." Tears blurred my path.

"Which way did he head out?"

I fell silent, trying to remember where the sun had thrown shadows as Dell rode from the camp. I glanced at my hands and away. They were purple and dead-looking and felt as if fire ants were attacking. The cuffs of my shirt were caked with blood and body fluids. "North, I think. The hatchery is between two steep ridges." Yo nodded to indicate her knowledge of the locale.

"I was on the south side of the creek near the hatchery manager's cabin foundation and saw Dell move out directly in front of me, shadows falling to his left, so…" I tried to think. "That would make his direction north. I can show you when we get back. But he was on horseback, so he should be easy to follow."

"North will take him out of the park, onto state and private land. If he makes thirty miles as the crow flies, he'll leave North Carolina. We'll need local backup, both here and in Tennessee," she said. "I don't have freqs for them on the portable, so Joel will have to call in the Mounties." She keyed her portable radio again while I tried to make sense of her words. The "Mounties" reference was facetious, but using terms like "SAR" and "county boys," she requested search and rescue teams and local law enforcement.

From her words, I figured "EM freqs" must mean emergency management radio frequencies, and that she was relaying for more help. More help was good. And if the Canadian Mounties were in the area, they could jump in, too. Anything to help my IsaBella. A hysterical laugh tickled at the back of my throat, but I swallowed it down. If I let it go, I'd never stop the tears. I'd fall apart.

On the radio, another voice took over asking pertinent questions. Finding some still-functioning part of my rational mind, I gave as much information as I could remember. When the radio fell silent, Yo turned back to me. "Tell me about him burying you."

A shiver ran through me. To buy time as the weakness passed, I asked, "Can you get this hair out of my face? I can't see."

We paused as Yo tied my hair back with a scrunchy she pulled off her own head. When we resumed our walk toward help, I told her about the attack. About how I got out of the pile of stones. We were interrupted repeatedly. While we made the last tenth of a mile, her radio crackled constantly with relayed information about search and rescue activity.

When we finally reached the parking site, the throbbing in my hands, back, arms and head was like football-field-size bass drums sounding in my bloodstream. But tears no longer ran down my face, and I appeared as calm as I was able in my bedraggled, bruised, swollen condition.

There were law enforcement cars waiting and an ambulance had just arrived. Two EMTs ran to me, carrying a stretcher. Afraid I might not be able to get back up, I refused their offer of a ride even for a few feet and trudged on to the sidewalk beside the ambulance unit.

I fell against its steel side and slid down the vertical wall. "Just clean me up and let me go back to the campsite. I have to get back up there," I said as I collapsed to the concrete.

"You aren't going anywhere except to a hospital," the female EMT said.

"See if you can talk her into being sensible," Yo said. "I have to check in with Joel and see about getting things started for the SAR."

"I'm not going to a hospital," I said as Yo walked off. "I'm going back up the mountain. I have to." My voice broke on the last words.

Intercepting the look passed between the two emergency workers, I realized they would only allow me to refuse treatment if they believed I was in my right mind. If not, then they could—and would—force me to go to a hospital. I held out my arms and glanced at her name tag. "Ruth, do I have a pulse in each hand?" I demanded.

Ruth bent over me, folded back the cuffs of the camp shirt and the thermal T-shirt underneath. It was a slow process, as the cloth stuck to my skin and open tissue beneath. My hands were still dark, but the color was better, less blue and more red. Red had to be good. Fresh blood seeped down over my knuckles. That was the first time I saw the extent of the damage to my wrists. The rawhide had chewed into my flesh, the ligature marks were burned and worn through the skin. A wide gash composed of multiple slashes scored the tissue over my wrists, carved so deeply that the white of bone shone through the clotted scab. If Dell had tied the bonds over the shirts the damage would have been less extensive. I knew how bad it really was when Ruth's partner sucked air between his teeth.

"That must hurt like a son-of-gun. How long were you tied?" he asked, passing me a bottle of water and an ice pack for my eye. With a cool expression, he watched me try to work my hands to accept them. I was clumsy, hands on fire with pain.

"What time is it now?"

Ruth checked her watch. "Ten-o-five."

"Seven o'clock, maybe, is when he reached camp." I shrugged my shoulders to ease a cramp, but it didn't help much. "I was probably free just after nine. I don't know. An hour tied at the ankles?" I guessed. I fought to remember the time, the sequence of events. I fought harder to sound coherent, rational. If I didn't, they might tie me to a stretcher, sedate me. I didn't have the time. Taking a steadying breath, I said, "Maybe two hours tied at the wrists. Maybe less," I amended when I saw the look they exchanged. "Three hours tied at the elbows."

Ruth stopped folding back the cloth of my shirts and cut the sleeves along the seam to above my elbows, nearly to my armpits, before removing them and tossing them aside. The flesh above my elbows was horribly bruised and blackened. Other bruises marked my arms, purplish places where I guessed Dell had tossed rocks to cover me.

"He used a wide band here. That's good. But your wrists and hands look bad," she said. Ruth put her fingers at pulse points on my swollen skin. Long minutes passed while I drank and the other EMT checked respiration and blood pressure and reflexes, pulled off my shoe to inspect the gash on my foot. Blood pooled beneath it onto his gloved fingers, but it was slowing now that I was off my feet. "Okay, you have adequate pulses, but—"

Relief slammed into me and I blocked out the rest of her words. I wouldn't lose my hands. I'd had images of stumps and prosthetics, surgery, which would have meant not going after Bella anytime soon, if ever. I sagged and a bolt of pain from my ribs stunned me. Sucking in a ragged breath, I straightened and forced my expression to remain unaffected. From the look on Ruth's face, I wasn't sure I was fooling anyone.

"Good. Get me some more water, some Tylenol and some food, and I'll be heading back up."

"But adequate pulses aren't the main thing," she said. "You could have what's called compartment syndrome. Or even Volkmann's ischemic contracture."

"What's all that?"

"Volkmann's is where you have blood flow, but the tissue is dead. But I don't think you were tied long enough for that, if you're right about the time." Ruth didn't meet my eyes, her own on my limbs.

"Ruth's like our resident doc. She reads medical books for fun," the man said, his tone letting me know that her being a resident doctor was a joke and reading books was a weird pastime.

"Compartment syndrome, though… I think you may need treatment for that. It's where the pressure distal to—lower than—the ligature is enough to stop all blood flow *from* the hands but not enough to stop it *to* the hands—"

I shook my head, interrupting her. I wasn't able to follow the medical jargon.

She tried again. "Your hands are swollen so badly they may not be able go down by themselves. You may need surgery to open up the skin and allow the fluid to escape. And you've got damage to the muscles and the tendons and underlying tissue."

I turned my hands over and tried to make a fist; I couldn't curl my fingers closed. But I could bend them enough to hold the water bottle between them clumsily, like a child, which I figured meant she was wrong in her analysis. Ruth watched and said, "Even with dead muscles, you can still move them some. But they develop a woody feel. Full function never returns."

"Ruth's also our resident doom and gloom expert," her partner said. "Let me see." He took my arms and turned them over, inspecting the tissue, telling me to move and bend and try to make fists, which I did despite the pain.

"If I don't have this compartment syndrome, then the only thing a doctor can do is clean me up, maybe give me some stitches, bandage me, X ray me for broken ribs, which I already know I have. Right? If all that waits, it won't kill me any faster. If you really want to help, get me some more water, some Tylenol and some food."

"Not so. With a broken rib you could have a pneumothorax and end up with a collapsed lung," Ruth said. "And I'm not giving you meds or food because then you couldn't have surgery to fix anything that might be wrong with a lung, or to treat for the ligature."

I closed my eyes. "Do you have a child, Ruth?"

"That's a low blow," she said softly.

Opening my eyes, I connected with her brown ones. "I'm going back up the mountain, Ruth. That man took my daughter." She shook her head in response and I knew I had won. "I can get to a hospital in a couple of hours," I said, mentally adding *or a bit more, after I get the film developed.*

Ruth sighed and glanced at her partner, who avoided

her stare. "I'll bandage you, get you some Tylenol and ibuprofen to treat the pain and the inflammation and give you the fluids, though if you lose your hand function, I'll kick myself later for not taking you in to the E.R. Maybe we can get someone to bring an ATV up. If the park service permits it, you can ride to the hatchery and back here, and drive yourself into town."

I was feeling much better as the water made its way into my bloodstream, more like myself, more alert and alive, less like a victim. I had to be at my best, and fast, if I wanted to help my daughter. "You know a good photographer with his own darkroom? I need one for a few hours."

The male EMT pulled a pair of black-plastic-handled scissors off his belt and said, "I'm going to have to cut away your camp shirt."

"What? And ruin this perfectly good outfit?"

He smiled grimly as he applied the sharp edges of the scissors to the ripped cloth. My purple undershirt was exposed as he worked; it was caked with creek sand. "You really should let us take you in," he said.

"I'll give you this much, guys. After I get food, find the film and get it processed, I'll see about stitches and X rays and peeing in that cup they always make you use when you go to the E.R. Until then, I'm kinda occupied."

"Rick?" Ruth's tone held a warning or a demand I couldn't translate.

The man smiled harshly and glanced up at her. "Okay, okay. I'll get her back to the fishery. I got some time coming. Could you have tried to be a bit more subtle? All that talk about ATVs? So, I'm taking off the rest of the day to go out with the SAR team."

"Thank you, Rick," I said.

"I got kids, too," he said simply as he pulled up my undershirt, exposing my bruised sides. I watched his eyes meet Ruth's. Both faces gave away what they were thinking, and Rick put it into words. "Hematomas, lacerations, contusion, abrasions. Looks like you got hit by a truck."

"Boots with pointed toes."

"Um. Steel-toed is more like it." He applied a stethoscope to my ribs and commanded me to breathe deeply. I managed it without squeaking or crying, but it was close. When he was finished with my examination, he said, "Rate 20 and slowing with good breath sounds, equal on both sides. Pupils equal and reactive, BP 140 over 96, pulse 98. But the neuro checks in her arms suck." I didn't know what that meant, but it didn't sound good.

A car pulled out behind us and Rick stood, waving the driver to a stop. I didn't turn to see who had been hailed. I couldn't twist my body. When he came back to us, Rick said, "Ruth, I'm heading in with a county boy, to get my gear and a couple ATVs. I'll stop in on the way and make sure we have permission to take one backcountry. That'll get our patient back to the campsite without any more damage to her."

"Call and see if old Doc McElhaney will share his darkroom," she said without looking up.

"Me?" Rick asked, his tone odd. When Ruth nodded, he said, "Sure, if you want me to." And he was gone.

Ruth pulled out a liter of IV fluids and a needle as big as a cannon. "Smile, honey, or I'll think you might be about to pass out."

"I'm not real crazy about needles."

"You cry and it'll spoil my vision of you as Superwoman."

I managed a weak laugh as she prepped my arm for stabbing.

6

In short order, Ruth had started a saline IV, found my spare key attached to the bumper of the Bronco, given me two Tylenol and two ibuprofen with a liter of water to drink, and opened a pop-top can of Beenie Weenies from my stash in the Ford. While the fluids percolated and I ate, the paramedic bandaged my wrists and listened to my story. I had a feeling I would be telling it often in the next few hours. Around us, cars and trucks had begun to arrive. Off-road vehicles, county sheriff's deputy cars, emergency management vehicles—everything in sight was four-wheel-drive, steered by tough-faced men and women, each as capable and rugged-looking as the conveyances they owned.

The fluid and the calories enriched my bloodstream, and I was feeling stronger as the parking area filled. I even opened a second pop-top can of ravioli all by myself when the first can left me hungry. Ruth's practical treatment seemed to work. My head began to clear, and my hands and side ached a little less.

More importantly, I was no longer crying as if I could never stop; I felt calmer, more like my usual somewhat

dour public image. In private and behind the camera I
was carefree and lighthearted, with a quick and biting
sense of humor, but I had a different face for the public
and business. And getting IsaBella back was business of
the most consequential kind. When the press discovered
that Rachael Morgan's granddaughter was kidnapped
and missing, the public persona might get rough usage.

As part of her pragmatic approach to medical care,
Ruth helped me into a pair of Isotoner gloves she spotted in the back of my Bronco, thinking the tight Lycra
might help alleviate the swelling in my hands. And finally, she handed me a liter of fluid in a clear plastic con-
tainer and said, "Wash your face? The sheriff just pulled
up with Joel, who'll likely be the IC."

"IC?"

"Incident commander. Joel Durkowitz. My boss."

My baby was an incident.

I rose from the stretcher, which I had agreed to sit on
to make Ruth's job easier, without too much difficulty,
lifted the IV bag and the bottle of water and hobbled to
my Ford utility vehicle. Over its roof, I saw two men beside a marked sheriff's car, heads together. Propping the
bag on the roof of the Bronco, I found a comb and another
clean shirt, took the bottled water and poured it over me
while standing in the middle of the parking lot. I couldn't
do anything with my hair, though. The wild curls were
too snarled with dried creek water, mud and bits of veg-
etable flotsam.

Pulling a shirt over my head was impossible, too, but
I had a less-than-clean button-down that worked, one
with sleeves that were loose enough to accommodate
passing the IV bag through as I put it on. And new hiking boots and socks, though I had too little finger coor-
dination to tie the laces. No one seemed to notice, too
busy admiring one another's equipment and dogs,

studying maps of the area, attaching compasses, beepers and satellite phones to belts and backpacks, and assembling an amazing array of equipment and weapons. To a city girl with my history, it was more than scary. Yet I was glad all the guns, ammo and machismo were on Bella's side.

Friday
1110 hours

Over an hour had passed since I'd reached the clearing with Yo. I wanted to scream at the searchers to hurry up, head up the mountain, get pursuit under way, stop wasting time that Dell was using to flee. I wanted to give in to feelings of helpless impotence, the sense of being confined, paralyzed, useless. I wanted to shriek with agony and misery, to weep and rail, succumb to a thoroughly female case of hysteria. But I understood that a well-organized search crew would be more likely to find Bella than a hurried, disorganized one. And I knew I still had to appear to be in control, or even now I would be promptly packed off to a hospital for treatment of shock. So I didn't rage and screech and curse them to speed up. Being married to Marlow had given me that much—intense control. I watched them and I prayed as best I was able with a soul that had frozen solid hours ago.

With a flunky tailing behind him, the sheriff talked to Yo and Ruth before he approached me. I watched him, automatically framing him for a shot I would never take. He was big and burly, with a gut that would have appeared monstrous on a smaller man but seemed just right perched beneath the broad shoulders and the beefy arms. His uniform shirt had been tailored to cover his torso, his pants tapering down over nonexistent hindquarters.

Propping a foot on the bumper of the Bronco, he exhaled noisily through his nose and said, "I'm Sheriff Harman Harschell the Fourth," he said. "Folks call me Harschell."

"No, they don't. They call you Har Har," a passing man quipped.

"Not to my face they don't," he said to me, his expression equable.

I smiled. It was the first time in hours, and moving the muscles made my face ache. "A man calling himself Dell Shirley took my daughter. I have a roll of film back up the mountain with photos of him. I need to get to the campsite and find it and get it developed."

Har Har nodded thoughtfully. "You ever seen him before?" The flunky behind the sheriff opened a notepad and poised a pen at the bigger man's question.

"No." I was surprised. "Why would I?"

"No chance he knew your daughter?" Har Har propped an elbow on his raised knee, a feat to get around his gut. I knew a pose when I saw one. He was settling down for a lengthy chat. I was photographer and businesswoman enough to note that he had positioned his face in the shadow with me looking into the sun. The pompous ass was posturing, playing games while my daughter was lost in the hills. I wanted to kick him. Instead, I took a calming breath through the pain. I hated the thought, but my daughter's life might depend on how I managed this interview. The sheriff added, "Any chance that this was a rendezvous gone bad?"

"No," I said. "No chance." Using the excuse of finding more water, I hefted the IV bag, much lighter now than only minutes past, moved around into the shade of the ambulance, found a water bottle left by Ruth and drank. Put the ice pack on my eye. I could almost open it again and was relieved that the site wasn't damaged.

Pursing his lips, his body language telling me he was

fully aware of why I had moved, the sheriff had no choice but to follow me, placing us on equal terms regarding the light. Satisfied, I told the story of Dell's approach and the events at the campsite. When I mentioned the gun, he perked up. "Registration for the gun is in the glove box," I said before he could ask.

"Did he take the gun? Is he armed?"

I hadn't thought about a theft, and considered now the possibility that all the searchers could be in danger. "I don't know if he even saw me drop the .38. He was too busy trying to beat me to death," I said dryly.

Har Har looked puzzled for a moment, the expression somehow contrived. "And why did you take pictures, ma'am? I mean, if you had a gun. Why not just pull the gun and order him away?"

The question speared me, a bright searing pain. "I should have," I whispered. "I should have."

"Did he have a hunting rifle?"

The question seemed out of sequence, the kind of query a disordered mind might make. But I didn't think Har Har was disorganized at all. I dragged my fractured thoughts back together. "I didn't notice, but if he did, it'll appear in the photos I took as he rode down the mountain."

"Any other reason someone might have taken your daughter? Custody battle? Enemies out for revenge? Ransom?" Har asked.

I had been shaking my head steadily, as much as my stiff neck allowed, but arrested the motion at the last question. Ransom? Had Dell known that Bella was the granddaughter of Rachael Morgan? "Her father just came into a large estate. But I didn't get the feeling that money was part of Dell's plan. If he had wanted money, he would have made sure I was alive and well to carry down a ransom demand to Bella's father, wouldn't he? I think—" Dread took my heart in a clawed grip. Tears gathered again. I forced breath into my lungs and said, "I think he just wanted Bella."

As I spoke, Rick maneuvered a pickup pulling a flatbed trailer through the quickly filling parking lot, and stopped near us. Wordlessly, he got out of the cab, lowered the tailgate and dropped two two-by-tens into a ramp position on the trailer before wobbling his way to the back. With a roar of ignition, he turned on the first ATV and backed it down to the ground.

I wiped at a tear with my shoulder, shrugging it up to my cheek in a motion that was as painful as any I had made. "I'd love to stay and chat, Sheriff, but we need to get up to the campsite and back. You want to talk, we can do it on the move."

"You aren't going anywhere, little lady. First of all, the IC needs to talk to you. Second, you're what we call a material witness, and I'm holding you for questioning."

I had always hated being called little lady, or any other derogatory term for woman. Wonder how he'd feel if I called him little man? Probably find it funny. I took a steadying breath. "I realize you need to ask questions, and I'll answer every one. And I realize you have to rule out all obvious suspects, including me. But tell me, could I have tied myself? Who else here can find specific rolls of film out of dozens I left at the site, two rolls that went tumbling down a hill, one in a pile of stones? Who else can direct your men where to look for the .38? Who else can point out exactly where Dell rode out of camp?

"And I can guarantee you that I'm the best person in a hundred miles to develop that roll of film to obtain the best qualities. You can stick to me and ask any question you want. I'll answer. But please..." Tears welled up anew. "Please, let's get this search under way."

The sheriff watched my face as I spoke, gauging my

reactions. Finally he nodded. "Robbie?" he called. When a plainclothes deputy wearing a cheap polyester suit ambled over on bowed legs, the sheriff said, "Detective Robbie Wightman will accompany you to the campsite and assist you in finding the film. Mrs. Morgan is not to touch anything else at the site, not to take anything from the camp except the film."

Harschell was still watching my face as he spoke, and I recognized that the moniker Har Har disguised a mind that was sharp and serpentine and infinitely clever. I hoped he'd turn that mind to finding my daughter and the stranger who took her, once he was convinced I wasn't somehow a suspect in the disappearance of Bella. "She is to return to the incident command post with you or the officer of your choice and make herself available for any questions the IC may have. You are to question Mrs. Morgan about her daughter and the events of this morning, see she gets all necessary medical attention, and see she gets cleaned up. And she is not to leave town.

"Mrs. Morgan, may we have permission to search your vehicle?" he asked by way of ending his monologue.

Tit for tat, I thought. The man was into power games. "Help yourself. May I take some clothes and some personal items out first to help me clean up? You can look through them to make sure I'm not hiding clues, contraband or illegal aliens." The words were perhaps a bit snarky, but I kept my tone easy.

The sheriff smiled. "Detective Wightman will observe and tally anything you remove."

7

The trip back to the fishery didn't happen fast. It wasn't simply a matter of hopping on an all-terrain vehicle and roaring up the mountain. Rick needed to have a SAR discussion with the other searchers first; Detective Wightman had to change clothes. They told me I had a half hour to twiddle my thumbs. Instead, Ruth discovered that the park had a bathhouse and insisted I clean up. Wightman was agreeable to my removing some belongings from my truck and taking a hot shower, during which I finally had a chance to inspect my body. Unfortunately, Wightman also insisted that I have a female officer watch me in the shower and then photograph my bruises. Naked. For the record.

Standing in the icy damp of the bathhouse, I realized that I was a mess—abraded, bruised, trampled, lacerated and battered. Except for the layer of body fat, I looked like an escapee from a WWII torture camp. Discarding the bandages Rick and Ruth had so carefully applied, I stood on a clean evidence sheet and shook, brushing off the detritus that adhered to my flesh. Then, finally, I was allowed to lather up as hot, steamy water sluiced sand and dried blood down the drain. Officer E. L. Latham's back remained turned enough to afford me some privacy.

Afterward, shivering in the cool air, I stood as ordered by the middle-aged uniformed policewoman. The ibuprofen and Tylenol began taking affect; my bruised and cracked ribs were becoming marginally less painful as I held my arms to the sides, to the front, higher, lower, the IV bag supported on a wall hook positioned out of the shots as I posed at Sheriff Deputy Latham's directions. Her face giving away nothing as she worked, the female cop took full body shots, followed by some close-ups of my ribs, arms, stomach, face and back. For these, I held a tape measure positioned to show exact bruise size.

It seemed all the cops had hearts of stone, that nothing moved them, nothing affected them. I was having my picture taken—by a cheap digital camera and a Polaroid, no less—while Bella was taken farther and farther away from me. Again and again, I fought down panic as the minutes passed, my pulse rising, breath growing faster, shallower. If I became hysterical, it would help no one, Bella least of all. During the shower and portrait session, I found the mantra from the morning's icy swim. "Anything for Bella. Anything for Bella," I chanted softly under my breath.

The shower and photography didn't take long, perhaps twenty minutes, during which my fingers were beginning to move more easily, and when I pulled on a clean, dark teal long-sleeved undershirt, I was able to lift my arms over my head, though E.L. had to tie my new hiking boots, which were yet to be broken in properly, and button my camp shirt over a Velcro brace she helped strap around my ribs. The brace had been Marlow's, something he wore when carrying heavy equipment deep into backcountry on a shoot. He wouldn't be needing it, any more than he would need the Kevlar bulletproof vest, the clothes or the camping and photography equipment he had left in the Ford, or the wristwatch I now had strapped through a belt loop. I figured anything he'd left when he abandoned us was mine.

My hair, though, was ruined. Not even with heavyduty conditioner had I been able to get the tangles out, and there wasn't time to fiddle with it. So I called Ruth over from the ambulance and asked her to cut it off.

"Are you out of your freaking mind?" she said.

"No. I'm in a hurry. It'll grow back in six months. Cut."

Griping to the cop about women with thick curly hair who have no more appreciation of it than to whack it off, she did. I watched as she cut into the first locks, the medical scissors grinding. In the polished steel mirror, I saw that the skin encircling my injured eye was purple and swollen, the white on the inside was bloodshot. My face was scratched and raw, a dark circle marred the flesh beneath my good eye and dense damp curls sprang up wildly around my head as she cut, catching the morning sun with red highlights. On the wet concrete at my feet long strands of damp reddish-brown hair landed, still twisted and knotted with creek debris.

Inspecting her work, Ruth said, "I hate you, you know. Beat up all to…ah, heck, hair clipped with dull scissors and you're still gorgeous. Well, except for the eye, the bruises and the scrapes. You could use some concealer and lipstick. A lot of concealer," she conceded. "Maybe a bucket of paint to cover those bruises." E. L. Latham seemed to find that amusing, but I didn't look her way, sweeping the last long hair off my shoulders.

"I'll do without makeup. I can get pretty when I get Bella back. We can go for a spa day and spend the whole day getting beautiful. Till then…" I fought tears, turning away from my reflection. I hadn't cried in almost half an hour. A new record.

"Yeah? Well, Rick got you set up to use Doc's darkroom. He can check out your ribs, sew up your wrists and generally do whatever the E.R. would do, while your film is developing. He's a good guy. You'll like him."

"Thank you, Ruth." I sniffed and wiped my damaged eyes on a sleeve cuff.

"You're welcome. I still hate you. Come on, I'll reapply the bandages to your wrists and foot and stuff your fat hands back into the Isotoners. Don't know why I bothered to bandage you in the first place, if all you intended to do was to strip them off the first chance you got. No one appreciates all the effort that goes into a good field dressing." I stuttered a laugh and she tucked a slip of paper into my pocket. "If you need anything, you give me a call, okay? My cell number's on it."

"I need to call Bella's father. Tell him what's happened."

"You're divorced, right? So this is gonna be loads of fun." Ruth exchanged a glance with the cop.

"Almost divorced. And yes, it'll be a delightful experience. A memory to treasure. You mind listening in? According to my lawyer, I need a witness for all phone conversations."

"Oh, fun, fun, fun. I like this even less than I did cutting off your beautiful hair."

"Mind if I'm a party to this, too?" E.L. asked while she stuffed my discarded clothing into an evidence bag.

"Why not?" I said, my chest hurting too much to sigh. "It's not like I have any secrets from you after the last half hour. You might as well listen in on all the family skeletons. I'll have a constant audience later, anyway." I didn't elaborate and no one asked me to, but I knew the press would be here within hours of Marlow's arrival, and after that, nothing I said would be private, not with telephoto lenses and long-range listening devices. My life would be ripped open and laid bare.

Back at the Bronco, I pulled out my IV drip, let a still-grumbling Ruth reapply soft dressings, gauze and tape, and found Bella's cell phone, which I plugged into the vehicle's cigarette lighter socket and set on speaker mode. The purple phone speed-dialed Marlow out in Aspen as I held more ice to my eye. I wasn't thinking about the time difference and didn't really care if I woke him up. But when a woman answered Marlow's personal line, in his private suite in Rachael Morgan's palatial home high in the mountains, I got a bit hot under the collar.

"Let me speak with Marlow."

"May I ask who's calling?" she said, her words blurred with sleep.

"You can ask all you want. Now get Mar on the phone, or I'll have the local sheriff out to wake up his sorry butt."

"Oh. It's you."

"Yeah. It's me, the wife he dumped to get you." I could hear the bitterness in my tone. "And his daughter's in trouble, so put him on." She didn't reply, but there was muted conversation in the background before Marlow came on.

"So what's she done? She in jail?" he asked. "I refuse to bail her out and she knows that. We had this talk on her last visit when she went on that little joyride with the Phillips' boy and the cops had to bring her home at 2:00 a.m."

My mouth fell open at his selfishness, and at a bit of knowledge that had not been shared with me. "No. She's not in jail. We were taking photos of the fishery—the shoot you set up when you still were part of this family—

and she was…" I stopped, the word refusing to leave my tongue, as if saying it would make it too real. I took a breath. "Bella was kidnapped."

"What?" I heard him shift, heard the alteration in his thinking processes. Heard the old Marlow come to life in that one single word for a least a moment. I knew it wouldn't last, but while I had his total attention, I told him about the attack, leaving out only the condition I was in. That was more than I wanted to share with the man who should have been on the shoot with us, the man who could have protected us.

Marlow was nearly silent though my spiel, saying little even when my voice clogged with tears. I could hear nothing but his breathing, which got louder and faster as I spoke, and I should have recognized that his selfless reaction had passed. I should have. I'd had enough experience timing his moods. But I missed the cues. I finished with, "I'm heading back up the mountain to find the roll of film, which I'll develop. Then…well, I'm not sure what then. But you should be here."

"How could you let this happen!" he spat.

"What?"

"You're not fit to be a mother. How could you let a strange man ride into camp and take our daughter?"

"I—"

"How could you be so stupid? So totally thoughtless? What did you think you were doing? Did you even bother to bring the gun? The gun you hate so much, the one that could have saved us this trouble? Not to mention the damage to Bella." His words bashed me, bitter indictments. "Has there been a ransom demand? Word from the kidnapper? Hell!" he shouted. "I don't have time for this. And the press will be all over it." The last phrase was the final accusation, my most important sin.

Tears were falling down my face and wetting my shirtfront. When I took a breath I sucked them up my nose and down my throat, making my voice raspy. "Yes, I had the gun. But there wasn't a chance to use it without hitting Bella. And what was I doing?" I took another tear-drenched breath, forced the words out, not hiding from them. Never again hiding behind fear of dealing with Marlow. "I was living up to my responsibilities. I was doing my job, the job you signed up for and then walked out on."

"Oh, here we go again."

"No. We are going nowhere. You have been informed about the situation. I've done my duty." I pulled the phone from my ear and positioned my finger to end the call, but heard his voice. "What?" I said, more a demand than a question.

"We'll fly out on the next flight."

"We?"

"Sure. Gianna's going to be Bella's stepmother. She has a stake in this, too."

"Your snow bunny is not welcome," I said through a tear-clogged throat. "And she has no stake in Bella's life, not now, not ever."

"This is my decision, not yours. And Gianna Parker Smythe was my mother's nurse as she lay dying, not a snow bunny. I expect you to be civil to her when she's around."

"I'm warning you—"

"I'll call when we get in."

The call ended. I was left holding the phone, crying like a kid. As always, the loser in conversations with Marlow Morgan. Maybe I should have been embarrassed; at one time I would have been. My lawyer said I should be angry at times like this. Right now I was just defeated.

"Well. That was fun," Ruth said as she stepped from

the Bronco to the ambulance and brought back a box of facial tissues.

"Yeah, he's a real sweetheart," E.L. said.

I dabbed my skin, the tissue sticking to my face and coming away in clumps.

"The county purchases cheap paper products for half the price and then we use three times more than if they bought name brand. Typical county accounting practices. You okay?"

"Yeah. Just ducky." A breath shuddered down my spine.

"So it's your fault?" E.L. asked.

"Oh, yes. My fault. The affair is my fault, the divorce is my fault. The fact that he can't keep a job anymore is my fault. The fact than his mother died and left a complicated will is my fault. He missed three deadlines and now his career is in the toilet and no one will hire him, that's my fault. And now Bella's abduction is my fault."

"Man, you are one powerful woman," Ruth said. "A voodoo queen. You killed a chicken and cursed him, right? Can you stop the sun in the sky, heal the sick and the lame, and create new life with your bare hands?"

Ignoring the wisdom in the pithy questions, I said, "The sad part is, he's right. I did bring Bella out here, away from civilization, to a place where she got hurt and kidnapped. He's right. He's always right."

"You sound like a dishrag some man stomped on, not the Superwoman who dug herself out of a grave and hiked down a mountain alone."

I controlled a jerk in reaction to both descriptions. This was the second time I had been referred to as Superwoman. A strange tingle swept through me, but before I could respond to it, analyze it, Ruth continued.

"She could have been kidnapped on the way home

from a movie. You aren't God. You can't hide her from the world. You can't foresee the future. And if you can, I want to know who wins the next Super Bowl."

"I could handle some of that action, too," E.L. said. "Maybe like who's going to be next year's NBA champs, while you're giving away good betting tips."

I laughed shakily, but put my shoulders back a bit. "Okay. You made your point."

"Which was?" E.L. said.

"It's not my fault."

Ruth took the box of tissues and stored them in the unit with a careless toss. "You say that like you don't believe it. I got an ex myself, and while he's more likely to use his fists than a sharp tongue, he's pretty vicious, too. You did okay. But if you want a bit of advice?" Before I could reply, she went on. "If you stop acting as if the snow bunny—good name, by the way—is important, and stop accusing him, he'll likely start feeling guilty. And a guilty man is a good thing."

I laughed again, this time sounding more like my normal self. "Thanks, I'll try that."

"One other thing. The sheriff may stay on you a bit about the possibility of Bella's kidnapping being something she planned. Last year we had a double homicide where the victim's daughter disappeared. We all thought she was kidnapped, and it turned into a three-state manhunt. But she turned up living with her boyfriend over in Tennessee, spending the parents' money. They planned and carried out the whole thing. The fact that the girl was his godchild made it hard on him."

I met Ruth's gaze, acknowledging that I understood. She nodded to the side, and I turned my head to see Rick standing beside an ATV.

"You ready?" he asked, turning the key and destroying the silence of the parking area.

I nodded and shouted, "I'm ready."

"Climb on behind me. Wightman and Yo and a couple crime scene techs are heading up with us. Let's move."

8

Friday
1210 hours

The ride back to the fishery was torture and disproved Ruth's Superwoman claim. Every bounce and jostle was sheer agony, sending waves of pain around my chest until I was scarcely able to breathe at all. My arms stretched around Rick's waist while spasms of pain twisted my rib cage like a noose, through both shoulders and down into my fingertips. I couldn't imagine how bad it would have been had I not worn the gloves and Marlow's brace. My brace, now.

The camp was just as I'd left it, packs and equipment scattered all over, ground dappled with sunlight, silent except for the remembered sounds of my screams and Bella's crying. I couldn't stop shaking even after the ATV engines were cut, my eyes darting from the creek to the empty packs, to the place where I thought I saw Dell ride into the trees, his packhorse and Bella in tow. There were already two people at the camp, and they had circled the area with yellow crime scene tape.

Wightman, dressed in camouflage hunting clothes of much better quality than his suit had been, got off the ATV he had been riding and walked over to me. "You okay, ma'am?"

"I've had much better days." I licked lips that were cracked and now bleeding, torn where I had grimaced with pain on the ride up. Rick handed me a small vial of petroleum jelly and I smeared it on my mouth as Wightman and I spoke.

"Will you show me where you were when you first saw the man you claimed—where the subject came into the clearing."

"Thank you for that," I said.

He shrugged. "Like you said, you didn't tie yourself up."

"I didn't leave the horse droppings, either."

"Reckon you didn't at that, ma'am," he said with an unwilling smile. "I need to know where you stood, what you were shooting at each spot."

It seemed a needless waste of time to me, but Yo, two other rangers and the SAR volunteers were busy discussing details of the search, pointing out roads and trails on a series of maps they'd spread on the ground, comparing miniature Global Positioning Satellite devices that looked like cell phones, and the crime scene people were working on a plan of their own. So I humored the detective and crossed under the yellow tape. "I was taking shots from here," I said, moving to the spot in the clearing where the first morning light had illuminated the distant hills and cast mottled shadows into the tumbled stones of the fishery.

"I took two bricks of film, thirty-eight rolls, in twenty-four hours, some yesterday evening, most this morning, moving roughly from here to the manager's cabin, into the creek and back." I pointed out the route I had mapped the afternoon before, while Bella set up camp. It seemed so long ago. Another lifetime. I fought tears and lost. They stung where they coursed over my broken flesh.

As if he didn't notice my reaction, Wightman pulled out a pad, drew a quick map and sketched where I had stood, what I was shooting from each vantage point. "I was on the next to last roll, I think, when Bella spotted a man coming down a trail on the far hill. You can't see it, but there's a trail there, curving down the mountain-side."

"Yo? There a trail there?" he called.

The ranger rose from her knees and dusted herself off as she followed my pointing hand.

"The trail curved down to the right, then to the left." I demonstrated with pointed finger. "He was in sunlight the whole time, so he was riding east. I have his descent on film."

"Yeah. That's state land starting at that big oak there—" she pointed "—but I've walked the surrounding hills. There's a trail down that slope, but it's steep as all get-out. Maybe a forty, forty-five degree incline. Not something a horse could do easily."

"We'll want that film," Wightman said, a hint of suspicion in his voice.

"Ruth—the EMT—made arrangements for me to use a lab in town. I can have shots of everything for you tonight. That's faster than you could get them processed."

"As part of a crime scene, SOP is we confiscate all film and make our own photos." At my confused look he said, "Standard operating procedure. The film is evidence and it belongs to us as long as there is a criminal investigation."

Giving up the film meant losing what little I could still do to help Bella. It cut across everything I was as a mother to give away that morsel of power, control of the last film I had taken of my daughter. "You want to process fourteen hundred negatives to get twenty or thirty usable photos? You've got a better budget than I have if you can afford the lab costs when you don't have to. Why not assign a cop to help me?" I bargained. "I'll cover all lab costs and you'll still get your photographs."

"I guess that'll be up to the sheriff," Wightman said, stone-faced. "Show me where the alleged kidnaper entered camp."

For the next forty minutes, I walked Wightman through the sequence of events and quoted as much of our dialogue as I could remember. I ended at the place on the leaf-strewn ground where Dell had kicked me senseless. Despite my bruised face, Wightman didn't seem to believe how brutal the attack had been until I pulled up both sleeves and the hem of my shirts. He couldn't quite cover a wince at the purpled hematomas. Wimp. Even E.L. had done a better job than that.

"Looks like something was dragged off," he said, nodding to the tracks pulled toward the pile of stones.

"Me. He pulled me into the lee of the foundation wall and knocked it over. I heard him tell Bella I was dead. Or maybe he said that before he buried me—it's all getting confused. But I know this—the roll of black-and-white film is in that pile of rocks somewhere. The color rolls are scattered all over." I toed one with my new boot.

"How the heck did you get out from under the rocks?" Yo asked. "The smaller ones probably weigh fifteen pounds each. The larger must weigh at least fifty-five." When Wightman looked at her quizzically, she said, "I've been hauling rocks for months building a rock garden. I've developed a feel for their weight. You do know how lucky you are to be alive, don't you?" Yo asked me.

"Yes." I turned and found the trail where Dell had taken my daughter. "I'm the luckiest mother in the world."

"If you weren't lucky, you'd still be buried and Bella would be gone forever. Now she has a chance."

I wished everyone would stop trying to help me see the positives. I wished it heartily.

Wightman called over the crime scene techs and walked them through the sequence of events as I had explained them to him, then told the technicians to start with the pile of rocks and small boulders, photographing and measuring, establishing the position of each rock in its present location, because they would have to dismantle the pile to find a valuable piece of evidence—film of the subject and victim.

My watch was gone, lost in the beating or in the stones or in the creek along with my boot, but luckily I had Marlow's castoff. It was early afternoon, close to 2:00 p.m. If Dell had taken my daughter between seven and eight, he'd now had six hours on the run. And the search was still not officially underway.

"Yo?" I asked when I could stand it no more. "When is the search going to start?"

She looked at me strangely. "Chopper flyovers started half an hour after I found you, close to ten hundred hours," she said, using military time. "Three men on ATVs took the trail here half an hour after that and set off on foot. They've been after your bad guy for hours."

Relief ran though me, clinging, hot and sticky as caramel. When I sobbed, a hand over my mouth, Yo shook her head and put her arm about my shoulders. "You thought we were dic—ah, wasting time here waiting for the crews to hit the woods? Mac, honey, we been on this guy's track all day. Come here."

She unfolded a map and spread it on a large stone. "Soon as you said the horses were heading north from the fishery, we got a three-man hasty team with an SAR main tracker up here to scout out locations. He coordinated with the searchers back at the incident command post and they divided up, each taking different routes along the mountain, putting people where the main tracker thought they could do the most good. Here's where we are." She indicated a place on the map. "We got three six-man teams—here, here and here—so far, with more heading out every minute."

I sobbed harder and she hugged me. "You hang in there. We'll find her. If anyone in three states can find her, Caleb Howell can. He's practically a legend here 'bouts. If the FBI'd had his help in the early days of the search for Eric Rudolph—the man allegedly responsible for the bombing at the Atlanta Olympics, among other things— that boy would have been caught in the first week."

When the mention of a week brought on more tears, Yo.said, "And Rudolph was on foot, alone, and moving fast. Your daughter is on horseback, leaving spoor and tracks as big as a bear'd make. You stick by me and I'll update you on the search as soon as I know something. Your girl's practically home."

Breathing got easier knowing that someone was already on the trail. *Caleb Howell.* I had a name to hang my hope on now. I took more Tylenol and ibuprofen and followed Yo, listening as she showed me where other parties were being positioned. And finally, I identified, far off, the sound of a helicopter, the chopper making flyovers, its distinctive whomp-whomp a noise I hadn't distinguished until now. Bella wasn't alone out there. She had help. The Mounties had arrived and I hadn't even noticed.

Friday
1530 hours

A crime scene tech wearing latex gloves handed me a scratched and slightly dented roll of black-and-white film. On a chain-of-custody sheet she initialed for thirty-nine rolls of film, the single black-and-white and thirty-eight color rolls, and put them into a Ziploc bag along with the form. I was ready to head out, ready to do battle with the sheriff over who would develop the film and provide photographs of Bella and Dell. My daughter had been gone eight hours.

Friday
1605 hours

The sheriff wasn't at the ICP when Rick—who was a volunteer law enforcement officer, a volunteer firefighter, a paramedic and part of the search and rescue team— dropped me off at the ranger station with an amused glance at the film bag. The glance said he hadn't been put in charge of it. The cops who were at the parking area didn't show any particular interest in me, so though I knew I was supposed to find a cop, turn over the film and find the incident commander for a Q&A session, I found Ruth instead and asked for directions to Doc McElhaney's in town.

Climbing into my Ford utility truck, contemplating the problems that might arise from stealing my own film from the cops, I started the old motor and it chugged a bit. It had needed a tune-up for weeks, but that could wait, along with all the other things that could wait until Bella was back and safe with me. Black smoke blew from the tailpipe for a while and I idled until it cleared. Still no sheriff, no cops, no incident commander. I slid a pair of good quality polarized sunglasses onto my face and drove down the hill toward the small town.

Friday
1632 hours

The old man who opened the door to the stone-and-clapboard house built into the hill wasn't what I might have expected of a retired mountain doctor. He wasn't the wizened gnome his steep-roofed Swiss-chalet-style home suggested, either. Doc McElhaney was big and rawboned, with a florid face and callused hands that shook mine gingerly. "Got beat up a bit, did you?" he asked by way of greeting.

"Yes," I stated, but got no further.

"Men are pigs. Just ask my wife, she'll tell you so! Rick called. Said you needed a darkroom and a medical checkup. Let's get the chemical process started and then we'll take a look at your injuries. I've been both physician and a photographer in these hills for sixty years. Bet you didn't know that, did you?"

"No, I—"

"Watch your head—well, that won't be a problem— you're as little as my Beth. We've been together for almost fifty years. We met in the courthouse during a murder trial where we both had to testify. Man got the death penalty for killing his wife and I got the best little woman left in three whole states! Like you, she can't be five feet tall."

I was several inches taller than five feet, but I understood that my part in the conversation was to listen; I shut up. As we wound through the narrow corridors of the tiny house and down a cramped staircase, I learned he was a sixth generation mountain man with a bum knee, a ready laugh and a degree in orthopedic surgery. He also had the weirdest darkroom I had ever seen, mine included, buried in the back of his basement. Even with Bella missing, I could appreciate the eccentricity of the room. He told me about his workshop as we circled around to a sturdy table under the stairs.

The little house was built against and over a huge boulder that intruded into the spacious underground chamber, and the doctor had chiseled out niches in the stone, the rough shelves filled with an assortment of photography and medical equipment. A huge fireproof cabinet housed his chemicals, a twelve-by-eight space sealed against the light was used for the actual development process, and an ancient X-ray machine stood against the other wall beside an examination table right out of an old Frankenstein flick.

Both medical and photography equipment hung on

the walls, dangling from tarnished brass hooks set into boulder and timber. The only thing missing from the scene was the expected scent of mold, flickering lighting and a pieced-together body on the antique table. The subterranean room was dry, well-illuminated and body-free.

I handed Doc the bag of colored film and the black-and-white roll from my pocket. He looked at me, perplexed, silent for the first time. Not able to interpret his speechlessness, I said, "I'm a photographer. I was doing a shoot and a man came out of the hills and beat me up and kidnapped my daughter." It was the first time I hadn't cried when saying the words, and it was made easier by his conspicuous lack of sympathy. Taking a breath, I continued. "I got his face on the black-and-white roll. I need that first. Actually, most of the rest can wait until later. Except for two color rolls, I can finish processing them at home. Each roll is inscribed with a number in black marker, and we need the rolls numbered thirty-seven and thirty-eight. And this one." I tapped the black and white.

"And this?" He held up the police chain-of-custody form Wightman had tossed into the bag. "It usually comes with a police officer attached."

Oops. Busted. I had meant to leave it in the Bronco. Taking a chance, I asked, "What would you have done if someone took your daughter and you had the best chance of getting the film processed properly, the best chance of getting good quality photos?"

"You mean instead of letting some police lackey have a go at them?"

"Or some anonymous lab in the state capital."

Doc set the document on the table. "You're in luck. I'm the police lackey at the anonymous lab," he said dryly. When I sent him a confused look he said, "I develop film for the local police. So you did fine in bringing it to me. Now I understand why Rick called on me instead of one of the artsy types in town."

"I'm not sure I understand."

"Ruth is Rick's partner. Ruth is my daughter. Machiavellian little thing." He fished in the bag of color film as he spoke and tossed me roll number thirty-seven. "Always looking for intrigue and trouble. And finding it most times."

"She reads medical books. She wanted me to go to the hospital and I refused," I said, putting two and two together.

"And according to Rick, you could have compartment syndrome. Sounds like one of Ruth's notions. She's probably right—she usually is when she makes these off-the-cuff diagnoses." He tossed me number thirty-eight. "But you caught both rolls, which I wouldn't expect to see with compartment syndrome. So perhaps she was wrong this time. She sent you here to kill three birds with one stone." He ticked them off on his fingers. "Verify her diagnosis, treat as necessary, and develop the film. And it keeps you out of trouble with the local police, who would not have looked kindly on your stealing the evidence." This last he said with a droll tone, and I smiled. "Let's get to work, shall we?"

Locking ourselves in the darkroom, we started with the black-and-white roll. When Doc discovered I couldn't use my hands with the necessary dexterity, he took over for me, edging me out of the place of power in the darkroom and into a small chair in the corner, away from his work space. I wasn't used to sitting and watching, but Doc had a way with film that put me at ease. And with someone else to do the work, I was free to call Ruth every half hour for an update on the search.

By 8:00 p.m., Doc and I had four good quality black-

and-white photographs, one of Dell, one of Dell and Bella, one showing the hindquarters of the horses and the pack, and one shot of the horses and Polly. Perfect. Or it was, until I looked at the image of Dell, captured when he'd first realized I was taking photographs. The flash of anger, unreasoning and volatile. The heat and fury in his eyes…. This was the man who had my baby. I could have shot him. And I hadn't. Guilt and fear, old companions, almost a way of life, landed heavily on me.

The photographer in me wanted to work the negative, wanted to squeeze out every bit of light and shadow to expose more of the soul of the man who had taken my daughter, as if the photograph could show me where he had taken her and if he would harm her. Such efforts would have required a week of trying different paper and techniques. But the pictures we pulled from the print dryer were good enough for the searchers and the cops, and I needed to get back to the station.

I walked from the cozy house with multiple copies of the four photos. I also had twenty stitches in one wrist and seventeen in the other, six in the side of my heel, a set of X rays that proved I had four cracked ribs but no complete breaks, and a bag containing medicine samples for pain relief, an antibiotic ointment, muscle relaxers, muscle rubs and herbal tea for stress. Determining that I did not have a surgical need for relief of compartment syndrome, Doc helped me back into the Lycra gloves and into my truck for the drive back to the ranger station, leaving me with plenty of admonitions and advice for rest, none of which I was likely to follow.

Night had fallen and it was frigid when I drove up from the mountain house buried in the hill. I pulled on a lightweight down jacket and stopped at the local café for a travel cup of homemade tomato soup and a large hot herbal tea. I had a long day behind me and a longer night ahead. I needed something to warm my frozen soul, and food would have to suffice. It was my first meal since the Beenie Weenies. I wondered if Bella was hungry tonight. I wondered if she was safe. I prayed she would do whatever she had to do to stay alive…. Whatever she had to do.

9

Back at headquarters, two television vans and one bread-truck-style radio van were pulled off to the side of the parking area. A cameraman trained a camera on me as I eased from the Bronco, but lowered it almost immediately. I didn't look important. So far the press didn't know I was Bella's mother and had not drawn the conclusion of whose granddaughter was a victim of a kidnapping. Things would be different once they had.

With three dozen prints of Dell's face and photocopies of the shots of Dell, Bella, the horses and Polly under my arm, I entered the room the park officials had designated as a search and rescue command center. There were tables and chairs scattered across the space, maps on the walls and the scent of burned coffee in the air. I heard the words *incident command post, main tracker* and *incident commander* within seconds of entering, and my blood warmed. This was the place where Bella would be brought when she was found. Here, or a hospital, a small part of my mind whispered.

The sheriff looked up at my entrance and stormed over, his face a thundercloud, his flunky close behind. "Where the devil have you been, Mrs. Morgan?"

Handing him the photos with the amended and signed chain-of-custody form on top, I managed the partial lie I had practiced on the drive back. "Doc said these should do, and he'll make more when required. I left him making copies of some color shots. He has the rest of the film with him, so you can have it as needed, and the divided chains-of-custody should hold up in court. And personally speaking, I want you to thank the uniform who gave me such good directions into town."

"One of *my* men let you take the film? And gave you directions into town?"

I shrugged, my expression bland. That was the lie part. But of course, Ruth had been in uniform. The flunky, whose name tag read Ira Schwartz, lifted his brows as if he knew I was being creative with the truth. I ignored Schwartz, while Har Har paged through the stack of photos. The sheriff grunted with frustration one moment and then made a small *hmm* sound in the back of his throat. "This is the man who took your daughter?"

"Dell Shirley, if that's his real name. And that's Bella." I pointed to another shot. "That shows the hindquarters of his horses, and that's Polly."

"Rifle stock," Har Har said, studying the photo that had caught the back half of the two horses. Pulling a small magnifying glass on a string from his pocket, he said to Schwartz, "Based on how short the stock is, looks like a high-tech hunting rifle. Black plastic composite stock, brushed stainless steel construction to kill the shine."

"Joel," he bellowed, "we got intel."

"Scope could be a two-by-seven variable Leupold, likely waterproof," Schwartz said, his voice unexpectedly deep. "Maybe a mountain rifle."

Har tilted the photo as if looking for the rest of the pack I hadn't captured. Joel, a tall gangly man, joined them, his ranger-brown setting him apart from local law enforcement. "Whatcha got, Har?" he asked, his voice high-pitched. My first, irreverent thought was that with a fourth man, they could do a pretty good barbershop quartet.

Har nodded to me. "The mother," he said, and then explained about the rifle stock visible in the photograph. "And maybe this little spot of black here is another rifle stock. If it is a mountain rifle…" He didn't finish the sentence.

"That's bad, isn't it?" I asked, guessing from his tone.

"It ain't good," Har said, sounding like a local boy rather than a politician.

Joel said, "My men expect there to be an element of danger in a search and rescue, but gunfire from a .308 isn't part of the usual bargain."

Har thumped the photo and looked at me. "Nice photograph. Too bad you didn't just shoot the bastard with your .38 when he rode into camp."

His words landed like a slap, echoing my own conviction. The thick feeling of guilt washed over me, a tumbling, suffocating shame. I had made a mistake. And Bella was paying for it.

Har seemed to read my reaction, his face reddening as he lifted the shot of Dell and Bella sitting side by side. "Course, if he was sitting this close to your daughter, you coulda killed her instead. That woulda been a shi—ah, bad, huh?"

Still feeling sick, the soup rising like acid, I turned away and sat at a table, the pain in my shoulders and hands soaring. *My fault, my fault.* The words whispered in my veins with the beat of my blood. Har Har dropped a rough hand on my shoulder for a moment. "It's all right, missus. You done the best you could."

I nodded, knowing my best hadn't been good enough. When I could think again, I looked for Yolanda. She wasn't here, but Ruth was sitting in a corner with another EMT, the two drinking from foam cups. A man with a Bible open on his knee sat against a wall, his eyes closed, praying or sleeping. I spotted a woman on the far side of the room working a radio, alternately keying notes into a computer and drawing with a red wax pencil onto a plastic wall map on a corkboard at her elbow. I assumed she was in charge of communications, notifying everyone as information came in from the searchers.

Har Har and Joel called Robbie Wightman over to discuss the type of equipment Dell had and the precautions the men in the field would need to take. The three men studied the photo of the rifle together, and Wightman agreed with Har Har's assessment. Dell had a .308 rifle, which was a nasty gun in the hands of a desperate man.

"Tell me what kind of precautions our men need to take against this kind of firepower," Har asked the cop. "Kevlar vests?"

"Mountain rifles fire .243 or .308 caliber bullets. They're designed to fire on a fast, flat trajectory that can hit an egg at two hundred yards. And no matter which his rifle shoots, vests aren't designed to deal with that kind of power. And this scope…" Wightman cursed. Pulling the hat off his head, he slapped it to the table. The smell of day-old male sweat drifted from him with the motion. "With that scope, he'll be able to see us in almost total darkness."

I closed my eyes as the headache I had throbbed stronger. I didn't want anyone to die trying to save Bella. I just wanted my daughter back.

"Suggestions?" Har demanded.

"I'd put all the men in the front lines in Kevlar, anyway. The vests will protect them from a glancing blow or a shot from a greater distance," Wightman said instantly. "Tell 'em to keep a wary eye out for ambush. Caleb should reposition anyone without a vest to the backtrack or intersecting roads," he continued. "No one intercepts the suspect. He is to be considered armed and dangerous. Make sure all the searchers know that. But deputize 'em to use force if necessary."

"Make it happen," Har said.

Wightman called the order to the radio operator. The tension level in the room increased with the words, a scent like fresh blood and the sweat of fear.

Armed and dangerous. The enormity of the words struck me like a fist, stealing my breath and heartbeat. I opened the bag of medical supplies provided by Doc and swallowed two little pain pills dry.

"This guy isn't a fool," Har Har said. "He thought he got away scot-free, but he has to be aware of the flyovers. And the SAR teams on the ATVs aren't exactly silent, even if they're only on roadways and established paths. He knows he has pursuit, and that might make him unpredictable."

"Them the pictures the mother shot?" Wightman asked, holding up the photo of Dell and Bella, the one that showed the flash of fury in Dell's eyes. I realized he hadn't seen me, sitting still, partially hidden behind Har Har.

"Yep. She's a pistol, ain't she?"

"Good thing she didn't use the .38 to try and stop the guy," Wightman said, studying the photo. "If this camera had been a gun, she coulda missed and killed the kid. A shortbarrel .38 is really only good at eight to ten feet. After that, it's useless for target work."

I put my head on the tabletop, an arm beneath my forehead. The position made my head pound harder, but I needed the privacy. I had done the right thing, but Bella had still been taken from me. Tears gathered and fell, splattering on the scarred wood. I pulled in a breath trying to stifle the sound of crying, as guilt and worry, shame and fear, blended within me.

"You find her gun?" Har Har asked.

"Yeah. Little .38, matches the registration in the Ford Bronco she drives. A cookstove and a hiking pack had been tossed in the creek below the dam, along with some other stuff that probably came from the women's camp. Looks like it was all dumped in the water to hide the fact that a camp was abandoned. Found a boot about a hundred yards downstream that matches the one in the evidence bag with the mother's clothes. No rawhide strips yet, but tears in the shoe leather match the leather thongs Yolanda cut off her elbows. The mother wasn't responsible for this, Har."

"Don't look like it. But we can't rule out the daughter."

"Sheriff?" a woman called. "Caleb's coming in. He's ordering all the hasty teams on the front lines in for replacements and supplies. None of the folks out today wore vests, and with the cloud cover, it'll be too dark soon to make any more headway, anyway."

I looked up at that. The voice belonged to the woman at the radio, and I stood and moved with the sheriff, the IC and Wightman to the other side of the room. Detective Wightman looked at me, surprised when I appeared from behind the bulk of the sheriff. I nodded to him and he tilted his head to me.

"We got a report from the weather service," the radio woman added. "Fifty percent chance of rain is expected by tomorrow night, unless it veers north. We got storms building to the west already. Caleb wants the chopper to make grid runs east and west at these coordinates—" she handed a scrap of paper to the sheriff "—using night vision equipment to look for the guy's horses and for campfires not in regular campsites."

"As if this guy's dumb enough to light one. He's cold-camping tonight, dead sure," Wightman said, his eyes on the photo that revealed Dell's pack. "He's holed up in a cave or under an overhang. But what the hell. It's only money."

"Language," Har Har said, with a glance at me. "Civilians. And the preacher's here."

Friday
2203 hours

I had finally been grilled by the IC, had been put in my place for leaving the search site to process the photos and had learned most of the names and some of the history of the people in the command center. The radio woman was Evelyn, Robbie Wightman's wife. The EMT with Ruth was Mason Bartholomew. The two spent time removing a splinter as big as my hand from a man's thigh and bandaging the wound, then treating other minor scratches and bumps as injured searchers came in for the night. There was Oline and another woman named Pearl, who were SAR support. Sherman, Sheridan and Shelby Smythe were all cops in early retirement and brothers who had purchased and settled on an old apple farm. The preacher was Otis Bumgardner, a farmer, reformed hard drinker and Baptist minister.

Listening to the conversations around me, I learned that Ira Schwartz, the sheriff's lackey and right-hand man, had a life partner named Silas Newton, and they were the talk of the county. So far, though, no one had had the courage to tell Har Har his most trusted officer was gay, a lifestyle that would be a serious flaw in the sheriff's eyes. Silas took over the food table, making sure it was kept fresh, warm or cold, as health standards required, and attractively laid out.

Silas, the Smythe brothers and Otis had broken out a pack of cards for a game of rummy when voices sounded on the nighttime air.

The brothers dropped the cards in the middle of the first hand. Silas left the food. The female SAR supporters stopped a chatty discussion about the weather and all moved as one to the door. The room fell silent as boots sounded on the steps outside.

10

A lone man walked into the ranger station and was instantly surrounded by officers, rangers and plainclothes people, all babbling again at once. All I could see was the crown of his black cowboy hat, a creased relic stained with salt and ancient sweat. I stood and moved toward the crowd on limbs that felt like putty.

The crowd parted, moved to the table closest to where I stood, and the man spread out a laminated map as creased and worn as his headgear. He shoved the hat back on his head and I got my first glimpse of Caleb Howell. He was tall, nearly six-two in his riding boots. Sandy wisps of hair escaped from beneath the hat's brim. His dark eyes emerged, the irises not brown but a dark blue, like the ocean on the far horizon as the sun glints off the incoming tide. A craggy face, weatherworn, he had creases beside his mouth and down his cheeks to his jaw. He wore a thin black denim shirt over a charcoal-gray thermal, black jeans and a belt with a tarnished silver buckle. Caleb had been in the saddle at some point, and carried the scents of horse and male and woods, a faint underlying tang of oak, cedar and rich earth.

I felt myself unwind at the sight of him. A curious feeling of calm came over me, a sense of security, of sanctuary. And I understood why Yo had said Caleb Howell could find my daughter. *Could.* And, if she was alive, would.

To either side of him, others spread their own maps, but it was Caleb's I examined. The map was old, crushed, stained with moisture. Dozens of landmarks had been drawn on before it had been laminated, and others had been added later in ballpoint, the markings pushed into the plastic with a heavy hand, notations for latitude and longitude in the margins made the same way. Several others had been made with black marker. Over them all he had drawn with red wax pencil. An X at the fishery. A red trail leading off to the north. *Bella's trail.*

Heat and hope shot through me. For the first time in hours, I smiled with genuine emotion. *Bella's trail.* This was the man who could find my daughter. I was no longer tracking shadows.

His voice was soft, a burry mountain drawl that picked up the Scotch-Irish brogue of the original settlers. "Got anything on the flyovers?"

"Not yet," Wightman said.

"What do we have on the backtrack?" he asked.

"Campsite on the top of the hill. Looks like he spent a couple days there," another man answered. "Not sure, but it's possible he could see the fishery from the hilltop. Maybe see a campfire at night."

"So, if he had a good set of lenses, he could have seen the women the day before," Caleb said.

"Maybe. We got a team there tonight. We'll check that out. Sheriff, we'll need to set a campfire where the women had one," Wightman said. "May need to do it again at dawn, too, to see if it was visible both times."

Har Har nodded his approval. Wightman walked to

Evelyn and bent close to her. She began speaking into the radio mike.

"He could have planned out the whole thing the night before," Har Har said, rubbing his raspy beard.

"Could have. We got an ID on the man yet?" Caleb asked.

"No. But the mother got pictures. I sent one to head-quarters for comparison to mug shots on file. Had it scanned and sent to local law in neighboring counties. And the state law boys are itching to get into this, so I sent them a copy, too. We got the broken cameras and stuff he touched in the camp for fingerprinting, but that'll take days."

"Let me see the photos."

Har handed Caleb a sheaf of four and the SAR tracker studied Dell's face carefully. "Something…something's familiar. Can't say what." He went through the other photos, pausing at the one that showed the pack in best detail. Turning on a boot heel, he moved to better light.

"Man look familiar, Caleb? Maybe you boinked his sister back in high school," Sherman said to my left. The tracker flashed him a distracted smile.

"If not, then she was the only one," Sheridan said.

Shelby laughed. "You're just jealous because you never figured out if he had Jeannine before you did."

"Maybe. But I'm the one who got her in the end."

"Oh, kinky!"

I moved away from the brothers before talk became more ribald. I wanted to hear Caleb speak, not hear about long-past teenage sexual triumphs.

"You're the mother?" he asked, setting the photos on a table when I edged closer.

I looked up into Caleb Howell's rugged face, the feeling of refuge once again slipping around me like a warm shawl. "Yes," I said, taking the hand he offered.

"You did real good to get the photographs. I'm so sorry about your daughter. I'll do my best to get her back." His palm was warm, long fingers wrapping around my gloved ones in a grip that was meant to comfort. "MacKenzie Morgan, right?"

Tears sprang to my eyes. "Yes, but it's Mac. Thank you." The words sounded trite, so banal, the phrase lacking true meaning for the return of the most important thing on earth. "Can you tell me anything? Can you tell me if—" I took as deep a breath as my ribs would permit "—if she's still alive."

"She was alive and walking as of three or four hours after he took her. We found a place where they stopped." His face was gentle, sympathetic, but with an adamantine edge he took no pains to conceal. "There were two sets of human tracks. Some personal things left behind."

Elation replaced the pounding in my head for a long moment and I shuddered a relieved laugh, gripping his hand harder with both my gloved ones.

"He hurt you, didn't he?" Without asking permission, Caleb turned up the cuffs on my shirt to expose the bandages put in place by Doc McElhaney. I saw his eyes linger on my lower chest at the bulky band of the brace beneath my shirt before his gaze came back to my face. "Got a shiner a boxer would be proud of."

"One of the EMTs offered me a gallon of paint to cover up the bruises."

Teeth showed in his grin. "Ma'am, may I ask you some personal questions about your daughter? I know Har likely asked lots of questions, but I need different things from what law enforcement would want to know."

"Yes. Anything." I sniffed and gingerly wiped my face with a cuff. The swelling was down, but the pain had reached a new peak in the last few hours and even Doc's little pills hadn't made a dent in it. Near the door, more searchers were arriving, and Oline and Silas had pulled out a huge tray of sandwiches prepared by the preacher's congregation. Fresh coffee was being brewed. Caleb led me to a quiet part of the room.

"Can your daughter—"

"Bella."

"Can Bella ride?"

"Like the wind. She can stay on any animal that has a back. But she told Dell she couldn't. That she was afraid of horses."

"Smart girl. She sounds resourceful."

"She is."

"And is she…" Caleb looked uncomfortable, a red flush rising on his neck. "Is she in her…woman time?" He stumbled over the words.

"In her period?" I asked pointedly. To avoid my eyes, Caleb pulled off his hat, exposing light ash-brown hair pressed flat by hours of sweat, grayed at the temples, sun-bleached blond at the tips, curling raggedly around his neck. Straddling a bench, he pulled me down beside him. "Yes," I said. "She started last night. Why?"

"We found some…evidence of…of that, ma'am. Pads. Buried." His flush spread. "I just wanted to be sure she hadn't been injured and was bleeding."

Tears gathered again as I looked up, catching the over-head fluorescent lights and sparkling on my lashes. The tears fell as I considered Bella being…attacked, what the blood could really mean. I licked my dry lips and tasted salt. "He's going to hurt her." I swallowed past the knot in my throat. "Rape her," I said, finally speaking the word. "Isn't he?"

His hand tightened on mine. "Ma'am, in all honesty, I have no idea what that kind of man might do. And frankly?" He paused, his eyes on my face. I nodded, encouraging him to continue, but I heard the shift in tone and I knew he would say something else, changing his mind at the last instant. "They're moving fast. Too fast to stop for…" his lips moved oddly as he choose his words "…physical violence. I'd say it gives you some hope, if you need it."

"But?" I asked, steeling myself. "There's a but in there. I heard it."

Caleb searched my face before answering, his words slow and measuring. "But I wouldn't count on anything like mercy from him." After a beat, his eyes softened. "I'll do my best to get your daughter back, ma'am."

I felt the weight in my heart grow heavier, but I kept my expression calm. "Thank you for the honesty."

"Is she an experienced camper?" He changed the subject to ground that was safer for us both.

For the next twenty minutes, I answered questions about Bella's expertise in the wild, what she might do if she saw the chance to get free, her ability to tell north from south by foliage and stars, how she would handle it if she were injured. I told Caleb about the Red Cross first-aid course we took together. "She did far better than I. I don't care much for the sight of blood. Bella just gets more efficient." I told him she was sneaky, mischievous, afraid of nothing. And somehow, without a word, Caleb Howell convinced me that Bella might survive. Fresh inside me bloomed a feeling of hope that had been wilted for too many hours.

A crash sounded. I jerked my gaze away from Caleb to see Marlow framed in the open doorway, blond hair on end. The sound of voices stilled in an expanding ring of silence as the searchers looked up. My soon-to-be-ex was haggard, clothes rumpled and wrinkled, pale blue eyes an angry red, yet he still dazzled. Marlow was always beautiful, no matter the circumstances.

Shoving a hand through his hair, he found me in the

mass of people. A pang shot through me, an old ache of betrayal and lost love. I pulled my hand from Caleb's, where it still rested.

Eyes locked on me, Marlow swung a suitcase in a long arc and threw it across the room. It swung away in a low curve and crashed into furniture. Lightweight metal folding chairs collapsed or skittered across the floor. He lifted an accusing finger, pointing at me, his face constricted in a mask of hatred. "You should never have brought her with you," he said in the too-calm tone he always used just before he exploded.

I felt the old reflexes kick in, felt myself closing up, shutting down, withdrawing. And I fought the fear, the unearned guilt, the need to run. Clenched my aching hands into fists as Marlow descended on me. The name *Superwoman* echoed mockingly in my mind. I would not run. Not this time. Never again.

"You should have left her at home where she was safe. You acted like a fool, like a stupid child, bringing her here."

My head came up, fear burning into anger. He'd never lost control like this before. In front of strangers. In front of a crowd. Not image-conscious Marlow.

"You idiot," he said.

Anger flamed hotter, singeing the bands of control I'd built over too many years.

"My lawyer says this demonstrates a serious lack of judgment."

The anger snapped, an almost audible ping inside my head. "Serious lack of judgment?" The words hissed from my mouth. His eyes widened at my temerity. "Our daughter is lost on a mountain and you took time to call your lawyer?" I whispered into the shocked silence, slowly standing. "If you'd been here doing your job instead of sleeping with that woman in Aspen, Bella would

be safe. Don't you *dare* blame me for your deficiencies."
I jerked as he took a step toward me, raised my voice
from a whisper, raised my chin to him as I had never
done before. "I refuse to take blame that rests on you and
that Gianna."

"Don't you start in again," he roared, and charged
me.

Caleb stepped in front of Marlow, taking the brunt of
the lighter man's attack. "Control yourself, man," he said,
voice dead calm.

A cameraman had followed Marlow and his clamor to
the door of the room, standing there with the heavy,
shoulder-supported lens trained on us. I turned away
quickly, but Marlow shoved at Caleb, who braced his
legs against the thrust.

And then the sheriff and the IC were there. Wightman
was shooing the newspeople out of the room. Caleb was
forcing Marlow into a chair, while others were righting
furniture and restoring interrupted conversations. After
a moment, a woman edged closer to Marlow, as always,
drawn by his magnetism even in the midst of his rage.
The mountain folk slid surreptitious glances over us that
I pretended not to notice. Slowly the room returned to its
low rumble of conversation, the sheriff keeping Marlow
in a corner away from me, asking him about his financial state, wanting to know about possible reasons someone might kidnap his daughter.

It hadn't always been this way. I remembered a time
when we had been madly in love, his devotion so complete, so all consuming, that it seemed we had become
one another's whole life, whole world.

The first time he hurt me had been more a shock than
a physical pain, and he had been devastated at his own
actions, so full of shame for his loss of control that I had
forgiven him instantly. As I looked back, I realized that

had been my first mistake. That moment of absolution had set a pattern in place, warping our relationship a bit more each time he lost his temper, each time I forgave or took the blame for his violence.

I had been in counseling since he left, and had learned much about my own co-dependent actions and destructive patterns in our lives. Superwoman, huh? I wondered...

The radio crackled. "Evelyn, 'ess is Bayard up at the last camp used by the kidnapper. Le' me talk to the shurff. I think we got us a old grave here."

11

Sheriff Harman Harschell IV, took the standing mike and identified himself. "What've you got?"

"It's been here awhile, but it must still have a smell. The dogs found it. Size about four-by-two feet, big enough for a person curled on a side if they was limber."

"Crime scene been there?"

"Been and gone. The grave is off to the side, down from the edge of the camp."

"Keep the dogs out of it. I'll get you a forensics team up there by morning."

"I want to see it too, Har," Caleb said. "Can the team be ready to leave half an hour before sunup?"

"They can be here by then." Har gave further instructions to the team at Dell's old campsite and signed off. Facing the room, he said, "That's it till o-five-thirty. Be back here for a 6:00 a.m. start, those who can. Breakfast, a half hour before that, will be provided by the ladies of the Stove Creek Baptist Church."

The crowd began to thin immediately as tired searchers made for the door and a few hours of shut-eye. A hand rested on my shoulder. When I faced Ruth, I smiled. It was the first time all evening we had been close enough to speak.

"You still look like death warmed over. Here's a key to my house." She pressed a warm brass key on a silver ring into my gloved hand. "No, don't argue. Ervin's on the mountain, I'm pulling a twenty-four hour shift and the kids are at my sister's place across the road. No one's there and you need a hot bath and a few hours rest in a real bed. The guest bedroom is to the right of the front door, a little suite my father-in-law used until he had to go into a home. Use the tub, it's got jets that'll sooth your muscles, and you can turn on the gas logs for warmth. Consider the place yours until this is over. Shut up," she said when I tried to interrupt. "Just check to see if the dogs have water in the bowl at the back door. The puppy keeps turning it over. And for God's sake, stop crying."

I hiccuped a laugh. "I have Marlow's old sleeping bag in the back of the Bronco."

"Yeah? Well, why didn't you say so. That sounds so much more comfy than my guest suite with a real bed and full bath." Ruth curled my fingers around her key and gave me directions to her house in town. "If you want company and if the puppy doesn't smell too bad, let him in. He likes to sleep on the foot of the bed. He'll keep your feet warm. Do not—" she held up a hand when I started to speak "—argue."

"I was going to say thank you."

Shrugging off my thanks, Ruth called to her partner and they left the building. As I walked to my truck, I heard Marlow's voice, strident and hostile, questioning Har and Joel. In all the years together, I had never realized how big a pain in the backside my ex was. I hoped the snow bunny was capable of being a competent buffer between Marlow's temper and the world, now that he didn't have me to do the job. If not, he might never hold a photography commission again.

When Marlow was charming, he was God's gift to the world, reading every nuance of a person or a room and responding to it perfectly, a glittering, captivating angel of a man. But when he was stressed, it was a very different story. His temper had already damaged his standing in the rarefied domain of professional wildlife photographers. Of course, with his mama's estate coming to him and his brother, Marlow didn't need to work, unlike the rest of us poor souls who still had to make a living.

Putting my nearly ex-husband out of my thoughts, I climbed into the Bronco and headed toward Ruth's to try and rest until the search could begin again.

Saturday
0058 hours

At Ruth's, I took a long bath in the swirling water, rewashed my hair in the huge shower and curled beneath a down comforter with her puppy over my feet. Restless, frightened, envisioning things I didn't want to see or think about, I lay in the warming covers. I had lost my baby. Tears fell onto the cotton pillowcase as I thought of her alone with Dell Shirley. *I had lost my baby.*

Knowing I wouldn't sleep, I prayed instead. It had been a long time since I had bothered to pray, and the formal words were almost forgotten. Stumbling over uncertain phrases, I abandoned them and simply cried for protection for my baby out under the stars. Begged God's forgiveness for letting her be taken away from me, for not moving faster, not shooting the gun, not finding a way to free myself and go after her.

Sensing my distress, the puppy crawled up my body and licked my face. My reaction was more sob than laughter, but I took the wiggling dog and resettled him beneath my arm.

I whispered into the dark every name I could remember from the long day. I especially called God's goodwill down on Caleb Howell. I wanted angels and good vibes and lots of heavenly favors on his head. I didn't know what God thought He was doing, letting my baby get taken by Dell. Maybe it was the devil, not God, who had a hand in this. But I figured God would forgive me eventually, and Caleb could be used to right a wrong, to save my Bella. Exhausted, I fell into troubled dreams with the puppy snoring softly beside me.

Saturday
0400 hours

Awake early, I soaked for an hour in the tub before cleaning the bath and making the bed. I moved like a ninety-eight-year-old woman and felt as if I'd been hit by a truck. The bruises were black and purple across my chest and hips, and my hands had swelled again in the night. The swelling in my fingers was worse than I expected, but there were gloves for that, so I treated my cuts and injuries and dressed in warm clothes and the new, stiff hiking boots. Pulling on Isotoners with convenient leather strips across the palms, I let myself out into the chill gray of predawn. I was sure I could find someone at headquarters to tie my shoelaces, tighten my rib brace and button my shirt for me.

The cold sliced through my chest like an icy saw, grinding deeper with each breath, and the puppy whined in discontent until I let him back with the bigger dogs and he found a warm place against a heated side. I relocked the doors, still quietly amazed at the kindness of strangers.

Before I drove off, I tore through the back of the Bronco, hunting for Marlow's Kevlar vest, worn when he went into dangerous South American territory for photos of endangered wildlife species. I found the vest, left there months ago along with the rest of Marlow's life, an old F3 Nikon camera Bella had packed, Marlow's padded sleep roll and camp kit, a sun visor constructed to withstand wind, and a half-dozen other things I might need on the trail. I tossed them all onto the passenger seat. I was going to the campsite and then on the search with Caleb, come death or dirty water. My daddy's old saying. The unexpected memory of the man who had raised me brought solace.

Buttoned and tied and properly dressed by Oline, I ate eggs and bacon, cheese grits and oatmeal with the searchers, listening to snippets of the previous day's activities, learning that roads were to be blocked off and trails to be covered by scores of men and women. The searchers were trying to keep Dell from getting to a place called Satan's Tombstone, a hill that had been ravaged by fire in the early part of the twentieth century and had never recovered. If he reached that hillside, there were myriad trails out, from old logging roads to railroad tracks left from the logging camp days to narrow trails difficult for one man to traverse, let alone a man with horses and a girl.

Caleb rose from a table near the front and I observed him as he worked the room, speaking to every man and woman under his command, touching the shoulders of most, thumping the backs of others, asking about kids and wives and husbands, businesses left unattended, jobs deserted for the search. He was a natural leader with a quiet sense of command, an ease in his own skin that made me itch to take candid shots. And though the night had left me with a sense of desolation and anguish that I couldn't dislodge, it seemed to diminish as I watched him.

While it was still dark out, I gathered with the

searchers and the forensics teams for the day's work. Not once meeting my eyes, feigning that he didn't see me standing with the others, Caleb divided up the group into seven search teams based on experience and equipment, the number of Kevlar vests and the available number of rangers with their strong park radios.

"No teams without vests north or west of the old Hindenlaurel Trail. Instead, you folks are the brush beaters we hope will guide and direct the subjects toward the northwest. Try to make enough noise to move them away from the Tombstone, into areas where they're less likely to slip by us. Make enough noise to be heard but not enough to be obvious. ATVs on open roads and permitted trails are a good idea here. Shout instead of using radios. Let him think we're overconfident or stupid, but keep your eyes open.

"All teams with vests are to work as three or four man hasty teams, with one park ranger per group. We have enough vests to make four teams. Divide up according to expertise and move out with Stubbs." A tall, pole-thin man wearing ranger-brown standing beside Caleb lifted a hand. "He'll position you to begin a northward push. You are to move silently horseback and on foot, radio and cell phone communication only. Two teams will head out by truck to the intersection of Singing Rock Road and move into the woods. You guys are our eyes and ears. When you find the trail again, mark it, call me and stay put. Don't screw up."

"Ya mean like Bubba Stevens did in '98, when he fell in the creek and near 'bout froze to death?" a voice called.

"Come on, y'all. Let me live that one down, why don't you?"

"Yeah, like that," Caleb said with a flash of white teeth in the graying light. "Or like getting yourselves shot. Try not to do that, will you? Blood always ruins a perfectly good trail for the dogs."

"We'll try to oblige, Caleb," Stubbs said, his voice an amused bass rumble.

"And remember that the subject has a girl with him. You spot the man, you call in. Do not approach. No heroics that could get her hurt."

"Yeah, but we get to shoot him later, right? When no one's looking?" The crowd laughed, good-natured banter between them. I wasn't so sure it was entirely a joke.

But I wasn't part of their crowd, and Caleb Howell was still determined to ignore me. Whether he liked it or not, I was not going to be left behind.

12

As the groups moved away in small clusters, I stepped up to the tracker. "I'd like to go to the camp with you. To the grave site."

He sighed, the single breath saying that he'd been hoping to be on his way by the time I spoke up. "Hasty teams have to wear Kevlar vests." His tone was reasonable, flat and final, as if that fact alone would remove me from the search.

"I have a bulletproof vest." Caleb's brow went up a fraction of an inch in surprise. "It was my ex's. He kept it stored with all the camping gear in the back of the Bronco."

The tracker looked me over from head to foot, the glance not sexual or insulting but studious, as if taking stock. "I talked to the sheriff about your injuries," Caleb said, pushing up the brim of his hat to see me better. "He showed me photographs of the bruises. You're beat all to heck. No way you'd make it."

My face flamed in the darkness. "The sheriff had no right flashing photos of me like a centerfold."

Caleb stepped back, surprised. "Wasn't like that. Not

at all. I asked about your ribs and— It's a tough hike and... Listen. I—"

"Let me be less polite. I either go up with you and the forensics team or I'll find a way up on my own." My words startled both of us. I had never been the sort of woman to stand on my own two feet if there was a shoulder close by to lean on. Maybe that failing was part of what had ruined my marriage and caused me to lose my daughter, but it wouldn't keep me from finding Bella again.

"You right-handed?" he asked.

"Yes. Why?"

Caleb grabbed my left hand and squeezed hard. I couldn't stop the gasp of pain that hissed through my teeth. "How about here?" He poked me in the ribs over one of the worst of the bruises. "Or here?"

I caught his hand and thrust it to the left, brought my right leg forward, behind his, and shoved. Caleb hit the ground with a whoof of breath and I stepped back three steps, as stunned as he. The words that followed my unexpected action were just as startling. "That first-aid course I mentioned? There was a self-defense course after it. You poke me in my sore ribs again, and I'll leave you talking like a ten-year-old boy."

Applause and catcalls echoed, bouncing through the night. "Spitfire," and "You met your match, Caleb," and "My kinda woman." I ignored them, my eyes on the tracker.

Caleb lay on the ground before me, too far away to grab an ankle or hook my leg with his. He laughed instead, rose to a squat and stood, waving to the entertained search and rescue audience. I noticed he was wearing hiking boots today and camouflage hunting clothes to blend in and make less of a target. The Kevlar vest added bulk to his thin frame.

"Try to keep up," was all he said as he moved to his

truck in the darkness. Unable to breathe without hissing from pain, I followed Caleb to a Jeep CJ newer than my vehicle by five years or so. The four-wheel-drive CJ was popular in the hills, and this one had the look of a vehicle that was regularly used off-road—scratched finish dulled by the elements, a coating of mud under the wheel wells. I bet his Jeep didn't need a tune-up.

"Do you poke all the parents of lost children in the ribs?"

"Nope. Just the ones I think might get in the way."

"I won't get in the way," I said.

He didn't bother to reply. Instead, he hopped onto a trailer hitched to the Jeep, where he started a camo-painted ATV and eased it down a portable ramp to the parking lot. It looked like an expensive toy, but it suited the tracker.

"This way," he said, over the noise of the tough little machine. Caleb ordered me onto an ATV behind Yolanda, and I wedged my Kevlar vest, supplies and camera beside a pack she had strapped to the four-wheel-drive unit. Straddling the padded back of the long seat, I held on around her waist as we took the rough ride up to the fish hatchery. Six other ATVs loaded with gear and people made the first climb with us, including Wightman and Oline.

A second group gathered in the wake of our exhaust fumes to bring up the crime scene and forensics team. It was slow-going today in the dull light, but the bouncing was still severe and my ribs screeched with pain that threatened to bring up my breakfast. I prayed I wouldn't have to stop on the way up. Not have to give up before I even got started.

But I survived the nearly five mile ride to the old fish hatchery and kept my breakfast down, too. I credited the long soak in the tub and a few hours of rest for my success.

From the fishery, where we parked the ATVs in an irregular sprawl, we began the hike to Dell's previous camp, up a steep hillside on the narrow trail. I couldn't believe that anything four-legged could have made the climb down, but signs of horse droppings and deep, sliding hoofprints convinced me otherwise. In several spots, I had to grab trees to either side of the path to lever my bodyweight up, and twice I braced my feet on saplings for the next step. Breathing was icy torture in the early spring cold, and my hand hurt where Caleb had squeezed it. I told myself he'd done it for Bella, but it still made me mad.

Anger following physical abuse was a new sensation for me, an emotional reaction so fresh I wasn't certain how to deal with it. I probed the feeling as we hiked, the way a tongue might inspect a fresh lip wound or broken tooth. The anger was strange. Or perhaps I was.

The tracker, carrying a full pack with aluminum struts, was deep in conversation with Wightman and Yo, both also weighted down with supplies. He never looked my way. I had no doubt if I dropped out, Caleb would leave me on the side of the trail and keep going. But my legs were less bruised than my upper body, and I had always been an excellent hiker. I reached the campsite with the others.

The spot was about ten feet wide, fourteen feet long, a flat patch of dirt on the side of the mountain. It smelled of horse and cedar and fecund earth as the rising sun warmed away the chill. A fire pit nestled in the side of the hill, protected from wind and the view of any casual observer.

Standing next to Yo, I heard her speak into the radio. "Light it," she said. Following her gaze, I saw a spark far down the hill and realized it was at the fishery. It was our campsite.

I had spent literally hours at the hatchery the afternoon and early evening of our overnight stay, plotting the morning's shoot, taking a few photos of the fishery with the sun in the west. Bella had lit a fire early in the evening, when the light was little brighter than now. Dell could have spotted its glow or my movements at any time as I circled the site, moving upstream and down, searching out the shots I wanted to take.

He had seen us. Stalked us. Like prey.

"I see it." Caleb lifted binoculars from his pack and trained them on the distant light. "So, he could have spotted them either the day or night before and watched their camp. Likely knew the terrain well, and took the girl at first light. Well-planned assault, not a blitz attack." Lowering the field glasses, he asked, "Where's the grave?"

A woman in camo-brown hogwashers and a corduroy shirt said, "This way," and started down a narrow path about twenty feet straight down the mountain. Leaving all the packs, four of us took the trail, navigating the drop silently. The path was well traveled, but so narrow a rabbit would find it tight passage. Pine trees were a ribbon of darker green across the hillside. I remembered the pine needle that had appeared in our campsite at the hatchery. Dell had been down this path. Recently.

The grave was beside a boulder with laurel sprouting from crevices and from the hillside. The grave itself was bare, the slight depression scored with dog tracks and littered with wilted greenery. Caleb lifted a stem and inspected its end. It had been cut. "A bouquet?" he asked. No one answered, and he stared out over the vista provided by the location, twirling the cut stem in his fingers.

"He came here to mourn. Comes frequently, if the path down here is an indication. Grave's been here two, three years, maybe less. Means he's been around at least that long, but he may make the trek for special reasons, or he may be a local boy, gone for years and come home." Caleb spoke in a low tone, the words musing, almost pensive, but the theory made sense. "Yo, how long before the forensic team's up here?"

"Less than two. They're cresting the hill now," she said.

"Dell's got a Charleston accent," I stated.

"Not a local boy, then. Or he spent a big part of his youth away," Caleb murmured.

We made the steep climb back up to the campsite, meeting the crime scene and forensics team. They were blowing hard as they entered the camp, and two men and a woman fell to the ground, heaving for breath, easing out of their packs to get relief. Seeing them made me feel better about my own endurance. Even with cracked ribs I had stayed on my feet. Of course, I hadn't carried a pack up the incline. There were six packs altogether, filled with supplies for the crime teams.

"How long before we know what's inside the grave?" Caleb asked the woman.

She waved him away a moment and drank from a quart bottle of water she carried in her pack. When she'd caught her breath, she said, "Even with a rush job it will be hours before we know anything, and likely months before we know everything about the remains."

"I just want to know if it's human and female and if it died from obvious trauma," Wightman said.

"We'll know that by dark."

"Dark is too late. Harschell needs it by afternoon."

She shrugged and climbed to her feet. She was overweight and out of shape but clearly the person in charge of the site. "You'll get it when I get it. And tell Hardy Har Har if he bugs me while I'm working, it'll take an extra half day. I beat his butt in grade school and I can beat his butt today."

Wightman smiled, his expression rueful. "I'd rather not pass that along, if you don't mind."

"Whatever. Okay, people. Let's get a work area set up and equipment ready. I want out of here by nightfall, latest."

Caleb and Yolanda started back down the hill and I followed slowly. Wightman remained behind with the others. The cops wanted to know if the body was human, female, and had died from obvious trauma. The cops wanted to know if they had a serial…serial something on their hands. I couldn't wrap my mind around the thought of a serial what.

Saturday
0827 hours

Back at the fishery, I was about to mount the ATV with Yo when I paused and went back to the campsite. "What?" she called to me. A moment later she joined me and I could almost feel her gaze boring into the side of my face. "What?"

I let my eyes go slowly out of focus, scanning the site. The clothing and pack remains had been removed to a law enforcement center somewhere, the bear bag was gone. Nothing was left to show we had been there, that I'd nearly died there, that Bella had been abducted.

"What?" Yo demanded, a tinge of frustration in her voice.

"I never found it. I never had time to look."

"Found what?"

Rather than answer, I moved toward the fire pit and turned in a slow circle. Uncertain, I went left a few paces and knelt at the foundation of the manager's cabin, searched with my fingers along the ground for loose soil. Nothing. Pulling off the right Isotoner, I searched again. Still nothing. I stepped around to the other side of what was left of the wall. Nothing.

"The dam…." I said, little more than a whisper. I studied the old barrier, the tumbled stones, the trickle and roar of water over and through them. I crossed the dam, jumping the space where water had long ago broken through and knelt at the far side, digging in the soft soil. Until my fingers felt the crackle of paper.

Using careful strokes, I unearthed the single folded sheet. Opened it. Bella's handwriting leaped from the page.

> *Well, you found it. Tag, you're it.*
> *Love you, Mama!*
> *P.S. When Dad started dating I got a new horse.*
> *When you start dating, do I get a convertible?*
> *A guilt car?*

Tears blurred the words and they seemed to waver across the page. *Tag, you're it.* An old game begun by Marlow and me while teaching our three-year-old daughter to read. At every job site we'd hide a note, and when she had found it and deciphered it properly, she won a prize. When she got old enough to participate, we played tag with her, one of us hiding a note until the other found it. The prize would be a foolish wish, granted in the future when we someday got rich.

"Mac?"

I looked up into Yo's concerned face and explained the note game.

"The police will want to see that," she said gently.

"Would Bella leave notes now? On the road with this man?" Caleb asked.

I turned at his words, breath freezing in my heart. "She might," I whispered, looking into his dark blue eyes on a level with mine. I hadn't heard him approach or kneel down. "If she thought I survived. If she had her pad, she might." I remembered my scream of rage as I came out of the stones. Had I shouted her name? Had it resounded up the mountain to her?

"Yo, call in and see if Har and the crime scene recovered a notepad about five by seven inches, the kind with an adhesive coating at the top holding the sheets together." He fingered the paper. "Always purple?"

My tears had dried. "It's her favorite color right now. You ought to see the wild grape shade she painted her bedroom. She bought us matching purple thermals for this trip."

Yo eased up from the ground and spoke into the radio, asking if a purple pad had been recovered from my belongings removed from the fishery.

"Where would she hide them?" Caleb asked. "Can you tell me where to look?"

"No. Not without seeing the site. Every place is different. That's part of the game."

"No pad," Yo said, sliding the radio into a pocket. "She must still have it with her."

"Then I hope your ribs feel all right, MacKenzie Morgan, because you're going up the mountain with me to the place where Dell and Bella stopped for a break." He pulled me to my feet and, with a long rangy stride, crossed to his ATV. "Yo, get us permission to take the ATVs up this trail and get it fast." He pulled a handheld GPS topographical device from a zippered belt pouch and started stabbing buttons.

Looking at me, he said, "Climb on behind Yo. We have a little ride and a little hike. And then we're heading out on horseback. You just joined the Howell Hasty Team." To Yo he said, "You got permission? If so, let's go."

She pulled the radio from her ear. "I got it." Her tone said someone wasn't happy at the thought of ATVs on the mountainside. "I'm up for a relaxed ride, sure. There a four-star resort at the top?"

Caleb nodded his head. "Chef, silk sheets, Oriental carpets on all the floors."

"I'm in then, you sweet-talker, you." She straddled her ATV. "I've been up that trail once on foot. You can handle the extra weight of a pillion rider better than I can. Mac's yours this time."

The cops could have the note later. I tucked the purple page into my shirt pocket and retrieved my vest and camera from Yo's ATV. Climbing on behind Caleb, I encircled his waist with my arms and held on. The stiff fabric of his Kevlar vest made holding him seem like holding a sturdy oak. The ATV roared and took off up the steep incline to the north, where Dell had disappeared with Bella.

13

I held on to Caleb for the most grueling half hour of my life. The repeated impacts from the stiff suspension of the ATV as it crawled over roots, rocks, ground scored by the elements and by man in his search for true wilderness, together with the vibration of the engine, delivered agony beyond what I could endure. But I did. Somehow I held on, minute by moment, bounce by bump.

Breathing was a luxury. Pain and torment again became my world. And when we stopped, Caleb didn't allow me to catch my breath or dry the tears and mucous that had run down my face. He led the way uphill on foot, following no path I could see, crossing a steep gully with a rill of water between boulders big as houses. Near the top of a rise, on a blacktop roadway that hadn't been visited by a maintenance crew in a decade at least, he boosted me into the saddle of a horse, turned east and again led the way uphill. Yo brought up the rear.

I wasn't in riding boots and my feet barely fit into the stirrups of the ancient saddle. I held on by muscle memory and determination, not balance and skill. I didn't see the scenery, paid no attention to the beauty around me. I just survived as the animal beneath me climbed the steep grade.

After a time, as the angle of ascent leveled off a bit, inhaling and exhaling became easier and I managed a deep, complete breath of the pure air, felt the cramps in my chest and abdomen loosen, felt an awareness of myself and my surroundings begin to return. We were climbing at a thirty degree angle on a narrow path, trees and air to our left as the slope fell away; wet stone, moss, lichen, stunted trees to our right as the mountain towered above us.

The horse beneath me was a surefooted, short-legged creature with a dun-colored coat and a dark stubby mane. His too-long ears twitched back and forward as if he was curious about the trail and the people with him. Several times he even turned his neck, angling his head back to look at me. I spoke to him and he twitched his ears to show he heard me before returning his attention to the trail. I finally fell into the rhythm of his gait, and breathing was almost tolerable by the time we reached the overlook.

Caleb pulled off to the side and dismounted, tying his horse to a low limb. After a single glance my way, he took pity on me and captured my reins, easing them over my horse's head and tying them off. Reaching up, he grabbed my leg with one hand as his other encircled my waist and eased me from the saddle to the ground. He held me while I tried to stand, and the warmth of his body was a furnace to my chilled one. I clutched him, gloves against his Kevlar vest. "How long since you spent any time in the saddle?" he asked, his breath against my hair.

"I'm always in the saddle. Little jaunts like this are part of my everyday life. This mountain is nothing. A ride in the park. Are we there yet?"

Caleb laughed and I felt the sound through his body, the soft notes absorbed by the silence of the trees and rock and earth around us. "Can you stand?"

"Yes," I said as I transferred my weight from his arms to my feet. "Sure, I can stand." When he released me I wavered for a moment, discovering I could indeed carry my own weight, and my eyes found the view to my left. The mountain fell away at an acute angle, deep into the tight, narrow valley below. Trees, the green of new spring, imbued the hillsides with life. Pine trees, decimated by beetles, were a long brown wound down the western slope. I studied the scene, trying to see it as Bella might. Frightened. A strange man, one who may have killed my mother, keeping me prisoner. Had I heard my mom's scream? Could she get help? Would my father come after me? Would anyone? Thoughts of what Dell would do to me.

I shivered, put a hand on the saddle to steady myself.

Yo came up behind on a brown horse and dismounted. "We'll get her back," the ranger said softly, reading my fear. "We'll find her."

Caleb said, "Bella was tied belly-down to the pack-horse when they left the fishery?" I nodded and he continued. "This is the first stop they made. Looks like they spent some time here, ate, rested the horses."

"We went overland to this spot, didn't we?" I asked, fighting for clarity, for lucid and analytical thoughts.

"Shaved about two hours off the trip. Yesterday, I went the way they did, step by step. But that's how we'll catch them. Once we know where they're going, we can move ahead, box them in."

Caleb had stopped the horses just before the path widened—Dell and Bella's resting place. I moved from the horses and stood in the center of the meager patch of flat ground and turned slowly. The view out over the valley was probably spectacular, but I kept my attention on the small space itself.

"Where is the latrine?" I asked.

Caleb pointed off to the side and I moved to it. It was a miniscule patch of dirt hidden behind a laurel, the long leaves offering some privacy. At least he hadn't watched her…. I looked back to the view, down at the horses, up higher to the next stretch of trail. "Why didn't she run?" I asked, more to myself than to him.

"I think she was still tied." His craggy face watchful, Caleb added, "There were traces of something dragging in the dirt between her footprints when we first got here, before we marked it all up with our own."

Tied, shackled. Just enough slack in the rope or rawhide for her to take a step. Would he have allowed her time to rest? To write in a journal? I didn't think so, but I studied the site just the same, considering where Bella might have hidden a note. Behind me, Yo spoke into the radio, a hushed conversation.

I flipped over a rock with my toe. Moved aside a fern. And my gaze was drawn to the rock face of the mountain beside me. Cracked and broken by the elements and time, it offered crevices and crannies and dark places where something could be stuffed, hoping to be found. I moved to the face and touched it with my gloved fingers, paused and pulled the Isotoners off, pressing my fingertips to the stone. Dragging them across the rough rock. And I saw it. A space long and narrow, close to the latrine, where a hand might rest on the way by. Perfect for stuffing a bit of paper. Something pliable. Anything supple. I put my fingers to the space, angled my head. And caught a flash of purple.

Excitement raced through me, like an electric shock running from my fingertips to deep inside my belly. I turned to Caleb. "I need something to drag it out with."

"You found something?" he asked in surprise.

"I think."

Motioning me aside, he took a thin pocketknife from his thigh pocket and opened the blade. Inserting it, he scraped and teased the scrap of paper from the crevice. When a corner of purple was exposed, he took it in thumb and forefinger and eased it out. I could tell he wanted to open the stiff paper first, perhaps to save me from the contents, but he handed it to me.

I slowly opened the scrap of paper, sliced along the bottom by the knife.

> *Mom's alive. I heard her scream. She sounds mad,*
> *which may be good.*
> *We left a trail so I know someone will come.*
> *Come fast. Please.*
> *IsaBella Morgan*

I wanted to kiss the paper. Weep over it. Instead I passed it to Caleb and turned back to the horses and Yo. "Let's go. We have a long day ahead of us," I said, fighting tears, almost boiling with adrenaline.

"You'll never make it," Yo said, her voice pitched low. "And there's no point in it until there's some progress from where we left off last night. Please don't take this wrong, but, well, you'd be in the way. You'd slow us down."

The insult and the truth of it sliced into my raw soul. I had lost my baby and no one was going to let me help bring her back. Without giving me a chance to reply, Yo gestured with her radio. "Caleb, they need you and the dogs up ahead. The subjects took to a stream and the searchers are breaking up into two groups to head both upstream and down. But dogs will make it easier."

The two professionals pulled out maps and notebooks and compared them with Caleb's GPS device. They conferred with each other, with the searchers and the ICP, all the conversation in jargon—place names and coordinates of longitude and latitude and compass points that I couldn't begin to follow. They located on Caleb's map where the trail had gone stale. Found a passage near the location from another old tertiary road, one overgrown and out of use, but still accessible by four-wheel-drive truck.

Caleb noted the direction and said, "Take Miz Morgan back to headquarters and bring back the dogs and fresh horses. Join us as soon as you can. I'll meet the forward searchers in maybe an hour and a half, and you can catch up with us with the mounts. Sound good?"

"Best use of resources," Yo agreed.

I said nothing. I wanted to go with them, but I knew Yo was right. I was too stiff and sore to help. I would hold them up. I would be a hindrance. I couldn't even get into the saddle by myself.

I had packed the pills given me by Doc, and swallowed a painkiller and a muscle relaxer with the water handed me by Yolanda. And accepted her boost into the saddle. When we left the site, it was with Caleb's horse on a lead. On foot, the main tracker had taken off overland on a trail only he could see, to meet the searchers.

Saturday
1240 hours

Back at the ranger station parking lot, Yo and I found little excitement. All the action had taken place while we were coming back down the mountain. The handlers and their dogs had left and fresh horses were tethered in the shade with a chip of hay and water, ready to be loaded for the ride to the search area. We parked the ATVs on the far side of the station building, where the noise and movement wouldn't spook the animals, and I followed Yo up the walk.

"I'm going to have a bite and then take off. I'll make sure you know anything the minute we know," she said.

Dissatisfied, but powerless to change things, I said, "Thank you," and canted my face away from the cameras and the vans that lined the curved road to the station door, hanging my head so hair would partially cover my face.

"Why do you do that?" she asked.

"What?"

"Hide your face."

I tried for humor. "If you had a shiner like this, wouldn't you hide your face from TV cameras?"

"You have a point. But I don't think it's the real answer."

"I'm not a wanted felon, if that's what you're asking."

Yo opened the door and held it for me, laugh lines creasing her face. "Tell me the truth when you can trust me."

Surprised at the words, I started to say, "I trust you now." But Har Har called my name. The sheriff knew I had two notes written by Bella, knew how the search had progressed. He was tired, distracted and brusque when he demanded the purple pages. I gave them up with an unwilling hand. More links to Bella gone.

Keeping a watch on the purple sheets, I stopped at the snack table and loaded up on Krispy Kreme doughnuts. They had glazed and chocolate-covered cream-filled, Bella's favorite. Standing at the table, I ate one of my daughter's "bestest in the whole world" treats, blinking back tears that threatened to fall, the sweet cake and cream turning to dust in my mouth. I wanted my daughter back.

"Enough. Enough of this," I said aloud, and brushed my hands free of crumbs, knocked the tears out of my eyes with a careless wrist that brought pain to both black eye and hand. I squared my shoulders and poured a foam cup of hot water, adding an herbal tea bag from

Doc's stash. The bag was hand tied and I knew it would taste like tree bark, so I added a pink packet of sweetener while it steeped. Carrying my cup, I sat beside Evelyn Wightman, who was manning the radio again. Her graying blond hair was tied in a ponytail on the top of her head but she was younger than her hair color made her seem, with an unlined face and eyes that I could only describe as happy. She would photograph as perpetually good-natured, the emotion shining from the print.

"Anything?" I asked her.

She swiveled in her chair and twinkled at me. "It's murder sitting around, not able to do anything, isn't it. I always think it's harder on the families than on the searchers. Here, let me show you the position of the teams." She pointed to the map beside her. "We got a hasty team and dog team combo here, near the gorge, and two ATV teams circling the Tombstone, to drive him away. And we had two more hasties up here where the horses entered the creek, one heading upstream and one down. Got a second dog team heading in on foot, and I just got word that Caleb is on site, and has requested Glenn Team circle around to the west. Seems he picked up the trail pretty quick."

"He's good, isn't he?"

"Good man, better tracker. He's a main tracker, maybe the best main tracker ever. And got the most beautiful eyes in the county, but don't tell my Robbie I said so. Some of the local boys never quite got over their teenage jealousy. When Caleb was growing up, the girls just went gaga over him."

I pulled out a chair and sat. "You, too?"

"Honey, I ain't blind. And if I was, there's that voice. 'Course, your husband—ex?" she questioned, "is something to look at, too. Got some of the local gals in a tizzy."

"Marlow is my soon-to-be-ex. And he's always looking for a woman to put in a tizzy, even when we were married."

"They need a word for that. We got fiancée for soon-to-be-husband, but no word for soon-to-be-ex. Maybe I'll coin a term for that. How about fiancex." She grinned happily when I almost laughed. "Or we could take it from politics. A lame duck is the outgoing politician, so maybe we could call him a limp duck."

I did laugh at that one, and the weight of worry shifted from my shoulders a bit.

"See, I knew I could get you to smile."

"Evelyn, I need to *do* something. Not just sit around here, waiting."

"Go talk to your limp duck. He just came in. And for some reason he's got reporters all over him." Evelyn cocked her head, a sparrowlike movement. "You folks are somebody important, aren't you."

Turning my head to the doorway, I sighed. It had started. Three photographers and a cameraman were trying to block the door, trying to keep Marlow outside. Questions were being tossed his way that had nothing to do with his daughter and more to do with his mother and her money and his impending divorce. It would be a three-ring circus from now on.

"Marlow and his family are important. I'm just a photographer."

I rose when the sheriff and a deputy intervened, sent the paparazzi packing and pulled Marlow in by an arm. Shutting the door firmly against the press, Har Har turned to my soon-to-be limp duck. "Who the Sam Hill are you, man?"

"I'm Marlow Morgan." He spotted me across the room and gave a gesture that told me to come to him, one of those long-practiced motions that one recognizes even after the marriage ends. On well-trained legs that moved when I was summoned, I crossed the room as he continued speaking. "My mother was Rachael Morgan."

"The movie actress?" Evelyn asked from the radio. "I am *such* a fan. I was so sorry when she passed. Y'all got all my sympathy."

"Rachael Morgan," Har said. "So that makes the kidnap victim the granddaughter of a Hollywood legend." Looking in the sheriff's eyes, I could see the wheels turning. He was an elected official, and this search and rescue operation could make or break the next election. He didn't say, *"Well, that puts a different spin on things,"* but he might as well have. Our moment of anonymity was over. "How much chance the kidnapper knew that? Knew he was taking the grandkid of a Hollywood movie star?"

"None. Until now, I've managed to keep my child in the background, out of the limelight and out of the press," Marlow said. "He'd have to be a major player in the film industry or have access to deep background on my mother to discover Bella. She wasn't even referred to by name in the autobiography that came out just after Mother's death. But even if he did have access to that kind of information, there would be no way he'd have known she would be up in the mountains. The only people who knew that were family."

I stood at Marlow's side and waited, knowing what he would do, what he would say. He didn't disappoint. Taking my hand, wearing a solemn look, he addressed the room.

"Bella's anonymity is over now, however. We'll need to hold a press conference this afternoon to deal with the questions and satisfy the media hounds, otherwise they'll be all over this, getting in the way of the searchers. They'll be up in the hills looking for Bella themselves. They'll pester the rangers, the tourists and the people in town for on-the-street interviews. And they'll make our lives a living hell."

"I'm not part of the press conference," I said softly. He squeezed my fingers lightly in warning. I wasn't supposed to refuse the command of the press. Morgans never rejected the lure of the crowd or free publicity. But though I was keeping the name, for Bella's sake, I no longer had to be part of the spectacle. "The interview is for you and the sheriff. Not for me." The hand holding mine squeezed hard.

"You're hurting me," I said, not trying to be quiet, and pulling my hand from Marlow's. His face blazed with anger at the public embarrassment my comment would cause, but I no longer had to care about that, either, and curled my injured hand into the curve of the other elbow to protect it.

"Mrs. Morgan was pretty well beaten up by the kidnapper," Har said, correctly reading the reactions on Marlow's face. "If she doesn't want to appear on camera, that seems a mother's and victim's prerogative. Maybe when her pain level eases up a bit, she'll reconsider."

Marlow looked at me, really looked at me, and I realized that in his self-absorbed fashion, he had not noticed the damage to my face until now. In that fluid, mercurial manner of the Morgans, his expression changed, softened, acquired the look of intense tenderness that had made me fall in love with him so long ago. My stomach clenched.

"Oh, baby. Your poor face." He curved his hand along my jaw in a cool caress and touched my curls with a finger.

I went still beneath his hand, resisted pressing my cheek into his palm, resisted the tenderness in the gesture. It wasn't real. It wasn't real at all. But, oh, some part of me still wished it was.

"You went back to red, and cut it short," he said, exuding charm as he always did after I capitulated to his and the Morgans' needs. I could sense the small crowd easing back, out of the apparent *family reunion*, and ground my teeth. He touched my shirt and felt the brace against my ribs. "My God," he breathed. "What did he do to you?" I understood that Marlow expected me to give in this time, too, even though there was no marriage, no relationship to protect.

"Dell Shirley kicked me until I passed out, buried me in a pile of fifty-pound rocks and left me for dead," I said baldly. "Then he tied our daughter across a horse, belly down, and took her with him. He left a message for you but it's best given in private." Marlow's eyes flashed crystal fire at my tone, which was anything but wifely and soothing.

"The kidnapper left a message for your husband?" Har asked. He hadn't gone very far and was listening, clearly angry. "You didn't say anything about that when I questioned you."

"It wasn't important," I said.

"Anything he said may be of importance, ma'am. I need to know everything he did, every word he said."

I knew how Marlow would react to the sheriff hearing Dell's words, and backed away a step from my limp duck. Somehow the phrase and the image gave me courage. Softly I said, "He said that useless man of mine should know how dangerous it is in these hills. That no real man would allow his women into the wilderness alone." Harschell was writing the words in a notebook he carried, his flunky behind him also writing. The sheriff raised his head and looked from Marlow to me and back in surprise. "Then he said that he was taking Bella because her father wasn't worthy of her, and because Dell never wasted a good woman."

Marlow's color flamed again and I backed up another step, cradling my arms against me, the familiar fear rising up in my throat like bile. Unable to help myself, unable to resist the conditioning of half a lifetime, I added, "But if you hadn't called the ranger station and reported us missing, I may not have made it back. Thank you, Marlow." My tone grew louder so the appreciation would be overheard by all, and though I hated the weakness that made me want to pacify him even now, I continued, "I took Bella into a situation that I couldn't control and I accept the total blame." Which I did. Well and truly.

The choler in Marlow's face cleared a bit, diminishing to almost normal even though I hadn't said the magic words, "I'm sorry." I couldn't and wouldn't go that far to anyone but Bella. And to my daughter, I'd be eternally repentant.

"Anything else you haven't mentioned, Mrs. Morgan?"

"Nothing I can think of. But if I remember anything else, I'll tell you," I said, watching Marlow.

"No matter how insignificant it may seem," Har repeated.

Marlow softened and took my gloved hands. "What happened here?" he asked.

"The man tied me. My hands will take a week or more to get back to normal."

"Have you been to the hospital? Let me drive you."

"I saw a doctor. I'll be fine."

Marlow touched my face again in a gesture I had once loved. "The bruises will fade. You'll be lovely again. And you can always put the rinse back in your hair to tone down the color."

My jaw wanted to drop at the words, but I simply turned and found a seat. I liked my red hair. The darker color I had worn for years had been to please Marlow, who liked it auburn, not its natural old-copper-penny reddish-brown.

"Burgess is here." When I looked up in surprise, he nodded to the elegant man stepping into the ICP. "He flew in today. He has a room in the Falls Chapel Inn, just down from my room. We've become close in the last months. I think watching Mother struggle for every last breath gave us a chance to talk. Brought us closure on the past. He wants to join the search team as a peace offering to me."

Marlow straddled the bench beside me, resting an elbow on the table in a motion that was as fluid as his mood changes and that begged the camera to photograph him. And Burgess Morgan was even more beautiful than Marlow. The elder Morgan brother found the sheriff and shook his hand, his expression engaging, as if the law officer warranted his total attention and complete fascination. It was a trait shared by the brothers and their famous mother, a gift that usually got them whatever they might want or whoever they might want.

"You and Burgess? That's…unexpected, but great."

"It feels a little odd. We talked more in the last few months than since we were children." He watched his brother move to Joel with the same effortless attention. "Mother was pleased. I think it helped her to pass on more peacefully because we were reconciled."

At Marlow's elbow was a photograph of Dell Shirley, the one showing the anger and fury. Marlow lifted it and said, "This is a great shot. You captured him perfectly." I said nothing, always the safest bet around Marlow in one of his volatile moods. "This is a dangerous man. A very dangerous man. And he has Bella." Tears gathered in my soon-to-be-ex's eyes. A look of shock settled on his face. "He has Bella."

Feeling the ancient, familiar tension drain out of me, I said, "Yes. He does." Marlow finally understood.

14

With nothing to do as the day wore on, and the need to be doing something, anything, clawing me like a buzzard at a corpse, I pulled Bella's small Nikon to me and loaded it with fingers still clumsy from the swelling. I framed and snapped shots of the searchers and the townspeople who came to assist, catching moments of the day on film: worry, laughter, exhaustion, fear, anger. Once pain, as a woman who had burned her calf on an ATV exhaust pipe was bandaged by the paramedics on duty.

A local vet made a trip out to check on the horses still stabled at the ranger station, and to make sure the dogs in the field were offered water and food. He volunteered his services for the duration of the search. A food service van painted with a company logo delivered free sandwiches and colas, and the delivery man promised to return every day at noon. Perhaps I'd been around media types too long, but I knew that the free press exposure alone was worth the loss of day-old sandwich revenue.

At noon, Marlow, Joel and Har Har gave a press conference, during which the searchers were praised, Marlow begged the kidnapper for his daughter back, and I was described as brave, bruised, distraught—eulogized for the heroism and quick thinking that saved my life after I had been left for dead, unconscious and buried. Morgan was milking the crowd. He gave away far too many details of my ordeal, some of which he had to have learned from Har Har or Yo, but perhaps the graphic details were enough to content the press for a while and allow me a day or two of freedom from the hounding for in-depth exclusives that was sure to follow. And who knows, Bella being Rachael Morgan's granddaughter might attract more searchers, might actually save her life.

When the questions turned from the search for his daughter to his divorce and his new girlfriend, Marlow skillfully turned the questions back to the pursuit of the kidnapper. He was adroit with the press. Always had been. It was only in his private life that he displayed little emotional control, only in his private life that he had needed me to soothe and calm, to be agreeable.

Still unrecognized by the press, I photographed the event from the fringes of the crowd, catching the liquid changes of emotion on Marlow's face with an ancient telephoto lens, a sun visor hiding my face. The camera was a distraction, and kept the hounds of worry at bay, but the need to be on the search myself was growing even as the pain from my beating was beginning to ease.

I took photographs of the press conference for nearly an hour, until I caught a glimpse of Gianna, the snow bunny, standing in the crowd, staring at Marlow, moon-eyed. Long, lithe legs in jeans, big boobs, a bright, happy smile and highlighted blond hair flying in the slight breeze. I took four or five shots of her before I caught myself. She was pretty, in an overblown, curvaceous-hoyden kind of way.

Dell and Bella's photographs were given out to the press; grainy copies made by the police department were pasted on CNN, Fox News, local channels, and would likely be picked up by the networks. Marlow made sure I was given the photo credits, and at one time that would have sent me into a paroxysm of professional delight. But no longer.

TV and press crews had taken every available hotel room to be had in a hundred miles. Restaurants hired temporary help. Residents rented out their extra rooms. It wasn't even autumn and the locals were cashing in. Televisions were brought in by the park service to monitor the national reaction. The search made breaking news on the West Coast, where media interest in Rachael Morgan was still high even months after her demise.

Local law enforcement offered the park service the use of three police volunteers to help man the phones, and local city council members offered to assist. Workers in the black-and-gray uniforms of the sheriff's office set up a table and ran phone lines to the far corner of the room where the volunteers answered six phones, which began to ring not long after the news conference took place. First a trickle, then a steady flow of tips and crank calls began to come in.

I was still on the outside, useless, a passive, powerless figurine as action swirled around me and left me untouched and uninvolved. A boulder in a stream around which the water parted. I may as well have died at the fishery, for all the good I was doing Bella. Despair gathered itself around me, a growing dark shroud.

At two in the afternoon, Doc McElhaney hand-delivered the color photos of Dell's trek down the hillside to the hatchery. They were exquisite, perfect, two of them blown up by Doc to show the details of Dell's pack. The sheriff took them and distributed them to law enforcement and media alike, again giving me credit and telling how and when I'd obtained the shots. Making me sound like a hero, instead of a woman who'd lost her daughter.

I said nothing. The cops could have the entire brick of film and my head on a platter, if it would help get Bella back.

Doc searched me out, pulled me aside and insisted that I allow him to test my arm and hand reflexes. Once we were sitting on the uncomfortable metal chairs, he thumped me with a little rubber-tipped hammer and did a weird check where he simply pushed his fingertips into my skin and mumbled things like "Hmm," "Beautiful shade of purple. Bruises like storm clouds," and "Yes, I see."

He made me follow his finger with my eyes, checked my blood pressure and pulses in both arms, wrists and thumbs. When he was finished with the physical exam, he said, "Depressed, are you? Not sleeping? On edge?"

"Getting there," I said, instead of the tart words that hovered on my tongue. "Maybe two hours."

"Dumb questions?" He smiled, as amused as if he had heard my internal answers. "Drink the tea I gave you. It'll help with brain chemistry as well as stress. Now, describe my darkroom and basement," he said, the lack of segue throwing me for a second.

"Okay, this is really weird. You forgot what it looks like?" I asked, only half-serious, and touched by his concern.

"No. I remember. I want to see if *you* remember details from yesterday. In case you have a concussion or subdural hematoma I overlooked on the X rays."

"I don't have a concussion or a sub anything." But when he simply sat and waited, I described the strange rock-hewn place with its macabre atmosphere.

"Not bad. A little whimsical and imaginative, especially the part about Boris Karloff and reanimated body parts, but accurate enough in its own way. Do you hurt?"

"Yes. I hurt. And the longer I sit here doing nothing, the more I stiffen up. But your little pills help. And you can tell Ruth I'll live."

"That obvious, was I? She won't be satisfied unless I put you in the hospital, but I have to say, I think you're healing fine."

Rather than simply agree, I said, "Thank you, Doc. I appreciate the help."

He stood, patted my hand and disappeared out the door, calling a hello and goodbye to each person he passed. When his booming voice was gone, there was a strange empty space inside me where his presence had been. I stood and paced through my own internal fogbank. There was nothing else to do.

Saturday
1613 hours

I was sitting three tables up from the phones, trying to find an appetite for the pear butter and homemade bread brought to me by Ruth's husband, Ervin. The food was a nice gesture, but inactivity and fear had stolen my ability to put anything in my mouth. Nibbling at the crust of bread, I heard the change in tone when a phone operator said, "You recognize him? You're sure? Tell me." Leaving the food on the table, I stood and moved closer, my eyes glued to the woman.

"Dell Shirley. You're sure?" she questioned. A tense chill ran up my back. She had something. "Sometimes Alton Shirley? Yes, I got that."

Lifting her head, she waved to the rangers and cops as the room slowed, quieted, and every ear turned her way. Taking notes, she nodded continually. "Right. And he called himself Dell Shirley. You're sure," she clarified. "An officer will be out that way shortly. What was that last date again? Right. Got it. And you say he was a regular customer, coming in three or four times a year until this year. What did he buy? You do? That would be great if we could have copies. Fax would be perfect." She recited a phone number.

I moved closer until I could see what she was writing on the pad in front of her. It was a shopping list. Foodstuffs, both canned and dried. Ammunition. Cloth. Fishing supplies. "He did?" The woman's tone was surprised. "How often? How much?" She wrote, "Every six mo., supply of 'female items' purchs'd by Emma Hansen, for Shirley's wife. Clothes, shoes, etc. Until Dec. last year. Asheville." She handed the list to the sheriff.

Finding a chair with one hand, I sat down hard. Around me, others moved in, crowding close, obscuring her from my sight. "Thank you so much," she said. "An officer will be there before closing. Yes. We appreciate it. Bye."

The room was filled with questions, and Harschell called for silence. "What do you have?"

"His name is Oral Hansen and he owns a small chain of specialty stores between here and Asheville, catering to hunter and survivalist types. He says he saw the photo on CNN and recognized the subject as Dell Shirley immediately. Subject packs in on horseback three or four times a year to pick up supplies. Mr. Hansen acts as an unofficial mailbox for him and takes messages that are delivered on each visit."

"Is there mail to be picked up now?"

"Affirmative. And three phone messages waiting. He's calling Emma at the store here in town to tell her to give us anything they have on file for him. No subpoena needed. He's happy to help." She recited an address, and behind me a call went out to law enforcement in the area to make a pickup. "He also says he went online with a computer network last year and he has nearly a year's worth of purchases made by Dell, backed up on file. He's going to fax them to us, along with a set of duplicate receipts and information his wife has kept. She's been shopping for Dell's wife for six years. A wife no one has ever seen, by the way."

The chill had settled deep inside me, an icy mass, a frozen tumor, malignant and virulent, spreading a frigid cancer through me. My arms gripping my chest tightly, I rocked back and forth, a drunken, numb rhythm. Darkness closed in around me, leaving only the voices talking.

"Emma is supposed to be the closest thing to a friend Dell Shirley has. He told her last fall his wife was sick, and then he missed the usual November phone call where he orders things for Mrs. Shirley. She thinks he's been grieving for his wife. Maybe went off the deep end. Mr. Hansen says Dell shops at two other stores near his. Here's the addresses for them."

I blinked as water splashed. The brown Formica of the tabletop in front of me was chipped, the surface rough and dull from years of use. There was water on it. Tears. My tears. I stared at the wet table, as if it might have secrets hidden in its scars, as if it might save my baby. I was quivering, shaking deep in my brittle bones. I was going to splinter into a thousand ice shards, melt and vanish. I was dying, I knew it. I felt a hand on my shoulder. I couldn't move, not even to acknowledge the solace.

At my back, Burgess said, "You're not alone, Mackie. We're here." A long shudder passed though me, a silent sob that seemed to be absorbed by the comfort of his hand.

"Wightman? We need an investigator to talk to Mrs. Hansen," Har said. "Take Curtis and a car, code three. Lucas, stop the uniform from making a pickup and see Judge Kirshbaum for a subpoena. Let's make sure we do this right." Scuffs and scrapes proved that the cops were following orders. Motion I could follow at the edges of my vision.

"Fax is coming through," someone called. "We got shopping lists and receipts and all kinds of stuff over here."

"Hey, this is weird!" a woman's voice said. "The wife must a lost a lot of weight. She went down three dress sizes about two, two and a half years ago."

"Something ain't right here, Sheriff. Dell's wife lost about four inches in height about the same time. She went from a standard misses size twelve to a petite size six. And changed shoe size from an eight to a six."

The tone of the last sentence was strained. No one answered, but I felt eyes on me where I sat and rocked, the hand anchoring me to the chair warm, solid. But I knew what they all were thinking. No matter how much weight a woman lost, she didn't shrink in height, and her feet didn't get smaller. Dell Shirley had changed wives once. Now, it seemed he had changed wives again.

15

Burgess stayed close, his palm the only steady compass point in my universe for long minutes that seemed to stretch into hours. Then Ruth shooed him away and sat beside me, holding my hand. She wasn't working with the emergency service but with a SAR team, and she'd brought in an injured team member for treatment. She elected to stay and keep me company rather than go back into the hills alone, and I knew she was treating me for shock, because after she took my pulse and blood pressure, she wrapped me in a blanket she heated in a microwave and forced me to drink her father's vile hot tea.

Ruth was still holding my hand when the forensic team came in, the heavyset, middle-aged anthropologist practically falling into a chair in exhaustion. The sheriff sat beside her, straddling a flimsy folding chair and propping his chin on his hands, his backside hanging off the chair edge to make room for his belly, booted feet spread wide.

"Maxine, you and me got to lose some weight or we're gonna pop a gasket."

"My daughter's been after me to join a weight program, but they hold meetings. I hate meetings," she said, still gasping for breath.

"How about Atkins? All the bacon and steak we can eat."

"I don't know, Har, I'd be such a sex goddess I'd have to beat 'em away with a stick. And you know what kind of frivolous lawsuits I'd have to deal with then."

"There is that. And I'd hate to lock you away for inciting to riot," Har deadpanned.

"You say the sweetest things, you silver-tongued devil."

"As an officer of the law, it is my responsibility to warn even sex goddesses against illegal activity of any kind. And it's true, we have become a litigious society. I don't reckon your medical malpractice would cover sex-goddess nymphomaniac activity."

Maxine laughed and seemed to finally catch her breath. "Not last I heard."

"Maybe as a favor to society we should just stay chubby. You up to telling me what you got up there?"

"Down here." She heaved a deep breath and faced the sheriff squarely. "We finished at the site and brought it back with us. Anything I have is preliminary, and subject to change."

"So noted. At this point, I'll take what I can get. In English, if you please, instead of Latin this time."

"Spoilsport. Body was buried under two feet of soil and a foot of rocks. Crime scene crew opened the grave and recovered some fiber and physical evidence. When they finished with the little hand brooms and tweezers, an extensive photo shoot and site measurements, I took over. I did a few preliminary measurements on the remains, and I'd say she was female, age seventeen to twenty-five at time of death, been in the ground two, two and a half years. Height between five-five and five-eight. She had bad teeth, with signs of long-term infection at two molars that had to cause her pain."

The room was almost silent, only the sounds of the radio buzz in the background and the muted purr of machines breaking the stillness. Ruth again moved closer to me, encircling my shoulders with her arm. She stroked the back of my chilled hand with her thumb in a gesture that was meant to be reassuring, but was only chafing. Yet I didn't tell her to stop. If the irritating scouring stopped, I might cease to exist. I was so light, so cold, I thought I might die if she stopped rubbing my hand. The body in the grave fit the size of the woman Dell had bought supplies for before he'd changed to the smaller woman. My teeth started to chatter and I bit down to stop them.

"COD?"

"Best guess at this time for cause of death is sepsis, secondary to a broken right tibia. The edges of the bone are practically disintegrated, she had it so long. I'll say this, that girl suffered, likely for a long time, without medical help. We found a rough splint in the grave with her, so it wasn't like someone didn't know she was hurt."

"How 'bout an ID?"

"She had some dental work as a child. I'll compare it to old dental records of missing females. If she was reported missing, we should be able to do something for you, but it won't be quick."

"It never is. Put a preliminary report in writing for me?"

"It's what I live for," she said, heaving herself to her feet.

"We could change that if we got skinny."

"Too risky. I'll take my chances with diabetes and heart disease. I'll see you later, Harschell."

A woman tapped the sheriff on the shoulder and said,

"We got a possible confirmation on an ID. The head of the geology department at the University of South Carolina at Columbia thinks he recognized the photo on CNN. Dell may have been an assistant professor back in the early nineties. The caller has to locate another man who might recognize the photo to be sure of the ID."

"You got a number?" When she nodded, Har said, "Dial him back. I want to talk to him." Pushing himself up from the flimsy chair, Har stood and stretched, his hands at his lower back, gut sticking out in front as if he had swallowed a massive medicine ball.

"You okay?" Ruth asked me.

"No. I'm not okay," I said, my voice sounding tinny and distant to me. "I'm dying."

"You are not dying. But you are in shock. Lie down and put your feet up."

Unable to find a reason to disagree, I swiveled on the bench, twisted my legs to the left and put my feet on the table. Tears began running into my ears as Ruth disappeared for a few moments, and when she returned, I was lucid enough to ask, "He's hurt girls in the past, hasn't he?"

The EMT slowly sat on the bench beside my head. "It seems so."

"He'll hurt my baby."

"If he does, she'll need her mother. So you can't die."

"I need to do something, anything." I could hear the pleading tone in my voice and knew I was really begging for someone to help Bella. "Sitting here doing nothing is killing me."

After a long moment, Ruth said, almost reluctantly, "Why don't you join the searchers?"

An electric spark zinged through me. A sleepwalker waking, I swung my legs to the floor. "I can join the searchers?" Suddenly I could hear my heart beating, a thready, too-fast rhythm.

She shrugged. "Why not? You've got the equipment. You've got hiking and survival skills. Stamina, if the walk down the mountain with your arms bound behind you is any indication. And I can't see where sitting around is helping you any. Yolanda and Caleb are together on the far side of the Tombstone and don't intend to come back in tonight. Why don't you join them in the morning when supplies, replacements and reinforcements go out."

"I can go out?"

"Well, your soon-to-be-ex-brother-in-law is going out with a team hoping to herd Dell to the north. Family members have joined the search before."

"And Marlow?" I didn't want to ask, but the habit was so long ingrained, I couldn't help myself.

"I heard him tell one of the cops he was going back to the hotel. He sounded tired." Her tone implied that he was milking the situation. That he may have hidden reasons for his actions. But then, he was a Morgan. They always had ulterior motives. Like looking for women or sleeping with women or placating one woman while keeping another on hold for a later tryst.

"To check on his snow bunny."

Ruth grinned. "Your color looks better just now. Seems talking about Marlow makes you angry and when you're angry your blood pressure improves. Maybe I should keep you talking about him."

"I think my color is better because I can help on the search."

"Whatever. You up to hearing the rest of the news that came in while you were crashing?"

I grabbed her wrist, unable to hide my excitement. "News?"

"Not necessarily good news, but not bad news. Just news. A backtrack team found Dell's previous campsite, about ten miles from the one with the grave, south of where he first started stalking you. No graves that they've discovered, just a small campsite. He seems to have stayed there for a week or so. Just waiting."

I didn't understand the significance of that, but I nodded for her to go on.

"In the other direction, where Caleb and his hasty team is working, the helicopter's been making flyovers but they haven't seen anything, not with the tree canopy. Even a week ago, they would have had better results, but with last week's rain, spring has come in full force, and the leaves are opening fast. They'll make flights again tonight with infrared scopes and low-light vision equipment, but that's seldom successful. The FBI used special equipment for Eric Rudolph and they never got lucky. And Caleb and Yo found the campsite used by Dell and Bella last night. They want you there tomorrow, if you're able, to look for a hiding place for a note."

"Me? Not Marlow?"

"Let's just say that Marlow has made a distinct impression on the searchers and it isn't all good. You, on the other hand—"

"Well, why didn't you say so?" I stood and wavered only a little, holding to the table with a desperate grip. "I can go now."

"In the morning is soon enough," she said wryly. "I promised Yo you'd get some sleep tonight and be rested for an arduous hike tomorrow. Come on. You're going home with Ervin and me tonight. And if you argue, I'll have no choice but to deck you and have my hubby carry you home. You *are* coming with us."

I lifted a hand to Ruth's, my touch tentative. "Thank you."

Seeming uncomfortable with my words, she jerked

her head toward the door. "Let's get out of here and get some steak into you. You need protein for the uphill climb tomorrow."

16

Long before dawn, I was dressed and pacing the dew-damp grass of Ruth and Ervin's front yard, the puppy gamboling beside me in the cold darkness, chasing my bouncing bootlaces. Bootlaces I had tied myself. In fact, I had dressed myself entirely, not that it had been easy. If anything, I was more stiff and sore than the day before, but today I had both pain pills and adrenaline coursing through me, and two hour-long soaks and a good night's sleep behind me. If you can call four and a half hours a night's sleep.

"Come on come on come on come on," I said to the darkness. And to the dog, "Watch it, little guy. There's a hundred-thirty pounds of woman on top of that foot. What's taking them so long?" I stopped and studied the house. It was a two-story A-frame with a roof pitched to allow snow to fall off instead of accumulating. The wing where I had spent two restless nights was off to the side, and dormers shone brightly as the household prepared for the day, two teenagers getting ready for school and Ruth and Ervin preparing for the SAR.

When they finally appeared, I had worked myself into

a frenzy, though I concealed it well enough. Years of prac-
tice hiding emotions from Marlow had made me an expert in hiding lots of things. His eyes only half-focused,
Ervin passed me a travel mug filled with sweetened
herbal tea and pushed me toward the Bronco. "Ruth says
drink this. Don't argue."

Getting in my sport ute and following their truck up
the winding roads, I drank. It was more of the awful tree
bark prescribed by Doc, but it did seem to settle my system. By the time we reached the park station, I was
calmer, feeling hungry. I joined the searchers in a huge
breakfast donated by a fast-food restaurant in town:
bacon-egg-and-cheese biscuits, hash-brown patties, OJ in
little plastic cups with foil tops and glazed fruit pastries.

"You going up with the searchers today?" Oline asked
when I sat at a table, her wrinkled face reminding me of
a dried apple doll.

"Yes."

"Well, you be careful. And take some riding boots, so
you can stay in the saddle," she advised, looking over my
jeans, flannel shirts and hiking boots.

"Saddle?" I put down the greasy breakfast on its paper
wrapper. "I thought I'd be hiking."

"Only until you meet up with the forward team. How
do you think Caleb is gaining on your daughter and that
awful man? He's pushing the horses as if the devil is
after him. That's why they call it a hasty team," she said,
her eyes bird-sharp. "If you want to keep up, you'll be
on horseback, too."

Before I could formulate a reply that might have included the saddle sores that had blistered my backside already, I heard a voice not far away say, "Yes, I was in that
film. My brother and I were stunt doubles for the twins.
We both ended up with broken arms—my right, Burgess's
left. You have a good memory for trivia, to recall that."

It was Marlow, his trained voice carrying across the large space. Other people looked up and I followed their gazes to my soon-to-be.

"Thanks," I said to Oline, and swiveled on the bench to listen.

"And how many movies were you in altogether?" The speaker was the cute woman who had gravitated to him on Friday night, even in the midst of his rage. A few others sitting nearby listened in on their conversation, as well.

"Twenty-seven. But never in the altogether," Marlow quipped, his pale eyes sparkling. She giggled. "And of course, when I reached puberty I was no longer suitable for child roles, and I had seen what a film career could do—had done—to my mother's life. I wasn't interested."

A different voice said, "Yeah, okay, but I don't watch movies and I *know* I know you. You were here not more'n two months past. Talking 'bout the fish hatchery."

"You're mistaken. I haven't been in this area for months," Marlow said. "Not since last fall."

"Sure you were. We had a long talk up near Haskell Falls," the man said, surprised. "Two months ago."

I stood and watched the two, several tables over. It was Sheridan, one of the Smythe brothers. I noticed Wightman watching them also. He glanced at Har Har, whose eyes narrowed, communicating something I couldn't decipher.

"Sorry," Marlow said, his tone amused, crystal-blue eyes sparkling, "but my mother was on her deathbed in Aspen about then, and I was holding vigil. But you may have seen me when I was here in late October, doing preliminary work for a photo shoot. Or in the summer, when my wife and I were shooting the lakes and ponds of the highlands. Maybe we spoke then."

"Well. Maybe. Could of sworn it was you, though."

"Sorry," Marlow repeated. "Not me." As he spoke, he spotted me and smiled that blinding, dazzling smile passed down by Rachael to all the Morgans. Lifting his brows sheepishly, he said, "Guess I should have said ex-wife."

"We were married then," I said without emotion.

"Guess so. Still are, for a while." Marlow stood and moved to my table, carrying his breakfast. He was having an apple and the egg from a biscuit. No greasy bread that might ruin his complexion, which was flawless, or that trim form. He settled beside me and lowered his voice. "Sheriff wants me to go up with you today to the campsite where Bella spent the first night after she was kidnapped. I saw the fishery and the overlook yesterday afternoon late, and I agree with you that if Bella left one note, she may leave others that only we could find."

"You're going with the SAR team?" I asked in surprise.

"I considered it, since Harschell was willing, but because Burgess is with a team already, maybe one of us should stay here, deal with the media and the official side of the search." Marlow ran a hand through hair that fell back as if each strand had been ordained to its place. "I figured you would rather it be me who deals with the media, but if you want—"

"I'll go with the searchers. I have your Kevlar vest."

"Yeah. You have lots of things of mine. I'd like to get them someday soon."

Over my dead body. The thought jolted me, fed by the morning's adrenaline rush. It left a strange reverberation inside, almost a resonance, a buoyant energy. Yet I was supremely happy that I hadn't said the words aloud; Marlow would have shifted from his current easygoing mood to fury in an instant. And then, even more surprised, I wondered where the words had come from.

Over my dead body. They sounded like Bella. Or an ancient echo of…of me. Of my teenage years.

A hot flush speared me. Words spoken by an old self? By a person I had once been? Marlow was still talking and from habit I forced my thoughts back to him for an instant. He was making a speech about the press, and so I let my attention drift again. *Over my dead body.* Even my fingers were burning with the power of the phrase.

I'd give his things back *over my dead body,* which had been kicked into a stupor and buried. Left as dead. A death I had defeated. Maybe I had angels looking out for me. I fought a smile for a moment until I realized I didn't want to fight it. Letting the grin take my entire face, I stood up in the middle of whatever Marlow had been saying and walked away.

Over my dead body.

Marlow was a limp duck. Not my husband.

Walking to Ruth, I said, "Are you part of the group going to the frontline team?"

Her eyes widening, she gripped my upper arm and led me to the doorway. "What'd you do to him?"

I glanced back at Marlow, who was staring at me across heads, his face twisted in rage. "I walked away from a limp duck. So, are you?"

"Yes." She closed her mouth and looked at me. "He ever hit you?"

"Not so it would show. Let's get going."

"Yeah. Sure."

I led the way outside and to my sport ute, where I pulled out a knapsack of essentials I had put together from Marlow's old camping supplies. I added the Kevlar vest, Marlow's old bedroll, an aged telephoto lens that worked with the Nikon F3 I slung over my shoulder, a change of shirts, an old pair of Bella's riding boots and socks that had once been Marlow's. "Let's head out before the press wakes up and realizes Marlow is here."

"Truck's there." She led the way. "We have a thirty mile ride around the far side of the mountains to meet up with Caleb's team. You're staying with them? The team?" she asked, eyeing my gear in the graying light.

"Until I get my daughter back."

"Stop." She put a hand on my arm, halting me as I tossed my pack in the back of her truck. "Something's happened to you. Just in the last few minutes, something's happened. You're different. What's going on with you and Marlow?"

"You ever lose something and then find it in the most unlikely place? Like finding your sunglasses in the refrigerator or your favorite coffee cup mixed in with the dirty clothes?"

"Yeah." She drew the word out as if she didn't see the connection between our questions. At a noise, Ruth looked to the ranger station and I followed her gaze. Marlow stood framed in the doorway, his golden hair catching the sun. He was beautiful, ethereal, an angel from heaven. But it was all false, a trick of the light.

I looked around, spotting Burgess in the back of a loaded pickup that was driving away. As they roared past, he lifted a hand to Marlow, who ignored the gesture. Burgess's mouth turned down and he shook his head in what might have been disgust with his younger brother. Perhaps things weren't as cozy between them as Marlow thought.

Studying my limp duck, I said, "Well, I just found myself. And I didn't even know I was missing. Let's go." And I once again turned my back on Marlow Morgan and climbed into Ruth's truck, my things and a pack of SAR gear stowed in its bed with bungee cords for the ride to come.

Sunday
0700 hours

It was daylight when we reached the bottom of a steep hill and pulled to a stop in a small grassy pasture. This early in the season, the north and south sides of the same mountain were in different stages of spring, the warm south side already budded out in bright green, leafy fullness, the north side still pale yellow-green, early leaves velvety soft.

This particular spot, shielded from the warming sun by steep hills on three sides, was still stuck in winter, the grass seared-brown, the trees bearing small tight buds, the breeze holding the ice of January. The air smelled of truck exhaust and winter and that indefinable scent that always said mountain wilderness, a tang of pine and spruce, perhaps a hint of primeval earth.

Days like this translated well to film, and I recalled long mornings spent with Marlow in the field, the two of us photographing secluded sites in the hills of the Blue Ridge or Smoky Mountains, the high peaks of the Rockies, even cold mornings in the Sahara at a desert oasis. There had been sweltering sunrises on the Amazon, the air redolent of rotting vegetation, fried fish from breakfast and spent diesel fuel. Or deep in the cavernlike dawn of the Grand Canyon, with Bella on a donkey's back, her small heels slapping at the beast beneath her. Gone. All gone. Never to be again. But I still had a life and work and a daughter to find, rescue and raise.

I took a few shots of a family of turkeys scratching in the hard ground. They watched me as I walked closer, the lead bird lifting wings in warning. I sidestepped to catch the shadow of the wings on the earth. The turkeys turned and scurried into the underbrush of a laurel thicket, the long shadows and bright sun making a brown-and-gold perspective, like a sepia print.

Spoiling the moment and sending the turkeys rushing out of sight, two other trucks pulled up beside us and disgorged four men with a hound dog on a long, sturdy, knotted leather leash, the knots placed so the handler could easily lengthen or shorten the leash with a single motion. Possibly smelling Ruth's puppy, the huge hound came to me, putting his head and damp jowls against my knee and sighing in contentment, his sad eyes resting on my face.

The hound was wearing a figure-eight harness with a breastplate and shoulder protectors. It looked more uncomfortable than an underwire bra, but the dog seemed to notice no discomfort. He closed his eyes in ecstasy when I rubbed his long, black ears. The hound and I stayed in position, his head against me, the two of us enjoying the cold snap in the air and distant bird calls, as the men and Ruth broke open the pack of supplies.

And it was odd—I wasn't feeling anything. Not the paralyzing fear I had nursed for two days, not worry over Marlow and my impending divorce, not anything but a sense of calm that seemed both foreign and yet distantly familiar to my soul. The strange calm was due to four simple words: *Over my dead body.* It was astounding.

The men and Ruth each donned heavy aluminum strut packs, struggling under the weight, while I carried only my few belongings stuffed into Marlow's knapsack. Though I wanted to protest that I could carry a pack, too, I knew the hike we were facing would be a strain on my bruises and ribs even without the extra weight of a resupply pack, so I remained silent.

In unspoken accord, we all headed into the shadow of the steep hill, the hound beside me, his handler just behind. The first step from level ground to hillside was almost vertical, the path narrow and twisting. Trees with bowed trunks marked where climbers' feet had pressed until the shape had conformed to the weight over time. Within ten minutes I was huffing, the brace holding my ribs making me breathe too fast, too shallowly. But I knew I'd never be able to climb without it.

"No one can convince me that horses made this climb," I panted to Ruth, who was trudging just ahead of me.

"No way," she said, her voice nearly as breathless as mine. "We're trekking in overland on the old Coolidge Trail. It was blazed by a logging man, Jake Coolidge, in the nineteenth century. It was said he could walk into a stand of trees and tell you how many board feet of lumber you'd get out of it just by looking."

The dog handler behind me added, "Truth. Once Coolidge's reputation got around, there were experiments by different logging companies. And bettin' to rival any on a horse track anywhere. They'd take Coolidge blindfolded to a piece of property, and he'd look around. The only thing they'd tell him was the property markers. He always got it right. I'm Jedidiah Wilkins. Jake Coolidge was my great-granddaddy on my mama's side," he finished.

I gasped my name and he nodded, not breathless at all, seeming content to let me concentrate on the climb rather than on his stories. But he added after a moment, "That's Ed there, by your leg. He seems to took a liking to you."

"Hi, Ed," I said, patting the dog's head once between handholds on trees. Ed whuffed and plowed on, taking the hill in bits and spurts, running ahead to the limit of his leash and waiting for us to catch up before running on again.

17

It took the small party two hours to reach the intersection of the Coolidge Trail and the narrow horse trail on the far side of the hill. Though Jedidiah and Ed took several breaks, and we went on without them each time, the intersection was the first break for the rest of us, and I drank more water than I should have, gagging as I swallowed down pain pills. We ate granola bars, the high fat kind loaded with chocolate and marshmallows, rested for ten minutes and went on.

Two hours after that, when my stomach was rumbling, my heart aching and my ribs blazing with agony, we finally sighted the Howell Hasty Team on the north side of a hill across a small valley, their horses resting. On this side, only yards above and beyond us, partially obscured by foliage, was a splashing cataract and Caleb Howell.

His rangy form was squatted down on a huge boulder, his back turned. He stared out and away from us, though I was certain he knew exactly where we were. He was relaxed in the pose, half in shadow, yet a steady energy thrummed through him, power and stamina so apparent, so constant, it was as if I could see it pulse beneath his skin. When we reached the boulder he turned and looked down at us, his face grave, as unyielding as the stone. His light brown hair notwithstanding, I thought there was Cherokee in the lines of his face, the bones of his nose and jaw.

"Jedidiah, good to see you and Ed."

The dog whuffed at his name and flopped on the ground. Jedidiah joined him and began the process of looking for thorns and debris in the dog's feet. The big hound rolled over, exposing his belly for a good scratch, too. Caleb nodded to the rest of the team members and greeted them, all but me. "Old Nyla is coming up lame," he said. "She needs to see the vet back at the ICP. If you folks'll take the supplies on to the team across the valley, they'll be ready to move on. Mrs. Morgan." He might have smiled, but the expression was lost in the shadow of his hat brim. "I imagine you're a mite tuckered out. But if you can handle another climb uphill and back, Bella's first night camp is up that way about a quarter mile."

I remembered the mantra I had half chanted on the trek down from the fishery, my arms bound, my sight half-gone. *Anything for Bella. Anything for Bella.* "I can make it." It might have been more believable if my voice hadn't rasped like old leaves.

He did smile then and stood, swinging down from the boulder hand-over-hand, using saplings as handholds, never touching ground until he landed lightly on the balls of his feet. He was in hiking boots and camouflage, the Kevlar vest loose, Velcro straps hanging.

"Meet you later on then," Ruth said, and the others moved down the trail, where horse hooves deeply marked the soft soil. To make the climb, I dropped the small pack I had strapped to my back, and Bella's camera, and jammed them between a fallen log and the base of the boulder where Caleb had knelt. Maybe a bear might get my stuff, but nothing else.

Holding out a hand, Caleb waited for me to join him, taking my gloved palm in his. Turning me, he placed both hands on my bottom and pushed me up the hill. It was a hard climb, almost vertical. Above me, I saw a faint track, but horses had never made it. I wasn't sure I could have climbed it except for the trees I used and Caleb's hand that steadied and guided.

"Horses?" I questioned when I was able to catch a breath.

"They were hobbled in the valley overnight for forage. He separated them so they'd look like big deer or elk, not two horses at a camp. The dogs kept watch over them. Dell and Bella climbed up to this vantage point to camp."

Camp. Dell and Bella. Alone that first night. The pain strumming against my ribs tightened and wailed. And then we crested a ledge.

The space opened up, offering a dramatic view, fog rising in spirals over the treetops. I hated it. Hated everything about it. This was where my baby suffered at the hands of the man I should have shot to protect her. Fighting tears and the chill that suffused my bones as sweat from the climb dried, I looked over the camp. The fire pit was against the rock wall of the mountain. The water source trickled down the vertical height. The overhang of boulder provided protection from rain with a sleeping site beneath—a thin layer of soil and a thick layer of leaves and brush atop a flat stone floor. There was enough room for two bedrolls. I couldn't take my gaze away.

"Looks like he uses this site from time to time," Caleb said, his voice dispassionate, his eyes on my face. "Fire pit is well used, but they cold-camped. Water just to the right. Latrine to the left. Protected from the prevailing westerly and north winds and minimal protection from rain and flyovers if needed." When I said nothing, he added, "Good surveillance point for the entire valley, back up the trail and down."

I struggled with a breath that wanted to freeze in my lungs. When it came it was painful, ragged, tearing, a sound like rotten fabric ripping. I felt Caleb move closer, his hand on my shoulder, so hot it burned. Unable to accept the comfort of the small gesture, I stepped away and walked to the sleeping space. The second breath, when it came, was harder, a coarse groan. I erupted, kicking into the pile of brush again and again, movement so vicious it sent leaves spiraling down the heights in a lazy windmill. There was no sound on the mountain but the frenzied rustle and my breathing. I kicked and kicked until every last leaf was gone, until the spot was cleared of evidence of that first night Bella had spent with Dell Shirley.

But I didn't cry. Not one tear.

"So much for the cops doing a crime-scene workup of this place later on," he muttered under his breath, half laughing. The laughter died and he was solemn when he spoke again. "Come on. I'll take you down again and Ruth can get you back to the ranger station."

Whirling, I speared the tracker with my eyes. "Over my dead body." My voice was raspy and pitted as old stone, carrying grief that vibrated in the air between us. Caleb's face didn't change, expression didn't waver. "Over my dead, putrefied and decaying body." I heaved a breath so deep it growled. "I came up here to look for a note. To find my daughter. And I'll do that or die trying."

Something flickered in Caleb's eyes at my words, emotion moving so fast it was gone long before I could identify it. He canted his head to one side, the shadow of the hat brim shifting to reveal his cheek and jaw, and after a long moment, nodded once. "Do what needs doing. Then regroup and move on," he said, the strange phrases ruminative. Louder, he added, "Hope the message wasn't in the pile of leaves."

"It won't be. Part of the game is that the note can't be easily dislodged. It can't blow away." I jutted my chin toward the fire pit. "I'll start there."

Caleb moved out of my way and I pulled the tight Lycra gloves off my hands, tucked them in my waistband and plunged my fingers into the ashes and stones of the pit. Moving each rock, each charred splinter of wood that had escaped the flames, I made sure nothing was secreted beneath the outer stones. When I was certain that no note was hidden there, I moved to the latrine, though normally that would have been construed as cheating, to hide a second note in the same type of spot as the first. But though I searched every fissure in the stone, there was nothing.

I went to the side of the camp where water flowed. Water for washing and perhaps for cooking, if a camper let it boil long enough. It trickled down and gathered into a shallow stone bowl that looked as if it had been placed for just that purpose. A makeshift cistern. Had Indians placed it, using this spot as a lookout during tribal wars or when fighting the European interlopers? Or had Dell positioned it? I knelt and searched every loose pebble, bending over, my hair hanging around my face in tight curls. The hollowed stone looked as if it had been there since the beginning of time. Maybe God had set it here....

Nothing. No note. Had she been injured? Too emotionally battered to leave a message? I washed my hands in the icy water, letting the char from the fire pit sluice off before moving to the vertical rock at the side of the mountain, wet fingers growing colder in contact with the stone. Bella wouldn't have hidden the note anywhere she couldn't touch easily, would not have hidden it where Dell could see her. It had to be a place she could reach without giving herself away.

I stopped and looked at the overhang that protected the sleeping site. He would have put her against the wall so she couldn't get away in the night. He would have crowded her against the boulder, where the leaves were deepest and would crackle each time she turned over. I walked straight to the back of the sleeping area and ran my hands along the rock, but it was smooth, not broken. Scoured by wind for centuries, it was a single solid granite slab.

At the base, where she could have reached from a prone position, was a small, soil-clogged gap. I knelt and dug, tearing flesh on the ragged rock as I worked my fingers back and forth. Until they encountered a texture that wasn't soil or stem or stone. It was paper, folded over and over into a triangle.

18

With a small sound, I gripped and pulled, easing it out of the hiding place. As it came, it exposed another piece, this one folded in half, and I pulled it from the dirt, too, purple treasures. Falling back, I sat, my spine against the granite. Moving oddly, Caleb sat beside me, his warmth a furnace at my side. Unfolding the half page first, I read.

> *Mama would laugh and laugh.*
> *The curse protects me, for once.*
> *He won't touch me as long as I have it.*
> *Says I'm defiled.*
> *Four days more. Five if I'm lucky.*
> *Please God. Let someone come.*

I did laugh, just as Bella had known I would—the sound a joyous and exultant peal. I met Caleb's startled, dark blue gaze, handed him the note and threw my arms around him, hugging him so hard my ribs groaned beneath the brace. "She's okay," I half shouted into his ear. "He didn't rape her. He didn't hurt my baby. Not yet. Not yet." I pulled away as the tracker read the note, a little half smile on his lips. "You've got three or four days to find my baby," I said. "I expect you to pull a miracle out of that tracker's bag of tricks I've heard so much about, and get her by then."

"Yes, ma'am. Well, I'll do my best. Why does she say you'll laugh?"

"Bella always whines and moans and gripes about being a woman. And now it's saving her. Of course I'll laugh."

"You like irony."

"I like it when life works out," I said happily, removing my left hand from his shoulder, where it rested. "I got blood on your shirt. I'm sorry."

Caleb took my hand and turned it, seeing the scrape. He pushed at the skin, squeezing lightly until cleansing blood flowed freely. I let him hold my hand, his palm still so warm it cooked my cold skin. How could he have warm skin on this chilly day? But he did.

"And the marriage? That didn't work out."

Breath whooshed from me. "*What…?* That's none of your business." The words sifted between us, settling into the cold. Caleb Howell said nothing, eyes like lapis stones, hard on my face. I didn't intend to reply to his question, but words came from some secluded, shadowed place inside me. "The nurse who took care of Rachael Morgan got to live on the fancy estate, under a Hollywood idol's roof." I heard the bitterness in my tone, astringent, malignant. "She shared three-star meals with the family, slept in a deluxe suite set aside for guests, answered the phone for family, talking to the press when they got through. She lived in luxury she'd never had before. And she never wanted it to end. So she seduced my husband, not that it was a difficult task for her. Not that it was the first time he looked for and found something on the side. It was just the first time a woman ever got him to fall in love with her. And he left. No. It didn't work out."

"Sometimes good comes from evil," Caleb said, the phrase cryptic. Pulling me to my feet, still holding my hand, he led me to the cistern and washed the scrape in the shallow water before making it bleed again. When he had it bleeding in a steady stream, he took my right hand, inspected it carefully and washed it, too. Pulling out a handkerchief so white it shone in the sunshine, he dried my right hand on one corner, the injured left on another, keeping the scrape clean.

My hands were both still puffy, a peculiar reddish color, and Caleb turned them, exploring them curiously. Shoving up the cuffs and peeling back the bandages, he looked at the stitches that bound together the torn flesh. I let him examine me, enjoying the strange feel of his touch. His hands were callused, skin mottled by sun and years. His fingers were long and well-formed, as if they should be holding a mandolin or lute in some grand medieval castle.

The peculiar warmth of his hands pulsed into mine, up my wrists and arms, deep into bones that had turned to ice on the day Dell entered my camp. The moment was piercing as a keen blade, yet oddly comforting. Caleb's heat radiated deeper, as if into the soul that had frozen and shattered when Bella had been stolen from me. I watched his face as he warmed my hands, his eyes intent in the shadow of his hat brim.

Satisfied, Caleb pulled my cuffs back into place and bound my injured hand in the handkerchief. Taking the gloves from my waistband, he pulled the first over the swollen flesh and handkerchief bandage, then pulled the other on as well. "Put ointment on that spot when we get to the others. You don't want it to get infected." His voice was resonant and steady.

"No. I wouldn't want that."

He met my eyes for a moment, and there was something in the ocean-blue depths that I didn't comprehend. Something that was part of the warmth of his skin, part of the heat of his spirit. A vitality all his own.

"You want to try to open the other note with these hands or you want me to?" And the bizarre moment was gone.

I focused on the tightly folded purple triangle he held and didn't remember giving it to him. It was folded so tightly it was a curved, puffy thing, the kind of toy made by bored boys in class to toss through goalposts formed by a friend's hands. A football. "I don't think I can do it without tearing the paper."

Caleb rotated the wad of paper until the sun caught the seam of the toy, and with nails that were clean even after a day in the wild, he picked at it until he'd worked it loose enough to unfold. "I used to make these things when I was in grade school," he said. "Toy footballs. I was pretty good at flicking them through goalposts my friends made with their hands."

Caleb handed me the creased paper, letting me read it first. The words were lined up on the left margin with indentations, different from her usual centered, almost poetic structure. And the shape of her letters were different, as if some parts of the note were written at different times. Perhaps at night, by moonlight? Or with damaged hands, like mine, tied too long? My earlier joy evaporated in wisps of anxiety.

I'll leave this when I can and pray someone finds it. Dell Shirley's taking me to his home. This is what I've learned:

The horses are specially trained to the terrain. Other horses wouldn't make it all the way. We're heading north and west, toward Tennessee, but he says we'll be there in a few days.

He has a cabin in a steep valley. His family lived on the land on and off for generations but they moved away for good when he was a child.

There's a springhouse, a garden, but no power.

He calls me Belinda. I think that was his wife. She used to draw, and he thinks that's what I'm doing.

Polly was Belinda's dog, given by her daddy when they married.

He really is a geologist. Talks about USC and the Citadel, and the army, so I think that part was true.

He's about two inches taller than Daddy, and solid muscle. He has green eyes, light hair. Two guns.

He thinks he killed my mama. I thought he did, too, until I heard her scream my name. My mama's alive. I know she is. And my parents will come after me. They have to.

IsaBella Morgan

Not sure what the letter was for, I handed it to Caleb. He scanned the note and a slow grin spread across his face. Lifting a hand, he pulled off the battered hat and heaved a deep breath. "Smart girl. Good for you, Bella."

"What?"

"Your daughter left us some clues. Yolanda or I will radio back this information." He tapped the purple paper. "Har can ask around the old-timers about a family that moved a generation or so back, who lived north and west of here. Maybe pull out old maps before the park took over and see what was abandoned or sold. Ask after marriage records between a Belinda and a Dell Shirley, in case they were married here. See if the U.S. government has any record of him."

Excitement shot through my veins. Bella had given us all that?

"As soon as we get to the others, I'll take a look at some maps and see where the horse-accessible trails end. 'Course, Dell has managed some places I'd never have tried, and he obviously blazed the last three miles of trail himself in the past five years or so, 'cause they're not on my maps. Lady, your daughter is something else."

I laughed, relief soaring through me again. "It's the home-schooling and the only-child complex. My Bella is the most resourceful girl on the face of the earth."

"She'll need to be. Let's go." Facing the mountainside, hands and feet in crevices and gripping trees, we worked our way down the steep hill, Caleb below me to catch me in case I slipped. I found breathing easier on the way down, the relief of knowing my daughter had been alive and well for the past thirty-six hours like a shot of pure oxygen to starved lungs. Less breathless, I asked, "How did you find the site where they camped? Did you know it was there?"

"Nope. I saw where someone left a gash in the hillside, where a foot slipped or something. It could have been natural, from a branch falling, but I couldn't find a branch. And there were others higher up. So I started climbing. Found the site."

"Super Tracker," I said. "All you need is a cape—" The tree I was holding gave way. I slammed into Caleb just behind and below me. He absorbed my fall with a little grunt and halted my plunge. Soil and debris rained over us and Caleb shoved me into the hill to protect me.

My heart raced, thudded, an arrhythmic pace against my chest wall. My body was cradled in his, his arms above me, gripping tree and rock, his thighs beneath mine, feet wedged in crevices I hadn't seen. My cheek was pressed into the loam and moss; the scent of the mountain filled my senses.

Placing my hand on another sapling, Caleb nudged

my right leg to a tree, where I settled a foot and slowly lifted my weight from him. "Okay?" he asked.

Unable to speak, I nodded, and he eased his body from mine and down. I followed, continued the downward climb, grabbing a dogwood sapling with one gloved hand, a small oak with the other.

The near fall had roused me as if from a deep sleep. The world around me plunged into my mind, my senses. For the first time I was aware of the wilderness, its scents and its burgeoning life, both spring and winter at once. The earth, only inches from my face, was split by roots that crawled over rock and down deep. Small ferns uncoiled from the black soil, leaves tight spirals. Birds called, a crow to our right, laughing, a mockingbird far off. Several black snakes lay on exposed roots in a natural cave created by erosion. The mountains were alive. Bella was alive. Not injured. Her fighting spirit was intact and unbroken.

When we reached the trail again, I retrieved my things and slung Bella's camera around my neck within easy access. I was hungry. Starving. I drank and tasted the cold water, the taint of plastic from the bottle. *My baby was alive.*

As we walked, the pace hard but not impossible, I saw late-blooming daffodils and purple periwinkle, an early bloodroot. A sharp-lobed hepatica was open in a shaft of sunlight and I framed and snapped a shot of it just as a golden-brown butterfly settled on its petals. An eastern box turtle sunned on a warm rock. A pileated woodpecker tapped a ringing cadence, marking his territory with sound.

As we moved from the south side of the hill around to the north, we crossed a lonely blacktop road, with houses visible among the trees. A searcher on an ATV waved to us and gave us a thumbs-up as we reentered the woods. Here, the trees offered less shade and tighter buds, the redbud and serviceberry still trying to bloom. Two male cardinals fought, aloft in a tight ball that dropped sharply as each bird tried to gain dominance. I got three shots of them before they disappeared, but the film was wrong for the light and I hadn't had time to adjust the settings, so I didn't think they would come out except as a red blur.

Marlow had the knack, almost a gift, of capturing wild animals in motion. My specialty was light and shadow, the intricacies of proportion and balance in a well-framed photograph. And in the darkroom I had a special talent. I could bring out nuances of composition that were not apparent in the hand of another photographer.

MarMac Inc. had been a great team, our work bringing a premium, often placed with magazines for cover shots, the coveted goal of any wildlife photographer. Without him, my work might be less vital, less alive, but I was learning that I could go on without Marlow, professionally as well as personally. I could still get work without him. Could still make a living. Could make a good life for Bella without him, too.

And I took several photographs of Caleb as he hiked the trail in front of me, framed a shot looking up at him as he crossed over a long-unused logging road. Maybe when this was all over, I'd inspect the photos for insight into the man. Perhaps understand what had happened when he held my hands and warmed them. What had happened when he caught my body with his as I fell.

Sunday
1145 hours

No one shouted to us as we neared the rest of the Howell Hasty Team, the restriction for silence holding even though they plainly saw us. Yo, who had led the team on around and up the hill, following the tracks on the blazed trail, waved to us from above, her fit form standing on a boulder, one foot on a large, exposed root. I waved back, and Caleb, who had remained silent since my near fall, increased his speed.

I let him pull ahead, and when I neared the level spot where the team waited, I framed and took a roll of film, the sunlight slanting in, catching faces creased with excitement and exhaustion, bodies moving quickly with the natural energy of a search team reunited, horses dozing, standing at rest.

"Put the camera down, already, and eat."

I turned instead and took a close-up of Ruth's face, her soft eyes shadowed, mouth curved in an amused smile. "Caleb told us about the notes. You go, girl! No wonder Bella is a stick of dynamite. She's got you for a mother."

"Not me. Marlow's the one with the strong personality."

"Marlow is a seriously unstable man. And if I wasn't such a nice woman I'd use language a lot stronger."

I dropped the camera and accepted the plate of cold food she held out to me. "He's a Morgan. That alone makes him famous in some circles. He was in something like twenty-five movies by the time he turned eighteen. And while that was a long time ago, he's been rich and privileged all his life."

"According to Evelyn, he's a limp duck. And don't offer excuses for him. Eat."

"Yes, ma'am. I'm eating," I said around a mouthful of beans. They were right out of the can, nestled next to a cold MRE reconstituted with bottled water. "Heaven."

Ruth rolled her eyes. "Meal Ready to Eat—cardboard. Marlow—limp duck. Remember that."

19

I changed out of the new boots, putting antibiotic ointment on the stitches in my heel and wrists, and on the new abrasion on my finger. I found a blister starting on my big toe and greased it up well, too, adding a padded Band-Aid. In Bella's riding boots, my gear tied with rawhide strips behind the deep-seated western saddle, I let Yo boost me onto the horse's back, and joined the others on the upward trek. I had put ointment and padded Band-Aids on all my blisters that morning, but the ones between my bones and the saddle leather squished beneath me and I knew they'd burst soon.

Having consulted the maps, a state-of-the-art GPS topography device, the sheriff, and Joel back at the ICP, Caleb left us, going overland to try and meet up with the new trail farther on. He was attempting to give us an advantage, take a few miles off the lead Bella and Dell had on us. It might mean leaving the horses behind, but we'd eventually make better time than the two we were after if Caleb could make a few such directional leaps.

We rode all day. Some of the blisters on my backside began to break in early afternoon, the sticky liquid within causing my skin to adhere to the cotton and denim. I was miserable, and popped painkillers and muscle relaxers as often as Doc's directions would allow. But I wasn't quitting. Not for anything.

Two hours before dusk, after miles of arduous travel, Caleb radioed in. I was riding behind Yo, horses slipping down a steep ridge, when the radio crackled and I heard his voice. Kneeing the horse beneath me, I closed the short distance so I could overhear.

"Is your twenty anywhere near the Ramsay Ridge Horse Trail?" he asked. "If so, you want to stop before you cross over it."

"Affirmative. Ramsay Ridge is maybe a klick ahead. Why?"

"Looks like they crossed the trail, doubled back overland and met up with Ramsay again. Ran the horses for a while, until the trail crossed over a creek, a minor feeder of Sampson's Branch. Then they turned hard south, off the trail and took the feeder again. I think."

"South? He's spotted us?"

"No," I breathed, gripping the reins in shock. My horse tossed his head, missed a step.

"I need Jedidiah and Ed. Put them along the water as soon as you cross over the feeder to Sampson's, heading downstream. I'll watch for them."

"Ten-four. What do you want us to do?"

"Stay at the juncture of Ramsay's Horse Trail and Shirley's previous path. I'll let you know."

"Will do." Yo turned her head to me and asked me to pass the word that we would soon be taking a break. "And ask Jed to head up here for Caleb's orders."

I nodded and gave the message to Ruth behind me. As we rode, I changed back into hiking boots and untied my gear from the saddle. I debated putting on the Kevlar vest and decided to carry it instead, added two MREs, a half-dozen granola bars and a large bottle of water. If Caleb Howell thought I was going to be left behind, he was seriously mistaken.

Moments later, I heard a chopper in the distance and looked up into the cloudy sky. When had clouds moved in? Was that another reason for the change in procedure? Rain on the way? Caleb had given up on the pretense of silence. He had called in reinforcements.

A slight shiver took me as I considered the implications of a noisy pursuit. Either it was good because he was close to Dell and thought to spook the man out, or it was bad because Caleb had no other recourse but to try spooking a desperate man. Strapping my knapsack and bedroll to my back, I slid to the ground when we reached the little rill of water that was a feeder for Sampson's Branch. Waving to Yo, ignoring her questions, I followed Jedidiah and Ed into the brush.

The dog handler, who was holding Ed's leash on the shortest knot to keep the dog close to his knee, glanced back once, and I thought he might try to send me packing. Might try to say I wouldn't be able to keep up. Might consider me a liability on a fast and dirty search. Something in my face must have dissuaded him, though, because he shrugged and clicked his tongue to Ed. I followed them, and the trail and horses and Yo's frustrated tone were soon lost behind me. Also lost was the handy-dandy ranger radio on Yo's belt, and Ruth. Now, like my baby, I was cut off from the rest of the world.

Jedidiah and Ed went into the water quickly, the handler holding a soiled red T-shirt I recognized as Bella's to the hound's nose. The dog put his snout almost to the water and searched back and forth from bank to bank in a widening circle, but even I could tell he picked up no scent. With a command I couldn't hear, the handler pulled the dog off the scent-search and plowed downstream. On the bracken-covered bank, I chased them with as much speed as I could, but was quickly left behind. I wondered where my hip waders were and envied the thigh-high rubber overshoes worn by Jedidiah, and the hound's ability to disregard the cold water. I could go into the water, too, if I wanted to get sent packing the moment Caleb saw wet hiking boots.

The course of the feeder twisted hard to the left and took a twenty foot drop as the sound of splashing footsteps faded. Using tree handholds and footholds, I made fast time, nearly catching up with Jed, who had to carry Ed down.

I was panting and flushed when the handler and the hound greeted me, and Jed had an amused look on his face. I didn't ask why. I had run through old spiderwebs, scratched my already abused chin, and had worked up a good sweat. I was a sight to make men smile, but that probably wasn't a good thing.

Jedidiah sped up again as the bank widened out. Moments later we spotted a third person stopped on the bank. It was Caleb, standing relaxed and watchful. Breathing like a bellows, I joined the men, bent over and gripped my knees for a long moment as oxygen found my lungs again.

When I stood straight, Caleb Howell's dark eyes met mine. He didn't waste time with pleasantries. "From here on out, Jedidiah'll be in the water. I'll be on the ridges and in gullies, out of sight. You can't keep up with me, and if you tried, you'd slow me down. You'll get separated from us and I'll have to come back for you. You're a liability. Go back to Yo and the team."

"If you lose sight of me, just forget that I was here until you find my daughter. If I get separated from Jedidiah, I'll head back upstream to the trail and hike back to the team or the ICP. If I get turned around, I'll stick close to the feeder until I get found by someone or find my way back. I've seen the maps. I can't get lost up here. There are roads everywhere. I have food and water so I won't die of hunger if I get separated. I'm going with you."

Caleb's dark eyes were on me, his expression unreadable. "When I first met you…" He paused a beat. "I thought you were a meek little mouse."

"Before this happened, I *was* a meek little mouse. Getting divorced, kicked almost to death and having your daughter stolen can change a person," I said, with only a little squeak in my breathing.

"I reckon it can." He almost smiled when he said the words, but it was so fleeting I could have imagined it. "Hope you don't need that first-aid training. You get lost, I'll find you later. Against my better judgment, let's move."

"I appreciate it."

"Don't." Like a will-o-the-wisp he was suddenly gone, disappearing uphill into a laurel thicket.

The trail wasn't a well-used track, or even a path. We hiked in a zigzag overland pattern approaching the sound of water. I kept up while on flatter earth, and by the time the sound of the falls grew to a roar, I had caught my breath, even with the fast pace.

Sampson's Branch wasn't moving a lot of water, but it did take a long drop between solid rock walls. The thunder of the falls made it sound like the Nile was dropping down the chasm. I saw no horse tracks, smelled no horse spoor, and Ed didn't look very interested in anything except a long drink. The main tracker turned uphill and back overland again for a rugged half mile hike before we met up with slower moving water. And this time there were deeply pressed horse tracks and fainter tracks of dog.

They entered and exited the branch, moving downstream. Jedidiah called a short halt to rest the hound. He rolled Ed over and made sure the chest protector had not snagged anything that might chafe the tracker dog. Lifting each foot in turn, he inspected between each pad, pulling on the long hairs that separated them. Caleb was lost to sight, not willing to stop, even if the rest of us had to. Super Tracker.

"What are you doing?" I asked Jed when I caught my breath.

"Looking for thorns. Tracker hounds like Ed can get a thorn embedded and not show it till the next day. He'll catch himself a scent and run it till he drops dead if I don't stop him time to time. Rest him." Jedidiah pulled a bag of Redman tobacco from a pouch at his waist and tucked a pinch in his cheek. Around the wad, he said, "I got me a feeling about them tracks. When Ed takes a pull of the scent article this time, we gonna get a hit. Jist got a feel for it."

Too exhausted to react, I nodded and tried to catch up on my oxygen deprivation. After a fifteen minute rest, Jed again held the red T to the dog's nose. "Check it," Jedidiah said.

Ed's ears did a little twitch and he buried his nose in the shirt. The black-and-brown hound huffed twice, quivering.

"Find it," Jed said. Ed put his nose to the ground and pulled the handler forward, then right in a small circle. Circling out in a continuous spiral, the dog led the man around and around.

"What's he doing?" I asked.

"Scent pool's got him squirrelly. See how his ruff is standing straight up, all excited like? He got hisself something he likes and he's following the smell that's laying on the ground, searching till he finds where it originates. Then he'll take off after it. Same thing if there ain't a scent, except without the excitement. He'll look around a bit, mostly in circles, like he's doing." Ed pulled the handler off the spiral and toward the tracks on the bank, sniffed with more excitement than I thought him capable of, and stuck his nose into the water. Came up dripping, pulling hard downstream.

Ed scented Bella.

"Hunt 'er up good now, Ed. Hunt 'er up. Good boy," Jedidiah said, as excited as the hound.

The pace became a slow run and I took longer strides, following along the bank of the stream. The water was too deep to cross without getting wet to the thighs, and was always too wide to jump. I glanced up once and saw Caleb, but he disappeared, moving into the heights, looking for a better vantage point, hoping to catch sight of the fleeing horses.

Sunday
1800 hours

It was near dusk and my muscles were aching with a pain I hadn't felt in years. It was similar to the pain of childbirth, long aching ripples dancing along my thighs and down my calves, up my spine in undulating waves into my ribs. I was a single spasm of misery. The light was failing. We would have to stop, I knew, and damned the short spring days. The threatening rain. My traitorous body.

"We got something weird up ahead."

I jerked so hard my shoulders wrenched. Caleb stood overhead, perched on a rock overhang, his hat in hand. Appearing above us was becoming a habit. I stopped when Jedidiah pulled Ed in and forced the tracker hound to stop.

"What?" Jed asked over the rasp of my breath and the sound of water.

"Not sure yet. Prints are muddied and Ed'll make 'em worse. Stay put till I figure it out." And he was gone.

The handler and dog stepped from the water's edge

and joined me on the bank. Ed shook hard, throwing a gallon of icy water from his coat. Jedidiah pursed his lips and shrugged before settling on a fallen tree, giving Ed a crunchy tidbit and drinking from a water bottle. Then he lifted one of Ed's feet, peering at it carefully, pulling the pads apart and ruffling the wet hair between. He pulled gently and removed a burr no bigger than a pencil eraser and held it to the light. "Thorn. Stupid dog. You'd get so busy with a hunt, you'll hurt yourself and not let me know till the next day when you come up lame."

"What does that mean? The things Caleb said."

Jedidiah spat a brown stream of tobacco juice onto the bank. "Something with the trail changed? They was moving downstream in a single line. Ed's been scenting it fine, even with them in the water most times. But if something changed, and they left the water, Ed's big feet could mess it up. Maybe."

I had figured that much out myself. "Okay." Turning, I slipped around the upended tree roots and moved on downstream. Jedidiah and Ed stayed put and the handler didn't call me back. But then, Caleb had said nothing about *me* staying put.

20

A hundred yards farther I spotted Caleb through the trees, squatted down, hands hanging loosely between his knees, his hat dangling from a branch nearby. When the foliage thinned again, I slowed, watching as his eyes followed a track on the earth into the forest and back to the stream, then seemed to follow it in a different direction. Squinting back and forth, he scanned the ground, deep, sun-burnished furrows in his temples and cheeks. With a long index finger, Caleb moved a leaf, then traced something pressed into the earth. I couldn't hear him sigh, but I saw his chest move and saw the smile touch the corners of his lips.

"Your daughter is something else."

I started at his low words, surprised he had seen me. "How so?"

"Looks to me like she got away." He stood in a single, fluid movement. "Which, if we can divide up into two parties, may make our job a lot easier."

"She got away?" A heated flush burst inside. "Yes!" I thrust a fisted hand into the air, the delight scorching through me like raw lightning. The pain of the movement snapped through my ribs, but I ignored it. *Bella was free!* "What do we do?"

Caleb's grin blazed. "You do nothing, Mac. Not a thing. Tonight we make a camp there—" he indicated a flat space up the hill "—and before dawn I make tracks to the rest of the team. Tomorrow, by sunrise, we'll be on the trail again. Half of us after the packhorse and Bella, the others, with a new dog team, after the man on foot and the other horse. Which aren't together, by the way. She was on horseback and Dell was on the ground, likely leading the horses across the creek. My guess is she did something and the horse Dell was leading bolted. She went the other way, straight uphill, and managed to stay on."

Caleb put the hat back on his head and crushed it in place, looking gratified. "We're a half day behind them, to this point, but now's when we gain on them. Just pray for the rain to hold off."

I followed his eyes to the darkening sky and lowering clouds, heavy with moisture. I imagined Bella alone on a mountain in the rain. Tears gathered in my eyes and I turned away from the tracker to the flat place up the hill. "I'll get Jed and Ed to the campsite. Can we have a fire?"

"Don't see why not. A hot meal sounds mighty nice." His voice held a tone that confirmed he knew I was near tears.

"I'm not much of a cook." I battled the tears back down. My baby was free. That was the only thing that mattered. "But it would be nice to have something better than MREs to work with."

"I'll see if I can bring back a rabbit. You're crying, aren't you?"

"Rabbit stew would be nice. And of course I'm crying. Bella got away, but she's alone and it might rain and—"

A shot echoed through the hills. Whirling, I saw Caleb

swivel his head, following the sound as it reverberated off the mountainside. A second shot followed. When the sound died, Caleb had the radio in one hand and was unfolding his ancient map on the ground with the other. "Howell Hasty One here. Check in all teams. We have rifle fire to the north. Report."

"Howell Hasty Team Two," Yo said. "We're at Ramsay Horse Trail. All okay, not our fire. Seemed to come from the west."

"Chandler Dog Team. Just south of Spotted Cow Creek. All okay. Didn't hear anything."

"Perkins Backtrack Team, heading to the ICP. Nothing."

Avoiding the tracks in the earth, I edged closer. Caleb was making notations on the map with a stub of red-wax pencil. I realized he was trying to triangulate to find the origin of the shots.

"Rebart ATV Team at Tombstone. Heard it off in the distance. No direction."

"Nesbitt ATV Team. East of Tombstone on a logging road within sight of Steely Rock Road. I can see the chimney top of the old Sweatt place." I watched Caleb find the location on his map. Squatting, he placed the map on the heavily tracked earth. "Sound came from the east."

"Stevens ATV team. Nothing."

"Stubbs Hasty Team. To our east."

"Buddin Hasty Team, here. We're about two klicks from Howell Hasty Two, south of Sampson's Branch. Shot came from the north. No doubt. Where are you, Howell One?"

Caleb pressed the button on the side of the park radio. "I'm south of Howell Two. They spotted us or you this morning and took to Sampson's, moving downstream to get behind us. I figure he was trying to backtrack to Tombstone and then head north on a different track. But it looks like they had a little altercation and the girl got away." There was satisfaction in Caleb's voice and multiple clicks over the radio. He glanced up at me. "Clicks. That's radio for applause."

I smiled and squatted down beside him in the increasing darkness.

"Since those shots weren't ours, and didn't seem directed at us, and the girl is heading off in a different direction and they weren't directed at her, and it ain't hunting season, and of course there's no poaching in these hills, I'm guessing our bad guy was taking down dinner or trying to flush out the girl. Make her bolt so he could spot her."

There were more clicks on the radio. Caleb glanced at me, amusement in his eyes. "That set of clicks was laughter. About no poaching." Into the radio, he said, "Stubbs, can you convert to a backtrack team? Find Howell Two's current location at Ramsay Trail tomorrow and head back from there? You're looking for the suspect's second night camp. I pushed overland and missed it. When you find the camp, contact the mother with Howell One or Two and see if she can talk you through a search for a note the girl might have left."

"Rebart can assist as backtrack team," a voice said. "We're close in but we'll need a dog if it rains."

"Buddin Hasty is to meet up with Howell Hasty and spend the night," Caleb ordered. "Then, come morning, Buddin can take one set of tracks and we'll take another. No fires unless you find a site protected by a north-facing wall."

"Affirmative," three different voices said, the crackle of overlapping transmissions breaking up the words.

"Five bucks says we'll have her before nightfall tomorrow," a fourth voice said. "I'll notify ICP of all locations and plans when we get back. Perkins Backtrack out." The radio traffic went silent a moment later with no one taking the bet.

Sunday
1827 hours

In the gathering shadows, Caleb folded his map, pocketed the radio. Around his eyes the skin in the depths of the fine lines was white. A shock of hair fell over his forehead, which was whiter than the rest of his face, a tan achieved by the daily wearing of a hat instead of sunscreen. He met my eyes. His were dark with a fierce glee, a dangerous, predatory expression that shocked me to my core. We both heard my slow intake of breath. My mouth opened and his eyes fastened on it.

In the distance, an owl trumpeted, the sound a three-note call. Farther off, another answered twice. Leaves rustled overhead, the water murmured nearby. An early insect buzzed drunkenly in the cooling air. The smell of nighttime was different, a return to winter crispness, strangely touched with spring rain.

The warmth that had started with Bella winning her freedom continued to spread through me and I took another breath, feeling deprived of oxygen, of something elemental and vital. Caleb lifted a fist and gently brushed my cheek. I blinked in surprise, feeling the residual chill of my skin beneath his, but I didn't pull away. When he turned his hand, the remains of a tear glistened on the pad of his thumb. "I'll get Bella back." His voice was a burr of sound, lower than the susurrus of water.

"I know." The words came out whispered, a seed of strange sensitivity taking root inside my newfound warmth. An odd combination of heat and cold, spring and winter, hope and fear. Bella was free. We might have her by tomorrow night. It might rain. She could fall off the horse and break a leg. She could die.

Dell would find her first, take her back. Hurt her.

Taking my hands, Caleb rose to his feet, drawing me

up with him. "Tell me about Bella. Anything that comes to mind." He curled a fist about my hands, warming them.

"We were at a grocery store, down near Buckhead. In Atlanta," I added at his quizzical look. "The manager was an older, grayer Tom Cruise look-alike. My age. Bella told me he was hot, and I could have sworn she was staring at his backside where he was bent over a box of canned goods being shelved." I shook my head, remembering my audacious daughter's behavior. Caleb lifted a hand and pushed away a tendril of hair that blew into my eyes on the cold breeze. "She has this odd need to see me dating, married, so I won't be alone when she goes off to school. Some misplaced guilt a child of divorced parents must feel.

"Anyway, when I just shrugged, without halfway looking at the guy, she walked up to him and asked him if he was married. Told him her mother was available and would like a date for Friday night." Caleb chuckled, and I could tell he liked Bella's reckless spirit. Just what I needed, a main tracker with a crazy streak. "It wasn't funny. I just about sank into the floor in embarrassment."

"She's tough. Bold. Fearless. That's good. You get Jedidiah and Ed, tell Jed he can make a fire. I'll get us some supper."

Not trusting my voice, I nodded and watched as Caleb Howell strode downstream and was swallowed by the darkness.

The fire was deep in a bowl of stones, wood sliding into hot coals. The owls had kept up a chorus for hours, changing position several times in the trees overhead as they hunted. Bats flew into the small bit of light, attracted by heat perhaps as much as illumination. The night air was cold, but warmth from the piled rocks was a radiant pleasure, and a comfortable drowsiness pulled at my eyelids. The scent of smoke, stew and drying dog seemed to say safety and home as Ed and Jed snored softly across the fire. My remaining saddle blisters hadn't popped yet and I had enough Band-Aids to repair the wounds for another day. I was warm and fed, wearing clean underwear and socks. And my baby was free tonight. My certainty that I'd have her tomorrow was growing.

The rabbit stew that filled my belly would have been better with something besides an MRE and a pinch of salt to season it, and my taste buds wanted a huge slice of toasted Italian bread slathered with garlic butter and a frosted mug of dark beer, but I was satisfied. I was picturing my baby perched on the side of a mountain, horse hobbled nearby, Bella's belly filled from Dell's packhorse stores, a couple of warm bedrolls wrapped around her. Maybe a poncho rigged as a tent against possible rain. I'd have her back by tomorrow. I would.

The radio crackled. Jedidiah's right eyelid lifted. I rolled just enough to see Caleb in the darkness, sitting slightly behind me, to my left, as he pulled the park radio from a pocket. Adjusted something on its side. The connection was scratchy, but I recognized Joel Durkowitz's voice.

"This is the IC, broadcast to all field SAR teams. Howell, got your message. Good work. The sheriff just handed me an ID on our guy." I sat up. Caleb watched me in the flickering light. "Name's Delano Alton Gregory. His mother was a Shirley. Only wife of record is Belinda Little Gregory, no death certificate on record in three counties we've contacted so far. The Gregorys were property owners about twenty-five miles from Gladdenton during the time of the Vanderbilts. Made it rich in industry, railroads and mining until the crash of '29. We're looking through land and property records for a map of the time. Soon as we have one, I'll send someone in with it to Howell Hasty One or Two. Hang on a sec."

The radio went quiet. I felt Caleb's eyes on me, felt the solace that seemed to leak from his pores and surround me. He gave that almost-smile, a lifting of flesh over his cheekbones, the shift in expression that didn't have to touch his lips to be called a smile.

"Got word back from USC. Gregory was an assistant professor of geology until early 1997. He had a breakdown and left the school, supposedly joined a nihilist, back-to-nature group out west that broke up in the patriotism aftermath of 9/11. But Gregory was back here by then, with the wife. We got someone getting dental records for the wife to compare with the body in the grave, and we're checking out the rest of his history. We should have more by morning. We'll check in then. ICP out."

"Ten-four. Howell One out." The other teams checked out one by one. Silence fell once again, and this time only the crackle of fire marred the absolute stillness. Jed's eyelid closed. He had made no other movement, no acknowledgment.

Caleb's eyes stayed on me, warm in the night. "You all right? Warm enough?"

"I will be. Tomorrow, when you find Bella." I could feel the heat of his smile. I closed my eyes and slid into slumber.

21

I woke to find a hand on my arm, a face only inches from mine. A scream opened my lips. And then I felt the heat of his body and recognized Caleb. "It'll be dawn in an hour. I'm heading out to get the other teams. Back fast."

"Breakfast'll be ready and camp struck when you get here."

"Coffee would be nice, if you're feeling womanly." I could hear a trace of teasing in his voice.

"Macho male pig. Maybe Ed will be feeling womanly."

Caleb laughed, the sound a gentle breath of air though his nostrils. "That's a mental picture I wish I'd never had. I put water on to heat for washing. There's plenty left." And he was gone, boots silent on the forest floor.

True to my word, I was washed, dressed, and breakfast was still hot on last night's coals when I heard the noisy tromp of the hasty teams returning with Caleb. Ed and Jed looked up when I did and began the last minute jobs of striking camp, which included tossing water on the coals and Ed marking his new territory. The smell of wet wood and smoke mingled with the fainter scents of breakfast.

The main tracker's face was creased with worry when he entered the camp ahead of the others. He made no eye contact at all, simply held out his hand for the plate I clutched. Feeling last night's elation fade, I gave him the plate of reconstituted eggs and pan-heated Hungry Jack biscuits, and a plastic cup of coffee. He ate three fast bites of food and downed half of the coffee before he took my arm and led me away from camp, back to the stream. He shoveled food as he walked, the motions not crude, but industrious, mechanical, a man who had little interest in the use of food except as fuel. He cleaned the plate, stopped and turned me to face him. Gently, he seated me on a rock beside Sampson's Branch.

"The IC contacted us as I got to Hasty Two. We got a report back on Dell Gregory." His tone was devoid of emotion, as automated as his eating. A cold fear caught at me with ragged claws. "When his records came back, Joel discovered he had been kept in a private hospital specializing in emotional and mental disorders for about eighteen months back in the nineties. He was diagnosed as bipolar, paranoid schizophrenic with delusional episodes. Don't really know what that means medically, but in Gregory's case, without his medications, he becomes violent. Loses touch with reality. And according to his doctor, who was tracked down about two this morning, Gregory's been off his meds for a couple months now."

I gripped the boulder beneath me as it seemed to tilt. Caleb caught me in one arm, dropping the plate. "Hang on. We'll get her back. Mac." I looked into his dark blue gaze, the predatory expression so fierce it seemed to slice into all my fears. A blue laser of purpose. "I'll get her back for you. I promise." I managed to nod. "You want to go back to the ICP?"

"No. No way," I said, hating that my voice was so breathless, so fragile. I pushed him away, found a center of balance and stood, supporting myself with one hand on the boulder. "Bella will need me. I have to be there for her."

Caleb released my arm, his fingers sliding reluctantly from me. "I should have told you some other way. I'm sorry. Your ex took it pretty bad when they told him. You sure you're okay?"

"I'm fine." I spotted horses moving through the trees. "Howell Hasty's here. Let's go."

"Mac?"

When I looked at him again, Caleb said, "It's pretty clear who the strong one in that marriage was. Bella's lucky to have you for a mother."

Not trusting myself to speak again, I nodded.

"I gave up on promises ten years ago, Mac. But I'll get Bella back." Once again, Caleb Howell moved into the trees and was gone, taking his warmth with him.

The teams met in the campsite, above the bank of Sampson's Branch, a motley crew of men and women, dogs and horses. There was Jed and Ed, Yo and Ruth, four horses, Buddin Hasty Team, which was now comprised of the dog from Chandler Dog Team, Buddy Buddin, Ned Gorman, and my brother-in-law, Burgess Morgan.

He walked to me with that smooth, dancer's grace I remembered so well, no visual evidence remaining of the damage that had ended his dancing career. He smiled, whiter than white teeth blazing in the early sun. "Mackie!"

"Burgess." I managed a smile just as he grasped me in a hug. He had never been a demonstrative man and the affection caught me by surprise, as did the pain in my ribs. I grunted and Burgess eased back, concern etching his face.

"My God, look at your face. Are you hurt? No one told me you were injured so badly. Are you all right?"

"I'm fine. Bruised, but fine. Easy on the hand. It's bruised, too," I said, sliding my gloved hand out of his too-tight grip.

"You look like you got hit by a truck."

As this wasn't the first time I'd heard the comparison, I merely shrugged and slid from the residual circle of Burgess's arms.

Except for the moments at the incident command post, I hadn't seen my brother-in-law in three years, not since the Morgan siblings discovered the contents of Rachael Morgan's will and the already strained relationship was thrown into discord. He was the elder, the taller of the two Morgan boys, the one who had been a dancer in his younger years and then ran the family business after an injury mangled one knee. There could never be any doubt that he was a Morgan. His hair was darker, his eyes a clear green, his willowy frame less delicate than Marlow's, yet they were similar enough in appearance that he and Marlow had often been mistaken for twins while growing up and acting in movies as child extras and in supporting roles.

"Thank you for coming," I said, the words not conveying the surprise I felt at seeing him on the wilderness trail. In another time, Burgess would have been called a dandy. Even here, he was decked out in the latest L.L. Bean microfiber down-filled jacket, an Egyptian cotton shirt, undyed, natural, woven khakis. And a brand-new Kevlar vest.

"You should be back at headquarters. This is no place for an injured woman." Burgess's jade eyes were compassionate, but his mouth pulled down at the corners. "Marlow should be here instead of you."

"Marlow is better with the press," I said, hearing the

inadequate excuse. "He's…" I shrugged again, suddenly embarrassed for my soon-to-be-ex. Why hadn't Marlow joined the search? This far out in the backcountry, the media getting in the way seemed a foolish concept. Bella's father was back at the ICP, safe, while his daughter was out in the wild, lost. And his brother and wife went into danger. Ex-wife, soon-to-be.

"I love my brother, but he's a self-involved, egocentric man," Burgess said bitterly. "He should be here, looking for his daughter, but he's too busy looking out for the Morgan image." Burgess turned from me to the hillsides, misery on his face. "Mama saw it in the final days of her life. She saw how self-seeking he'd become. It broke her heart. If she hadn't been so sick, she would have cut him from her will. Only her falling into the coma so suddenly saved him."

Marlow had always been selfish. I knew that. I had known it when we met. But he was magnetic, charming, the kind of man a woman would sell her soul to have. Perhaps I had done so. Or perhaps I had sold my daughter's soul and safety to have him.

"Okay, listen up, people." Caleb's voice broke into the conversation. "I got a lot to say and not much time to say it."

Uncomfortable with the direction of my thoughts, I turned to Caleb. Hat in hand, he was standing with his weight on one leg, the other bent slightly at the knee, in a pose I recognized as characteristic. His eyes roamed the small group. "With the latest information on the kidnapper, we now know we're facing an unpredictable, violent man. One who is well-armed, familiar with these backwoods and has nothing to lose. The sheriff is sending in more law enforcement, but as you know, he has officially deputized us and authorized the use of force as needed in the rescue of Bella Morgan and the capture of Dell Gregory.

"As the girl is now free, that may make Gregory even more unpredictable, more dangerous to any of us who get in his way. Don't hesitate to shoot if you have the need. Just make sure you don't have one of us in your sights instead." The groups chuckled, but it was an uneasy sound, full of the knowledge that friendly fire was a dangerous problem in the woods.

"Howell One and Two will follow the faster-moving horse tracks, the mount most likely carrying Bella Morgan. Buddin Hasty Team will take the trail of the injured horse, the one being pursued by Gregory. Both teams will go armed, moving as quietly as possible."

Armed? I spotted a rifle slung across Buddin's back. And what horse was injured? Why hadn't anyone mentioned that to me? What else didn't I know?

Caleb went on. "Until we find evidence to prove Dell Gregory is permanently out of the picture or captured, we are to adhere to all safety measures. Everyone in Kevlar vests.

"I'll be sticking with Howell Hasty Two, but moving at point. We're running out of horse-accessible trails and the mounts may need to be left behind soon. The stormfront got stuck over the Tennessee border, but it won't stay put much longer. Move with all speed, people. But keep safe."

Angry and not sure why, I whirled on a heel and found Ruth. "Same horse?" I asked her. And without waiting for an answer, I lifted a booted foot and pulled myself into the saddle of the ugly, raw-boned little beast. It was only much later that I realized I had mounted without assistance. I pulled my sunglasses out of my knapsack and slid them and my visor into place.

The teams separated, Burgess lifting a hand in farewell as the Buddin Team picked up the trail of the injured horse, and Howell Two Team started off after the main tracker, who had conveniently vanished into the foliage at an up-hill run before I could state my annoyance at being uninformed.

We chased Caleb at a steady clip, moving through the more sparsely spaced trees, Ed and Jedidiah out front of the horses, the hound's nose to the tracks. The horse Bella was surely on had moved out fast, irregular-spaced hoofprints digging into the soft earth as she kicked him up-hill, away from Dell. There was no trail here, just hazardous, severely steep mountainside, rock strewn loam, gullies that opened out on either side and closed up as rapidly, thickly treed, with laurel thickets dotting any open space. Our horses were quickly an encumbrance, sliding back down hills, the pack animal caught twice in a thicket that seemed to close in from each side. My mount looked back at me once, his eyes rolling in fear. I tried to comfort him with hands and voice, but he was terrified.

Caleb reappeared. "Leave the horses. Ruth, can you get them back down the mountain to the stream? Get someone in to pick them up? Then rejoin us if you can."

"Sure. I think the horses have had enough, anyway. Dismount I'll take mine down, then the others one by one. And then back to Ramsay Horse Trail. How 'bout I head north with fresh mounts just in case?"

"Fine. Logan Lowell Road winds through. Suggest Joel make a secondary command post somewhere on it." To Yo, Jedidiah and me, he said, "Shoulder small packs and move out, people."

I hit the ground hard, jarring my ribs, but the horse seemed to calm immediately, as if my weight had been a source of trouble to him. "It's okay. My fat is a source of trouble to me, too," I confided in his ear as I stripped him of gear I needed. "You were a good mount, for all of an hour and a half. Thanks." I slapped his rump and half ran up the thirty-five degree slope, my feet in Yo's tracks.

Adrenaline was shooting through my veins in red-hot spurts, my breathing loud, fighting to keep up with my body's needs. Sweat broke out beneath my shirts and poured down my back to puddle at my waistband. The stitches and blister on my foot cried out, weeping into my sock. The blisters on my backside chafed open again, hurting with every step. My ribs complained and my heart beat like a drum pounded by a two-year-old. I had left the camera with the horse, carrying only the essentials, yet the weight of the pack and the angle of ascent strained my legs beyond anything I had done since high school track. Ahead of me, Yo dug her feet into the loam and pushed upward like an automaton, beneath the heavier pack she carried.

When we crested the hill, my blood was pounding in my ears, and even the hound we followed was huffing for breath. The north side of the hill was shaped totally different from the steep south side, composed of rolling laurel thickets fifteen to twenty feet high, the ground beneath unseen, impenetrable. Yet horse tracks descended in a straight line. Bella in a panic? Horse out of control? There were dog prints pressed on top of the horse prints. Only one set. Rufus? Yo plunged after them. I followed, keeping close.

"Why do we know the other horse was injured?" I asked Yo when I found a gasp of breath I could spare.

"Blood trail. Caleb thinks she stabbed it with a stick or something and took off. 'Course, the horse could have injured itself in a fall, and she took advantage of it and ran." Yo was out of breath, too, but she was concise. "And then there's the possibility that she injured Dell and it's his blood Buddin is following. Now that would be a kicker, wouldn't it?" Yo sounded as if that possibility would please her immensely.

"Bella told Dell she was afraid of horses. But she loves them. She might have hit a man, but she wouldn't have hurt a horse."

"My feelings exactly. I've met dozens of men I'd like to whack upside the head, but never an animal."

I laughed and my feet slipped out from under me. In a single wild skid I slammed into Yo's legs and we rolled together, uncontrolled, for several yards before she managed to grab a laurel tree and stop our descent.

"Glad that wasn't on horseback," she said when she'd caught her breath. "Come on. Back up a bit. Jed and Ed went that way."

We repositioned our packs and trudged uphill, found where the horse and dog tracks made a path down a less steep slope, the hoofprints growing closer together, a more compact stride. Bella had gained control just here, drawing the animal up, making him feel her power, her authority. Pride swelled inside me when Yo pointed out what I had deduced from the tracks. I was learning to read the ground, discern its secrets. Her radio tweaked, Buddin's voice calling for Howell Hasty One and Two. Still moving, she pulled out the radio and said, "Howell Two here."

"Our boy Gregory found his mount after 'bout a half mile and turned him into the water. We've lost him."

"Howell One. You splitting up?" Caleb asked.

"Yeah. We got the dog, the handler and Gorman going one way, with Morgan, Raymond, Hamilton and me going the other. But you need to know, Dell's moving fast. And my feeling, given where he entered the water, is that he's going back after the girl."

"Ten-four," Caleb said. "Out."

A low rumble of far-off thunder sounded, and I risked a glance up, away from my feet. The clouds were swirling shades of gray, angry-looking, as if they were seeking whatever trouble they could cause mankind.

"Don't rain. Please don't rain...." I breathed.

22

Except for Ed, who was forced by Jedidiah to rest every forty-five minutes, there was no stopping for breaks or lunch, just a hurried breather on a spit of rock overlooking a deep valley I was too winded to notice. A moment for a wilderness toilet stop and to wash my face and massage muscle rub into my calves and thighs, and we were back at it. While on the well-marked trail with the horses, I hadn't concentrated on the speed we were making. Now, on foot and moving almost as fast, I learned why the groups were called hasty teams.

We saw Caleb four times that day, once at the breather, and the other times unexpectedly, when he would circle back and speak to us from the brush at the side or from a perch above or below. Yo and I were following Bella's horse's tracks step by step. The main tracker was covering three or four times our distance, crossing back and forth, looking for ways to read Bella's path, to get ahead of her, to cut time off our chase. Twice during the day he called us from the tracks to an unmarked race across ground that hadn't felt a human footstep in a hundred years, cutting time off our run by moving ahead on foot in a different path from what Bella had been forced to use on horseback. Each time, we sliced minutes off our pursuit, and were now only hours behind her. Even I could tell the horse droppings were moist and aromatic, still drawing flies.

With a drizzle of rain in our faces, we discovered the sheltered site where Bella had spent the night. She had cold-camped, but the well-used latrine, and the pile of leaves and brush she had collected to put beneath her sleeping bag, gave evidence of a long rest. And Caleb found the note Bella left, this one folded into a purple football and stuffed into the heart of a living tree once torched by lightning.

My fingers had swelled again and I was unable to open it, so like the last time, Caleb unfolded the delicate purple paper and gave it to me to read first.

Well, this is the pits. I am IsaBella Angeleena Morgan. I was kidnapped and got away from a guy who is certifiable, and I mean that literally. He's nuts. I found some empty medicine bottles in the bottom of a bag. Zyprexa is the name I remember, but there were four bottles. The doctor's name on the bottles was A.P. Patel, or maybe it was P.A. Patel. The patient's name was Delano A. Gregory. Dell Al Shirley Gregory or any combination of those is what he calls himself. I'm not sure he knows who he is anymore.

Anyway, I got away, but now I'm lost. I know there's supposed to be no way a moving, uninjured adult can stay lost in these mountains, that civilization is just too close by, and man has made too many encroachments and all that. But I haven't seen a path or a road or a house on a hilltop all day. It's dark now and clouds are moving in. It'll rain tonight or tomorrow. And I'm afraid.

Tears started, gathering and falling so fast I held the paper away from me to keep the words legible. I took a breath that sounded suspiciously like a sob and Yo put an arm around me, reading over my shoulder. Caleb was a furnace on my other side, though he wasn't touching me, and I knew he was reading, too.

Not of the bogeyman, or space aliens, or bears, or snakes, or even mountain cougars. But of being alone. I miss my mom. I miss the stupid lessons she and Dad always made me do in the stupid home-schooling they forced on me. I miss her making me clean my room or do the laundry or wash the cars. I miss the dogs and my horse and my bedroom, though Rufus has stayed with me and I'm not totally alone. I like the little mutt.

I miss a bath! Ahh! That's me screaming. I stink! Dell could find me by my smell. Tomorrow I'll find a stream and bathe, I don't care how cold it gets.

I laughed then, and Caleb chuckled beside me.

I'm heading roughly southeast, but the mare is in trouble. She has a limp but no obvious injury. If it doesn't get better, I'll have to ditch her tomorrow, leave her someplace safe. If there is any place that's safe. I put on wraps for the night. I miss my mom.
IsaBella Morgan

I held the note to my chest and cried, the others moving away to give me as much privacy as the small clearing allowed. Bella sounded so strong and so afraid, and so…so Bella. "I miss you too, sweetheart," I whispered. "I miss you, too."

"Move out, people," Caleb said, looking at the sky, the

direction of Bella's horse's tracks and finally at me. "We need to read this to the ICP, but there's no signal."

I crushed the note into my bra and took off after the tracker, who had decided to take us out of second gear and into overdrive, straight uphill. When we reached a height where the radios worked, I splayed onto the cold ground, muscles so tired they felt like rubber bands, lungs so spent they sounded as if I had asthma or a serious infection.

Ed, no doubt thinking that my legs looked like his bed, fell across them and grunted with pleasure. I was too tired to push him away. Jedidiah fell beside him, and at least *he* seemed tired. Of course, the dog handler was pushing sixty.

Still looking fresh, Caleb held out his hand for the note, called in to the ICP and read it to Evelyn, who was again manning the radio. She, in turn, shared what information they had on the police part of the search before calling the incident commander to the unit. I was so tired, I could only summon the energy to listen if I had my eyes closed.

The connection faint, Joel told us that a man who sometimes bought gold from Dell and took phone messages for the reclusive hill man had a message from an out-of-state number. It was being looked into by the phone company to determine who the owner of the number was. When he read it to us, I froze. Then lifted a hand to Caleb, who was looking at me already.

"It has to be a mistake. It has to be," I said.

"What? The number?" Yo asked.

I nodded and forced the words through the stricture in my throat. Past the pain that lodged there, anchored by betrayal. In little more than a whisper, I said, "I know that number." Tears blurred the dull day, made the laurel waver on the hillside. "It's a Colorado area code," I said, my voice sounding strained and foreign. "Followed…" I took a breath that ached. "Followed by a number with an Aspen prefix." My eyes held Caleb's, shock rippling through me.

"Hang on a sec, IC." He lowered the radio, pressing it against his thigh "Mac?"

"It's at the estate of Rachael Morgan. It's Marlow's private line."

23

Caleb quoted my words back to Evelyn, the syllables falling like the blade of an executioner's ax. I could hear the sheriff's voice in the background, but the signal was too weak for me to understand until he took over the radio and spoke into the mike. "You sure, Missus Morgan? You absolutely sure about that?" He repeated the number.

Feeling wooden, thick-brained, I just nodded, blinking away my tears, trying to read Caleb's face, trying to make sense of the number. *Marlow had called Dell? Why?* Parts of questions flowed through my mind. Fragments of nonsense. Slivers of fear. *When? And why? Why had Marlow called Dell? It had to be a mistake.*

The world seemed to slow and narrow, darkness closing in from the sides until there was nothing left but fear and a single link to reality—the blue of Caleb Howell's eyes. A black vacuum of space lit only by twin blue suns. The realization that I was passing out occurred to me, a gradual insight, a slow-motion discernment.

"She's sure, Har," Caleb said, his eyes giving nothing away.

"Please ask Missus Morgan to keep this knowledge to

herself and not discuss this with Mr. Morgan," the sheriff said, "at least until we dig a little bit."

Numb, I nodded. Discuss it with Marlow? With Burgess? Why would I? And if Burgess's team was on a hilltop, he'd know already. This didn't make sense. *Marlow had called Dell?*

"Will do, Har. Howell One and Two, out." I heard soft clicks and the sound of a radio sliding into its leather sheath. Caleb, his eyes still on mine, knelt beside me and held out his hands. I placed mine into his and felt the warmth of him—a radiant heat that seemed to fill me. To force back the darkness. "Take a breath," he said. I breathed. And the vacuum receded.

He pulled me to my feet. My legs were feeble, unsteady, like those of a child who would fall. Caleb held me, sliding an arm around my waist and pulling me to him. His eyes pierced into mine, his gaze securing me as tightly as his arms. Without looking away, he said, "Yo, you and Jed and Ed head back down the hill to the trail. We'll catch up."

Trapped in the dark blaze of his eyes, I heard the quiet departure of the others. And then there was only the mountain, the sky and Caleb Howell. "You okay?" he asked.

"Why?" I asked, though there was no way he could answer that.

Caleb shook his head once, a slight motion. "Are you okay?" he repeated.

"No. I'm not okay." I watched his face as the muscles moved beneath his skin, anger and a savage protectiveness taking root. "I'm just…numb. He couldn't have been part of this. He couldn't have. It has to be a mistake." Caleb's steady gaze held mine. "Did he…" My throat closed on the question. "Did Marlow…?"

"I don't know. I can't speak to that right now. But I'll get Bella back. And I'll find out from Dell Gregory who set this up. And why. I'll do that for you. For Bella." I stared wonderingly at Caleb, letting him convince me with the fervor of his certainty, with his promise. No one had promised me anything in years, not anything I could believe in. I felt his strength flowing into me.

"If you can't keep up, you'll slow me down. So, if you can't go on, if you need to go back, I'll see you get to a place where you can be picked up."

I smiled then, knowing he was pushing me because otherwise I would have fallen. I stood, holding my own weight. I held him away from me. "Over my dead body."

White teeth flashed in a grin. "Figured you might say that. Try to keep up."

He tossed my glasses at me and I caught them one-handed. At a dead run, Caleb Howell, the best main tracker in the state, a local legend, flew down the hillside. I followed in his wake.

Monday
1600 hours

When the spurt of strength, the jet-spring of euphoria, had worn off and left me so tired I could barely put one foot in front of the other, Bella took a page from Dell's book and entered the water of a stream. And Ed lost her. Ed lost Bella's scent. She was gone.

Heaving breaths so loud they sounded like a steel rasp against raw meat, fighting cramps so intense I feared my legs might draw up under my chin and solidify there, I fell against a downed tree, its bark stripped off, leaving smooth marbled wood with a long tight grain. Black walnut, with its characteristic dark striations. Supine, my head turned to follow the motion of the three other searchers, I watched and prayed and cursed my mutinous body.

Ed pulled Jedidiah up and down the stream, the hound splashing water with his big paws, searching for the scent. Jed held the scent article in one hand, the knotted leash in the other. Yo walked slowly down one bank, studying the ground, her eyes snapping back and forth from side to side. And Caleb ran higher up, searching for signs of the dog or something we might miss at water level. Into the silence of the frantic hunt, Yo's radio squawked. It was Ruth, and she sounded desperate.

"This is Ferguson Horse Team, requesting assistance. Ferguson Horse Team requesting assistance. I have an animal down. Repeat, I have an animal down." In the crackle of static behind her words, I could hear the blowing, grunting breath of an injured horse.

Caleb said, "What's your twenty, Horse Team?"

"I'm halfway to Ramsay Horse Trail with the last of the horses. Something spooked them and the last animal in the train reared and slipped. He fell about twenty feet down a narrow gully." I could hear tears and suffering in her voice. Anguish. "He impaled himself on a branch." I knew what was coming next. I could feel it in the poignant pause of her speech. "I can't get the branch to break off. There's no way to free the horse without a crane or a chopper with a sling even if I did get him free." She sucked in air through tears. "I need a gun." She swallowed, the sound audible over the airwaves. "And someone who knows how to use it."

A voice I recognized as Perkins, from the Perkins Backtrack Team, came over the radio. "I can get back in there to Ramsay Horse Trail and I got a .308 Winchester. It'll take him out with a single shot. I know how to do it right, too, Miz Ruth. He won't suffer." There was compassion in his tone, at odds with the callous choice of words. "It'll take me an hour to get to Ramsay. Can you walk me through finding you?"

"Yes," Ruth sniffed. "Hurry. He's hurting bad." The sounds of the horse struggling sliced deep. Over the airwaves I could hear him battling to live, could hear it in the fierceness of his breathing, the untiring fight of his legs as he tried to free himself, hooves hitting trees and stone. "Hurry," Ruth said. The radio traffic went silent.

Ruth was suffering because of me. Hurting because of the search to find Bella. And a horse would die. Was it the ugly little animal that had carried me up the steep slopes? I hadn't even known that Ruth's last name was Ferguson. Would a person die before this was over? These strangers were risking everything to find my baby. Chaotic thoughts twisted through my mind.

From fifty yards off, too far away to know there was a problem, Jedidiah shouted to Yo. "You got anything? 'Cause I got nothing. I need to go upstream and back down, make a few loops." His speech seemed dull and prosaic after the torment in Ruth's words.

Yo shook her head to Jed and made a circular motion with an upraised arm, as the radio crackled again. "ICP, this is Buddin. ICP, this is Buddy Buddin. We got an injured horse, too. We tracked the subject's mount, found where the subject caught it, turned it and rode it hard till it came up lame. She's got a swollen canon bone and needs vet care before we try to walk her out."

We heard no answer from the incident command post. But after a moment, Buddin said, "Ten-four, IC. Will do. Buddin out."

Yo glanced at me. "We can receive the nearby teams, but we've moved so far from the ICP we can't always pick it up. The signal gets blocked by the mountain ridges."

I nodded to show I understood, but I didn't care. It didn't matter. Nothing seemed to matter at the moment. Might not matter ever again.

"Joel'll likely set up a TCP closer in soon." Before I could ask what she meant, she pressed the transmit button and spoke into the radio. "Caleb, I got nothing. I'll start downstream, away from Jed and Ed, and I'll stay on the west side of the creek. If I spot something I'll call you and you can come back for Jedidiah."

"Sounds good. I'll follow this ridge to the cleft about a klick ahead where the water joins up with a smaller branch and forms a creek. If she went that way, I should spot her. Keep your heads up. This is nasty land, lots of ravines."

"Yo?" Jedidiah called from the creek edge.

"Ten-four." Again moving her arm in a long arc that encompassed the stream bed both up and downstream, Yo indicated to Jed he should do what he thought best. He stuck a thumb in the air to show he understood, and moved out of sight. To me, Yo said, "You coming? Or you just going to hold that tree down?"

"I'm gonna lie right here and think about dying," I said, tears trickling down my face in cold wet runnels. "My legs seem to think that already happened when I stopped. I'm numb."

"Don't lie there too long or you'll have to be carried out. Sit tight. One of us will pass this way again and you can join up then. Drink a lot of water, rehydrate your muscles and take a couple ibuprofen. Keep an eye on the pack." She removed the heavy pack and dropped it on the ground beside the tree.

I gave a little salute with two fingers, the only parts of my body able to move, and heard Yo push through brush. She was gone and I was alone. Tears coursed harder, pooling in one ear and trickling down my neck on the opposite side.

We had a dying horse. And we had lost Bella. And I was going to have to drop out of the search. Hours before dark, hours left to search, and I was now a liability. Perhaps I always had been.

The silence of the forest closed in around me, the only sounds distant birdcalls and the soughing of leaves overhead. Deep in my mind images were torturing me. Images of Bella on horseback, sliding into a deep ravine, crushed in a tight gully, unconscious, as her horse kicked her slowly to death. Images of Bella lying in the water, fallen from a startled horse, hitting her head and going under to drown. Images of Bella when she was four, sitting astride her first pony, her eyes wild, alight with joy so intense I had felt it slide along my spine, through my body, into my toes, my own joy in my daughter resonating with her. Images of Bella sparring for the first time in karate class, her yellow belt tied proudly around her waist, her white pj's moving with the fierce movements of her twelve-year-old body. Images of Bella pleading to be let free from lessons *just for today, only today, please, Mama, please,* so she could go riding on her new horse with the girl next door when she was fourteen. Visions of Bella taking a six foot deep, eight foot wide ditch on the same horse, her face euphoric, triumphant and fearless. And her shock when the horse died of colic last fall, after eighteen hours of walking the animal, moving without ceasing. Her horror and indignation when a neighbor pulled up in a truck and offered to haul the carcass off instead of giving him a decent burial.

My baby was lost. She had been so close. And now she was lost again. And I knew, deep in bones that ached and in lungs that worked only with pain, that we would not find her tonight. Bella would not be found before the rain came and washed away tracks that she was trying to obscure.

Bella would not be found today.

As I lay there, the first spattering sprinkles fell on my sweating skin, cooling, chilling, stealing what little life I had left, splotching my lenses. Thunder rumbled far off. And I cried as the rain fell, drenching my clothes, washing my face free of tears. Bella was lost.

24

I lay on the log as the rain pattered to a stop, as the clouds thickened and dropped, as the afternoon wore toward night. My muscles stiffened, my clothes half dried. My body forgot to be cold, the shivers coming, passing, and leaving me slightly blue with fatigue and a low-level hypothermia. Finally, I stood, went through my small pack and found clean underclothes and a clean shirt. With my few toiletries, bandages, ointment, facial soap, I made my way to the creek and stripped, washing off the smell of old sweat and fear in the frigid water, massaging a heavy coat of muscle rub into my legs. Addressing the burst blisters on my backside—what the saddle hadn't ruptured, the run today had. In clean clothes, heartsore, physically exhausted, in pain I hadn't admitted till now, I washed out the filthy shirts and panties.

Close to the creek, I found a level, sheltered site and gathered dry wood for a fire—some broken limbs from the black walnut where I'd taken my rest, some cedar kindling, a few oak lengths that would have to burn at an angle unless someone had brought a saw or an ax.

Building a ring of stones pulled from the creek, I started the fire with supplies from Yo's pack. Put on water to heat. If I'd been thinking, I'd have used heated water to wash, but my brain wasn't functioning. Not that it mattered. I had ceased to feel the cold. I had ceased to feel anything at all.

I assembled a spit, bracketed it over the flames, started coffee in a tin percolator and added another pot for water to hydrate MREs for supper. I found a bag of beans and dumped them in with three packets of salt advertising a fast-food chain. They'd boil for hours before they were soft enough to eat, and might have to be simply tossed out or carried to a different site for the night if Caleb found a better one. Or if... But I knew Bella would not be found. Not today.

Yo was first back to the campsite I'd chosen. She stood at the edge and looked it over, seeing the pile of leaves to cushion our bedrolls, checked the scant shelter for protection against wind and rain. Bent and added a stick of wood to the fire.

"We won't be able to pick up the ICP from here, but it's a good campsite. And Caleb can climb the ridge to report, or relay a report through another team."

I felt her eyes on me as she spoke, but I didn't look up from stringing a line for clothes to hang and dry. Refused to meet her gaze. I didn't want to hear what she had to say. I knew it already. Bad news. No Bella. I didn't need specifics. As she stood there, her radio crackled. I heard a report on the horse that had fallen. It was out of its misery but couldn't be retrieved. It was carrion, wedged in the steep walls of the crevasse. Ruth sounded shattered, broken, as if she had lost a personal pet. Or a child, though I was the only one who had done that.

Obviously uncomfortable with my silence, Yo took

the warm wash water, her radio and a small bag from the larger pack she had carried, and moved out of sight, toward the creek. When she came back, her face was shiny and free of sweat. She was dressed in a clean green thermal shirt and sweater, but like me, still wore dirty jeans. She hung her hand-washed clothes beside mine and sat, her gaze hooded but watching me.

Jedidiah came in later, as darkness was flooding in and a heavy cloud settled down upon us. He made Ed sit near the fire, and the rank smell of half-dry dog rose into a fog that was so thick it hissed in the fire and held the smoke close. The white haze picked up the red glow of the fire, swaying and swirling as we moved, like silk scarves in a choreographed dance. It muted the night sounds, not that there were many. Few predators would hunt tonight. Not until the fog cleared.

Near six-forty, Yo tried to call headquarters and was surprised to get through. She reported our present location from her handheld compass and local landmarks, and told the IC, in careful terms, that we had lost the trail. "Temporarily," she said. "We'll pick it up in the morning." She stayed on, listening to the locations of the other SAR camps and marking them on her map. When she signed off for the night, she looked at me and waggled the radio. "Atmospheric conditions do strange stuff. We shouldn't have been able to call in from down here."

It was seven, pitch-black when Caleb radioed in, his voice holding no elation, no joy, just a defeated exhaustion as thick as the low cloud that pressed down on the mountain. Yo told him how to find us by following the creek, described the fire and the mist, which seemed to be localized, as Caleb had no fog where he was. By the time he reached us, the beans were edible, though bland, Jed had rigged protection from possible rain in the form of a length of tenting material strung across the campsite, and we were on our second pot of boiled, instant coffee. No one was speaking. I couldn't make myself look at the team members. Fear and failure wrapped around me, layered like a mummy swathed for the tomb.

Caleb came in from the night like a wraith, like a vampire in an old film, mist-woven cape swirling behind him. He strode across the camp to where I was standing, looking out into the night, the sound of his boots swallowed by the haze. He stood too close, his form blocking out the light from the fire, throwing me into shadow, a deeper silence settling on the small clearing. When he realized I wasn't able to look up at him, Caleb touched my chin, pulling my unwilling face up to his with a fingertip.

All in darkness, he held me there by the tip of one finger, his expression hidden by the night, the top of my head just brushing his hat brim. "I meant what I said." His voice was low, a hoarse murmur. "I *will* find her."

I closed my eyes, tears leaking out beneath my lids. "Still?"

He laughed, the sound desolate, yet certain, a strange combination of emotions surging together. "Still." And then he was gone.

The failure that had sat like a weight upon me for hours lightened, lifted. I shuddered a breath, another. I was certain I hadn't breathed since we'd lost Bella's trail. I hadn't asked him what he had found. Hadn't asked how he would find my baby. But I believed him. Somehow, I still believed him.

"What did he say?"

Yo's voice made me jump. I found her in the darkness, her body wreathed by diffuse light, a mystical, fire-touched hue, blurred and indistinct, her dark hair a gold-streaked halo around her head, her form so strange I longed for a camera to capture the image.

When I spoke, I kept my voice soft, as if a loud tone might mutate the vision she presented. "He promised to find Bella for me. He wanted to know if I still believed him."

"Caleb *promised* to find Bella?" Yo and Jed exchanged a glance I couldn't interpret.

"What?" I asked.

"Caleb Howell ain't promised anyone anything in ten years," Jedidiah said.

The main tracker had used that time frame with me, too. "Why? Why ten years?"

They looked again at each other and Yo shrugged, as if telling Jedidiah the explanation was up to him, that she didn't care to start it. He looked from her to me, his gaze reflective. Moved a chaw of tobacco from one cheek to the other. Spat into the fire and sucked at the chaw. "His kid was lost over to Glass Mountain 'bout ten years back. Son, maybe four, five years old. Caleb promised his wife he'd bring him back. Promised her he'd find him. Shoved his own pain down deep inside somewhere and did the things that needed doing. Never found the kid. After six months, his wife give up. She'd lost Caleb and the kid, too, see, with him being gone." Jed spat again. "She left him. Some say it took him another six months to notice."

"He lost his job with the park service when he wouldn't give up looking and go back to work," Yo said.

"Obsessed, is what he was." Jed scratched Ed behind the ears and the hound sighed, his black lips fluttering with the breath. "He lost his son, his marriage, his house, his whole life. When he came up for air, two years had passed, and he finally admitted defeat of a sorts. He took a job teaching forestry and conservation, stuff like that, in Asheville, and became a SAR main tracker so he could help other folks who lost someone. But he never promises he'll find 'em. Never."

"He still goes to Glass every year for a month, looking, hoping to find something," Yo said.

Chilled from the tale, I came forward to the flames, added a few small sticks and a larger branch, one that fit in at an angle, poised on the rocks I had piled. *Caleb Howell was obsessive….* Pulling my bedroll around to use as a padded seat in front of the fire, I sat beside Ed and stirred the beans, the scents of dog and beans and forest sharp and pure. *He promised nothing….*

I wanted to ask, why me? Why Bella? But I was honest enough with myself to know why. Honest enough to know that Caleb Howell wanted more than just to find my baby. The realization should have made me uncomfortable, but it didn't.

Caleb and I had connected, somehow, in the rare quiet moments of the SAR. Connected on an elemental level I was only now recognizing. Connected enough for him to break a decade of fear and failure and promise what only he could bring, what only an obsessive main tracker could give.

The thought warmed me just as his hands had. When Caleb entered camp again, I looked up at him and smiled. And saw the release in his eyes, the relief on his face. Tentatively, he sat on the damp pad beside me and took the fork and the plate of beans I offered.

Because I was honest, I had to ask myself, what if even this obsessive, never-give-up, never-say-never man didn't find Bella? What then? Could I live with that? Would I become as obsessed as he? Yeah. Probably. I passed around more plates and beans, including one for Ed, pulled five MREs out and checked the temperature of the water. It was near boiling.

I leaned against Caleb Howell's back while we ate, his warmth seeping into me, the silence in the campsite at last companionable.

25

Just as we were about to bed down, a cell phone rang. We all twitched and Ed barked, startled at the modern, tinny, automated sound. It was coming from my small pack. I dug through the loose pile of belongings, finding Bella's purple phone. Having been left on for several days, it was low on battery power, so low it wouldn't work for long. And with the steep hillsides blocking the signal, it shouldn't have worked, anyhow. I glanced in surprise at Yo.

"Atmospheric conditions," she reminded me.

I punched Send. "Hello?"

"Mac?"

A strange electric quiver ran through me at the sound of his voice, a brittle agitation. "Marlow," I said.

Caleb tilted his head up at me, his dark blue eyes a cool flame.

"I want…" Marlow's words trailed off. He was never without words. The phone was still working, a faint hum of white noise, so I waited. "Mac?"

"I'm here."

"I want to come home."

Sudden rage scorched through me, so fierce and hot it left me breathless. I closed my eyes against my reaction, trying to contain it, to hold it in.

"I want to be with you and Bella. I was wrong and cruel and I know that, but I want you to forgive me. I want to come home."

I gripped the little phone in my hand and had to force my fingers to relax on the smooth metal and plastic. "Oh?" It was all I could force myself to say, all that made its way past the crumpled mass of anger blocking my breathing and voice.

"We…we could get counseling. Family counseling."

Only you need counseling. Bella and I are fine…. Only, Bella wasn't. Not really. Not now. I opened my eyes, stared into the dark and pulled in a single breath. I wanted to tell Marlow to go to hell, that he had put me through hell, that he had put his daughter through hell. I wanted to see him hurt as I had been hurt, wanted to see him miserable. *He had called Dell.* Why and when and…if. *If* he had called Dell.

It could be a mistake. Mistakes happened all the time. "Counseling?" And yet, if it wasn't a mistake, then it was possible that Marlow was connected to Dell Gregory and what had happened at the fish hatchery. And now he wanted to come back. *Over my dead body.* The words fought their way up from the depths of my broken soul, crawling up through the fragments of the woman I had been for almost two decades. I stood and walked away from the light of the fire. Moved into the cold dark.

I opened my mouth to say the words, and the memory of Bella's face appeared in front of me, so winsome, so lonely on the night we'd camped at the fishery. For once without the dauntless vivacity that was so remarkably her own. I had forgotten that look, that conversation, that empty need. Forgotten it in the coil of horror and fear since.

Afraid of hurting me, yet wanting something I couldn't give her, Bella had confessed that she missed her dad. Missed him fiercely and wanted him back. Confessed that she didn't really want to find me a boyfriend. And I had told her that I understood, but that the choice wasn't mine to make. And it hadn't been. Until now.

"I'll find a good counselor, Mac, and we can all go together. We'll find a way to heal our marriage. And heal Bella, too, help her over this ordeal."

Something in his words didn't ring true. Some note of falsehood tainted the tones. He was trying to manipulate me once again, trying to get me to see him in a different light. He always did that; I understood the tactic. But why now? Why did it matter what I thought about him? Why did he claim to want to come home?

Yet, did I have the selfish right to refuse what my daughter needed? Bella would require counseling and more than just her mother's love to get over this experience. She would need both her parents. So I forced down the refusal that hovered on my lips. Bella would need all the charm and healing that Marlow could bring someone who was damaged, hurt, as once upon a time he had helped to heal me after the death of my father.

And if Marlow had indeed called Dell? Then my promise would mean little, as it would have been given to a shadow of a man. I wasn't very good at prevarication and Marlow would know if I lied, just as Dell had known I lied, back at the fishery.

"Mac? Are you there?"

"I'm here," I said, feeling my cracked ribs move with my breathing. "Counseling is good. But you can't come home, not just like that, out of the blue."

"Mac, I—"

"You can get an apartment in Atlanta, someplace near us. And we can go to counseling. I'll agree to that."

"Thank you, Mac." There was relief and gratitude in his tone, emotions I had never thought to hear from Marlow Morgan. "You won't regret this, I promise. I've missed you both. Didn't realize how much till Bella was kidnapped."

Relief and gratitude? Why? Had the sheriff already asked him about his Aspen number and Dell Gregory? Suspicion wormed into me like acid, eating a corrosive path to my heart, clearing a dull rancid place amid the broken pieces of myself. *Over my dead body…*, The phrase was cleansing, a sticky glue that pulled me back to myself. "It's not for me, Marlow. You need to know that. This is just for Bella."

"That's a start. That's all I'm asking. A chance to prove myself. I still love you, Mac. I still want—"

The phone beeped the "low battery" warning. "I have to go, Marlow. We'll talk later." The connection ended and the phone screen went black. I folded the small cell and looked down; though I couldn't see it in the dark, it was warm in my hand. I tucked it in a pocket of my jeans and shivered.

I was facing the misty black of night, my boots in the deep loam, the heat of the fire far behind me. I had walked away while talking to Marlow, as if my body and feet were restless, away from the fire and companionship and warmth. The creek tinkled and gurgled, chittering over rocks as it dropped a foot toward the sea so far away. A branch slid, fell and thumped to the ground with three distinct thuds and a sharp crack of breaking wood. A night bird called, the sound tremulous and tentative in the fog.

I stared into the nothingness of the dark, so like the nothingness of my marriage and my promise to Marlow, so like the emptiness of my heart. And despite my promise, I knew for the first time that my marriage to Marlow Morgan was really over. It had been over for a long time, and now I was finally breaking free. I sighed into the night.

26

Startled at the awareness, a sixth sense I hadn't known I possessed, I felt his presence behind me. I felt him before I saw or heard him, as if he was moored to me in some mystical way, a ship tethered close. And somehow I knew he had been there for long minutes, watching out for me, careful of me in the dark lest I get lost as Bella had. And that meant Caleb had heard my conversation with Marlow. Had heard my promise.

It was curiously important that he understand what the promise meant, what I was giving to the father of my child. I crossed my arms, feeling the cold and the damp of my shirts against my naked hands. I had removed the rib brace and gloves when I bathed, and hadn't put them back on. Without turning to try to find him in the milky night, I said, "The sheriff said not to let on that Marlow was being investigated for calling Dell. And Bella will need counseling. That much was true."

I felt Caleb draw nearer, and when he laid his hands on my shoulders, I leaned back into him, into the tenderness and solid, sure, craggy stillness that was Caleb Howell. His arms came around me, careful of ribs and bruises, finding my cold, swollen hands and interlacing his fingers gently with mine. It was the first time he'd touched me other than casually, an offhand gesture. And my pain slipped away in the heat of his arms.

He said nothing, content to let me lean into him as the mist swirled around us. The lonely bird called again, as if searching for something it had lost. The forest settled. Caleb rested his chin on my head and his breath stirred my curls.

I warmed, touching him, letting him carry my weight as he had shouldered the burden of finding Bella. The calm of the man rested against me, seeping in. Our breath came together, a soft synchrony, building something new between us, melding something fragile and shattered into some new thing, some feeling that was strong and extraordinary and beyond any words I knew.

"It's not too late," he said, his lips warm at my ear. "You can still go back."

"It is too late. It should have been too late the first time he found someone else. The first time he hurt me physically. But somewhere along the way, in my marriage to Marlow, in my dependence on him, I lost myself." It was so clear now, as I stared into the dark, what had happened to me, what I had become. My pride, my sense of self-worth, hadn't been so much stripped away as given away willingly into Marlow's callous care. I was the epitome of the abused wife who had never found the courage to leave.

I laughed once, the solitary sound hoarse and lonely, like the bird calling. My marriage had been pathetic. I had been stupid. I had turned a blind eye to his little flings, his one-night stands. I'd let him hit me, or twist my skin until it tore, or back me into a doorjamb until my spine ground into the wood. "I was a fool."

"But you loved him. A body will overlook an awful lot when the love is that strong."

"I reckon," I said, and Caleb chuckled against my back at my use of his words. "Where did you go to school?" I asked suddenly. "You know these mountains like the back of your hand, but you know GPS coordinates, and speak the cop lingo, and know horses, and—" I stopped. "You're not a backwoods good-ol'-boy."

He seemed to understand what I wanted to know, his voice vibrating against my spine as he answered. "I was born in these mountains to a couple of young hippies in a commune. Born on the dining room table while the commune members got stoned and chanted and played guitar."

I laughed, as he had intended.

"You should meet my mom and dad. They were into pot and free love and rock and roll and still are. They still have a commune down near Henderson. Pretty place, if you like ashram chanting and incense. But I went to school in Asheville. Spent six years with Uncle Sam's army, six more working in any low-paying blue-collar job I could get while I went to Clemson."

"A college boy."

He chuckled, the air from his laughter moving my hair, tickling. "Yes, ma'am. And graduated with two majors. Married. My son was born. I reckon you heard about my losing him," he said, his voice holding an accustomed grief.

"It's grown cold and I can feel the damp on you. Let's get you back where it's warm." But he didn't remove his arms or pull away, and I angled my head against the cloth of his shirt, hearing the brush of my curls against him. Releasing my hands, he turned me in his arms until my face was just below his. It was far too dark to see him, to watch his smile, but I knew it was there, that small tilt of lips, pull of skin over his cheekbones.

My hands were pressed to his chest, and I could count

his heartbeats, the soft intake of his breath. His lips touched mine, warm, velvety soft, and when I opened my lips, I learned his taste, the texture of his mouth. He pulled away to kiss my cheeks, my lids, my forehead, his mouth trailing a heated path across my skin.

"This is strange," I whispered.

"Yes." The word was husky against my skin as he sought control, for the gentleness I felt as he held my broken bones. When the silence stretched between us, he turned and led me back toward the light of the campfire, my hand safely in his.

When we finally reached the fire, he dropped my hand, yet Yo raised her brows at us, propped on one arm in her sleeping bag. Then she gave a half smile of delight, her eyes flicking back and forth between Caleb and me.

27

Tuesday
0540 hours

When I woke, long before sunup, I realized Caleb Howell had found me in the night. My face rested in the curve of his hand, his fingers against the back of my head, tangled in my hair. Only a fraction of an inch separated our sleeping bags, and we faced one another in the gray of false dawn, his eyes on mine. I smiled at him and he smiled back.

I heard someone stirring on the far side of the smoldering fire. Heard Yo yawn hugely and mutter something under her breath, cursing the hard ground. Heard Ed pad into the forest and the resulting sound of the dog's ablutions. Heard the radio crackle as Yo tried unsuccessfully to call in to the ICP. "So much for the atmospheric conditions," she said finally through a second yawn. "We need to go up."

"Time to break camp," Caleb said, the words unnecessary except to fracture the direction of his thoughts. He removed his hand from my face, slipped from the bedroll and into his boots.

Feeling stiff, heavy and old, I raised up on my arms and slid out of the sleeping bag, found my own boots, pulled them on and followed Yo to the creek to wash. I stretched as I walked, pulling on joints and muscles that had frozen overnight, that now creaked and popped as they became reaccustomed to action. As I washed and applied muscle rub to pretty much my whole body, excitement was building inside where last night had been only heartbreak. Today we would find Bella. Today would be the day. Caleb had done that. Somehow in the dark of the night, he had changed me.

Though the low-lying cloud was breaking up and patches of mountain forest were visible, it was still too foggy to track. After we broke camp and the fire was only a hissing steam in the dawn, three of us crawled to the tip of the nearest ridge so Yo could use her park radio and call for an update. Ed and Jedidiah waited below, near the creek, for light bright enough to track by.

Viewed from the top of the world, the forest below us was dark and shadowed, the peaks sun-touched. The golden ball of the new day balanced on a shelf of clouds, rising beyond a far ridge. The world smelled fresh and sharp. A dove called, mourning the passing night. Far to the east, an eagle soared before the red-gold clouds like an ebony promise. I longed for a camera and for Bella to share the view.

"ICP, this is Howell Hasty Two," Yo said. "Come in."

"ICP. Ah, Yo, how 'bout a Rabid Dog Two call."

Yo glanced at me and Caleb, but spoke into the radio. "Rabid Dog Two, confirmed. Howell Two out." She turned a dial on her radio, explaining, "Rabid Dog Two is Evelyn's personal jargon. It means she wants a private chat on channel twelve." Into the radio, Yo said, "Rabid Dog, Rabid Dog. Go ahead." Yo sat on a rock and Caleb leaned a shoulder against a tree.

"Rabid Dog Two confirmed," Evelyn said, her voice softer than before. "Har Har tells us the FBI's been burning the midnight oil. They confirmed the number of the fellow who left messages for Dell. It was Marlow Morgan's Aspen number, all right. They've got independent evidence that Marlow was calling someone in this area. Har's talking to him now. Can you hear?"

Yo turned a different knob on the radio and the volume rose. I could make out Marlow's indignant voice in the background as I found a rock to sit on, boneless with shock.

"You are clearly mistaken. What kind of backwoods investigation is this? Don't you understand who I am?"

"I reckon, Mr. Morgan," Har said, amused and bored, his local accent so firmly in place it sounded welded to him. "I think you made sure we all know who you are, not that the son of a dead Hollywood celebrity wields much power in these parts. Tell me, sir. This Gianna Smith you're traveling with. It's my understanding that she once worked at Maple Ridge, a private mental health institution near Boone."

"What of it? Gianna is a traveling nurse. It's a great service she provides, working at understaffed hospitals. Though it may not be common in a small town like this, it's what a lot of nurses do. They travel, work at one hospital for six months, and move on."

"Yes, Mr. Morgan. I know we're backcountry rubes—"

"That's not what I—"

"But though we're a small sheriff's department, we do have access to the most sophisticated FBI computers and research capabilities. Enough to learn that Maple Ridge is the same hospital where Dell Gregory was treated during his psychotic break and resultant evaluation and rehabilitation. Would you care to explain that to us?"

The silence was palpable even over the radio. When Marlow spoke, it was with a quiet voice, the one used when he was on the brink of losing control. "This is preposterous. I suggest you keep any more slanderous accusations to yourself unless you want to hear from my lawyer."

"Please feel free to have your lawyer present, Mr. Morgan. In fact, I suggest you retain one locally. I think you may need legal representation and advice."

"Are you accusing me of complicity in the disappearance of my daughter?" Marlow's voice rose, growing louder with each word. I had an instant of wanting to stop him, to place my hand on his shoulder, to help him remain calm.

"Can't say as I am. Not yet," Har said, his tone ruminative. "But I might before this is all said and done."

"You illiterate moron!" Marlow's voice grew with each word to a shout. In the background something crashed, as if a metal chair had been toppled. "I'll sue you and this backwoods county for harassment and slander and incompetence in the loss of my daughter. This interview is over."

"As you please, Mr. Morgan," Har said, his tone still amused, almost laconic. "Investigator Wightman, please take Mr. Morgan into custody and hold him for questioning."

My stomach roiled with conflicting needs and I pressed my hands against it to still the nausea.

"What? I demand to see a lawyer. Stop! You can't do this. I demand to see a lawyer. Take your hands off me or I'll—"

"I don't think you want to do that, Mr. Morgan. Unless you want to be taken out the front door of the ranger station in handcuffs in full view of all the cameras?" Har Har was enjoying himself. I could hear it in his voice.

Evelyn whispered, "I got to go. You got all that, Yo?"

"We got it. You take care, Evelyn."

"You bring that little girl and her mama back to us. You hear?"

"Ten-four. Howell Hasty, Rabid Dog Two out." Yo clicked off the radio, adjusted the dials, her eyes carefully not on me.

We sat in silence on top of the ridge, the wisps of fog swirling away around us. I could smell pine and spruce and damp earth. I could feel the cold of the stone beneath me, seeping into me, wetting my clothes and chilling my flesh. I could see the tip of another mountain to the left, standing like a block of stone turned at an angle, distant and obdurate and alone. I rubbed my stomach and swallowed against a sick sensation gathering inside. "Marlow—" My voice didn't work, and I cleared my throat and tried again. "Marlow was involved in what happened to us at the fishery, wasn't he?"

"Seems so," Caleb said, his eyes on me but his position unchanged, giving me time to absorb what I had heard.

"How? In what way is he…involved?" I thought I knew, but the concept, the image of Marlow as corrupt, as evil, stayed just at the edge of my conscious understanding, fleeting and transitory as the mist.

"Har will explain—"

"Don't." I held up my hand to stop Yo. "Don't placate me or say that the sheriff will handle it and let me know. Tell me what we just heard."

Yo looked away, out to the craggy mountain peak, her lips pressed together.

Caleb spoke, his voice low, words measured. They pierced me one by one, clarifying the new image of Marlow. "Har suspects Marlow of using Gianna Smith's contacts to hire or otherwise prompt Dell Gregory to hurt or kill you." The phrases fell on the thin air with the finality of steel against flint, drawing sparks from my newly mended soul.

His voice continued. "Maybe with the intent of leaving Bella alive, or to kidnap her, as he has. And maybe the plan was something else entirely, but went astray. But it's still in the investigative stages. Marlow hasn't been charged, hasn't been accused. Just held for questioning."

I looked up and met his eyes. "It looks bad, doesn't it? Bad for Marlow."

Caleb tilted his head once in acknowledgment, his posture still and calm, as much a part of the mountain as the peak across the cleft. And dived at me when a shot rang out.

28

With a lightning-quick motion Caleb shoved me down, pulling Yo with us behind the rock on which I had been sitting. He crouched over us, his own head raised, listening. "That was close by. Maybe across the—"

Another shot sounded. A third. Caleb whirled, his boots raking the earth, and was gone. The crack of rifle shots broke in echoes. Yo's radio crackled. "ICP, this is Ferguson Horse Team. We are under attack. Repeat. We are under attack!" Ruth shrieked.

Two more shots rang out.

"We have a man down. ICP, Perkins is down. He's been shot." A thudding sound like the radio being dropped was followed a moment later by a click and Ruth's muffled voice. "Get him behind it. Get him down. Bandages? Anyone got a— Good. That'll do. Oh Jesus, he's bleeding. We got an arterial hit here. Jesus, Jesus, Jesus," she prayed over the airwaves. "I need equipment. I need— Apply pressure here. Harder."

A muffled reply. The sound of someone grunting in pain.

"More. Give me something else. I don't care. Press. Harder."

And the voices on the radio went silent as Ruth let go of the talk button.

"Ferguson Horse Team, come in. Ferguson? This is the IC. Come in Howell teams."

Yo looked at me, her face only inches from mine as she clicked on her radio. "Howell Hasty Two here. We are secure."

When Caleb didn't call in and the uneasy silence lingered, Yo spoke into the radio again. "IC, Howell One is on the move. He said the shots were close by. He may be…" she searched for a word "…busy."

"Turned off his radio again," an unknown voice said.

"Maintain radio silence all units except requested teams," Joel barked into the mike, frustration and fear-laced anger spitting across the airwaves. "Come in, Buddin Team." When there was only a crackling silence, he said again, "Buddin Team, come in."

Two more shots rang out, the sounds so close together their echoes reverberated across the ridges in a complicated dance of sound. Yo pulled out her map and spread it between us. "We're here." She pointed. "Ramsay Horse Trail is here, with the spot they likely spent the night right about here." She placed a second finger on a different spot. "And Buddin was heading this way when they started out this morning." She placed a third finger. The groups were in a roughly triangular pattern.

"And here…" she paused, placing the forefinger of her other hand on a place equidistant between Buddin Hasty's supposed location and Ferguson's Horse Team "…is a ridge, a promontory that would make a dandy shooting position. He's got them pinned down." Fear raced along my spine with her words.

Yo clicked on the radio. "ICP, this is Howell Two. Possibility that Steader's Point might make a good shooting site for the sniper. He'd have clear sight of Buddin and Ferguson."

Ruth's voice overrode Yo's, crackling and half-audible. "ICP, I got a man needs immediate medevac transport to the nearest trauma center. Repeat, I need immediate transport. Over."

Joel said, "We've already called a chopper in, Ferguson. You got coordinates?"

"Negative. GPS took off with the horses. We're two miles south of Berkley Road and Staton Creek."

"You got a flare?"

"Wait a minute." The pause was an agony of white noise until she pressed the transmit button again. "Ten-four. Flare ready. You got an ETA?"

"Estimated time of arrival to your location is twenty minutes. Is there sufficient area for a chopper to set down?"

"Negative, IC. They'll have to drop a rescue cradle. Let 'em know, okay? And tell them to step on it. Perkins is losing blood fast. He's on Coumadin from that heart attack this winter and his clot formation stinks."

"Will do, Ferguson. Any other injuries?"

"Uh…well, now that you mention it—"

"What?" Joel barked.

"I sustained a minor flesh wound to the upper left arm. Nothing serious. And we got a horse with a major limp. Someone will check him out when we get time. The shots scattered the horses, so we may have more equine injuries to report later."

"Thank you for deigning to share that bit of information with us, Ferguson. Ervin is with us and he wants to know how minor your flesh wound is."

"Not bad enough to worry about till Perkins is outta here."

A shot rang out again, sounding this time as if it originated from a different place. The echoes were shorter, closer together. Three more shots sounded, the reports less crisp. Yo pressed my head down with her free hand and said, "Different gun. He had two, didn't he?"

I remembered back to the conversation with the sheriff and his men when they first saw my photographs of Dell Gregory. "Yes. Two rifles. One called a mountain rifle, I think."

"Yeah. That last was a mountain rifle. I'd bet my next paycheck that the first one we heard was a long range sniper's rifle of some sort. He's on the move and he's got two rifles. Ain't he the well-prepared kidnapper."

In the photos, the guns had been on Bella's packhorse. Had Dell relocated the weapons when he first took Bella prisoner? A feeling of cold seeped in through my exposed skin and I hugged myself, pressing against the rock.

Yo's radio crackled. "Uh, this is, uh, Buddin Team. Uh, anyone there?"

"That's Burgess," I said, surprised. He didn't sound like himself. He sounded unsure. Out of his element. Frightened. Not at all like a Morgan.

"Your brother-in-law?" When I nodded, Yo said, "He's got the transmit button pressed in. Hear the noise?"

There was a continuous buzz of sound coming from Yo's radio, abruptly cut off. Joel answered instantly. "This is the IC. Who is this?" When nothing was said in reply, Joel waited a beat and said again, "This is the IC. Report, Buddin."

A moment later he finally answered. "This is Burgess Morgan. Buddin is hit. I believe he's dead." There was an instant of stunned silence over the radio, a seamless moment of shock. Buddin was dead?

"And Raymond Hamilton is down, too, with a bullet through his leg. He's got the bleeding stopped. But, uh, we need help."

"Give me your location," Joel said.

"We're near a stream. The same one Caleb Howell sent us out on. There's a cliff on the left, and an open space on the right."

"That's a big, freaking help," Yo said. She pressed the button on the side of the radio. "Burgess, can you see a rock projection to your right as you face upstream, up high, shaped like a house turned on end? Or have you seen it today?"

"We could see it an hour ago, but there's too much tree cover to see it from he— Wait, I do see it. I'm sorry. Yes. I can see it. Why?"

"IC, he's on the north branch of Fortune Creek. We got two teams down at once, Joel. Who is this guy? He got a radio? Was there a report on military experience? 'Cause he's acting like he's got both intel and experience. He put himself between the teams in the night, in perfect position to take them both out at once at first light. What's going on?"

"Negative to time spent with Uncle Sam. And there's no information on the tactics used by the White Knights, the survivalist group he joined out west."

"Citadel has a sharpshooting team," a familiar voice said. "Anyone take a look at the graduation roster to see if he was part of it?"

"Negative, Stubbs. Good call. Har can check into that," Joel said.

"ICP, this is Howell Hasty One. He's gone." It was Caleb, winded, his voice carrying the hint of a whistle from exertion. I rose and mentally measured the distance from the ridge where we were to the peak across the mountain cut. It had to be a good two miles, maybe three, more than half the distance almost straight downhill, another mile straight uphill. Caleb Howell had made the run in less than half an hour. "He's shooting .308 caliber rounds, Joel. I found an empty cartridge. Must have gotten away from him. Ruth, was Perkins in a vest?"

"Negative." She was embarrassed, angry. "We thought we were too far from the path of the guy to need one."

"Burgess, you guys in Kevlar?" I could hear an edge of steel in Caleb's voice.

"Uh, no. Well, I am. But Buddin wasn't."

"Burgess," Joel said. "We have a team coming in via horse and foot. It'll take them half a day to reach you. Can Hamilton walk a half mile back downstream and then turn uphill to a ledge about six hundred feet?"

"You mean I should leave Buddin here? Alone?"

"Yeah. Leave Buddin."

"Well, I suppose. I mean, Hamilton can walk if I help him. But it doesn't seem proper to leave Buddin."

"You head back in overland to that ledge. We'll medevac Hamilton out and you can get back to Buddin by midafternoon. You can wait for extraction by the overland team."

"Uh…yes. That would work. I suppose." Burgess's reluctance was unmistakable. He didn't want to hike through woods where a sniper hid, possibly carrying a wounded man, hike back, and then sit and wait with Buddin's body. Not alone. And I didn't blame him.

"IC, this is Stubbs Hasty Team. We will move ahead to Kotter Ridge and resume search for the trail there. All in vests, with all possible safety precautions. All are agreed, we're not coming home."

Yo pressed the transmit button. "IC, this is Howell Two. Same here. Please keep me informed."

"Ten-four. Godspeed, Perkins."

Yolanda Perkins, the name recalled from the first sight of her name tag when I was bound and she caught me as I fell. I had forgotten it in the days since I met her. Putting out my hand, I stopped her. "Perkins? Your family?"

Yo looked away, up to the peak where Caleb had run. Her throat worked once. "Yeah. My uncle. My daddy's brother."

A sizzle of shock lanced through me. The searchers hunting for Bella were dying. Friends and family, good, innocent people. "I'm sorry."

"Not your fault. The fault of the bastard we're after. And if anyone can save him, Ruth can." She looked back at me, the ghost of a smile in her eyes. "Let's go find Bella."

Over Yo's radio came a strange voice, not one of the now-familiar searchers' voices that had intruded on the events of the last hours. "Ten. Channel ten. Channel ten." Two clicks answered the soft-voiced phrase. But when Yo adjusted the radio to channel ten, there was only white noise. Nothing else. She flipped channels, her fingers working the switches and dials, but the voice was gone. Shrugging, she gestured down the hill and plunged toward the creek. I followed, grabbing trees and vines on the way to keep from falling.

29

Yo, Jedidiah and I donned our Kevlar vests, mine over my rib brace, and divided up, a subdued Jedidiah and Ed going upstream, while Yo and I followed the current, our parties moving in opposite directions from the day before, hoping to pick up something the other had missed in the poor evening light. We had only one more day before supplies ran out and we were forced back to civilization to restock. Yo's shoulders were unbent, her pack much lighter than when we'd started out.

We didn't speak, Yo's attention fierce on the ground to either side of the trickle of water, as if she might compel the earth to give up secrets by the force of her will alone. I was constrained by guilt and by fear. What if Dell Gregory made the SAR so dangerous that searchers gave up, went home, declared Bella a lost cause? Caleb had said he would never give up. Caleb had promised to find my baby. But those words had less power by light of day and under threat of violence. Would he give up? Was Bella lost to me?

Tears obscured the landscape and I dashed them from my eyes, careless of my healing scrapes and bruises. I resecured my sunglasses and visor to protect me from the brightening glare. Shoving branches to the side and maneuvering around trees, we took a path away from the creek and back again as the landscape made following the water impossible unless we were wearing waders. I pulled off the gloves, heedless of the tender, still-swollen flesh of my palms, using my hands recklessly as I followed Yo, who moved like a dervish before me. Her breathing grew as labored as mine as our muscles worked without a break. The temperature rose as the sun sought the height of the sky. The shadows shortened, our way growing clearer.

The crackle of the radio reporting multiple missions was the only sound we could hear. Perkins was safely airlifted out, strapped into a rescue cradle and winched into the body of the chopper hovering overhead, an EMT riding atop him. The searcher was alive when he reached the hospital and a waiting surgeon. After that, no news came over the airwaves about Yo's uncle, as attention turned to Raymond Hamilton, the other injured SAR volunteer, and the recovery of Buddin's body. There was nothing we could do to help, and Yo channeled her fear and worry into the driving pistons of her legs and the ground that needed to be covered. Silence and the intensity of her questing eyes were the only indications of her mental state.

It was almost impossible to keep up at first, my body anything but limber. But as the minutes passed and I forced muscle and sinew to contract and expand, movement became easier. Breathing evened out. My heart rate stabilized and dropped into a steady pace instead of a jagged, mad rush of pain.

Yo turned away from the creek again and went uphill, back down, covering a grid of the hillside present only in her mind's eye. Lungs aching, watching her walk a mental diagram, I stopped and leaned my weight against a curved tree, half sitting on the trunk, the bole of which was bigger around than my arms could reach. Panting, I stretched my muscles to keep from freezing up. On one circuit, Yo paused and handed me a granola bar and a bottle of water. "Don't drink it all in one place. That's the last of the fresh stuff. We either get resupplied or we start drinking treated water. Stuff tastes like chemicals, so enjoy this while it lasts."

When she came back again, the water was gone. Her eyes lingered on the empty bottle for only an instant. "Bella didn't come this way. If she was still in the creek, still on horseback, she'd have to leave the water and go around the falls. There's no sign of hoofprints."

Yo sprayed a bit of orange paint high on the tree where I rested, on the north side of the trunk. I had noticed her marking trails before but never paid attention to the small orange can, too absorbed by my own pain. Yo and Caleb were leaving indicators of places Bella wasn't. With a final *psst* of sound, she turned to me. "Let's head back, meet up with Jed and Ed. Maybe they found a scent or something I missed yesterday."

Not waiting for my reply, she grabbed a root at shoulder level and swung her body in an arc, finding a foothold a yard higher, where she pulled herself up to another small tree and yet another flat foothold. Not managing Yo's grace or balance, I dragged myself after her. The wrong direction again? Had Bella ever entered this creek at all?

I glanced back at the small falls Yo had mentioned, registering the site for the first time—water crashing between broken rocks, splashing down a ten-foot drop between wet, black stone. Ferns and lichen clung to crevices in broken rocks, casting low shadows. A single twisted conifer rooted in the cracked stone had grown into a natural bonsai, leaning out over the spray, glistening with droplets from a mist born of water meeting rock. An old mountain spruce, its heart scorched by lightning, jagged splinters stabbing into the sky, soft fronds of darkest green draped like old lace, held on to the bank above with desperate fingers of roots.

I turned my back on the sight and pushed on. Once, I could have spent half a day here, photographing this one small area. But Bella had never been here. Nothing else mattered.

We had made it back to the previous night's campsite when the rescue chopper reached the area where Burgess should have been. Yo's radio crackled, Joel's voice calling. "Buddin Team, come in. Buddin Team, respond." The radio silence was ominous. "Buddin Team…Burgess Morgan, respond."

Falling to the damp earth, Yo shimmied out of the pack and dropped it on the ground behind her. We could hear other radio traffic in the background, all of it originating from the incident command post, but little of it on the single channel Yo could hear, and less of it intelligible to us so far away.

"Buddin Team, if you see the helicopter, please fire a flare into the sky," a different voice said, this one with the unmistakable sound of helicopter rotors beating in the background. "Buddin Team, come in. We are in position over the ledge to be used as an extraction site. Please acknowledge."

"He got them, too," Yo said, voice rough, her eyes shadowed with fear. "Son of a—" She stopped, fisted her hands and jabbed at the earth in frenzied punches, cursing vilely. Banging her head against a nearby tree with soft thunks like the throb of a bass drum, she cursed over and over, her anger turned inward and self-destructive. From her radio came the voice of the helicopter pilot, "—leaving the extraction site until such time as contact can be reestablished with Buddin Team."

As the chopper left the pickup site, Yolanda finally calmed, falling back onto her pack, staring into the leafy canopy overhead. Silent tears coursed down her face. Moving stiffly, I sat beside her, the ground cool beneath me. The smells of the recent fire and warming earth made a rich combination. Overhead, thunder rumbled, the sound rolling from far away. Beneath it, I thought I might hear the beat of the SAR chopper, but there was nothing. Yo ripped at her face with the sleeve of her flannel shirt, leaving streaks of dirt in the wake of tears. Her breath shuddered.

"If he thought to end this search, to run us off, he'll be sadly mistaken. When word of this gets out—and it will—" she beat the ground again with a dirty fist "—it'll spread like wildfire. Men will pour into these woods. Armed men, ready to shoot-to-kill anything that looks at them cross-eyed. And when they catch him, he'll never make it out of these mountains alive." Yo fixed me with cold, venomous eyes. "He's a dead man. I know these people. They have a singular brand of justice, unique to this one place. Mountain justice. And Dell crossed over a line into territory he never knew existed. He went after one of our own."

Yo wiped her face with her sleeve again and stood slowly, heaving on the pack. "Let's go find Bella," she said, slipping her arms through the straps and adjusting their fit.

"You're not giving up?" I asked, feeling bewildered.

"Are you out of your mind? He shot my uncle. If I had a gun I'd shoot Dell Gregory myself when I see him. Hell, honey. I'll never give up now. If a Perkins doesn't kill the bastard, a Bishop or a McHenry will. I just want to find Bella first so she doesn't get mistaken for the bad guy. Come on." She lowered a hand and I placed mine into it, letting her pull me to my feet. "Jedidiah and Ed will be moving upstream as fast as Ed's nose will lead them. Let's see if we can intersect his path." With that, Yo turned uphill.

"Why is it always uphill? Aren't there any downhill searches?"

Yo laughed. "Move it, city gal. We got a few miles yet to make before lunchtime."

Tuesday
1100 hours

We stopped for lunch at a picturesque spot upstream from where Ed and Jedidiah would emerge, having crossed uphill—always uphill—and gotten ahead of them. Yo and Jedidiah had been communicating through a series of whistles, and we knew we had a few minutes for rest and a meal. There wasn't much left to eat except for freeze-dried apples and beef jerky, a combination I would have scorned at any other time, but which tasted better than any steak and left my mouth watering for more. Yo had treated some water with little pills and let it jostle all morning in her pack. She was right. It was worse than vile. Sort of like chlorinated hot tub water after a family of chimpanzees had frolicked in it. But I drank it uncomplaining, washing down pills for pain and stiffness, happy to have the water and the meds. The only other option was to head back for new supplies.

I was stretched out with my feet up on a branch, my pack under my head, when Ed padded out of the creek, leash trailing. The wet dog plopped down beside me, treating me to a greeting with his slobbery tongue. I was too tired to fight it, and gave him my hand to lave. The dog seemed satisfied and so did his master, who trudged up a moment later. Jedidiah had a gleam in his eyes that caused Yo and me to sit up fast.

"You found her scent?" Yo asked.

"Ed's mama is the best bitch I've ever had. She can track a single possum baby being carried on its rat-mother's back for miles. She can scent a coon been raiding our garbage and follow it up trees, under holes, through water, and still have the energy to tree it. And Ed's got her gift. He picked up Bella's scent 'bout half a mile back. Found tracks three times when she left the stream to get around obstructions the horse couldn't manage. Got any of that jerky? I want to treat him."

Yo tossed three packets to Jedidiah, who tore them open with his teeth and fed the first one to his dog. As Ed wolfed down the tough meat, I rubbed his long, floppy black ears and crooned to him that he was the most beautiful dog in the world. He seemed to know that, and slobbered all over my hand again in agreement.

"Howell Two, come in." It was Joel, sounding tired and worn. I could picture him scrubbing his face with his palm, trying to remain alert.

Yo clicked in the transmit button. "Howell Two here."

"You seen Howell One?"

"Negative."

"Two horses are missing from Ferguson Horse Team. It's possible that they simply panicked, stampeded off and will be found in a day or two. It's also possible that Gregory took them and has fast transportation again. Pass that along to Howell One."

"Will do," Yo said.

"We're inserting a small team to locate Burgess Morgan, designation Nesbitt Dog Team. Tell Howell One to let them do their job. He's to stay on the girl until she's recovered."

"Understood," Yo said. "What dog is Nesbitt using?"

"A new one from over in Tennessee. You're so near the state line you could be sitting on it. I'm putting up a TCP and the Tennessee boys will handle that one with us jointly. We got so many volunteers right now, I can't beat 'em off with a stick."

"Not surprised," Yo said, cutting her eyes at me, satisfied and vengeful.

"We have news about the body in the shallow grave near the fish hatchery."

When Joel stopped there, Yo said, "Go ahead, ICP."

The IC sighed into the mike. "The bones in the grave have been identified. It's a missing girl, disappeared from a now-defunct family campground six years ago. You might remember the old Scarborough place, a primitive camp." He paused again, and I knew he didn't want to go on.

"Understood, IC," Yo said, her tone controlled and stiff. I could feel the weight of her gaze on me, but I didn't look at her. I couldn't. I stared unseeing over the valley floor, where the creek rushed, where Bella had taken refuge when she got away from a madman who was a…a what? A serial kidnapper?

"Julie Cravitz was five feet six, fifteen years old, brown hair, brown eyes, with poor dentition. She vanished after a chance meeting with a man on horseback, a man who showed her a collection of rocks and told her mama she had raised a pretty little daughter. FBI tracked down the girl's family this morning. They picked Dell Gregory's picture out of a standard batch of similar photos. He was in the campsite several days before the girl vanished. She looked like a runaway at the time. We're assuming now that Dell took her. FBI has already begun to look at all the cases of missing girls in the area."

"Marlow didn't do this, then? It was just a crazy man looking for a woman to take?" I asked, softly enough that my words were for Yo alone, not the harried incident commander. "And why can't I have a radio? Why do I have to wait and wonder and worry?"

Yo repeated my first two questions, her eyes still on me. What did she think I'd do? Wig out? Have a hissy-fit and throw things? That was Marlow's act, not mine.

Joel hesitated. "I couldn't reply to that, Perkins. The man in question is still talking to the police. I'll update you again when we know more. ICP out."

"Ten-four. Howell Two out." Yo looked at Ed, who had stretched his body, legs fully extended, his front paws near my knees, his back legs behind me. The dog was breathing heavily, eyes slitted, almost asleep. "How long before Ed can go again?" she asked his handler.

"He needs to be relieved now, spend a couple days in the sun eating some raw chicken and broccoli." When Yo laughed, he explained. "'Cept when he's working and I can't get to it, I got all my dogs on a modified Barf Diet. Keeps 'em healthy and limber as pups."

In the distance, thunder rumbled again, an ominous sound. We all looked at the sky, at the lowering clouds, darker than the fog that had caged us in last night, heavy with rain and swirling with intent.

"But I reckon he can go a bit more today. He needs an hour or two nap, but we need to beat that storm. Give him another twenty minutes and we'll get back in the water. Call Caleb. See, can he get ahead of us upstream."

Yo tried for five minutes, calling for Howell One on the radio, but Caleb didn't respond. Instead the ICP came in, Evelyn's voice sounding strained. "Howell Two, when you meet up with Howell One, he's to report to the IC on a secured channel."

"I'll pass along the message," she said into the radio, amused. "Howell Two out. Joel's not happy with our main tracker," Yo said to me as she stowed the radio in her belt.

"Never is, when the man turns off the radio," Jedidiah said. "But it ain't like Joel can find hisself another tracker with Caleb's success rate. So he can be unhappy much as he wants and he knows it. 'Sides, if Caleb is close to his quarry, he won't want a lot of air traffic alerting his prey. Radio chitchat don't mix real well with a hunt."

I closed my eyes and rested on my pack, my side pressed against the wet dog. I reeked with the stench of clothes slept in, too many days at a sweat-drenched run, and fear and worry. Now Ed added to my personal miasma, but I didn't care. The warmth of the hound was a comfort. I slept, dreaming of running uphill, pushing against the earth, only now, as is the way of dreams, I was heavy, paralyzed, sinking into the soil of the mountain, getting nowhere. And Bella was out there, alone, needing me.

I woke when Jedidiah called Ed. The dog and I rolled over, meeting each other's eyes, Ed's droopy and solemn, as if he had shared my dream. But he raised up on joints much more elastic than mine and trotted to his master, accepting the leash, the fresh reminder of Bella's scent in her red shirt, which he sucked deep into the tiny passages of his scent-hound nose. Putting his muzzle against the earth, Ed led the way back to the creek, as if he remembered where he'd last found the smell of my daughter. Together, dog and handler splashed through the creek to the other side. Dispirited and aching from the inadequate rest, I plunged after Yo, sticking to the banks, searching either side for signs of where Bella might have left the water. Overhead, thunder crashed closer, clouds rising with turbulence. Below us, the water began to rise as well, a warning of the storm upstream.

For an hour we scrambled through the underbrush along the creek, twice spotting places where Bella had left the water and taken to the bank. The hoofprints were uneven, and it was clear that the horse was injured, limping badly. Small size-seven boot prints indicated that Bella had led the animal for long distances.

At the end of the hour we found a place where she had lightened the packhorse's load, discarding two bags of flour; several sheets of good quality rawhide, still in the shape of the steers who had worn them; ammunition; rifle cases and a pack for cleaning weapons; an inflatable raft, which was odd; and camping equipment including a shovel, an ax and pots. A raccoon had rummaged through the pile, leaving bullets and discarded supplies strewn all over the ground, the telltale tracks of tiny humanlike hands pressed on the earth.

The creek was still rising, water lapping close to the rejected pile, and my heart beat painfully, an irregular ache against my ribs. "Please don't let it rain," I whispered, looking at the sky. "Please, don't let it rain." Lightning cracked across the sky, the answer to my plea. Wind whipped the trees fitfully, ripping loose spring leaves, slapping branch against branch, the forest calling for rain.

Sliding, slipping, falling on hands that should have been protected, I trailed Yo, keeping Jedidiah or Ed always in sight. The hound's relentless progress was vital. The angle of his ears, the position of his tail—all were signs that he still kept the scent. But now the creek was a rapids—fast, a muddy-brown river carrying branches and trash, tumbling over boulders and roaring through crevasses, the enemy as it rushed to wipe away traces of my baby.

"Oh please, please, please, don't let it rain. Don't let it rain. Don't let it rain," I breathed with each yard, begging God to hold off just a bit, just one more hour, just one more minute. And soft sprinkles pattered the canopy over me, a rare drop hitting me from above.

30

"Howell Team Two, this is Howell One. Give me your twenty. Howell Team Two, come in."

In front of me, Yo pulled out the radio without missing a step, her voice breathless when she answered. "This is Howell Two. We got messages for you from the IC."

I sprinted closer to hear the exchange.

"Later. Give me your twenty. Still on the creek where we camped last night?"

"Ten-four, moving upstream on the subject's track, generally north. Ed has a good scent but the water's rising." Yo slowed and looked around her. "If you came this way, there's sign of a landslide on the east slope of a ledge, where the rock face split and fell. Took out all the trees on its way down."

"I saw it. I'm nearly a klick ahead. If you're smart, you'll move inland, around the landslide. I've got tracks, so tell Jed to go around, too. I'll see you on the far side of the slide."

"Will do. Call the IC."

"Later."

I wondered about Joel's reaction to a conversation

that put his priorities and orders well below Caleb Howell's.

Yo shouted to Jedidiah and signaled him off the scent and uphill. The handler forced his hound away, and Ed resisted, his nose only inches from the ground, where I could see a single horse track. As a group, we crossed the creek, leaping from boulder to boulder, and crashed up the steep slope. Ed, freed from his leash, raced to my side and bounded up the hill beside me, his long muscles sleek beneath the wet brown coat, paws finding better purchase on the soft earth than my mud-caked soles.

The rain surged against the overhead leaves, wind slapping us with chilled, angry hands. The patter on the rich earth grew stronger. I no longer prayed that the rain would hold off. God wasn't in a mood to listen.

We reached the summit of the slide, the ground ripped and torn where the rock had split and fallen, shearing earth and vegetation away, leaving a raw wound in the mountainside. We edged beneath the remaining rock face, new stone exposed in a glory of yellows and browns, different from the black granite I had been buried beneath. It looked unstable, and only Ed raced past without a glance overhead.

And then we were plunging downhill, the pile of trees, stumps, ground-up rock and scored earth just to our left. Caleb stood high on a boulder, as always, his hat in hand waving in a slow arc to catch our attention. I shouted and pointed him out to Yo, who wasted no breath in reply, but flapped a free hand to show she had seen him. When she altered her course slightly north, Jedidiah and I made the same course correction, Jedidiah's feet slipping out from beneath him, sending him sliding and crashing for a dozen feet past me before he got them under him again. Ed thought the fall looked like play, and followed his master down, butting with paws and hip in a move that would have knocked me off my feet, but only caused the handler to laugh, the sound echoing off the split rock along with the thunder.

And the sky opened up and the rain fell—so thick it was a heavy sheet of water, pressing me to the earth. So dense it pounded back up from every flat surface, adding a white mist of microdrops to the mix. So hard the ground resisted the weight of it, didn't have time to absorb the deluge but tossed it back and downhill with us. So intense it blocked out all other sound, even the roaring creek. So strong it slammed through my clothes, icy against my skin, stealing my warmth and breath.

The runnel had become a hellish brew of destruction as wreckage from the landslide was carried down beside us, crashing into the backed-up water in the muddy pond produced by the rockslide. The newly created waterfall was wild and tempestuous, a monstrous, multilevel chute that changed as we watched, spouting through the piles of rock and debris in muddy arcs, carrying large gouts of stone and vegetation. Yo turned north and we followed, the falls lost to view.

Huge trees, ripped from the earth, whirled in the new pond, the flotsam swirling as water deep beneath became a whirlpool, sucking it down. A deer carcass corkscrewed in the eddies, bloated and days dead.

Yo slipped, falling back, feet shooting high. Suddenly Caleb was there, catching her and standing her upright in a single motion, graceful and balletic. He pulled her and then me under an overhang of torn rock, yanking at our packs as if to make us drop them.

"Leave the packs here and come on," he shouted over the sound of water and rain, making way as Jedidiah and Ed joined us. "I want you to see this before the rain washes it away. Hurry."

Dropping the packs, we followed the main tracker at

a dead run, away from the falls, upstream, past the sound of the cataract, beyond the new pond to where the water ran fast but clear again. And under a curved, smooth arch of stone, where the sound of rain was muted to a distant roar.

To a protected place where a fire had recently burned and a single bedroll had been spread and a woman's size seven boot had walked. I could see traces of the place where my daughter had rested, where she had groomed the horse and fed him, oats and rolled grains scattered on the tracked dirt. Ed went berserk, charging around and around the small space, spiraling in wider and wider circles, his tail stiff, his ruff like spikes.

Dripping, soaked, shivering in the icy wet, I fell at the rock wall, fingers searching in the soft soil for the note she had to have left. And then I saw it. The thing Caleb had brought us to see. The pile of rawhide strips beside the flattened sleeping spot. The larger footprints, coming to a point at the toe. A splatter of brown on the rock wall. Blood.

"No," I breathed, standing, my fingers on the brown stain. "Oh, God, no."

Caleb caught me, easing me down to my knees. "She's alive. He's got her again, but she's alive." He shook me, his face coming back into focus as he wrapped his arms around me, holding me as if afraid I might break into pieces and sail away.

"He caught her last night. Probably saw her fire. Took her and kept her tied most of the night, I'm guessing. Left her here while he scouted out a place to shoot from this morning. Then packed her up, headed back north, moving slow because of the fog, but chancing it. Man's crazy—got to be—to travel in that soup in the dark. He found another place between here and the shooting spot he chose. Dropped her off again, attacked the two teams,

and came back for her. But she's alive. Do you understand?" He shook me again, my head wobbling with the
action.

"Yes." I licked my lips. They were dry, cracked. I had
forgotten to drink for several hours and was dehydrated.
"I understand. He's had her all day. All day." A rivulet
of rainwater curled through the dirt at my feet, joined by
another. On the far side of the protected space another
tiny runlet purled in and lifted a thin skin of dry dust.
Pooling in the shelter. Washing away all traces of Bella.

"And he's on the run," Caleb said. "If he hurts her,
she's a liability, she'll slow him down. So he won't hurt
her. But the rain is going to obscure the tracks everywhere. We won't have a trail to follow tomorrow. We
don't have a trail to follow now. Are you listening to
me?"

"Yes." I struggled in his grip. "Let me go." I jerked
away, found my feet and stood on my own, on legs that
were rubbery and weak. Tremors of fear and exhaustion
ran through the length of my muscles. I heaved a breath
that billowed in the sudden cold, and ripped off the
Kevlar vest, throwing it to the dirt at my feet. "What
you're saying is that while I was sleeping at a warm fire
last night, my daughter was being kidnapped again."

"Yes. That's what I'm saying." Caleb's eyes were cold,
hard as lapis. He stepped away, trusting me to hold my
own weight. "You want to grieve, lay blame and wallow
in guilt, or get her back?"

Shivers took me and my teeth chattered. That wasn't
fair. Instead of pleasant company and a full belly last night,
I should have been wracked in anguish. Caught up in an
unnamable fear, some nightmare of horror. I should have
known, somehow known, that Bella was in danger. Sensed
it on the air, felt it in my marrow. I was evil and cold and
no fit mother. I had kissed a man while my baby suffered.

Yet Caleb was saying that my reaction to my own perfidy was wrong. How could he say that? How could he... I took a breath, the first in long minutes. I searched his eyes, his chiseled face on which no emotion showed. Nothing at all. No life, no warmth, nothing.

Caleb Howell had lost his son. Of all the people on this search, he understood. And he was saying I could be human later. Like him ten years ago, searching for his son. Do the things that need doing, regroup and move on. Wasn't that what he'd said? I took a second breath; it felt like betrayal, like treachery. "I want her back," I said. "Whatever it takes. Whatever I have to do. Come death or dirty water." Daddy's old saying. I could grieve and lay blame and hate myself when I had my baby back.

"Good," he said. "We're going back tonight for supplies and maps—"

"No!" I said.

"—and insertion tomorrow at a different point. I need to know where he's going. I need everything Joel and Harschell have dug up on his past and his family."

"No!" I shouted, squeezing my hands into fists.

"Yes! Mac, listen to me." He grabbed my shoulders again as freezing rain drenched me to the skin, slammed into the earth as lightning shook the whole world. "I could head off in the direction I think he's taken, but he's got horses from the shooting this morning. I found tracks. And I found the injured horse, the one Bella was riding. Dell left it behind. It needs help. The rain has washed away all traces of the scent trail. All traces! Look at the dog. He's frantic."

I looked at Ed. He was still circling, his paws muddy to the knees and elbows, huffing in desperation, a soft sound of panic escaping his throat. He smelled Bella. But she wasn't here. And the trail was gone beneath the heavy downpour.

"We have to go back. And you're going with us."

"That's why you made us come this way, isn't it. So I'd see this." I raked my arm across the expanse of the shelter, encompassing the tracks, the fire pit, the splatter of blood. "So I'd go with you like a good little woman and not make a scene. So I'd abandon my baby—" My voice broke, harsh and rough.

We had been close, so close to finding Bella. Separated by fog and darkness rather than miles. And now she was gone again and no matter what Caleb said about Dell not hurting her, there were ways a man could hurt a woman that still left her able to travel. And even if he did despise a woman in her curse, in his anger he might be tempted to claim her, to make her his.

"No…" I sobbed and hugged myself, feeling only cold and wet and the evil of this place. "No. Please, God, no." I reached out my arms, not certain what I needed, only that I needed something so desperately I couldn't think, couldn't feel. Caleb pulled me close and let me cry, his hard, angry, heated body seeming to soften against mine. And I realized he had been angry, too, laying blame. Angry with himself. Punishing himself. Perhaps all day.

And I cried, holding him tightly to me.

31

We recovered our packs even before the rain eased up, walking at times through the thin, dropping mist as the torrent died. Caleb knew where we were, where we had been, knew the distance to the nearest road. Knew it even in the rain, with the cloud so low we could touch it.

On the way out, Yo called in to the ICP, requesting Evelyn set up a Rabid Dog Four for Caleb and Joel, so they could have a private conversation on channel fourteen, or as private as an airwave dialogue can ever be.

Caleb walked away, his voice pitched low, and though I was sure he discussed things with Joel that were not mentioned to me or the rest of his team, I didn't care. I was beyond caring. Beyond any emotion. A frozen zombie, my feet like lead, squishing in my boots, I followed in the wake of the team, Ed beside me as if to offer comfort yet again as I stumbled forward, vibrating with huge quaking shivers. I rested my hand often on the hound's big head, stroking his warm wet pelt, using him for balance a few times when I couldn't find my own. The tired search and rescue dog seemed to like my attention. Or maybe he just smelled Bella on me and felt comfort in the scent.

It was late afternoon, with temperatures falling below freezing, when a crew picked us up in a battered, rusted truck, pulling between trees on a track so narrow I wasn't sure it was really even there. When the driver executed a three-point turn between saplings, the tires almost dropped off into a ravine. We climbed into the bed of the truck, Ed flopping his big body close to me as I sat on my pack. Caleb sat at an angle so he could see my face. Yo and Jedidiah rested against the pickup's cab, legs out straight and crossed at the ankles, as we jounced back down toward civilization.

We didn't end up back at the ICP, the park rangers' station where we had begun our search, but at a different place, a wide spot on a narrow, curving mountain road where someone had pulled a single-wide trailer and dropped off two porta-potties. Trucks and cars and a horse trailer were in the woods and parked beside the road, along with a vet van and a dozen ATVs and not a single media vehicle in sight.

This was the temporary command post, or TCP, Jedidiah explained to me, and the news folks hadn't found it yet. While it didn't have the comforts of home, there was a diner down the road, a gas station, a video store the size of a phone booth, and a small hotel. Ruth had reserved rooms for us, with a hot shower, a phone, a TV that accessed ten cable channels, and a bed, a real bed with a mattress made of foam and padding instead of sticks and leaves. It was heaven.

Bella had no such comforts, a small voice whispered in my head. Bella was alone with that man again. And we had lost the trail.

For now, another part of my mind whispered. *Only for now.*

The thoughtful EMT had sent along changes of clothes, toiletries and personal items, including my riding boots; a dry bedroll; an old down vest a couple of sizes too large, which had to be her own; a new pair of Isotoner gloves; a rain slicker; my remaining camera equipment; and my little .38, which I put away, determined not to carry it.

I was surprised to see the gun. On TV, the cops always confiscated guns. Beneath the revolver was a photo of Bella. It had been taken at the hatchery. My daughter was laughing, looking up at me as she poured coffee into a tin cup. My baby IsaBella. My heart stopped as I stared at her face. When it began to beat again, the rhythm was rough, uneven. I touched her face. "I'll get you back, I promise," I whispered to her. "Know that."

With frozen fingers I unbuttoned and pulled off my clothes, and as they landed, I spotted a flash of purple. Bella's note, soaked and crumpled, in my underclothes. I unfolded the crumpled pages gently, reread the blurred words, so full of excitement when she had gotten away from Dell. When she was free. And I placed it on the sink beside her photograph.

With Bella's note and photo propped in clear view, I showered away the chill that had invaded my body, washed until the accumulated filth was off me, until I was warm, my skin softened and pink—and blue and black and yellow and a yucky shade of green—my hair clean and hanging in curly dripping ringlets. I realized I had lost nearly ten pounds, my flesh hanging in thin, wrinkled sags. The muscles underneath were so swollen they were like painful steel bands. I was skinny for the first time in years, and if I kept up this pace, I'd be better toned than any gym could make me, fear and nonstop activity reshaping me. And I was too tired to care.

I had wanted to sleep the moment I saw the bed, but

the hanging skin convinced me I needed nourishment more than sleep, so I greased myself up with muscle rub and treated the blisters and stitches. Two stitches in my heel had popped open, and the wound oozed. I bandaged it tightly with antibiotic ointment and first-aid tape, combed out my hair and braided it as best I could with its shorter length. Warm, clean, I dressed in a thermal and a flannel shirt, both tucked neatly into clean jeans. I pulled on two pairs of socks and a pair of Marlow's sneakers Ruth had sent, and made my way to the diner while Yo showered and our boots and equipment steamed in front of the radiator.

It was an all-you-can-eat, home-style buffet for ten dollars, the price of eight dollars scratched through. When I saw the heaped plates of the searchers, I understood why. Ten dollars a plate and the owners would still lose money. But I stacked my own chipped china plate up with meat loaf, mashed potatoes—the real thing, not boxed—and gravy, green beans, two homemade biscuits, macaroni and cheese, yellow squash casserole, broccoli with cheese sauce, and then went back for more mac-and-cheese, chicken baked in golden mushroom soup, and a house salad with blue cheese dressing. When I found I somehow had room for dessert, I ordered a piping hot blackberry cobbler with vanilla ice cream, and coffee with extra sugar and cream. The cashier noted my appetite and said she wished she could eat like me and stay so skinny. So did I.

Sitting back while I sipped my coffee, I looked around. The diner was an old, single-wide trailer painted and wallpapered in pink and teal, sporting a Formica bar and red, swivel, backless bar stools. Formica-topped tables anchored the cracked-fake-leather booths. Dusty silk potted plants hung from the ceiling. The lighting was bare bulbs hanging from plastic bowl fixtures over each table.

A jukebox sat in the corner playing country and western at a bearable level, Clint crooning of lost love. Bella would have loved it.

When I had my daughter back, we would come here and take some shots of the place for a local interest story. The fact that my despair was gone again, and I was once more convinced I'd get her back, was not something I wanted to look at too closely. I knew I was an emotional wreck. I had to be. I was going through a divorce, trying to resurrect a photography business from the ashes of my limp duck's mismanagement, trying to build a new life from the dead fire of the old. Then my daughter was kidnapped, got free, then was kidnapped again. I had to be nuts or teetering on the edge. Believing I'd find her again fit in with my self-deception just about right. But I needed that just now, so I let the hope sit inside me, part of the full stomach and the taste of blackberries and coffee. I'd get her back. Tomorrow. I would.

Caleb Howell, showered, shaved and dressed in clean jeans, a denim shirt and cowboy boots, his hat left at the door, came in as I finished up, and joined me at my booth. I was happy that no one from Howell Hasty Team had been in the diner to see me make a pig of myself, but when Caleb proceeded to eat twice as much as I had, I felt my embarrassment ease, even when I had to loosen the button on my Levi's as the meal settled.

We didn't talk while he ate. He just shoveled food in, as methodically as he searched, with the same steady, economical, almost graceful moves. When he was done and the waitress had refreshed our coffees, he stretched out in the booth seat, his legs extended and crossed at the ankles, an angled barrier between me and the aisle. And finally he met my eyes, his glinting with something. "You get enough to eat?"

"Yes. Why?"

"The boys had a bet you'd go back for a third plate."

My mouth fell open as I scanned the room and realized the window beside me overlooked the parking lot. There were trucks parked in the dark, some with headlights on, and signs of men milling about, a dog with a slowly wagging tail. I closed my mouth. "You were taking bets on me?" I didn't know whether to be outraged, embarrassed or amused.

"Yep." He seemed satisfied with my reaction. "Seems the boys were being regaled by Jed about how you, a city gal, kept up with Yo and Ed and him for several days. Seems no one thought you'd make it past the first twelve hours. No outsider's ever lasted on a hasty team more than twenty-four hours. Not till now. You've made a few of the locals proud. And a mite richer."

"Glad I could oblige," I said dryly. "Were you one of the locals who got a mite richer?"

"Nope. I was backcountry. With you. But I told them they'd be fools to keep on betting against you. You won't give up. Not ever."

I understood that was high praise in Caleb's eyes. I fought a smile. "Remember the TV show *Survivor?*"

"Yep."

"Is this a bit like *Survivor,* mountain style?"

"A bit. But no one gets voted off, they just beg to leave. Usually."

"Glad I could entertain you boys."

Caleb laughed, the sound rich as the coffee, sweet as the blackberry cobbler. Then the smile slid from his face and I knew the main tracker had news. My china cup clattered into its saucer. I steeled myself for his words, gripping the table with clawed fingers.

"The searchers found Burgess's trail before the rain hit. Found the body of the injured man with him, Raymond

Hamilton. He was dead. Taken out by a hundred yard shot."

I felt the blood drain from my face. Limp hands fell into my lap. "You don't believe in sugarcoating things, do you, Caleb."

"You really want them sweetened up, Mac?" he asked, his face serious. "I could, if that's what you wanted. Just seems a waste of time to me. And you're stronger than that. Maybe the strongest female I've ever met. You don't give yourself credit enough by half, woman. Not by half."

"What else?"

Caleb almost smiled. "See? You know there's more and you're all ready to hear it." When I said nothing, the near smile vanished and he continued. "Seems Burgess might have been hit. There's a blood trail a little ways off from where they found Hamilton. And they lost the trail when the rain came. They'll see if they can find him tomorrow."

I nodded, picturing Burgess, freshly shaved, hair falling in perfect folds, dressed in his L.L. Bean microfiber down-filled jacket, Egyptian cotton shirts with the cuffs turned up to display both shades of green, and undyed, natural, woven khakis belted over them. And, of course, the brand-new Kevlar vest. New York's GQ version of a SAR tracker. Now lost in the woods in the freezing rain, unwashed and wounded.

If it had been a story of a stranger lost while camping and backpacking, I might have laughed in the way a successful hiker chuckles over the foolish neophyte. Instead, I was frightened for him. "The closest thing Burgess ever had to a wilderness experience was a commercial for a men's soap back in the early eighties. He practiced this frightful Irish accent for weeks. Dyed his hair blonder than Marlow's. He'll be miserable. Cold. Alone."

"After we find Bella, if he hasn't been found, I'll go back after him." Caleb met my eyes, and his were soft again, the gentle blue of the sunlit sea, not the hard lapis that had challenged me earlier in the day. "I'd never leave anyone in the wild, lost. Even a city slicker in designer duds."

Relief eased through me, as much because of the gentleness and teasing as the promise. Marlow had never been careful of me. Never kind. Certainly never praised me except for times when I followed his orders. He was always aware of image, of what others might think. He'd never have taken bets on how much I could eat. He'd have been horrified. I smiled and sipped coffee to hide my feelings. "Thank you."

"Get some sleep."

"I will. Don't tell the boys outside, but even my bones are aching."

"Your secret's safe with me." Caleb put down his empty coffee cup, stood and stretched, uncurling slowly and reaching to the low trailer ceiling, which his fingertips brushed. "That kind of information might drive up the bets."

"Funny man."

He bent and kissed me hard on the mouth, his hand curled behind my head, heating me from lips to toes in a single instant. I breathed out, eyes still open and staring into his. "I just blew some poor ol' mountain boy's tenner with that kiss, betcha. I got maps to pour over. See you in the morning."

I nodded. And heard the cheering outside the diner as he walked away, boots clomping on the hollow-sounding floor. Managing not to look out into the darkness, I gathered myself, buttoned my jeans and walked away from the window and out into the cold mountain air. Made it back to my room before the blush began to fade. Caleb Howell was an evil man. An evil, evil man.

But I was no longer afraid for Bella or Burgess. Caleb had the ability to remove my worries with a single touch. Sliding out of my clothes and into brand-new flannel pj's, I crawled into icy sheets on the bed against the radiator and fell instantly into dreamless, placid sleep. Tomorrow we would find Bella. Tomorrow.

32

Yo was up at five-thirty and I followed shortly, steaming away the night stiffness in a long, ten minute shower before braiding my hair and dressing again in the same clothes I had worn to supper, plus the rib brace. I rerolled my pack with the new sleeping bag, this one with a small pump on the side so I could inflate the air mattress at night. It added to the weight, but at the moment, I didn't care. I was sore from nights on the hard ground, bruises on top of the bruising from the beating. I needed a bit of pampering.

Into the sleeping bag I rolled the things I'd need for several days in the backcountry, and wrapped the whole bundle in the slicker before strapping it all tightly together in a well-worn pack Ruth had sent along. My knapsack was still too wet to use and had developed a sour odor. Dressed for a day in the wild, I slipped on the down vest.

Checking the room for anything I might have left behind, I found the gun. The little .38 Smith and Wesson revolver I had not used when Dell first came into camp.

"You going to take that?" Yo asked from the door to the bathroom. Steam leaked out around her, making her seem ethereal even in towels and bare feet.

I turned the small weapon over in my hands, careful to keep it pointed to the room's back wall. "Though cruel, as usual," I said, "Marlow was right about my aversion to guns. My father taught me to shoot. After my mother died. I guess he felt that a bit of handling a gun would cure me of the fear that had taken hold of me, maybe be a partial cure for the depression I went into after the funeral."

"How did she die?" Yo asked, pulling a comb through her hair.

"Mama was the victim of a convenience store holdup carried out by two fourteen-year-old boys. They came in on their bikes and pulled the gun. Said they needed all the money in the cash register. The manager tried to run them off."

Yo said nothing. She simply sat on the edge of the rumpled bed beside me and started pulling on socks. The ordinary action soothed me in the telling.

"According to the boys, the gun went off. The manager was shot by accident. But they panicked and shot Mama, too. She lay on the floor just inside the door, only feet from a phone, and bled to death. It took her two hours. I've hated guns ever since."

"Is that why you're here? Because you feel you should have pulled the gun and shot Dell Gregory? And you didn't?"

I shrugged. A "maybe" gesture.

Holding the cold weapon, I said, "I wonder how Ruth got it from Har Har?" Slowly, I turned the dull steel handgun over and over. Trying to decide.

Yo stood and pulled on jeans and a sweatshirt in armygreen. She handed me the photo of Bella and the nowdry purple note. "You did what you thought best then. Maybe if it happened now, you would do something else. Maybe not. But you aren't the same person you were a few days ago, MacKenzie Morgan."

I tucked the note back into my bra, a good luck piece, and put the photo in my bag. Opening the cylinder, I checked to see that the revolver had bullets, and closed it with a snap. "No. I'm not." I added the gun to the bedroll, wrapped in Marlow's old oversize T-shirt I sometimes used as a nightshirt. I should have shot to kill the moment Dell Gregory came into camp. At the very least, I should have held him at bay while we headed back to civilization. My fear of guns and death and violence had endangered my baby. Never again.

My old bedroll I left where Yo had thoughtfully draped it over a chair to dry. My filthy clothes I left piled in a corner with the sour, stinking knapsack.

Yo, looking over her own filthy clothes, tossed them with mine and called the desk, telling them we'd be discarding some things, to do with them as they pleased. Then we went to breakfast.

The all-you-can-eat breakfast buffet was eight dollars a person, and I heaped at least six eggs onto a plate, added a stack of hotcakes and butter, and grabbed the blueberry syrup. Before I sat down, I went back for a rasher of thick, country-style bacon, both sweet and peppery to the taste. The meal of the night before had melted away and I was ravenous. Yo brought a thermos of coffee to the table and poured for us both. We ate silently, simply nodding hello and scooting over when Caleb and a stranger joined us. Eating in the mountains on a SAR mission was serious business. There would be time for pleasantries later.

Stomach full, I was introduced to the stranger by Yo. "Mac, meet Lonnie Curbeam, from Tennessee. He'll be the dog handler working with the team looking for Burgess."

I offered my hand across the table and shook the handler's massive paw. "Thank you for anything you can do finding Burgess. He's not very accustomed to forests," I said, choosing words that might be kind to my brother-in-law's lack of wilderness experience.

"Buggy—that's my best hound, aka Bug Face, on account a he's so dang ugly—will find him. No fear," Lonnie assured me, displaying that he still had almost half of his teeth. "So far Buggy's got a seventy-five percent recovery rate. It'd be a hundred percent if he hadn't a got hisself hurt and been replaced by another dog on that last search."

I nodded, my smile in place even as I did the math. A seventy-five percent success rate, in this case, meant Buggy had been on four SAR events. Not the animal I wanted tracking my family, but I didn't think I got a vote. To Yo I asked, "And who is Howell Team's dog handler?"

Yo nodded to the door, where Jedidiah stood, his small pack sliding to the floor, a rifle and Kevlar vest strapped to it. His face lit up when he saw us, and he waved, but went to the buffet instead of coming over.

"I thought Ed was too tired to work again," I said.

Caleb gestured with his fork. "You got Big Bertha."

"Big Bertha?"

"Ed's mama. Best tracking dog in the country four years running, according to Jedidiah," Yo said in deference to the dog handler beside her. "She was the hound Caleb started out with the day Bella was kidnapped. She's well-rested and ready to rumble."

"Yeah, Big Bertha's the best hound for this job, but there's something about saying 'Ed and Jed' that was satisfying to the tongue," Caleb said. "'Jedidiah and Big Bertha' don't have the same ring to it."

"Go for 'Jed and Big B,'" Lonnie said. "That's what the judge at the state fair called 'em when they won the Best in Show two years past. Big B moved around the ring like a show queen, working the crowd like a striptease artist. She's more limber than a pole dancer, if you'll 'scuse the language, ladies."

Caleb shook his head and finished off his coffee. Yo and I laughed. The main tracker looked up at me, the laughter dying out of his eyes. "Har Har's called in a couple of FBI analysts to take a look at what we know about Dell Gregory. Fellas got in yesterday. My guess is that they'll agree Gregory's a nut case. Just so's you'd know."

I nodded uncertainly. Why did Dell Gregory need an FBI analyst? But before I could formulate the question, a voice called from the door. "Lonnie, your team is ready to move out. Howell, you folks ready?"

"Give us ten," Caleb called back.

Lonnie tossed a ten dollar bill on the table, stood and saluted us, leaving the diner in a small group of three others. Jedidiah took his place, hunched over his plate and dived into the food like a starving man. I had a feeling I had shown about as much restraint.

While our dog handler ate, Caleb addressed us. "We have a long ride ahead of us today in the back of a truck. Then, if Big B can pick up the trail, we'll be on horseback and foot until we find Dell and Bella."

"You know where they're headed, don't you?" I asked, as hope twisted deep in my gut. "Where?"

"Best guess Joel and Har Har gleaned from the old maps and land use information from the turn of the twentieth century says we got three possibilities. The Gregorys owned several properties and had homes on at least three. One burned down in 1894. Another was abandoned in 1927 when their money ran out and the land reverted to the state after back taxes couldn't be paid. Then there was a farm, a place they managed to hang on to. Family lived there for a number of years off and on when Dell was a child.

"Chopper made flyovers at all three sites yesterday, late. The first property is now a lodge and vineyard for tourists. I'm betting he's either heading to the farm or to the abandoned homestead. If he managed to locate one of his blazed horse trails and traveled part of last night, he could be within shooting distance of the closest place by this evening."

"Yolanda Perkins in here?" a voice called from the door.

"Yeah!" she shouted, peering around the still-hunched and eating form of Jed.

"Turn on your radio."

"Got it," she said, pulling the radio from its damp leather sheath, sliding switches and turning a dial.

Joel's voice was midspeech. "—has sighted two people traveling on horseback, spotted on the crest of a hill. Howell One, come in."

Lightning zinged through me, a hot, jagged path of excitement. My broken nails cut into my palms. Her eyes on mine, a smile fighting to spread, Yo handed Caleb the radio.

"Howell here," the main tracker said.

"Glad to see you got your unit turned on. Let's keep it that way." Caleb didn't reply and Joel went on, his voice full of static, as if the distance we had covered had rendered the radio nearly useless. "We got a location. You ready?"

One-handed, Caleb was folding open the ancient map he used, laying it flat on the table. "Go ahead, IC."

Joel gave Caleb directions that were meaningless to me because I had no idea where we were in the first place. "You can't get there from here. You got to go someplace else to start," I mumbled. Yo chuckled under her breath at the old punchline. I placed my fingertips on the edge of the map, straining to make sense of the directions and the landmarks, sliding forward in the cracked booth to see better.

"Got it." With his wax pencil, Caleb put a single red X at the far edge of his map. "They could still be heading to either place—if that was really them. Coulda been neighborhood kids out for a morning ride," he said, eyes slicing up to meet mine.

I knew he said that for me, to temper the rising excitement I was feeling. I tried to slow my breathing, tried to regulate my heart rate, but I was flushed, tingling all over and breathless. Bella had been seen. Really seen. She was more than boot prints in the dirt.

"I'd say he's marginally closer to the farm, Joel, but I'm not familiar with the region. I'll need a local man to join us. You got a main tracker who feels like a short hike?"

"Affirmative. And FBI hostage negotiators are standing by. They can be inserted by helicopter as needed."

I felt my excitement shatter like thin ice. *Hostage negotiators?*

"The local man is a fresh face, name of Adin Boone. He'll meet you at the site where the riders were spotted this morning."

"Understood, IC," Caleb said.

"The photographer there?"

"Ten-four," Caleb said, cutting his eyes to me, his tone cautious.

"Tell her we have news about the ex. The Hardy boys just phoned in with news that the FBI, in a certain town out west and up high, discovered photos of the individual and the subject. In the subject's personal belongings."

I looked at Caleb in confusion. He keyed the radio and said, "Understood, IC."

"Take care and godspeed."

"Ten-four, ICP. Howell One and Two out," Caleb said, handing the radio back to Yo. His eyes were compassionate when he said, "Sounds like this. The sheriff's department called Joel, told him the FBI found photos of Dell and Marlow in Marlow's room at Aspen. Har Har was trying to give you a heads-up before it hit the media."

My mouth formed a small O of understanding and dismay. Before the pain could sink in and do damage, Caleb added, "Let's roll, people."

I blinked. Pushed the shock and pain away, down deep inside. "Point made. Do the things that need doing now. Suffer at leisure," I said. "I'll have a screen saver made up with that on it when I get back to Atlanta."

Jedidiah shoveled the last forkful of hotcakes into his mouth and stood, wiping lips that dripped syrup. He burped long and loud as we crossed the room. And Howell Hasty and Dog Team went back to work.

Wednesday
0630 hours

The ride in the predawn light started out kinder than the ride in the dusk the night before. This time we were inside the cab, a little crushed, but warm and dry and on seats made for human bottoms instead of a grooved truck bed. As we sped over paved roads only slightly potholed from the previous winter's ice and melting snow, the radio blared with morning news of another bombing in Palestine, the discovery of a small nuclear device in a truck at the Mexico–U.S. border, a late blizzard in North Dakota, and the local news. The top story was the SAR for Bella Morgan, the arrest of her father on conspiracy charges—which shocked me—of a search that was going nowhere, according to the media. Too bad the media had no idea about Caleb Howell. They would have been more optimistic.

We made good time. Big Bertha, a massive reddish-brown hound, stood braced across the pickup bed behind us, poised in front of the saddles and packs, nose lifted into the air, scenting the rising sun. She was already in the tracking harness, the chest protector like a battle shield over her chest.

Full of carbs and fats, I half dozed several times, each time starting awake, my head on Caleb's shoulder, a contented smile hovering on his cheekbones. *Today would be the day. Please God, let today be the day.*

The sun was just beginning to creep over the horizon when we turned off the narrow main road onto a less well-kept one, a tertiary route that had last been paved in the fifties, if the number of repaired and deeply pitted potholes and the different shades of blacktop used to fix them were an indication We jounced along for two miles and then turned yet again, up a steep incline that demanded the use of the truck's four-wheel-drive capability and threw us closer together. In the back window, Big B stood, front paws on the bed edge, her body at an almost upright angle, scenting the air, nostrils spread wide with each whiff, jowls quivering. We passed a horse trailer and tow vehicle, both empty. I figured Big Bertha liked horses, the way her head turned as we passed them.

We pulled into a small yard at the very top of a rounded hillock, a tiny house and bigger barn visible in the pale light. A brown and two bay horses stood quietly, blowing steamy breath in the cold air. A dark gray mare was drinking from a bucket, near a row of saddles on the fence nearby. An old woman stood on her front porch, face pinched with irritation, a steaming coffee mug in one bony hand, her robe clutched closed.

We saddled our mounts—I was tickled to be able to lift and carry my own forty-plus-pound saddle—and checked their hooves for rocks or loose shoes, adjusted the stirrup lengths, and got to know the animals. Yo secured the weight on the packhorse and tucked a good-size first-aid kit into the pack where it would be within easy reach. I noted that Caleb had added a rifle in a long holster to his saddle, strapping it in place with lengths of rawhide wound through eyes in both saddle and sheath. The black plastic stock was near his hand, close to his thigh, in a position to be drawn in an instant. He saw me looking at the weapon and said, "Check your vest. Make sure it's secured." I nodded, understanding. This could be a dangerous day.

Yo adjusted the packhorse's load a final time, performed a radio check with headquarters and nodded a question to the main tracker. Caleb lifted his own radio and indicated it was working. "Call it in," he said. Yo called in to the ICP and indicated that we were ready to begin our SAR, giving position and GPS coordinates.

With the sun a huge golden ball behind us, fluffy clouds spreading out like fingers lifting the glowing orb above the earth, Jedidiah offered a pair of Bella's panties to Big Bertha. "Check it," he commanded.

The Best of Show hound buried her nose, the scent article, as I had learned it was called, and took several long sniffs. She pulled away and then sniffed again, a short sound, as if setting the scent in her memory.

"Find it," Jed said.

Putting her head down, Big Bertha scented along the ground, pulling Jed along behind her. He held her on the short leash, the first knot in his left hand, the last knot and the leash loop in his right.

We watched as the big dog began to circle back and forth around and around the property. Suddenly I understood that this all may have been for nothing. If the tracking dog didn't find the scent, then the riders spotted crossing the hillock had not been Bella and Dell and we would have to move again, start over.

Nervous, watching the big red hound, I yanked on my riding boots, let Yo check that my Kevlar vest was strapped on tightly, as I double-checked hers. Then I hefted my pack, which was considerably heavier than the small pack I had carried when on foot. We had a packhorse this time, and Yo made sure that everything was in place, with an eye to the load's balance, while I pestered her with hands that needed to help but had no idea what to do.

"Stop," she said, her voice gentle, one hand holding my left wrist, which had crossed in front of her face. "Get mounted. Please." Yo pointed to the mare when I started to object.

Not important, perhaps in the way, I pulled on the down vest and mounted the little gray mare I had saddled, a pretty thing Bella would have loved, with elegant, prancing legs and a black mane and tail. Yo was getting me out of her way.

I checked my watch. Twenty minutes had passed since Big Bertha had been told to find. And still nothing. I settled in the saddle, my blisters protesting beneath me, ignored.

Five more minutes passed and still Big B had not found the scent. Jedidiah steered the dog down the hill, around the barn, and began the process again. The dog pulled him, circling out of sight. Four minutes later, she yanked Jedidiah back into view, tugging on the leash with all her considerable might, nose firmly locked to the ground, tail straight out behind her like a flag. Jed whipped his free arm in an arc to get our attention, and nearly stumbled. Even I could tell that the hound was tracking Bella's scent. Big Bertha was squirrelly. My baby had passed this way this morning.

At a fast trot, we started down the hill, covered the distance to the dog and handler, crossed through a grassy field crisscrossed with narrow trails and spotted with clumps of dirty-looking sheep. We were on Bella's trail. And only hours behind.

33

We had reached the bottom of the hill and crossed a thin rill of spring water that wove through a flat, well-tracked, muddy spot used as a watering hole by the sheep when I heard hoofbeats behind us. A man wearing a camouflage hunting hat and army jungle fatigues was taking the hill quickly, demonstrating his mastery of the small quarter horse on the steep terrain. We had been found by the Tennessee main tracker. Slowing, we waited as he joined us, though my eyes kept returning to Big B and Jedidiah moving fast in the distance.

The young man reined his mount in when he reached us, the feisty animal snorting with delight at the speed and the obstacles and the cold air. He nudged the dark palomino up to Caleb, stuck out his hand and grinned, exposing large, tobacco-stained teeth the exact shade of his horse. "I'm Adin Boone. It's a pleasure to meet you, Mr. Howell. A pure pleasure."

"Same here, Adin," Caleb said, as the younger man gripped his hand hard.

Yo snorted softly at Adin's exuberance, at the light in his innocent brown eyes, at his unlined face. He couldn't have been twenty yet. Still a boy. And Adin Boone had a serious case of hero worship going for Caleb Howell. I wondered how that would affect our SAR for Bella.

Adin turned his enthusiastic energy to Yo. "Yolanda Perkins, I been wanting to meet you forever." He worked Yo's arm up and down like a pump lever as he spoke, a broad smile exposing the wad of tobacco in one cheek. "A pleasure, ma'am, I hear a man's got to work pretty hard to keep up with you in the field."

Yo's brows rose in surprise and pleasure at his words as she murmured a response. Maybe she hadn't heard that one yet.

"And you must be the mother. My brother lost a twenty on you yesterday, ma'am, 'cause you won't give up. 'Cause you're staying the course." He spit brown juice to the side and wiped his mouth with the back of one sleeve. "A mother's love is something else. Ain't no one betting against you this morning, that's for sure."

"Thank you," I said, glad my hand was too far away for him to manhandle it.

"Let's get going I hear we got Big Bertha on the trail. We'll push these horses pretty good just keeping up with that old bitch." He kicked his nimble horse in the sides and rode hard after Jed, his body stuck to the saddle as if hot-glued in place. Caleb followed, a half horse length behind, shaking his head.

Yo reined her horse after the others and said, "Oh, the energy of the young. It's totally wasted on them."

"But he does have a way with flattering words." I followed in the rear, trying to stay out of the way, but keeping close on the packhorse's hooves.

We covered two miles fast, up and down gullies, through brush so thick the trail hardly showed until we were on it, single file, riding hard. When we passed the first pile of horse droppings not left by our team, even I could tell they were still moist. Once again, we were half a day behind Bella. Maybe less.

We watered the horses in a creek with Jed and Big B, who was resting by the time we caught up, her sides heaving hard at the pace she had set. Adin and Caleb talked in low tones, looking over a map that crackled in Adin's hands. Yo and I walked off the stiffness from early hours in the saddle, drinking from plastic bottles of water.

Oddly, in this group of experienced trackers, I was the one who found the latrine. It was nothing more than turned-over earth, a single clump of black soil exposing a bit of white toilet paper in the shadow of a rounded, striated rock standing hip-high. I squatted over the disturbed ground. "Yo, is this what I think it is?" I could see a ridged left boot print in the dirt, the inside area beyond the arch, up to the big toe, pressed deeper into the soil.

A yard away, facing the print, were those of a man's pointed-toe, western boots. There was no privacy here. No brush to hide behind. Slowly, my mind made sense of what my eyes were seeing. Yo joined me, standing at my side. I pointed to the boot prints. "If Dell made her use this spot, then it was to punish her, wasn't it? He…watched her," I finished in a whisper.

I knew about this kind of punishment. Since my separation, I had studied it in books and on the Internet. It was a form of brainwashing, something all battered wives endure. Marlow had never been this vicious, but in his own, unique way, he had been a master at it, honing his skills, stripping away my individuality, my selfhood, until there was nothing left of the *me* I had once been. Until I was willing to tolerate anything to keep the peace, to keep Marlow happy and calm. And now Bella was suffering the same kind of treatment she had seen me endure for so many years. Had I made her a victim? Was I at fault here, in more than one way?

My lips felt numb, my hands tingling. *He'd watched her.* We would be too late finding her. Too late to save her the horror of being violated. Perhaps we were already too late. My breath came fast, anger zinging through me like lightning. Furious tears gathered and fell in scalding paths on my cold skin. There had been so many ups and downs on this trek, so many moments of hope that came crashing, shattering into dust. My heart had been broken and pasted back together with the plaster of belief in Caleb Howell, but the sight of this simple latrine with boot prints....

I had made her a victim. Bella had lived in the same house with Marlow and me. She had watched me step delicately around the fact of her father's instability, his anger, his violence, rather than confront it head-on.

Yet even though she had been aware of the abuse in our home, she had wanted me to go back to Marlow. Had she wanted me to fight him, too? Had her needs clashed and conflicted within her?

I turned away from the evidence of my daughter's psychological abuse. Forced my thoughts instead into still-life visuals of the torture deserved by the man who had done this to her. Hot burning coals. Slivers of steel under his fingernails. A skillful working over with a baseball bat in the hands of a pissed-off, drunken good-ol'-boy. Abuse themes that Bella herself might have thought up, things she would have said about the owners of a pet or horse left neglected or mistreated.

The ranger had bent over, hands on her knees. "I don't see what you—" The sentence was cut off as she measured the distance between the boot prints. "Sorry bastard," she said. For an instant, I thought she was talking about Marlow, and then my attention whipped back to the present, to Dell and the latrine. Her jaw worked hard for a moment, still considering, making sense of it all.

"Well, he could have just stood there to relieve himself. But…" She twisted her head up to me, her expression as stiff and unforgiving as mine. With a stick, she dug in the dirt, uncovering signs that Bella's curse was still with her. "You think Bella might leave a message here?"

"If she could." My mind occupied with images of Dell suffering, my head filled with the sounds of his screams, I squared my shoulders and knelt beside the latrine. Studied the rock, the soil. With Yo's stick, I prodded the base of the rock, peeling back the dirt, which hadn't been disturbed. I had no real hope of finding anything. The stick cracked, splintered and broke in two. I threw it into the woods.

The trees in the area were old-growth ones, most in this grove bigger around than my arms could reach, one or two bigger than Yo and I together could reach. I checked low branches, forks, the hollow hole in one where a branch had died and fallen and a sapsucker had pecked out a nest. I wandered around a nut tree, the ground beneath it scored where a wild boar had rooted for dinner with razor-sharp tusks. Except for the prints at the latrine, there was nothing, no indication that Bella had ever been here.

Up the hill, a white-tailed deer froze for a moment, watching, then bounded out of sight.

The largest tree at the site was an oak with a base twelve or fifteen feet in circumference. Six huge branches sprouted up from it, each as large and straight as a single tree.

I assumed they had all started out as individual trees, perhaps sprouting from a squirrel's stash, then growing together into one trunk over the years. It was the only such tree in the vicinity and I walked to the six branching limbs, running my palms over the ridged bark, smelling the scent of life and forest. I stepped around the tree, studying it as Bella might have. The photographer in me wanted to pull out the camera and frame the odd clump of oak. Instead, bending into the center of the wide root, I spotted a small wad of yellow paper, a Juicy Fruit wrapper, crushed as if to hold used gum. It was the only piece of human refuse I had seen on Dell Gregory's trail.

I reached in among the limbs and plucked up the wrapper. Unfolded it with fingers that worked almost as well as they used to, before I was tied up and left for dead. Inside, scratched into the wrapper with a narrow piece of charcoal, were hard-to-read words. *I'm hurt. Bella Morg—*

A small sound must have escaped me because Yo was by my side instantly, a supportive arm around me. I showed her the note.

"That's our girl," Yo said, giving my shoulders a squeeze. "Her mother's daughter. Come on. Now we know for sure we're on the right track.

"Caleb," she called out. "I think it's time to call in the chopper. Mac found another note from Bella. She's alive, but she's hurt." Yo handed the Juicy Fruit wrapper to the trackers as they hurried to us.

"Good work, Mac," Caleb said. Adin nodded and spat a long stream of tobacco brown. I nodded, seeing again the words. *I'm hurt.* My baby was hurt. What did that mean? What had he done to her? I remembered the long splatter of blood on the stone. The depressed sleeping place. I would kill Dell Gregory.

34

We mounted fast and rode hard, punishing our bodies and our mounts on the steep terrain, following the track blazed by Dell. The dog handler had moved out ahead of us and it took us over half an hour to catch up with Jedidiah and Big B, the dog seeming tireless, the handler looking beat. When he heard us, Jed turned and pulled the hound to a stop, forcing her off the track a few feet. He fell to the ground, the leash still held tightly in his hands.

The handler was breathing heavily, sweat running and smeared on his face. Forced off the hunt, Big Bertha found a pile of manure left by the horses we were pursuing and, lifting a leg like a male dog, bent and marked it with her own scent, then began to work the small space, her nose sniffing out every nuance of the trail. She found a place that smelled interesting and buried her nose in the dirt, puffing up dust with each breath, excited, her coat standing on end, slightly quivering.

Jed took a long drink from a bottle of water and handed the empty to Yo, who exchanged it for a full one. He pulled the hound to him, holding her still. Finally she settled, huffing in irritation, her pleasure ended before its proper conclusion.

"Something different just ahead," Jed said when he finished the second bottle of water. "I been getting glimpses of it through the trees. You got a map of this area? A map from, say, fifty years ago, maybe seventy-five?"

"I got maps," Caleb said, dropping his reins and sliding to the ground.

"Bogus." Adin followed suit, holding the quarter horse's reins.

"Bogus?" Yo said to me, hiding her grin. "I haven't heard that since the eighties."

The trackers knelt on the ground, spreading maps and speaking in low tones. I slid my foot from the stirrup and stretched my knees one at a time, hearing a faint grinding sound beneath one kneecap. I vaguely recalled injuring the knee the day I walked from the fish hatchery, down the mountain. The fall hadn't been good for it, the hikes since worse. Cinderella's evil stepsister, that was me, the one with the creaky knee.

"That it?" Jed pointed to the map Caleb held. "Old road?"

"Could be," Caleb said. "Let's you and me go ahead on foot. Adin, you willing to stay with the ladies?"

Adin pulled out a rifle case I hadn't noticed in his fast approach, and nodded, tying off his horse. Wordless, he spat, climbed onto a low limb and stood with a shoulder against the tree, scanning ahead, opening the case, withdrawing the gun. I wondered what I had missed by not dismounting and listening to the men's conference. Yo shrugged, lifting her eyebrows when I looked at her, questioning.

Her radio startled us when it buzzed with static and Evelyn said, "Rabid Dog Two, Rabid Dog Two."

Yo keyed the mike. "Ten-four. Confirmed Rabid Dog Two." When she had the radio on the proper channel, she said, "Go ahead, Rabid Dog."

"Got more federal stuff, girl, and plenty of prying ears, so listen up. The snow bunny is missing. Feds talked to the bunny's sister, who told them that, ah, the limp duck had talked about wanting a new lifelong mate and nest, without financial difficulty and without sharing custody of the duckling."

I closed my eyes, feeling nauseous as the saddle and horse swayed beneath me. Understanding the carefully worded statement this time, I gripped the saddle horn, staying up by willpower alone. Evelyn was talking about murder for hire. Marlow had wanted me dead and had paid Dell to handle it for him.

"There's evidence of funds being transferred to North Carolina bank accounts from out west in a...let's call it a hiring." I stiffened at the term. "It's being suggested that the plan went wrong when the drake the limp duck hired turned out to be rabid himself and flew off on his own path north. Got that?"

"Understood."

"And the limp duck? He's wigging out. Had to be hospitalized when he assaulted a guard and was taken down. He won't be paddling without a limp anytime soon. That's all, Rabid Dog."

"Understood," Yo said, sounding tired.

"Y'all take care. Rabid Dog out."

"Rabid Dog out," Yo confirmed. "You okay, Mac?"

"Just fine and dandy."

"Then why are you swaying in the saddle and looking white as a sheet? You gonna pass out or hurl?"

Horrified laughter spluttered out. "Hurl? No, I'm not going to hurl." I forced open my eyes, meeting her worried gaze. Darkness hovered at the edges of my vision.

The world moved in a slow eddy for a moment. "Pass out, maybe."

Yo swung from her horse and was at my side before I could stop her. "Breathe. Slow and easy." Her hands steadied me in the saddle. She was tall enough to hold me upright.

"You always seem to be here to catch me when I'm about to fall," I said. Yo snorted, the sound indelicate. Following orders, I took several slow breaths. "I just have trouble thinking about Marlow wanting me dead."

"Sorry bastard."

A whistle pierced the silence. Adin waved over his head and jumped to the ground, mounting his horse in a single graceful move. The animal was racing ahead before he settled in the saddle, man and beast a fluid act of nature.

I shook Yo off and indicated her horse with my chin. "If I get woozy again, I'll slide to the ground and catch my breath, then find you as fast as I can."

"Try to hit ground before you pass out, not after. The fall may not kill you, but being dragged by a horse might."

"Good point."

Yo was in the saddle and out of the small clearing in the blink of an eye, only slightly less graceful than Adin. And Yo was close to my age. So much for the energy of the young being wasted on them. Still gripping the saddle horn, I let the mare pick the trail, holding her to a much more sedate pace. She pricked her ears, wanting to keep up with the herd, not liking being left alone in a strange place. But she obeyed the pressure of the bit and reins, and we followed the others slowly.

They were gathered at a wide place among trees, Caleb and Adin each again with one knee on the ground, Jed and Big Bertha moving out of sight around the side of the mountain. Caleb was digging into the earth with

a shovel. The steel blade grated against stone—lots of
stone. Pebbles and cracked rock appeared with each
shovelful. He looked up at Yo as I drew within range and
said, "It's the road, all right. Old tintypes show it leads
to the Gregory family house, the big one built in the early
1900s. Should be that way." He pointed away from the
direction Jedidiah and Big Bertha had taken.

I looked left and right, following the old road, and
noted deep ruts. The tracks were parallel, the kind made
by wagon wheels in rain-softened soil and later by nar-
row-tired autos bringing family and guests to some
grand old house. Caleb stood, comparing his compass
and handheld GPS device to the map in his hand. "The
house should be that way about a klick. Since the dog
wanted to go both directions, let's divide up. Half of us
follow Big Bertha, the other half see can we find the remains of the house or why they came this way."

"Sounds good to me. Okay if I follow the dog? I got a
good feeling about Big B," Adin said, swinging into the
saddle as he spoke.

"Fine by me. Yo, since you have the radio—"

"I'll go with Adin. You keep an eye on Mac. She got
woozy a ways back."

Caleb fixed me with a piercing gaze as Yo reined her
horse and the pack animal after Adin, who was already
gone in a pounding of hooves.

"I'm fine. Really."

"If you get sick—"

"I'll sit down and stay put until you find Bella and
come back for me. Stop being so motherly."

"Now that's something I've never been called. And
that's nowhere near the way I feel about you." For an instant, his eyes glinted with something far from parental.
I felt an unexpected blush start on my neck and move up
my face.

"The bane of the redhead, pale skin and great blood flow," I said. Caleb laughed and mounted his horse, his action less limber than Adin's. Almost of their own volition, my eyes followed his movements.

Under better circumstances I would have liked the way Caleb Howell looked in the saddle, the way the cantle gripped his buttocks, the way his legs wrapped around the horse's barrel chest. The main tracker grinned at me, as if he knew the direction of my thoughts. I made a prissy face at him and nudged the mare forward. I had to find Bella before I could even think about a man or a new life. But Caleb made me aware of him, even when my mind was fiercely occupied by finding my daughter.

"Come on, Red. Let's see what was so fascinating about this place that Dell had to visit it, even though he knows we're on his tail."

The house was a mile up the road, the tracks we followed distinct in the disturbed leaves, the occasional print. In mud along the side of the old roadbed, Caleb found dog tracks, two sets. It seemed that Dell had both Rufus and Polly back with him.

The day was silent. There were few birds calling, no breeze to ruffle the leaves. Just clear mountain air and the thud of horse hooves, the sway of the mare beneath me.

The house was to our left on the south side of the mountain, protected from the harsh north and westerly winds. A long stone foundation and five chimneys had been built out of reddish-brown creek rock, the stones rounded, the mortar crumbling between. There was nothing left of the beams, nothing left of the roof. Only the gardens were still vital. A huge climbing rose engulfed one chimney and corner of the remains, and several ancient azaleas were sheltered by a south wall and three old oaks. A bulb of some kind poked through the cold ground, and blooming jonquils were placed near wildflowers. Trailing arbutus and a spreading carpet of periwinkle bloomed near a trout lily, and jack-in-the-pulpits had multiplied and moved away from their original plantings or perhaps taken over from the wild.

Caleb slid from the horse and this time I followed suit, letting him tie off the animals as I wandered to the foundation and through the gap of the centrally placed front door, stepping over a pile of last autumn's leaves into the sun-dappled enclosure. If only Bella and I were here to work, to photograph, this would have been a perfect spot, with the light falling like rain. Would she ever understand that this place, these mountains and woods, were not part of the horror she had undergone? Could I help her grow strong again?

Caleb jumped the low stone wall, one hand on the top. "No indication why he came here," he said, striding back and forth within the ruins. "Doesn't make sense. There's no—" His voice ceased so fast it sounded as if the words had been ripped out of his throat. I turned and watched him, his body frozen, one leg lifted off the ground, the other rock steady. His voice a low growl, he said, "Mac, don't move."

"What?"

"Don't move. There's something…" His voice trailed off, eyes scanning the ground. The foot in the air he carefully lowered, turning slowly, the unyielding earth grinding beneath his boot. I examined the ground, too, but spotted nothing that could have caused his reaction.

"I want you to get out of here," he said. "But go back exactly how you came in. Try to step in the same places you stepped on the way in—on bare ground. But get out!" His chest was rising and falling too fast, his limbs moving in slow motion as he searched out something only he could see.

I turned and walked to the front door, stopping as I

reached the gap in the foundation. Stretched across the opening, hidden by the piled leaves over which I had stepped, was a pale thin wire, glistening where it caught the sun.

35

I glanced back, seeing Caleb place his foot carefully on the ground behind him, his concentration complete. I stepped across the leaves that had hidden the wire, positioning my foot gingerly on hard, bare ground. Once beyond the walls, I ran to the horses.

With shaking hands I untied the reins from the low branch where Caleb had secured them, and turned away from the house, back to the road, running, pulling the horses behind me, around the curve that had hidden the ruin.

Booby trap. The words resounded in my mind. Dell had booby-trapped the place, knowing that we would walk through it. Knowing the main tracker would have to check out the reason for the deviation in course. I mounted my little gray mare. If the booby trap went off, I would have better control over her from her back than from the ground. With shaking fingers I pulled a woven fabric tie-down from Caleb's pack and attached it to his horse's halter and then to my saddle horn. I might get bruised, but the horse wouldn't get away if—

Boom. Boom, boom, boom.

The sounds came almost on top of one another. Shaking the earth.

The mare reared straight up, screaming. I dived forward, screaming with her, arms to either side of her head, yanking down. Forcing her neck to arch in, pulling her feet to the earth, reining her in a half circle. I banged my head on the mare's, my sunglasses hanging from one ear, my visor knocked off, trampled underfoot.

The explosive sounds echoed as I fought to control the horses, keeping the fabric tie-down from tangling around my waist. Caleb's horse kicked out, narrowly missing my thigh. He whinnied a high-pitched squeal and began to buck. The explosions reverberated through the hills. Smoke billowed from around the bend.

"Easy, girl. Easy, easy, easy," I murmured over and over, wishing I hadn't added my scream to the horse's fear. "Please don't let him be dead. Please don't let him be dead," I prayed as I pulled the mare around and around, following the panicked bucking of Caleb's horse. A sick feeling rose in my throat, acid hot.

The explosions had been dull sounds, multiple *huwomps* rather than cracks or bangs. They faded to nothing as the horses began to calm. Caleb's mount stood with legs splayed, as if drunk and searching for balance. My mare kept her front feet beneath her, hooves doing a jittery tap dance on top of the visor. There was no way I'd get it back without dismounting. And that wasn't happening if I could help it. I shoved my glasses back onto my nose and caught my breath.

Sweat trickled under my arms and down my back beneath the down vest, Kevlar vest and shirts. My hands were icy on the reins.

And still I prayed, knowing I'd have to go back to the site of the old house. I'd have to go find Caleb. Nausea rose and spread, a weakness in my hands and feet. "Oh,

Jesus, please don't make me have to do that," I murmured now, my shaking hands soothing the mare and Caleb's horse, trying to calm their wide-eyed fear. "Please don't make me—"

A soft whistle severed my prayer. The horses moved uneasily, ears twitching, eyes wild. Reining the mare around, I spotted Caleb, an arm over his head, waving his hat, his other hand holding his radio, speaking into it. "Oh," I breathed. "Oh, thank you. Thank you." Relief slithered along my skin like warm sap, coating me in an artificial calm that pulled anger along after it. "I'll kill him," I murmured. "I'll kill him for scaring me like that." That my promise was in direct opposition to my previous prayer didn't seem odd. Caleb deserved to die for my fright.

Gently applying pressure with one knee and both feet, I straightened the animals and nudged them into a walk, back toward the main tracker. Their hooves seemed barely to touch the ground as they pranced warily, eyes darting, ready to bolt. Caleb stood still, so as not to startle the animals.

"I'll kill you," I said to Caleb as I drew near, "if you ever scare me like that again."

He took his horse from me, motions slow, almost relaxed, calming the animal with long sweeps and gentle words. Though pitched in horse tones, his words were for me. "The son-of-a-gun wired a dozen places through the foundation. It's a miracle we weren't killed."

"Wired with what?"

"Hand grenades. Military issue stuff, I'm guessing. The FBI's criminal analysis people are having a field day with this info." He mounted with an unhurried gliding ascent, carefully easing his weight into the saddle. The horse beneath him moved anxiously.

"The who?"

"Investigators from the Criminal Investigative Analyst Unit were called in by the district—or maybe the state—FBI office. They flew in from the National Center for the Analysis of Violent Crime in Quantico." He glanced at me as his hands soothed the horse's neck. "I told you about 'em. Har Har called in the big boys."

"Okay." I remembered Caleb saying something over breakfast. Only, that had been a hundred years ago. "But who are they? The analysts."

"Profilers. But they hate to be called that. They like 'criminal investigative analysts.' Most are both behavioral scientists and cops. They like to get inside the head of a bad guy and try to predict what he'll do. Most aren't exactly as successful as the profilers you see on television. Far as I know, this is only the second time they've been called to these parts. The last time was for Eric Rudolph. And they didn't do so well nabbing him." Caleb seemed amused by the FBI's inability to capture the felon, who had spent five years in these hills, on the run.

I digested that, urging my mare to follow as Caleb turned his in the direction of the other team members. Something wasn't right here. I was missing something. Or I hadn't been told something…. I could smell cordite on the air, acrid and burned. The mare moved under me, still jittery with fear. "Why did they call in profilers?"

Caleb sighed and glanced back at me, seeming uncomfortable. "Harschell received a note from someone claiming to be a kidnapper, demanding a hundred thousand for the safe return of Bella. FBI negotiated, even though they thought it was a hoax. Someone hoping to cash in on Bella's disappearance."

A numb sensation was spreading through me, taking over my body, robbing me of my ability to think coherently. "Why do they think that? That the note's a hoax?"

"Cause the person writing it didn't seem to know anything about Bella except what's been in the papers. And 'cause it doesn't seem to ring true with what we knew about Dell Gregory." Caleb reined his horse until I was even with him. "And because it's one of maybe a dozen things Har Har's been working on, trying to rule out being part of Bella's disappearance."

"When did Har Har get the ransom note?"

"Thirty-six hours ago," he admitted.

"Why didn't you tell me?" I looked over at him, a feeling of betrayal slithering though me like cold sludge. "And what other things is Har working on that I haven't been told?"

"At the time, he still thought your daughter might be involved with her own disappearance, and ordered us not to discuss any of this with you. And I didn't want you feeling like you had to defend Bella, 'cause I knew she wasn't involved with Dell Gregory."

"How did you know that if the police didn't?" The mare moved in a quick sidestep, reacting to my unintended pressure on her sides and mouth. I calmed my body, soothing her with a soft word and long swipe down her neck.

"What if I had told you that, while one team of cops was working hard to prove your ex was involved up to his armpits in this mess, another team was looking for proof that Bella was involved with Dell and planned her own kidnapping?"

"I'd have denied it. I'd have—" The words stopped half-born. "I would have thrown things. Maybe had a screaming fit at the waste of time. At the impugning of Bella's name."

Caleb nodded. "Cops have to consider everything that crosses their table. But I knew you. And no daughter of yours could stand by while Dell tried to kick you to death. So I didn't waste your energy or emotions on something so obviously useless.

"And by last night, the feds and analysts seemed pretty certain the note was a hoax or a money-making scam instead of a real communiqué from Dell Gregory. It was a racket, along the lines of the psychic who wanted ten thousand dollars to tell you where Bella was, or the woman who promised to read the bumps on your head and tell you where she was—for a small fee, of course. You told me you didn't want to know anything stupid, and I believed you.

"Har's ruled out ten or twelve pranksters and frauds. Would you have wanted to know about every one of them, when you were here and couldn't help what was going on back there? Would you have wanted to hear about every stupid possibility or would you have wanted to concentrate on the reality of the situation?"

Before I could respond, he said, "We knew Big Bertha had the scent, and that we were on Bella's trail. Seemed no reason to burden you with things that were futile when you were doing the things that needed to be done. Till now, when I had a question for the specialists."

I was heartsore, confused, and said, "What question?"

"What does it mean to have Dell Gregory shooting at us, wounding us, and now setting off explosives in a nicely laid trap?"

As he spoke, I was inspecting my feelings, asking myself why I was so upset. Caleb had only been shielding me from things, useless events I couldn't deal with. And then suddenly it made sense. "You were protecting me."

He nodded slowly. "Maybe I was."

"That's what Marlow called it. He protected me, too, keeping a fence around me until I lost myself. I don't want to be protected from life, Caleb. From the truth. Not ever again."

He pulled off his hat, eyes wary but honest, vulnerable. "I'm sorry, Mac. You're right. You should have been told about everything going on back at the ICP. I get so tied up in an SAR I forget that what's going on in the civilized world might be important."

"What kind of trap did Dell set?"

Caleb hesitated an instant, as if remembering my statement about wanting the truth. He resettled his hat, movements deliberate and staid. "A complicated pattern of hand grenades, set up so that if one was triggered, it would set off the entire bunch." His voice was mild, almost offhand, but the import of his words was not. By sheer luck, I hadn't tripped the wire entering the foundation of the old house. If I hadn't seen it at the front door opening when I left, and had set it off, then Caleb and I would both be dead.

He reined his mount forward, lifting a branch for me to pass under. "The FBI and Har are certain that Gregory has no military experience, yet he set a trap any Special Forces soldier would have been proud of. They're looking into that paramilitary group Dell was part of out west. They want to know what kind of weapons were available to him, what he might have taken with him when he left."

"And what weapons he might have stashed along the way? Or back at his cabin?"

"You got it. The FBI want to know what weapons he's accumulated, and think there might be a hidey-hole back at the ruins he blew up. They're inserting a team there via chopper to check it out. They thought it might be nice if there weren't any little traps waiting for them, so when I got out of the foundation, I tossed in a rock and set it off. Mac…" He leaned over and touched my arm. "I didn't mean to insulate you needlessly or to frighten you. And I wasn't thinking about the effect of the noise on the horses. It was stupid. You did good keeping them from bolting."

I ducked my head at the compliment, but pursed my lips, considering. "If you think that means you're forgiven for scaring me to death, you're not."

Caleb chuckled, his voice still low. "'Course not."

"I'll still kill you if you ever scare me that way again."

"I promise to never set off half a dozen hand grenades near you ever again. At least not while you're on horseback."

"Gee, thanks."

He chuckled, pulled his hat lower over his brow and nudged his horse into a trot. I followed, letting the mare choose her own pace. She kept her nose near Caleb's knee, her body almost touching the lead horse, as if determined not to be alone, but part of a close pack. Her nearly black ears twitched constantly back and forward, her head moving slightly side to side to provide a total 360-degree range of vision. This was dangerous territory, and she was terrified. The mare wanted to go home, transmitting that fact to me with every quiver, each agitated step. She was smarter than I was. But then, she didn't have a baby lost in the hills.

Overhead, the distant sound of helicopter rotors was a deep heartbeat of flight and power. Caleb nudged his horse into a canter to expend some of the animal's nervous energy. His voice, when he spoke, reflected the rhythm of the jouncing gait. "They've started flyovers to see if they can spot a cabin not pictured on any maps, or placed on the property that was the old Gregory farm. The IC is also putting in two teams on the other side of the farm to make sure Dell doesn't vanish in the woods. You'll hear choppers all day, from now on." He urged his horse forward and my mare followed suit. We rounded a curve, climbed a hillock.

And the road petered out before us.

36

One moment the old roadbed was there, and the next it crossed a trickling creek and vanished, man's work stolen back by nature. Handing me the woven strap I had used to secure his horse to mine, Caleb dismounted and studied the ground, the trees nearby. His body tensed, quieted. I looked to the ground in front of him and saw nothing. Without a word, he remounted, but held his horse in check.

Caleb's eyes caught mine. "Back out nice and easy," he said softly. "Nice and easy."

My throat tightened. "More explosives?"

"No." He kneed the skittish horse past me. "Three bear cubs. Not more than two months old." He nodded his head to the right.

I glanced that way and after a moment saw a black ball of fur curled in front of a low, dark hole in the hillside. To the side, bathed in the sunlight, lay a second cub. A third sat upright in the dark entrance of the shallow cave. No mother bear was in sight. "I thought cubs didn't emerge until April."

"Apparently this mama bear didn't know that."

"You think this is funny, don't you?" I asked, as I guided my mare after him.

"Oh, yeah. A cluster fu—ah, bunch of problems all at once. Yeah, that's my idea of a fun way to spend the week." He looked back at me. "Meeting you was the only high point in it. And as high points in lousy weeks go, it was a doozy."

I smiled and glanced back at the cave. It was a shallow hole no more than two feet high and three feet deep, under some trailing roots. We had been upwind from the cubs and the horses hadn't reacted. Probably a good thing, in light of the last few minutes.

"Not only did we run into bears," he said, "we missed the trail. Nothing's come this way."

Keeping a sharp eye out for a wandering and hungry mama bear, we backtracked through the trees, found the place where Adin and Yo had left the track and entered the woods. There was no trail here. Nothing to show that Dell had blazed a path or that he had ever come this way. "This is the first time Gregory crossed overland on horseback," Caleb said when he finally remounted. "He either knows these woods like the back of his hand or he's desperate. I kinda hope it's both. And I hope Big Bertha's nose holds up to Jed's claims, 'cause if not, we're slowing down to a crawl."

Several yards later, Caleb reached up and touched a small notch in a tree. "Fresh." He rubbed his fingertips together as if they were moist with sap. "Looks like an SAR tracker's mark. Adin's leaving us a trail to follow. Come on. Maybe that boy's almost as good as he thinks he is." Caleb kneed his horse into a faster pace and my mare jumped a depression to stay at his side. I nearly came out of the saddle, and gripped the horn tightly. I'd have cramps in my fingers before noon, and blisters the size of saucers on my backside. But I refused to fall or quit.

We wove among the tightly spaced trees, Caleb tracking both the ground at our feet and the trees at shoulder height from horseback. Several times he touched a notch, seeming relieved to see the tracker's mark. The horses dislodged rocks as we traveled, the earth full of fist-size and bigger stones hidden in the old leaves. I began to spot the signs Caleb was watching for. Leaves turned over, exposing the damp side. Rocks kicked from their resting places. As I gazed ahead, my eyes slightly out of focus, I saw that the track we followed was faintly darker than the surrounding terrain. I could even trace it as we went, and pointed out a divergence to Caleb. He nodded. One party had gone left at a deep ravine, the other had gone right. We followed Adin's path, the notch on a tree crosshatched, as if to show this was the better trail, though nothing was obviously wrong with the other and Caleb didn't investigate to see why the tracker had made the decision.

Time seemed to shrink, dwindle to nothing as the sun heated the earth and the shadows changed length and position. My world was mountains and streams and decade-old trees, regrowth after clear-cutting by a logging company. Only a rare tree was mature, and then no more than twenty or twenty-five years old. Curving rock walls, little more than piled stones only two feet high, were randomly placed. We passed three, all following the gradient of the hillside.

The hills here were more softly rounded than the terrain in the first days of the search and rescue, but more stubbled with rock. If this land had been farmed, it must have been a torturous life for settlers, pulling rocks from the ground, making it smooth for plowing, then rising the next day and finding new rock, as if it crawled from the earth overnight or grew in place of crops.

We passed a foundation, a six by six area created by one huge, partly exposed boulder and piled rocks. I guessed it was for feed or equipment or maybe to shelter animals from inclement weather. A rock wall enclosed a wide space around it, the stones tumbled and fallen. It was picturesque, but I didn't pull out the camera.

It had been days since I'd framed a shot. Days since I'd felt the pull of the lens, the desire to stop and spend hours as the light changed, waiting to find just the right moment when the day illuminated some vista so perfectly it made me want to cry. I no longer cared about work or art. All I wanted was Bella back.

Wednesday
1220 hours

As we crested one low hill, we spotted the other searchers on the upward side of the far one. Judging the ground between us, Caleb kicked his horse into a slow canter and took the hill in long, almost jumping strides. I followed at the same speed only because I couldn't slow the mare. She was determined to ignore my commands and follow the lead horse. Partway down, I realized we had found a path again, and speed wasn't foolhardy. At the bottom of the hill, I finally relaxed my grip, peeling my fingers off the tooled leather as we passed several foundations sinking into the earth, a fallen chimney with nothing more than the firebox still standing. The remains of fencing wire were rolled in a ball of sharp rusted edges. Equipment left in the ground was corroded, an old farm, long abandoned.

And finally we reached the other group, positioned a quarter of the way up the hill beyond the old farm. It was a beautiful spot, a springhouse's foundations leaving a place for horses to rest and water. We dismounted, released the girths so the horses could relax, and ate a late lunch. I was silent for most of the half hour, remembering again the sound of the explosions when I thought Caleb had died.

The trackers spent the entire time discussing that event, Adin looking at his hero as if he would have given his left arm to have been there, sharing the fun. Jed's eyes held amusement. Men. Of course, Yo seemed to think it was pretty neat, too. I was clearly the only sane member of the group. I petted Big Bertha and checked her paws for thorns, pulling out one spur embedded in the hair between the pads of her left front foot.

After our rest, Jed and Big B did the sniff-and-find routine and took off, the dog trying to pull the handler off his feet and around the hill. They were quickly lost from sight. Caleb called for us to remount, and I tightened the girth of the gray's saddle, readjusting the pack and stroking the mare's neck. She nudged my chest with her nose and I scratched her under her long mane, gathered the reins and put my foot in the stirrup.

I was settling into the saddle when I heard two quick cracks of sound. And a man's scream.

The mare reared straight up, adding her scream to the echoing clamor. Caleb's horse kicked out and bucked once, sending the tracker and his loose saddle flying into my mare. The small horse shuddered and danced beneath me, down the hill in short hops, all four feet leaving the ground at once, landing hard. Again I threw my body forward, bringing her head down and in, preventing her from rearing. But if she bucked, I was a goner.

She suddenly drew to a stop, her neck bowed, ears laid back, tail down between her legs, lungs blowing hard. I turned her. Caleb was on the ground, groaning. I couldn't see the Tennessee tracker or his palomino. Fear pummeled me, making my breathing coarse and shallow. Yo dismounted fast and slapped her mount on the rump. "Get off the horse!" she shouted. I slid to the ground and raced up the hill, pulling the mare after me. And then I saw Adin.

The boy was holding his chest, low down, near his waist on the right side. Gouts of scarlet blood were flooding through his fingers. Looking uphill, I saw a flash of movement at the crest. The young tree near my head shattered, the round breaking the sapling off in a blast of splinters as the shot rang through the woods.

I fell hard to my knees. The mare squealed and whirled. I lost the reins as they cut through my palm. The gray followed Caleb's bucking horse down the slope and away.

Yo fell to the ground, pulling me with her. "Get down!" she yelled. "Caleb, you hit?" Blood from my palm seeped into the creases of my hand. I pressed it against my jeans to stanch the flow.

"No," he groaned, rolling behind a tree larger than most. "Just old and broke a mite."

"Well, quit whining and give us some cover fire."

"Right." He rolled to his knees, feeling for his rifle still in the saddle. "Adin?"

"He's hit." She keyed her mike. "Howell Team One and Two requesting backup and medevac out. Howell Team One and Two requesting backup and medevac out." She bent over Adin as she spoke, yanking loose the Velcro straps of the restricting Kevlar vest the tracker wore. She ripped her jacket over her head and wadded it into the wound. "We have one hit. Gunshot. A large caliber round penetrated the Kevlar vest."

She held out her bloody hand to me, demanding. I pulled Ruth's down jacket off, smearing it with my own blood. She bunched it and shoved it hard into Adin's wound. The tracker grunted. His face was pasty white. Crimson gore covered Adin's chest and spilled onto the leaves beneath him. "This is Howell One and Two calling the TCP or ICP. Does anyone read me?" To Caleb, she said, "Move it. He shoots again and we're all dead."

"I saw a man there." I pointed, my voice dry as dust, shaking with shock. "At the only tree of any size on the crest."

"Got it," Caleb said. "Keep your heads down." He crawled into the leaves on belly and elbows, the weapon held in front of him in both hands. He was quickly lost to sight.

"Adin, spit out your tobacco," Yo said. "If you swallow it or breathe it down, it'll be bad."

The young man spat to the side and groaned, "And that was brand-new fresh, too."

Across radio static a man said, "I read you, Howell Team." The voice was not familiar, almost lost beneath the sound of rotors on his end. "This is NC 1423, TV news chopper twelve. I don't have a medevac cradle, but I do have EMT training, and we are close to your last stated position. We have relayed your position and information to the ICP and they are responding. They are also setting up a radio relay so you can communicate with them, but it'll be a few minutes. Is the sniper neutralized?"

"Will be in two minutes," Yo promised, working the radio transmit button and pressing on Adin's wound.

"Any place to set this thing down?"

"Affirmative," she said. "An abandoned farm in the valley about a hundred yards southeast from the last GPS I gave."

A shot rang out.

"Yeah, it better be neutralized, Howell Team, 'cause I'm not setting this helo down till it is. Understood?"

"Understood," Yo said. Under her breath, she muttered, "Come on, Caleb. Do some magic here. I need help."

"On the way, Howell Team. ETA three minutes." Chopper rotors beat the air, faint in the distance.

A tree beside Yo exploded in splinters. From the hilltop, the shot sounded a split second behind. I dived behind an oak and hit the earth, slamming my cracked ribs against a rock the size of my fist. With a pained gasp, I rolled, curled up behind the tree.

More shots sounded—fire returned by Caleb. The crack of gun blasts skittered all about us.

Two more shots came from the hilltop. Five feet from me, Yo gargled a single note and tumbled over Adin.

"Yo!" I crawled across the ground, keeping low.

Blood pumped in a stream from somewhere. Her chest and arm were covered with it. Scarlet pumped again. "You're hit. Oh, God, you're hit." The blood spurted. Heartbeats. Arterial blood.

I had to get it stopped. *Pressure.* I reached for her arm and she jerked away. I rolled with her and pulled on her sleeve, finding the wound. Slapped my hand on it and compressed. Blood spurted between my fingers.

"Adin! Hold your wound," Yo demanded, her hand gripping her upper arm above my hands. "Mac, give me your belt. I said hold it, Adin, or you're dead."

The tracker lifted bloodred hands and applied pressure to his midsection. He was white as death.

Keeping as low as I could, waiting for the next shell to hit me, I unbuckled my belt and pulled it through the loops even as I argued with her plan. "You can't use a tourniquet. It'll shut off circulation to your arm."

"No choice. You can't hold my wound and Adin's, too. Squeeze harder on my arm. Hurry." Her voice was shaking, her eyes wide, struggling to focus. She was losing blood fast. I tightened my hands around her arm and pressed hard over the wound, just as I had been taught in the Red Cross course. I was instantly drenched in her blood. It pumped out in a deadly rhythm over my hands, hot and sticky where it splattered me. But as I watched, the blood flow slowed and fingers of relief stroked me.

One-handed, Yo pulled a Swiss Army knife from her front pocket and pried a blade out. Inserting into the sleeve of her shirt, she pulled hard, separating the fabric just above where the bullet had entered. She slid the sleeve off and placed the knife in her bared front teeth to hold it. Wadded the ripped cloth and nodded to me. I lifted my hands and Yo rammed the wad into the small wound. Bright red blood shot out around the cloth. It wasn't enough.

The bullet had clipped the inside of her right elbow in a two-inch gash, in and out. Her hand hung useless. I yanked off my Kevlar vest and ripped off the rib support. With a single pull, I opened my outer shirt, sending buttons flying. Rolling the garment, I placed it over the wound in Yo's arm and she clutched it in place. I could hear her breathing, fast and shallow. High-pitched sounds of shock came from her throat.

"Use the belt. Adin passed out. He'll die." Her voice was a whisper.

I cursed in frustration and slid the belt through the brass buckle, slipped it up her arm, over the bandage, pulling it tight. The bleeding had stopped, the wound closed off by the cloth and the tourniquet. Yo raised up and lay back down on the belt end, securing it in place. Freeing my hands for Adin.

She tucked the Swiss Army knife in my jeans pocket. "You may need it. In five minutes, if you can, loosen this thing, then retighten it." Her voice was weak and she dropped her head to the ground, breathing through her open mouth.

I checked the time. My watch was smeared with drying blood, but I could make out the hands. Three and a half minutes had passed since the shooting started. Five minutes might take an hour. It felt that long already.

I placed one hand over the saturated vest on Adin's chest and pushed. He grunted out a breath. His hands had fallen to his sides and his eyes were rolled up in his head, exposing only the whites. The tracker had passed out lying down. I knew that was a symptom of shock and blood loss. It was bad. But worse, unless the shooting stopped, the helicopter wouldn't land.

37

The helicopter was suddenly there, right on top of us, circling. A TV camera spotted us from above, the cameraman hanging out the door, a dish attached to the side of the machine. The backwash from the blades whipped leaves and dust into the sky. I squinted my eyes to protect them and bent low over Yo and Adin to shield them. The chopper moved away, up the hillside, and hovered for a moment. I could hear conversation from Yo's radio, but she had dropped it and I couldn't make out the words. The helicopter passed us again, rocking slightly back and forth, a delicate-looking thing far too small to take both the injured. It dropped lower, settled into the valley between two foundations. A man stepped from the passenger door and ran, his head bent away from the rotors. He carried a shoulder-mounted news camera.

It had been two minutes since the last gunshot. Was the sniper gone? Or just repositioning for a better angle of fire? Shutting down the helicopter fast, the pilot followed while the rotors still turned.

"What you got?" he asked, falling to his knees beside me. The first man held the camera on us, his feet firmly planted in a wide stance. We'd make the evening news. Might be live right now. For once, I didn't care.

"He's shot in the side," I said. "She's shot in the arm. He's in shock, I think. She's put a tourniquet on it to stop arterial bleeding."

"I don't have any supplies with me," the pilot said, checking Adin's pulse in his throat, lifting his pupils, counting the tracker's respirations all at once, "and there's no room on the holo for two more people. But I can apply pressure here and you can take care of the ranger. A medevac is on the way in."

"Okay." As the man placed his hands over mine, I eased up on Adin's side and scooted through the leaves to Yo. Yanking my watch from the belt loop, I listened for gunfire, loosened the tourniquet, removed the belt. Blood spurted into the wadded cloth. I gave it two beats before I pressed hard over the wound. Yo was white. Blood had splattered her face, up into her hair, a sharp contrast to the paleness of her skin.

Breathing in short shallow gasps, she was studying me with wide eyes, the sunlight catching green flecks in her irises. "You aren't wearing your vest." Her voice was breathy and rough.

"I was too busy keeping you alive to put it back on."

"Not smart, but thanks. I owe you one." She asked the cameraman, "How long before the medevac helicopter gets here?"

"ETA five. You're both going to make it. They got blood and fluids on the chopper for blood loss. Slow your breathing down, ma'am. You're hyperventilating." He turned to me. "What's her pulse rate?"

Adjusting the pressure on her arm, I put one hand on Yo's neck and counted against my watch, thinking, *she owes* me *one?* "One-o-two."

"How fast is she breathing?"

I counted for another full minute and said, "Twenty-seven breaths."

"Okay. You remember that and tell the paramedics and flight nurses on the chopper."

I nodded, feeling nauseous, shaking with reaction.

"Name's Bobby Lee Curtis. I'd offer to shake your hands, ladies, but it seems we're all tied up."

Yo chuckled hoarsely, the tone furious rather than amused. Tears gathered in her eyes; she blinked them away. "My hand's never going to work again, anyway. I've lost the feeling in it."

Bobby Lee looked up. "Try to move your fingers, make a fist."

"I can't. The nerve is right beside the artery, isn't it?"

Bobby Lee paused only a second to consider and said, "Yes, it is."

Yo asked, "And there's only one artery? One nerve?"

He nodded, the movement slow, as if he didn't want to agree, but had no choice.

"I think the round clipped it. That means I'll never use it again."

"No." The word slipped between my lips, a sound of horror.

"Microsurgery, ma'am. Then rehab. They can fix stuff like that nowadays."

"Yeah?" she said, uncertain, voice quavering, wanting to believe.

"They can," I said, remembering suddenly. "I know that. There was an injury to a guy's leg on a shoot, out west. A tourist-type cattle drive we covered for *National Geographic*. A steer gored one of the cowboys, mangled his leg. And a year later he was walking. I'll get you his doctor. He's supposed to be the best."

Yo laughed, the sound cutting, a sharp-edged tone of relief and hysteria tinged with disbelief.

The deeply beating pulse of a helicopter resounded through the woods, lower pitched than the news chopper had been. This was a basso roar, a dual-toned thunder of power. The big bird appeared over the far hill and moved to the open space. It settled gracefully to the earth about twenty yards from the smaller aircraft. The cameraman shouted and waved an arm wildly, then readjusted the camera on his shoulder for the next shot.

Forms in bright blue flight suits swarmed out of the medevac's sides and up to us. They were carrying a collapsible stretcher, boxes of equipment. Relief flowed through me in hot waves. At a shout from Bobby Lee, who held up two fingers, one turned and ran back to the open door, pulling out another stretcher, this one smaller. The cameraman swiveled back and forth, following the action. He was talking into the camera mike, and I knew we were going out live to the entire world.

A woman fell to the earth beside me and opened a rectangular tool chest filled with medical supplies. "Whatchya got?"

I told her what I was holding. Gave her Yo's respirations and pulse.

"She got a pulse in the injured hand?"

"I don't know. I didn't think to check."

"It's okay. No matter. We need to get her stabilized first, get her back to the trauma center, then we'll worry about the hand—hi, my name's Evangeline," she said all in a single breath to Yo and me. In the way of photographers, my brain took a quick snapshot of her, searing the details into my memory. The flight nurse had a round face with a straight black monobrow from temple to temple, and a compact, sturdy frame that eased next to me, relieving me of my charge. "I can take that now."

While backing away from Yo a few inches, I introduced us both, the words having an odd feel, as if I was at a small party instead of a shooting. "We're *so* happy to see you," I said. "You will never know." I looked down at my hands. They were shaking hard. Covered in blood. The blood of two people who were trying to help me. To help Bella. The cameraman maneuvered to get a close frame of my face. I ignored him, watching my hands.

"Ah. You're the mother and the ranger," Evangeline stated. "You're all over the news. The scumbag shot you?"

Please let him be gone, I thought, closing my eyes for a moment. Please let Caleb have shot him. "Yes," I said, and sat back hard, curling my legs under me, in a modified yoga position. I cradled my hands in my arms.

The cameraman moved in for a closer view of Evangeline, then focused again on me, on my crusted hands. "Can you tell us what happened?" he asked.

Tears gathered and fell, and I bowed my head. I was shaking. Shock, I figured. I didn't answer.

Yo laughed again, the sound not quite as hysterical as before. The cameraman swung to her. It was possible that the knowledge she might regain use of her arm had consoled her, because she seemed calmer, more her normal self. "He was up on the ridge," she said. "We had just taken a break and were mounting up. He fired twice and hit Adin. Then he fired a few more times and clipped me. The main tracker is up there now, trying to find him."

I followed the camera's motion and saw that Adin had been stripped from the waist up and two men were working over him, both with nursing emblems and wings embroidered on their chests. An IV was running, the blood bag hanging from a metal pole on the stretcher. As the camera and I watched, the two flight nurses rolled a sheet under Adin and lifted him to the stretcher, a well-practiced dance, reassuring in its casual pace. One paramedic affixed oxygen tubes in Adin's nose while the other started a second IV.

Adin turned his head and focused on me. "Where's Bonita?"

"Who?" I asked.

He blinked his eyes, the motion seeming forced and slow motion. "Bonita. My horse."

"She ran away."

"You got to find her." He licked his lips. "Please. She's my best friend."

I nodded once. "I'll find her. I promise." *Just as soon as I find my daughter.*

The flight nurses had covered Adin's wound, and all the fabric Yo and I had used to stanch the bleeding, with a large gauze dressing secured to his chest and abdomen with wide tape. It had already bled through, but they simply packed on more gauze. I wondered why they hadn't replaced the makeshift padding with fresh stuff and remembered the words from the nurse who had taught the first-aid course. *Clot formation.* The surgeon would replace it. Eventually.

"Tell Caleb I'm sorry I let him down," Adin said.

"We'll come see you in the hospital. And you didn't let anyone down." Not even Bella, I thought. *It was me. I let everyone down when I didn't stop Dell from taking my baby. It was my fault. All mine.*

"We're ready to move," one of the men said as he wrapped Adin in blankets and strapped him to the stretcher.

I looked at Yo, who now had an IV with clear fluid going into her left arm. The right was bandaged, in a sling, strapped to her chest at an angle. "Yolanda, can you get on the stretcher with my help, or do you need me to lift you?" Evangeline asked.

"I can do it," Yo said, but she looked pasty white, and stared at the nine inch rise from the forest floor to the lowered stretcher as if it were a mountain. She raised up; the nurse caught her good arm and lifted. Yo fell across the stretcher with a moan. She retched, heaving up clear fluid.

"Easy. Easy," Evangeline murmured, helping her turn her head to the side. "I can give you something for nausea when we get airborne."

The men stood, hefting the stretcher bearing Adin. "I'll be right back for you," one of them said to Evangeline.

"I'm ready here—"she nodded "—soon as I get her strapped in."

I rose to my knees and helped the nurse with the woven straps, which vaguely resembled seat belts. Behind me, the flight nurses carried Adin down the hill. "You'll be okay, Yo. I'll see you get the best nerve specialist in the world. Marlow can afford it," I said grimly. "And I'll see that he pays whatever the insurance doesn't cover."

Yo smiled up at me, the expression more grimace than joy. "MacKenzie Morgan, I wouldn't have missed this for the world. You get that girl back. And then you get me that doctor you promised."

I touched her forehead. "You got it."

"You don't have to wait for the other nurse. I can carry," the pilot of the small chopper said. He gripped the feet end of the stretcher as the cameraman focused in on the tableau. "On three."

Evangeline took the head of the stretcher and counted to three. Together they lifted it and stepped carefully down the hillside. The cameraman followed, turning one time to frame me in a shot. I looked back at him, too drained to shield myself. And then he, too, moved off. I was left, sitting on the damp earth with my bloody hands in my lap. My hair, freed from its braid, wisped against my face in the cold breeze.

The dual rotors on the medevac helicopter started turning, a whining thunder of mechanical might. I could feel the rush of air on my face. I shivered, the cold of shock squeezing down on me. My teeth started chattering.

After what seemed like ages, the medevac rose into the air and hovered above the valley for a long minute. The cameraman ran to his own helicopter, jumped into the fragile little bird. The rotors of the TV news chopper started to turn, the sound a thin whine without the bass undertones of the larger medevac.

And then it, too, was gone. I was alone.

38

I blinked, my vision focusing on the red-and-white things. I was staring at my bloodied hands resting in my lap. I had no idea how long I had been sitting, looking at them, or how long I had fuzzed out. But my shivers had stopped. The helicopters were gone. A cool breeze was blowing. A bird called.

Each breath ached along every nerve in my chest, down to my fingertips. I had bruised my ribs again and had no memory how. Holding the nearest tree, I pulled myself up, letting the world rock and waver into a steady construct. "Anything for Bella," I murmured to myself. "Anything for my baby."

When I finally stood, I looked around at the carnage of the woods. Two young trees were splintered, one that would surely die, as it listed far to the earth above the thin trunk where it had taken a direct hit. Blood was drying on the forest floor, still bright red but slowly sinking into the earth and darkening to a dull brown. A saddle was upended. Packs were everywhere. Paper and narrow plastic packages left by the flight crew were scattered around. The packhorse carrying the food and bedrolls was nowhere to be seen. The scent of vomit was sour in the air.

I was really alone. A squirrel played up and down a larger tree, scolding me, tail doing that up-and-down motion that nature had intended to be threatening and humans found so amusing. Jumping from branch to branch, he swung high and low as if the world were his personal playground. A bird called again, though I couldn't spot it in the leaves overhead. There was not a human in sight. Jedidiah had left before the shooting started. Caleb had gone after Dell. Had the mentally unstable mountain man killed the main tracker? Once again, I prayed. Funny how stress and horror and fear can drive you to God when all the good things in life can't.

I pulled the saddle over and opened Caleb's pack. I needed soap and water and food more than I needed to protect another's privacy. I dug past the treasured maps and papers Caleb worked over so faithfully, to the personal things deeper down, and found a bar of soap and a clean washrag in a Ziploc bag, rolled in a clean black undershirt. A soft flannel shirt in a shade of washed-out blue was next to it, with a clean pair of socks and briefs. I held the shirts to me and smelled the fresh scent. Not blood and death, but a mountain scent of conifers and wood. Fabric softener that could have been created for the man.

Moving like an old, rheumatic woman, I found the dammed-up spring where the springhouse had once stood when a family lived here, farming the land. There weren't many springhouses still standing, though they had once, prior to electricity, been the best way to keep butter and milk fresh; as the cold water gathered and ran, condensation chilled the inside of the house and everything stored there. I had photographed several of the small wooden buildings over the years. They were simple to design and make. A day's work for a farmer.

I sat on a large foundation stone and bent over the still pond, seeing myself reflected. I was a mess. I removed my shirt and bra and tossed them to the side. They were too coated with blood to ever be clean again. Blood never completely washes away. Not in my experience.

The purple note Bella had written, already water wrinkled, was now bloodstained. I set it aside to dry again while I washed.

Scooping up water with the rag, I washed my face, neck and chest. The cold water stung as I scrubbed my hands, digging into the cuticles to remove dried blood. When I was clean, I dried off with the flannel shirt and pulled the T over my head, strapped on my rib brace, then buttoned up the warm flannel and tucked it into my pants. They were so loose they hung on me. I had heard that stress and constant physical activity would melt off pounds. I was proof of that.

Locating the belt that had worked as a tourniquet on Yo's arm, I washed it and slid it, still wet, through the belt loops. If my pants hadn't been so baggy I would have thrown it away, but I was afraid I might find them around my ankles at an inopportune moment. The Kevlar went on last, feeling heavy and bulky and infinitely comforting.

I gathered all the packs I could find, and was pleased to discover Yo's personal pack where she must have pulled it off the saddle when she slapped the horse to get it away from the line of fire. Inside I found a comb and dragged it through my curls. Found a tube of lipstick I had never seen her wear, and rubbed a finger around the circumference, then dabbed it to my lips. Lost in the wilderness, alone with no horse, and I needed to feel pretty. I laughed, and the sound wasn't nearly as crazy as it might have been.

As I cleaned up, I kept hearing something tinny. As I gathered the last bit of useful detritus, I stumbled over the radio. Yo had dropped it in the leaves and someone had stepped on it, crushing it into the soil. A tinny voice emanated, half-buried.

"Howell One and Two, come in. Howell One and Two, come in." Joel was calling, sounding frantic.

I pressed the button on the side and said into the mike, "This is MacKenzie Morgan. What's left of Howell of One and Two. Over."

"Mac?" He sounded incredulous.

"Yeah. Just me left here."

"We heard the call for a medic. But we don't know what happened. The chopper was on a Tennessee 911 frequency. Why are you alone? Where's Caleb?"

Feeling guilty for forgetting the ICP, I said, "I don't know. Dell shot Adin, the tracker who joined us this morning. He's pretty bad." Even to my own ears, I sounded confused, my thoughts disorganized, chaotic. A robot, low on batteries. "The paramedics flew him and Yolanda out awhile ago." I looked at my watch, which was clean now. "Maybe twenty minutes? Yo took a bullet in the arm. Severed an artery and probably ruined the nerve in her hand." Tears fell and I sniffed, needing a handkerchief or a tissue and having only Caleb's sleeve. I wiped my nose with it, and told Joel what had happened.

"There was a cameraman and I think the feed from his camera went out live. He had one of those dishes on his helicopter. Maybe you should check the local stations. You can see for yourself."

"I'll send in another helicopter to extract you and Caleb. This is too dangerous for a SAR team. The FBI is willing to take over now and I'm letting them."

I looked at the radio. It was surprisingly heavy for its

size. And I thought about Joel's words while he asked me for my location, called my name, his tone growing more frantic and demanding. Finally I keyed the mike and said, "Joel. I'm not coming out. Not until I find IsaBella. This the last time you'll hear from me until I'm ready for extraction." I used his military-sounding term.

"Mac, that is not an acceptable or rational solution to this situation. You could be injured or killed. I can't allow you to stay backcountry. A helicopter is on the way. I was just given the coordinates from the news chopper."

Impatient, unyielding, I said, "I know the FBI can do wonders in a city, Joel. But this is no city. This is the same stretch of mountains where Eric Rudolph hid for five years until he was too tired of being alone and let himself be captured. The FBI couldn't find their butts with both hands in these woods." I looked over at Caleb's pack. "But I have Caleb's maps. And maybe Caleb, if I can find him. And Jed and Big Bertha are still out there somewhere. So I'm not coming in. Send out a helicopter if you want but I'll be long gone when they get here. And another one of those noisy things might make a tempting target for Dell's gun, if he's still around. Bye, Joel. I'll call when I find Bella." I clicked off the radio, severing his reply.

Standing, I looked at the ground beneath my feet and found where my little mare had dug her small hooves into the deep soil as she raced away. I located the place where the packhorse had panicked and run. And where Yo's horse had reacted to the slap and taken off in a panic. The tracks made by Caleb's horse when he started bucking again and tossed the loose saddle from his back had been obscured beneath human footprints.

Unaware I was using Caleb's tracking lessons, I followed the packhorse footprints uphill and found where they veered off hard left, back down a steep gully. A second set of tracks joined them. The horses had plunged down, and I slid after them, letting gravity pull me, breaking my fall with every tree I could catch.

At the bottom, they had crashed over a small creek, raced toward a nearly sheer wall and wheeled back to follow the runnel of water. The branch ran behind the small farm, and a crumbling outhouse had been built over it, so that rainwater could wash away the human waste. Just beyond, it joined a larger creek. As I rounded a curve, I heard the impact of water on stone. In a tangle of trees choked by silt and tumbled boulders from the recent floodwater, I found the horses, grazing in a narrow patch of early spring grass. The packhorse was still carrying its load, which, amazingly, hadn't shifted, and the little palomino tossed her head at me, mane flying. They were still hyperalert, ears twitching, hooves flashing when they saw me and tried to run. But unless they grew hands or wings, I was standing in front of the only way out. The horses circled the small space twice and came to a stop, snorting in displeasure.

With the sun warming me, I let them settle for long minutes. I sat unmoving on a warm boulder as a helicopter skirted overhead. When the horses were calmer, I approached the pack animal, moving at an oblique angle, not directly like a predator might, but sidling up slowly, toward her shoulder, as another horse would. She let me come, and when I reached out and took the lead rope, she nuzzled my neck, blowing out warm horse breath.

"I missed you, too," I said. "Let's head back to the old farm, how about it, and see if that little palomino will follow." The young mare did, picking her way after us on dainty feet. She had taken a tumble somewhere along the way and was muddy, her saddle hanging to the side. I didn't take them back up the steep slope, but followed the curve of the hills around to the farm. We heard a second helicopter during the trek overland, the horses' ears flicking. I didn't even look up. I was not going home.

When we were back on flat land, beside the foundation, I unsaddled and unpacked each animal, tying them to branches with tie-downs I located on the packhorse. Then I went through the supplies and set aside what I needed today, and what I might need tomorrow. And the day after that.

I found a curry brush and hoof pick in Adin's personal pack. The brush smelled like tobacco, perhaps because that was the only other thing in his personal stash. The hoof pick, brush, and the chew. Rubbing both horses down quickly, I removed burrs and twigs and cleaned their feet. And I gave them a bit of feed, piling the grain on the ground at their feet, more to settle them than to provide sustenance.

As I worked, I kept an eye on the gray mare, who pranced in the distance, watching. Finally, moving as if against her will, she approached. Let me feed her from my hand and take her reins.

When she was cleaned up, too, I resaddled her and strapped a much smaller pack to the packhorse, leaving bedrolls and supplies originally meant for Yo and Adin under a tarp. Along with my hiking boots, I tied Adin's rifle in its case to my saddle, though I had no idea how to use the weapon. I added an extra rifle I couldn't remember seeing anyone carry and secured it to the load on the packhorse, within easy reach.

"You manage to find my mount, too?"

I whirled, making a little squeal in the back of my throat. Caleb stood on a limb, relaxed, his rifle cradled in his arms, watching me work.

"'Cause I aim to shoot that horse first chance I get," he lied, a small grin warming his eyes. "You look mighty good in my shirts."

I crossed my arms, tapped my foot. "I'm the one with the food and the camp stove. You sneak up on me again and I'll put you on short rations." My tone was harsh from surprise, but I couldn't help but smile at the main tracker's return.

"I'll keep that in mind, ma'am." He leaped to the ground, landing bent-legged, rose and came down the hill to me. "You got any jerky I can chew as we ride, while I ponder my sins in penitent misery?"

I tossed him a pack, which he caught lefthanded. When he reached me, he gripped the back of my head. Kissed me soundly, sending heat flooding through me. My knees buckled and Caleb caught me against him, our bodies holding the rifle in place between us.

"I heard what you said to Joel. I've waited a lot of years to find a woman who wouldn't give up. We're not leaving here until we have Bella. I promise you that." He stepped back, grasping the rifle in one hand.

"And your son?" The words were out before I could stop them, but I didn't wish them back. I needed to know more about this man, this extraordinary man who never gave up, either.

For a moment, a film of sorrow crossed his face like rain clouds covering the sun. "I'll find him someday. I know I'll only find a skeleton, because I knew then, I knew in my heart, deep in my bones, that he was dead. Taken by a bear or some other wild predator, or fallen down a crevasse or into a hole so small it wasn't noticed by the searchers. Maybe hit his head. Died fast." His eyes were vivid, laser blue, electric in their intensity. "Want to help me search?"

"Yes."

"Good."

He boosted me onto the gray's back and swung his saddle onto the palomino. He cinched up the girth, putting a knee into her chest when she tried to hold air against the stricture, and sprang onto her back. "Easy, little lady," he said.

"Her name's Bonita."

"Yeah? She is pretty. Almost as pretty as Storm." He nodded to my mare. "She's mine. Been working with her for about two years and I'm mighty glad you got her back. Come on. I think we're only about five miles from the Gregory farm. We can be there in two hours."

I nudged Storm into motion, liking the fact I was riding Caleb's horse. "What about Jed and Big Bertha?"

"I spotted 'em on the far side of the hill, signaled to them. We'll catch up in an hour or so of hard riding."

"My blisters have blisters, you know."

"I'll rub some ointment into your butt first chance I get." He whirled the palomino mare and clamped heels to her sides. She took off like the wind, straight uphill. I followed more sedately, searing his wicked smile into my memory for later contemplation.

39

We caught up with Jedidiah and the indefatigable hound two hours later. They were taking a break with water and several packs of beef jerky, Jedidiah taking a bite from a stick, then the dog taking a bite, then Jed taking a bite. Sharing the stick. *Men.*

Jed watched us as we drew near, noting the palomino beneath Caleb, the absence of Yo and Adin. "Thought I heard shooting awhile back. You folks find some trouble?"

Caleb told him, ending with, "I found three trails, well-used and well-ridden. I figure the farm is close, that he took the girl there, thinking we'd be thrown in such confusion that we'd be pulled out. But he'll be back before long, just to make sure."

The dog handler nodded thoughtfully. "You're right. Man like that ain't leaving nothing to chance. I been smelling wood smoke off and on a bit. Seems to be coming from thataway." He nodded to the west. "That the direction of your trail? 'Cause I reckon it's the direction of the Gregory farm we been looking for."

Caleb crossed his hands over the saddle horn and

rested his weight forward. "Yep. I agree. And just so you know, Joel told us to pull out. Said it's too dangerous to continue."

Jedidiah opened a red bag of tobacco and tamped a wad into his cheek. Moved it around with his tongue as he thought. "Joel's an old woman. I ain't leaving that girl with no crazy man. And I don't aim to let him spend any extra time alone with her, either. Let's get moving. Big Bertha?" The hound turned soulful eyes up to him and sniffed the old panties that Bella had once worn. "Let's go huntin', you ol' sweet bitch. Find it," he commanded.

The dog stood a moment, nose in the air, as if scenting for Bella on the breeze. She lunged forward in a single leap. Jedidiah, prepared for her action, leaped with her. The horses seemed to know they were following the dog and man, and proceeded without urging, making me lunge with the unexpected motion.

I caught a whiff of wood smoke, just a hint, and then it was gone. Excitement surged up in me, whipping through my veins like lightning, crackling and burning. Bella was just ahead. This time there was no doubt.

The trail wound up and around steep ravines, deep gorges left by torrential rains in a time following heavy deforestation. I looked for the telltale signs of overturned leaves, horse droppings. There was nothing. Yet Big Bertha had a strong scent, her body nearly quivering with joy. She would have run full-tilt, had Jedidiah released her, and ended the search with her nose buried in Bella's lap, asking for praise. I could almost see it, the sad-eyed dog and Bella together.

I had never led a packhorse before, and found the lead line pressing into my thigh. I was sure there must be a better way to sit on a horse and pull one, too, but I hadn't bothered to watch how Yo did it. One more bruise to add to my collection. I was getting a pretty good stash of them by now.

The route turned uphill. The smell of wood smoke grew stronger as we neared the summit. Wind whipped up from the valley, spiraling and slapping, catching my hair in mischievous fingers and tossing it into my eyes. The trail widened out a bit into a flat place just below the apex of the hill, and Caleb handed me his reins. "Wait here. I'll be right back."

Jedidiah, Big Bertha and I waited below the crest with the horses, pummeled by the uncertain wind, while Caleb scouted ahead. When he returned after half an hour, his face was grim. "The trail's booby-trapped," he said without preamble. "We leave the horses here. Jed, you better hold Big B close in. I think I found all the traps and know when and where to go around, but I'd hate to have missed one."

Jedidiah spat the tobacco juice, a long stream that might have made Adin jealous. "I had me a dog in 'Nam could smell out traps. Never missed a single mine in two years with him. Maybe I need to train me up a new dog." He gathered the leash in tight, soothing the hound when she looked back with confused eyes.

"Unsaddle or not?" I asked, dismounting.

"Not. If we need a fast getaway, it'd be nice to have them ready to run. But we can loosen the girths and hobble them so they have some freedom. There's grass here. Leave them water and they'll likely stick around." He hung the binoculars around his neck and moved to hobble the palomino. "Let's make this fast, people."

Without further comment, I loosened the saddle girths on the gray mare and the packhorse and poured bottled water for them into a bucket, placing ten empties back in the pack.

From my personal pack, I pulled the .38, checking to

see that it was loaded. Snapped closed the cylinder. I felt Caleb's eyes on me as it clicked shut, but I didn't turn, simply tucked the gun into my pants pocket, praying that I wouldn't shoot myself. Untying my hiking boots from the saddle horn, I sat on the ground and replaced the smooth-bottomed riding boots with rubber-soled boots with a tread, watching as Caleb did the same.

I found more bottled water, three packs of beef jerky and the first-aid kit, which I wrapped up in a bedroll along with the ranger radio Yo had carried. A way to call for extraction and medical supplies for Bella, should she need them. I didn't dwell on my baby needing first aid. I couldn't. I held up Adin's rifle. "Jedidiah, can you use this thing?"

"I'm a fair shot, if need be." He took it, opened the case and inspected the weapon. "Good golly, Miss Molly. You seen this, Caleb?"

The main tracker chuckled. "I saw it. Big gun for such a little boy."

"'Ess is an AR 15." Jedidiah pulled the weapon halfway from its case. "It's got a brass catcher, extra clips, a scope on a see-through-style basement."

"Modified?" Caleb asked.

"Oh, yeah," Jedidiah said. "Fully."

"I thought AR 15s were banned," I said.

"Importing 'em is banned. So is modifying 'ese suckers to fully automatic. And I'm real glad our boy's a certifiable gun nut." Jed closed the case and slung it over his shoulder before he stepped to the packhorse and removed the webbed ties that secured the extra rifle I had found when I reorganized.

He inspected an ugly weapon that was something other than a hunting gun, closed its hard case, attached a strap and placed it across his back as well. Even to my untrained eye, the rifle was very different from Adin's.

It was lovingly cared for and well-used. "Much as I appreciate the volley of rounds the AR 15 can deliver, I'll bring this one, too. A Remington 700 bolt action, with a stainless steel Hart barrel, finished with Teflon. A .308 Winchester." He paused as if I should react to the description with awe. Bow, maybe, or curtsy.

Wanting to please, I said, "Wow," and nodded.

"Jedidiah's fairly well known in long-range target shooting circles," Caleb said. I had a feeling that was mountain man understatement.

I slung my pack over one shoulder and said, "Let's go."

With Caleb in the lead and Big Bertha thoroughly confused, we started down the mountain. At the last minute, acting on an impulse I didn't understand, I stopped and ran back for the camera, though it was stupid and could only get in the way. Running, I caught up, bouncing down the steep slope. There were abrasions in the earth where the horses Dell had stolen had slipped, unused to the terrain for which he had educated his own mounts.

I had a mental image of Bella crushed beneath a fallen horse, and shook my head to clear it away. Catching a young sapling, I swung down as I had seen Yo and Caleb do, feeling the stretch in shoulders and ribs. I was growing strong again, both in body and mind, finding power in muscles and bone no longer so bruised. Every mile I traveled from the beating at the fishery, and from Marlow and his abuse, the more I was coming home to myself. The real self I might have been, had my life and my husband been different. We would get Bella back. Today. Come death or dirty water. I had a feeling my daddy would have been proud.

Caleb led us away from the trail three times, off to the side and then back, discussing with Jedidiah things that I would never have noticed, like the way certain twigs were bent and some leaves were piled. Alone, I would have been dead four times over, just today. I was feeling strong, but I knew my weaknesses. And I would never find Bella alone. I needed this team.

At the bottom of the mountain, Caleb halted. "I've been no farther. How about you three waiting here? I'll move about twenty paces. Then you follow."

I realized he was suggesting that if he missed another trap, he would kill only himself. "Be careful," I said.

"I will. I got ointment plans for later in the week. Don't want to miss out on that 'cause I'm laid up in a hospital bed with my legs missing."

Jedidiah snorted, though he couldn't have understood the inviting quirk to Caleb's lips or the flash of blue fire in the glance he tossed me. The main tracker moved ahead, stepping carefully, his head swiveling. He moved with an almost preternatural caution, as if he had called up some primitive part of his being, moving the way humans had done eons ago, silently, cautiously, prepared for violence.

He lifted a hand, bent gingerly, lightly brushed away a collection of leaves. He stepped back, placing each foot with care, just as he had moved when he was backing out of the foundations Dell had wired. He moved right, eyes to the ground as if tracing something, and seemed to find it. He walked back and moved to the left, again concentrating on the ground as if it communicated knowledge only he could see. He signaled us forward, off the path. Big Bertha wanted to follow the scent, and pulled hard, trying to tell the human on the other end of the leash that he was going the wrong way. Jedidiah forced her into Caleb's alternate route. The hound was visibly relieved when she again found the special scent, her ruff relaxing, her tail wagging to thump once on Jedidiah's leg.

Detouring repeatedly, we crossed two small streams trickling down dark stone, and wound around a sheer wall. The downhill trek took an hour and a half of painstaking, slow travel, and suddenly the forest vanished and flat ground opened out before us. A makeshift pasture had been fenced off from the woods, with barbed wire wrapped around trees used as fence posts. A small shed was tucked under the trees, hidden in shadows.

I pulled out the camera and peered through the telephoto lens. In the open space, five horses, a mule and six goats grazed, the horses placid and sun-warmed, tails twitching. I focused on an ugly little horse standing in a shadow. It was the one I'd ridden when I found Bella's first and second notes. Had to be. There couldn't possibly be two such ugly horses in the world.

"We're close," I whispered to the wind. "So close." My breath came in short gasps as I studied the ugly horse. Dell had stolen him, just as he had stolen Bella.

40

Big Bertha put her nose to the air and sniffed deeply, her nostrils flaring and closing on the breeze. She came to attention, her legs stiffening, back straight.

"She's got herself a scent pool," Jedidiah said. "And that means the girl spent some time here, sittin' or standin'. Maybe takin' a rest. 'Cause the horses are pastured here, my bet is they's less than two mile away."

My heart pumped hard, a steady, fast beat in my chest. My curls lifted on the soft breeze, feathering against my cheeks. The dog led the way around the pasture, her nose up instead of to the ground, pulling in the scent that meant the end of her hunt.

We followed the animal along a dirt trail, crossing three different tracks leading into the hills. Big Bertha wasn't interested in any of them.

"Dell Gregory must have spent years blazing trails leading off to different locales," Caleb said. "It looks like he uses them regularly, too."

"Specially this'n," Jedidiah grunted, indicating a route leading south. "Betcha that's the one he usually takes to our neck of the woods, when he ain't on the run for stealing hisself a wife." He spat in disgust.

His head still turned in the direction of the tobacco spurt, he said, "Caleb? That what I think it is?"

Caleb moved slowly to the side of the trail, head lifting and dropping as he walked, checking both the ground and the view ahead. I followed slowly, while Jedidiah and Big Bertha waited on the path. My skin chilled in a wind that seemed to pick up and grow cold as I walked.

Four stone piles with crosses marked a patch of grassy ground, the grass left untended, sprouting up in long, dead tufts. The crosses were painted white with hand-written, black lettering, propped up in the rocks of each cairn. They all said the same thing. *Belinda. Beloved wife of Dell.*

I shivered violently as I stared at the proof of Dell's insanity. Four wives. All dead. All stolen and renamed Belinda. Two of the graves were old and sunken, with tumbled rocks and weathered crosses. Two were newer. One of those was still heaped high, the body beneath shaping the earth.

I remembered the information offered by the man in Asheville—Hansen, whose wife, Emma, had shopped for Dell's wife. The wife she had never seen, but who had changed dress and shoe sizes and then passed away last December. And the grave on the hillside overlooking the fish hatchery…wife number five.

Following Caleb, I reached the graves. On top of each was a small bouquet of spring flowers. Jonquils. Drying in the warmth of the day. I touched the curled, withered petal of a jonquil, the yellow so pale it was almost white. Had he killed all of them?

"Five dead, that we know about," Caleb said.

"And if this goes to trial, he'll get off because he's deranged," I murmured.

"He won't be going to trial. That much I know. This man ain't coming in without a fight. Jed or I'll have to kill him." He looked at me and tilted up his hat so I could see his eyes. There was little in them. No compassion, no clemency. And no willingness to wait, either. With a finger, he wiped away the tears I hadn't known were falling on my cheek. "That means we better get Bella away first," he said.

"Good idea."

"You know how to cook?"

I started. "Not worth a darn. But I make really great homemade bread."

"I'm a pretty good chef. I'll cook Bella a bang-up meal when we get her home. You can bake the bread and tear the lettuce. She gets to wash up."

"Deal," I said, knowing he was telling me everything would be all right. Bella was coming home. Caleb Howell was going to make it happen.

Searching the narrow horizon and the trail that dwindled in the distance, he led the way back to Jedidiah and Big Bertha, taking up position behind the dog. "Jed, that dog going to yap when she sees Bella?"

"Hounds don't yap, and you know it. They make a mighty howl. Like a wolf, but excited," he added to me. "Yap, my fat butt."

Caleb grinned, showing his teeth. "Either way, you better muzzle that dog, because I smell meat cooking on the smoke. Pork, unless I miss my guess. And we don't want to give ourselves away until we make a move to get the girl back."

"You got a plan?"

"Plans are determined by terrain and conditions, intel we don't have. We'll wing it."

Jed quickly pulled a leather contraption out of his shirtfront and slipped it on Big Bertha. The hound didn't seem to mind, even turning her head to make the process easier. Jedidiah passed a bit of jerky through the muzzle and the dog licked it in. "I reckon I'm glad we got us a extra gun, Caleb. 'Specially one what's been worked on a mite to remove certain firing restrictions."

Tingles started along my skin. A warm sweat broke out, dampening my palms. I fingered the .38 in my pocket.

"We move silent from now on," Caleb said. "Mac, you stay with me. Jed, you take Yo's radio. Sotto voce and hand signals only. Mac, you won't know the signals, so just move behind me. We know he has dogs, and we don't want to alert them. So we'll stay downwind as soon as we sight the house. Move out."

Jedidiah held the scrap of nylon once again to Big Bertha. "Check it." This time the hound only sniffed once. Instantly, she lunged forward with shoulder-wrenching might, pulling Jedidiah behind her.

We wound among trees with no foliage beneath. Jumped a manmade ditch carrying water to a wide stretch of tilled earth, the furrows looking fresh. A patch of marijuana was the only thing growing. "Tidy profit, right there," Jedidiah murmured.

"There's gold in them there hills, if you plant and harvest it right," Caleb said, his voice a burr of sound. The men acted amused, relaxed, while the sweat drained down my body and pooled in the waistband of my jeans. Again I touched the gun through the denim. And remembered the look on Dell's face when I'd first taken his photograph. Rage. Fury.

They were making jokes. I was thinking about shooting a man. A single hard shudder ran along my spine. *What if Bella wasn't here? What if it had all been for nothing?* The sweat chilled my skin in the fitful wind.

The path we traveled across the flat-bottomed valley was well-worn, the rich Appalachian soil deeply rutted. Mountains rose on either side of us, vertical walls running with water, heavy with moss and delicate ferns.

Birds sang. Flowers bloomed, yellow jonquils and lavender periwinkle. Climbing roses had tight buds, little knobs of green. Heaven on earth.

A low growl sounded from the side. A small yellow lab stood in the shadow of the roses, beneath the trailing stems, teeth bared. Face vicious, eyes full of warning. "Polly!" I hissed. "She'll give us—"

Big Bertha charged the dog, knocking Jedidiah to the ground. The leash flew free, his elbow impacting the earth with a thud. The lab jumped back, startled as the heavier dog hurtled into her with a hollow thump of muscle and bone.

His arm whipping in an arc, Caleb knocked the lab to the ground, binoculars swinging in a follow-through any athlete would have been proud of. Polly dropped like a rock. Caleb knelt beside the dog as Jedidiah gathered Big Bertha back to his side, rubbing his elbow and flexing his hand.

"Sorry, girl," Caleb said to Polly. "But you strike me as too well trained to let us by without a ruckus." He felt over the dog with long fingers, bringing them away bloody as he inspected the abrasion on her head. He wiped the red stain on his jeans. With a loop fashioned out of a handkerchief, Caleb created a muzzle much like the one the hound wore. Strapping it in place with a length of rope that then went around Polly's neck, he tied it to a nearby tree. "When she doesn't come when called, Dell might guess she's been taken out, but that's better than a sure alarm."

Slapping his hands together to clean them, he inspected the binoculars. They were bent slightly at the nose piece and he sighed. "That's a good hundred bucks out the window."

"Why didn't you use the rifle butt?" I asked.

Jedidiah snorted and Caleb met his eyes with amusement before answering. "Weapons have to be trued to fire properly, on target. You bump a gun and it can go out. Then you miss by several feet and can't understand why."

"Not like in the movies," I said, knowing I was out of my element.

"Around here, we spend entire action adventure movies spotting ways the hero got himself killed by sheer stupidity or carelessness," Caleb said. "Hollywood folks are stupid."

"Dumber than dirt," Jedidiah agreed, spitting. "Dog had to be in hearing distance of the house. We're close. Let's go kick us some woman-stealing, crazy-man butt."

As he spoke, the wind shifted and Big Bertha's head shot up, her nose in the air, nostrils flared. She did a little dance, her paws rocking on the ground, claws digging in.

"Bella," I breathed.

"Yeah. Let's go," Caleb said, holding his rifle at the ready.

We passed through a winter garden strung with loose mesh ghillie cloth, the stuff used by the military to camouflage cars and any sites that might receive cursory inspections. The ground beneath was dark with frost-ruined cabbage that still gave off a faint stink. We entered a patch of cane, where Caleb motioned us to follow him single file, and he moved one careful footstep at a time, watching for traps in the dark shadows.

As we eased out of the bamboo, the valley opened up again below us, falling away thirty feet to a small copse of trees hiding a log cabin and three outbuildings, one small enough to be an outhouse. Clothes hung on a line behind the house, moving in the rising wind. A fresh patch of turned earth in the shape of a wagon wheel marked the south side. A springhouse stood on the north, on a little rise near the mountain wall.

Thin smoke came from the cabin chimney. It did indeed smell like pork cooking, a mouthwatering scent. Big Bertha was panting in excitement.

I pulled the camera to me and focused it on the clothesline. Spotted Bella's purple thermal. We had been wearing matching thermal underwear the day Dell attacked. Bella's idea, for our mother-daughter trip. Dropping the camera and pack, I surged down the hill. But the breath blasted out of me in a strangled note. My feet flung out from under me as I was yanked back, my middle nearly broken in two. Plopped on the ground without ceremony, I tried to catch my breath, which had been knocked out of me.

"Sorry 'bout that, Miz Morgan. No disrespect intended. But I can't let you just run on up and knock on the front door," Jedidiah said, his voice calm. "After all this, I ain't aiming to take you and the girl home in body bags."

I groaned, pressing a hand to my chest where the camera had slung back and hit me. I rolled over the pack and left it in the dirt. "Bella," I managed to gasp. "That's her purple shirt. He's got her."

"We'll get her back," Jedidiah said, sighting through his rifle scope. He was stretched out on the ground beside me, having dropped there when I landed.

"But he could be—" I wanted to cry, but this time, I fisted my hands and hit the earth, pounding it with my words. "He could be *hurting* her. He could be hurting my baby!"

"He just walked out on the porch. Caleb, I need a better shooting angle to take him down," Jedidiah said, rising to a crouch. "You think I should go around, take up a position on the other side? Maybe that rock I see jutting out from the side of the cliff, beyond the trees."

Caleb nodded, both men ignoring me where I lay, feeling the first flickerings of anger. My baby was in that house. And I was going to get her.

"Don't get yourself shot or scented by the dogs. Looks like he's got three or more, besides the yellow one we left tied up, and at least two are on point. Well trained. Bet they hunt, too. I'd hate for you to have to kill 'em, but do it if you need to. You still throw a knife?"

Jedidiah spat hard, the juice landing with a splat. "I can hit a fly at twenty feet. Thirty if he's landed."

Caleb didn't even laugh at the boast, just gestured to the far side of the valley. "Give me a Rabid Dog on channel four when you get in position."

"Make it a Big Dog for me, Howell. Ain't nothin' 'bout my dogs that's rabid." Jedidiah repositioned his chaw with a thumb and secured his weapons and his dog in firm hands.

"We'll take him out before dusk," Caleb said. "But fair warning—if Gregory moves away from the cabin before you're in position, I'm taking him."

"You can't shoot worth a dang, boy. Leave the shootin' to the big dogs." Jedidiah spat again as dog and man moved into the shadows.

41

When Jedidiah had melted into the terrain, Caleb pulled out his radio, turned it on and pressed the transmit button. Speaking softly, he said, "Howell One to ICP. Howell One to ICP. Come in." After a moment he fiddled with the knobs and tried again. "Howell One to ICP. Howell One to ICP. Come in."

"This is the ICP," Evelyn said, her voice more clear and crisp than previously. "Hold for the IC, Howell One."

"Let's Rabid Dog, ICP."

"Understood, Howell One. Rabid Dog Three. Repeat, Rabid Dog Three. ICP out."

"Howell One out."

"What are you doing?" I asked.

"Just covering all the bases. A smart tracker knows his territory. And a long-distance incident commander can screw up an SAR faster than an armchair general can screw up a war." Caleb changed the dials again. "But then again, we may need Joel's help. Rabid Dog Three. Come in."

"Where the Sam Hill are you, Howell One." Joel sounded tired, disgusted and somehow not surprised to hear Caleb's voice.

"We're at the Gregory farm, IC, hidden in a little valley. Ready for GPS and compass coordinates?"

"Go ahead."

Caleb recited numbers and letters that still made no sense to me. Knowing they were indicators of longitude, latitude and altitude was little help.

"Rabid Dog, we have completed aerial reconnaissance of that position and found nothing."

"It's a small, two-tiered valley, more like a chasm between two sheer mountain faces. House is in the front gardens under ghillie cloth. The valley is narrow as the mind of a flat earther, and the winds are mighty fickle. I don't imagine they bothered to drop into the valley, not in a small spotter chopper. Likely just hovered over it and ruled it out. The mother has identified an article of clothing that belongs to the quarry, and Big Bertha has a confirmed scent. We have a hostage situation. Repeat, we have a hostage situation. How do you want us to proceed?"

"Good work, Howell. We'll drop a negotiator and guide into the next valley over and send them in with Tennessee law enforcement, along with ATF. Soon as they decide who has jurisdiction." Joel sounded even more disgusted. "You stay put until they get there. The FBI will take over at that point."

I raised my head, gripping Caleb's wrist. Joel wanted us to wait. We couldn't wait. Bella couldn't wait.

His eyes on me, unchanging, Caleb said, "Negative to a large team walking overland. Suspect has rigged booby traps all through the woods and in a cane patch. Suggest one negotiator and one guide, and I'll lead them in. You have to put down into the valley itself—" Caleb broke off. "Hold on, ICP. Situation is evolving."

He lifted the bent field glasses and peered through them. I was still seated where Jedidiah had tossed me, and I looked through the camera lens, finding a better picture of the log house below us. Oak trees shaded the entire structure, arching over the roof, which was metal, painted a dark camouflage green. The cabin was maybe two rooms, with a split-cedar rail designating the front porch, a wooden swing hanging from the beams overhead. Because we were at a higher elevation, looking down on the cabin, the upper half of the porch was hidden by the overhang of the roof.

A man stood there in shadow, propped against the front wall, one foot on the logs at his back, smoking a cigarette. A lithe form walked out to stand near him, arms crossed over his chest, stance antagonistic. Young man, or slender and old? I couldn't tell, but it meant Bella was alone with two men. Dread gripped me, swamped almost instantly by anger.

Two men. The slender man put a foot on the porch railing. Angry tones carried up to us on the wind, along with the sweet scent of marijuana. One voice was female. *A woman?* I realized the slender form's movements had been feminine. Confusion and weird possibilities swirled in with the anger and dread in my mind. What was going on here? A commune? White slavery? The kidnapping for money that had been ruled out by the profilers?

A dog trotted out of the house, sniffed at the slender form and sprang off the porch. It looked like Rufus, reddish, small. The mongrel put his nose to the wind and sniffed, his brown eyes moving along the mountain wall. I wondered if he was smelling Jedidiah and Big Bertha, and tensed. Instead, he turned and stared up the valley wall, directly at our position.

"I think we've been made, Mac," Caleb said.

"Please don't bark," I murmured. "Come on, Rufus. Just forget you ever sniffed me."

The dog wagged his tail, dropped to the earth and

rolled over on his back, feet in the air, for a good back scratch. When he was done, he lay there crookedly, belly to the sun, tongue lolling comically. The two on the porch continued arguing, only the tenor of their conversation reaching us over the distance.

"Good dog," I said, as if he had heard me and obeyed. "Now, go back inside to Bella. She needs company." Rather than follow my suggestion, Rufus seemed to fall asleep in the odd position. I had noted on our first meeting that he wasn't very well trained, so maybe I shouldn't have been surprised.

Caleb checked his watch. Looking at his wrist, I saw it was 1830 hours. Nearly dark. He pressed the radio's transmit button, looking up into the sky. "IC, it'll be totally dark in less than an hour. In this valley, with the high cliffs to block the sun's rays, it'll be dark sooner." Caleb looked around, considering the valley as he spoke. "Negative on the FBI or ATF tonight unless they do a blitz attack. And they don't have enough intelligence to do that successfully. It's too late to get them in place, what with explosives wired all over."

"Same stuff you found at the foundation this morning?"

"Affirmative. And I left them in place. There wasn't time to try and disarm them."

"We found a stash of explosives and weapons in an old cellar on the foundation property. We still have men on the site. *Federales.*" His voice was droll, as if the feds were losers in his book. "Alcohol, Tobacco and Firearm people. They want in, Howell, and with the explosives, it's their ball game."

"I'm not leaving Bella alone with him." I whispered, almost a growl. "I'll go down there without you before I do that."

Caleb met my eyes, his still giving nothing away.

"Your team comes in overland in the dark, they'll go home in zippered bags. They land in this valley and Gregory'll know they're here. No telling what weapons the man has with him in the house. The one thing they don't want to do is give him warning or they'll have a Waco all over again." He squinted into the shadows up and down the valley.

Into the mike he continued, "We may have no option but to handle this ourselves, IC. Gregory's unpredictable and the situation is volatile. We may not be able to wait for reinforcements."

Another man walked out onto the porch below us. I could hear the clop of wooden-heeled boots on the wood porch floor. He handed something to the man smoking. The smoker placed it along the railing. I focused in on it with the camera. It was long, blue metal with a black stock. A hunting rifle. Beside it, he placed a black matte weapon that looked like a toy. This one was compact, with a short muzzle and gun butt, and lethal looking, meant to kill humans, not dinner. The voices continued in a three-way conversation. The slender form—the woman?—removed her foot from the railing and paced back and forth.

"Send the feds in first thing in the morning, or in a blitz landing with the SWAT team before dusk," Caleb reiterated. "You got an hour of good light left. Let me know what you want to do. Howell One Rabid Dog out." He moved the dial again and spoke into the mouthpiece. "Big Dog, come in. Big Dog, come in."

"'Ess is Big Dog. Heard you pissing away time talking about getting feds in here tonight. You know we ain't leaving that little gal in there with them. Ain't happening. I'm in position. When we doing this?"

"Got to pacify the government. You see the man smoking?"

"You mean the one toking on the primo weed? I got him in my sights from the crotch down, which is fine if I want to take off his balls. His boots need polishing and his britches need washing. Onliest other thing I can see is the hooch when he drops his hand. The other man's closer to my side of the valley and I got a bead on his spine just below his shoulder blades. I'd take a head shot, but It's hidden behind the roofline. He has a rifle leaning against the house wall on this side of the door, along with something looks like a small machine gun. And I think I saw him hand something to the other man, but I didn't get a good look."

"Affirmative. Both men have what appear to be fully automatic weapons. Smoker's are on the railing, close by his hand."

"The pacer is a woman, blonde, maybe. Kinda busty. Be a shame to kill her, so I'll try to just wing her a mite."

"Why don't we try to hit the guns instead of the humans?"

"You ain't that good a shot, boy. Go for the chest and quitcher bellyaching. On three?"

"Hold on hold on hold on. What am I seeing?" Caleb asked.

A fourth form moved onto the porch, this one in an ankle-length white dress, walking awkwardly. She stepped off the porch and headed away from the cabin. I slid forward, straining. Watching. She paused by Rufus and bent to scratch his stomach. The dog squirmed in contentment. "Is it Bella?" I whispered.

The woman in the dress walked into the sunlight, throwing long shadows behind her. There was a bonnet on her head and dark, wet hair hanging down over her breasts. She walked as if the movement pained her. Walked toward me. "Lift your face. Lift your face."

42

The woman in the dress walked to the springhouse, picked up a metal bucket and bent over, her hands hidden from me. The sound of water falling was sharp and crisp.

"Her feet tied?" Jedidiah asked, his voice low over the radio.

"She's hobbled like a horse. Rope or rawhide ties."

As she stood, the woman lifted her face. Bruised. Scratched and pale. But it was my baby. "B—!"

Caleb wrenched my arm to keep me silent and still. "On three," he said, dropping the radio and my arm, steadying the rifle in the apex of his own. "One. Two. Three."

The shot blasted my ears, clawing all sound from the world.

"Run, Bella! Run!" I screamed into the silence of the blast concussion. "Run here! Here!" I was on my feet, arms waving wildly.

Bella looked up, her mouth open. A snapshot image of shock. Two more shots rang out, tinny pops of sound muted by the damage to my ears. She dropped the bucket, water splashing up and over her dress.

Dell Gregory stepped off the porch, lifting a rifle.

Bella grabbed up her skirts, shuffled toward me. Her first step covered eight inches, the rope confining her to baby steps. Her eyes were wide with fright, her mouth pulled back in a rictus of fear.

Dell trained the gun on Bella.

"Run!" I screamed, the breath ripping from my body. The weapon beside me fired again. Dell fell and spun, back to the porch.

"Mac! No!" Caleb shouted.

I dropped down the sharp rise, heels skidding for purchase on the nearly vertical wall, my hands grasping small trees, tufts of brush, a vine, anything to keep from simply falling straight down. I landed with a jolt that jarred my spine. The camera whammed into my chin, flinging stars. Bright instants of time, of pain, seared into my mind.

A bullet sang past my ear, smacked into the earth wall behind me. Caleb shouted again, his words lost under the barrage of staccato gunfire from the machine guns.

In ten strides I reached Bella and snatched her in my arms as she lurched forward, screaming. I felt the blow through my own body. Pounding into my chest. Bella had been hit.

Half lifting her, I towed her behind the springhouse and fell across her, tripping over Rufus, shielding her from the gunfire. "I can't breathe," she said, shoving at me, her voice almost lost beneath the ringing in my ears. "I can't breathe." I rotated my body, placing my weight on the ground, pulling her into my arms, her white dress tangling around us. Shots crashed into the springhouse, the vibrations boring into me, ignored.

"Bella. My Bella." With frantic hands I examined her, touched her face, her head, her shoulders, hugged her to me and pushed her away, touching her again and again.

She had two black eyes, fresh bruises on her jaw, a swollen lip. When my hands came away from her waist, the right one was wet.

Bloody.

I stared at the scarlet, felt the air leave my lungs. "Bella?"

"It hurts, Mama. It hurts." She was crying in awful, tearing sobs, her eyes on my hand and her blood.

My world slowed, skidded to a sluggish pace. A place where there was only the scarlet of blood on my hands. IsaBella's blood.

My heartbeats were rapid, an echo in my ears, my breath a wheeze of air. Rounds pumped into the spring-house, each a rich, harsh sound. Distinct and pure. Caleb shouted, angry. The main tracker was enraged. Bella was bleeding. The machine gun rat-a-tat was snare drum fast, striking the wood at my back, short bursts of ratcheting sound.

Nerveless, I turned Bella as if she weighed no more than a baby, my baby, newly born. She had an entrance wound and an exit wound on her waist on the left side. In a blinding moment of clarity, I knew what to do. And how to do it. Feeling nothing, hearing nothing, seeing only the wounds, I pulled the Swiss Army knife from my jeans pocket and cut away the bodice of the dress that hid them.

The entrance wound on her back was small, about three inches from her spine. The exit wound was much larger, left of her navel. The size of a silver dollar.

But I knew how to bandage them, how to apply pressure, the steps crystalline in my memory. With the knife, I sliced the skirt that had tripped Bella, ripping off a wide side panel. Then another. Exposing an old-fashioned, lace-edged slip beneath, and her bare feet, ankles tied with rawhide strips.

With another rip, holding the cloth in my teeth, I tore a long strip. Folded the panels into squares, roughly four-by-four, and clamped them on the wounds. "Hold this," I demanded, pressing Bella's hand on the front bandage as I positioned the back one. The long strip I wrapped around her waist, tying it off. It wasn't enough to create the pressure I needed. Blood soaked through the bandages. Spreading.

I shredded another panel of the dress, adding a second absorbent layer to both wounds. I pulled apart the Velcro bindings of the Kevlar vest I wore, yanked the blue shirt off, ripped the rib brace loose, wrapped the shirt around Bella, then the brace. Jerking it tight, securing it firmly over her wounds.

I turned the small knife in my hand and sliced through the rawhide that held her ankles together, tossing away the ties. The whole time I was muttering. Praying, calling on God. "Help, help, help, help!" My words were a litany of supplication.

I looked up at Bella. Her eyes were brimming with tears, her hands on my face, her lips moving. "You're alive. You're alive. You're alive." She had been saying the same thing over and over as I worked to stanch the bleeding. "You're alive. I knew it. I knew it. I told him so. You're alive. You're alive."

I laughed, the sound fevered, the tone vivid and sharp-edged as a sword. I put my hands on her face, too, pulled her to me and kissed her on both cheeks, her forehead, chin and mouth. When I pulled my hands away, I left bloody smears on her skin that I tried to wipe away. I only made it worse, and Bella laughed at my expression, her swollen lip splitting open, spilling a bright ruby drop of blood. Ignoring it, she hugged me hard.

Around us the battle raged, gunshots blistering the world with savage power. A whine sounded, high-pitched. The dog, terrified. But I wasn't. I was no longer afraid, not of anything.

"Mama?" Bella pushed me away and pointed to my shirt. There was a spot of blood there. Bright and widening. "Mama?"

I remembered the moment Bella had been shot. The pounding in my own chest.

Had the bullet passed through Bella, into me? I pulled up the T-shirt, exposing my skin, pale and white, grimed with my blood. There was no pain, a burning only when I concentrated, trying to feel. I touched the wound. It was jagged, mounded on top, just a little to the side of the hole where blood leaked out in a narrow trickle. I pushed on it. The mound was hard.

Bella was wracked with tears, panicked, her hands shaking, held before her as if to ward off a blow. Almost absently, I patted her shoulder with my bloody hand and reached for the Kevlar vest. When I lifted it, I saw the small rip in the odd fabric, a similar tear on the inside. The bullet had passed through Bella, pierced the vest and traveled into me.

I put my fingers back on the small knot on my chest. It was solid, located just over a rib, about a quarter inch from the entry point. "Think it's the bullet?" I pushed at it, moving it around on top of the rib. "Yeah. The bullet." It seemed so simple.

With the Swiss Army knife, I sliced across the top of the mound and popped the bullet out of my skin. It should have hurt, but there was no pain. Nothing. I held the bullet up in my grimy, bloodstained fingers. Spent bullets were ugly.

Bella looked at me as if seeing me for the first time in her life. Not recognizing me. Perhaps a bit afraid. Rufus cowered behind her, his tail between his legs, quaking. There was a pause in the firing, the silence as clamorous as the fusillade of gunfire had been. Bella turned to the side and vomited.

I held my daughter while she emptied her stomach, the stench acrid, harsh, explicit as a curse on the cordite-fouled breeze. When she sat back up, she mopped her mouth with a ragged scrap of her dress and looked at me, her eyes considering. As if deciding something. Something revolutionary or rebellious. I had seen that look before. It was dangerous. This time, I did nothing to stop the mental shift, the essence of transformation in her mind. Whatever it was, it was okay.

My baby pried open my hand and took the bullet from me, held it up, inspecting it. It was malformed, jagged. "That's a big-ass bullet."

"Ass isn't a nice word," I said automatically. Because it was expected.

"Ass is a small donkey," she retorted instantly. "It's a perfectly acceptable word." Grinning, she slid the bullet into my jeans pocket. Folded up and added the Swiss Army knife. "Family mementos." She watched me again, her gaze quick, taking in everything about me. She took a breath, gaining strength from someplace I wasn't privy to. "Now, take a photograph." She pointed to the camera that still hung around my neck on its thong, forgotten.

I raised the camera and framed a portrait of Bella and the small red dog, who chose that moment to crawl into her lap, whining. She lifted Rufus to her face for a second shot, looking into the lens with serious, thoughtful eyes.

"Belinda? You okay, honey?" Dell called.

Bella tensed, her muscles clenching in fear, her expression caught in the last shot. She dropped the dog, looking around in sudden panic. The world, the real world of a psychotic Dell Gregory and gun battles and blood, crashed back into me. While I had been working to stop Bella's bleeding, to bind her injuries, to gauge the wounds on her soul, I had blocked it all out. For long moments during the combat, it had ceased to exist. Like a rubber band, that world snapped back, an audible pop in my mind.

43

"Belinda?"

I had Bella back. For now. But how was I going to get her out of the valley safely? And were Caleb and Jedidiah still okay? Fear clamped its clammy hand on me. Hot sweat poured down my back.

"Belinda? Answer me!" The voice was closer, the words muted.

I put a finger over my lips and raised up one knee, finding the gun, the little .38. I pulled it out of my pocket, checked to see that it was still loaded, rotated the cylinder. A single shot came from above, shattering the silence. In finding Bella, I had lost all sense of time and place. A dislocation I couldn't afford, if Bella was to go home safely. The battle had grown silent, guns no longer blasting a constant hail of fire. Was Caleb out of ammunition? Injured?

"Belinda!" The single word was anguished, heartbroken. Crushed and conquered. The shadows were lengthening. The space behind the springhouse grew darker suddenly as the sun passed behind the mountain walls.

"Caleb!" I shouted. "How about those ATF boys about now!"

I heard him chuckle, anger and adrenaline lacing the laughter, the corrosive sound carried on the chill air. "You hit?"

"Now that you mention it, yes. So is Bella."

"How bad?"

"The wounds don't appear to be imminently life threatening," Bella called. First-aid-course language. "They just hurt like hell," she added. Softer, she asked, "Who's Caleb?"

"Hell's not a nice word." The phrase slipped out.

"Hell's a place. I know. I've been there." A haunted mist slithered behind her eyes, and she hugged me hard. I hugged her back, the dog trapped uncomplaining between us.

"Belinda!"

"Belinda's dead!" I shouted, protecting my baby with my body, shifting her quickly behind me. "Dead and buried and gone forever!"

The man screamed. Fired into the springhouse. Shots rang out around us, echoing down the valley, fierce and cracking. I grabbed the Kevlar vest and slipped it over Bella's head and side, securing the Velcro tightly. I pushed her back again, into the shadows of the dying day, down behind the security of the heavy wood girder that had protected us so far. I lifted the .38 in my right hand, braced it on my knee and gripped it in my left hand, curling my fingers around the butt just as my father had shown me, ready to fire.

"Who is the other man?" I asked. "And the woman?"

"It's Uncle Burgess," Bella said. "And Daddy's snow bunny."

I froze. The air was icy on my sweaty skin, the dusk still and shadowed. "Uncle Burgess? But he was shot. He's missing."

"I don't think so. He didn't look hurt to me. But he's

mad that Dell brought me here after he paid him all that money. I think Dell was supposed to kill me."

"Dell was supposed to kill you? For money? Burgess's money?" I felt thickheaded. Slow. I had missed something.

"Yeah," Bella said, her words bitter. "He was supposed to kill us both. So Daddy would go to jail and Burgess and Gianna could inherit the money from Gramma Rachael."

"I don't understand."

"Me, neither. But I heard Gianna say the cops had arrested Daddy. But Daddy didn't do this, Mama. Uncle Burgess did. And that bitch."

I didn't bother to correct Bella's language. Maybe this time she was right.

"Dell took me to protect me from Uncle Burgess. But he got mixed up in his head and started thinking I was his wife. I think. He isn't real clear on a lot of stuff."

From the corner of my eye, I saw her look down at the bloodied and ruined dress. She picked at the cut fabric with blood-sticky fingers.

"This was supposed to be my wedding dress. He was going to make me marry him tonight." Her voice was without inflection, the deadness of it piercing to my soul. She tried to take a deep breath but it seized in her chest, her face twisting. "Oh. Mama, I'm starting to hurt. Real bad."

"I know, baby.

"Caleb!" I screamed. "I need those helicopters *now!* Bella's hurt!"

"ETA four," he shouted, sounding relaxed and unconcerned that Dell might hear him.

"Belinda! I'm coming!"

Gunshots broke out again. This time there was screaming on the breeze, men shouting on the other side of the springhouse, the words twisted with the multiple concussions and the pervasive scents of cordite and hot metal. Something large slammed into the springhouse, the small structure shuddering. Bella yelped, rolling into a tight ball around the dog. I pivoted on one buttock just a half inch, still supporting the handgun on one knee. Steadied it in both hands, aimed at the opening beside me. Bella quivered in a long trembling shudder. I could hear her crying with pain. How much damage had the bullet done? Was she bleeding internally?

Shots were a cacophony, dirt blowing up in small puffs only feet from me. Just beyond the springhouse. Fired from above. Caleb was firing shots that landed near me. At someone I couldn't see. "Be still, Bella," I murmured. "Very, very still." The dirt was peppered with shots. One. Two. Three.

Screaming came from farther off. "Belinda!"

I saw the silhouette in the gathering night, a shadow within shadows. A smear of darkness resting on the earth. My world became that small pool of shadow. And then he moved. Lurched around the side of the springhouse.

The .38 was centered on his chest. I fired, squeezing the trigger smoothly. The recoil lifted my arms, bent my elbows. Straightening them, I instantly squeezed again.

A reddish blur streaked by me.

The form at the springhouse wall dropped back, his head snapping up. Mouth opening. *Burgess.*

He fell, arms thrown wide. Bounced on the earth, scrabbling at his neck with both hands. Deep snarling, screaming punctured the air. Rufus had attacked him. Rufus had him by the jaw and throat, snapping, biting.

Bella rose and stood at my back, her knees touching my shoulders, her hands fisted on either side of my face. "Rufus! Come."

The small dog broke off and trotted to her, tongue still hanging, a jester with a blood-splattered jaw. Burgess crawled away, holding his head. I was glad of the shadows that hid the destruction.

"Good dog. Good Rufus," my daughter said as the dog heeled at her left side.

"Belinda?" the voice called again. It was weak, strangled. I felt the quiver pass through her, fine as a stringed instrument, plucked once. I thought, for a single instant, that Bella might go to him. That he might have damaged her enough that she would feel his need and attend him. But she held steady, touching my hair with her fingers in a single caress.

44

A dual-rotor helicopter came on the wind, far off, the sounds capricious on the breeze. A scramble of boots sounded above. Bella tensed, fear quick in her bloodstream. "It's okay," I said, sliding the gun in the waistband of my jeans. Slowly, I stood, as rocks and dirt showered down around us. I wasn't sure how Bella was standing, but decided her reaction was adrenaline overload, and that the wound wasn't as bad as it looked. If she had been losing blood, she'd have been in shock. I thought. But what did I know? I caught her in my arms, pulling her toward the failing light, but still shielded by my body.

Eighteen inches from me, a man landed lightly, rebounding. He wore a hat that shadowed his face, dark jeans, boots. A rifle was in his right hand, long and lethal. Bella gasped. As if understanding her fear, he whipped off the hat, his eyes darting over us, and smiled. I had seen the full force of his smile only once, blinding and warm and solid as the earth. He stood still, hat and gun in either hand, held out to the sides, letting Bella accept his presence in her own time.

"Who's that?" she asked, her voice small.

"That's Caleb Howell. The main tracker. He's the reason we found you."

I felt the tremor that ran through her, but she shook herself, straightened and held out a hand. "Pleased to meet you, Mr. Howell. I'm IsaBella Morgan."

Caleb took her palm gently, held it for only a moment, careful of the emotions on her face. "Miss Morgan, you're the bravest young woman I ever met, but then, with a mama like Mac, I guess I'm not too surprised." He smiled again, this one softer, tender, as Bella pulled away her hand and hugged me. "I'd like to get you to a helicopter and to a hospital for treatment, IsaBella Morgan."

"And a shower? And my own clothes?"

"I reckon that might be on the agenda for tonight."

"And pizza." Bella held her side as pain writhed through her. I didn't think she'd be allowed a meal anytime soon, but now wasn't the time to mention that. "And I get to keep Rufus," she said, when the spasm passed. "He's coming with us."

"Any dog that protects his owner and master the way he did you, I guess deserves a good home. I'll bring him with me when I come." Caleb glanced at me, his eyes taking in everything, every detail, including the blood at my waist.

Kicking up dirt and dust, the helicopter landed in the higher valley, the chopper blades making the uncertain light flicker, a blue and red glow coming from above, spreading with the sound of voices and men, moving as they took the trail down. Others took up places on the ridge where we had waited.

Caleb put his hat back on, raised his radio and spoke. "This is main tracker Howell One. Our position is to the right of the cabin, behind the small wooden structure. One man and two women. Both women are hit, injuries not life threatening at this time. Request transport to the nearest trauma facility. And would appreciate not being shot."

"I think the SWAT team can arrange that, main tracker Howell One. Evelyn's relaying your message on the channel they're using," Joel said, relief and weariness in his voice. "Come on home, Howell Hasty." Cheers and whistles came over the radio.

"Sounds like a plan. Howell Hasty out."

Caleb slid the radio into the sheath at his waist and smiled again, gestured to the ridge with the hunting rifle in his hand. "We're not finished here just yet. They've holed up in the cabin and the cops are of a mind to make sure they come out tonight and visit the local jail. That's a SWAT team coming in. So if you'll walk in front of me, I'll cover you both until you're on the chopper."

"You're not coming with us?" I asked, falling into step, moving through the darkening night. Behind us, Caleb followed, his rifle at the ready, eyes scanning left and right and behind, back at the cabin.

"Not just yet. But soon." There was a tone in his voice, hard and slashing, that said he wasn't coming in until Dell Gregory was no longer a threat.

"Yeah, soon," Bella said, her voice weak, breathless. "You get to bring the pizza. Right?"

"Sounds like a plan to me. I think we got stories to swap. When you're ready," Caleb said.

"Mama? Where's Daddy?"

My heart gave a small lurch. What could I tell her? That her father was in jail, charged with her kidnapping, except he wasn't the person who was really responsible? "He'll be at the hospital as soon as he can, sweetheart. He misses you." It wasn't a lie. It just wasn't the whole truth.

With Caleb covering our backs, safeguarding us with

his body, we reached the path leading up to the helicopter. I went before her up the meager stairs, extending a hand to help her. In the deepening shadows, it was difficult to find the steps that had been cut into the hillside, shaped of the natural rock, laid with flat shale. I stumbled and levered myself up, and finally we reached the top of the thirty-foot elevation. A cop in SWAT-black pulled me over the ledge, and Caleb boosted Bella up behind me.

He stood below me, his face little more than a blur in the dusky light. "I'll be along directly. How about you two taking care of each other till I get there."

"We will. Thank you," I said, pulling my daughter back under the protection of my arm. "I don't know how to say it any better. Just…thank you."

"My pleasure, ma'am." With the simple words, he slipped away and blended into the night.

"Helo is that way, ma'am, if you'll follow the path," the shadow said at my side. He was visible only as a dark stain in the night, skin shining above and below the greasepaint on his face. "You need me to help you or can you make it on your own?"

I could see the red and blue lights through the fringe of cane. "We can make it. Is the ground cleared of booby traps?"

"I don't know about the area to the sides, but the path is fine. Try not to stray. There's a man positioned about twenty feet in. He knows you're coming through."

"Thank you," Bella said, a half second after I did.

Together we entered the stand of cane, the darkness absolute except for the glaring flashes of blue and red ahead. The shadows were intense. When I glanced up, there was only the concealing foliage, narrow leaves hiding the young moon and a single bright star in the cerulean sky; thick patches of thin cane stalks closed around us.

A darker shadow materialized out of the cane. "Ma'am," he said. "Stick to the path. We've found three separate explosive devices so far and none have been defused. That'll have to wait until morning."

"Thank you," Bella murmured, her body drooping as the certainty of her safety settled in. "Thank you so much," she whispered to me, her breath a warm breeze at my cheek. We moved through the dark, the chopper only yards ahead.

"Belinda."

The word whispered into the night. Cut right through me. Bella gasped, whipped away from me. In one movement, I slid my hand around the butt of the handgun, stepped in front of Bella and pulled the .38. Gripped it in both hands before me, the barrel unwavering, centered on the dark shape sliding through the cane.

"Belinda," Dell breathed, moving into the path, his face a pale blur, as insubstantial as the shadows around him. "It's all right now. I'm here." He reached for Bella, dark on dark, moving as if he didn't see me, as if I wasn't there.

"I'm not going with you!" she said, her voice ragged with fear.

"Belinda." His teeth were a white slash in the dark. "No!"

"Belinda. You know—I told you—no one leaves me." A blade glinted in the faint blue light from ahead. Lifted. "I'm taking you back."

"No one takes what's mine." I fired point-blank into him, squeezing the trigger just as Daddy had taught me, the motion easy and smooth as touching a lover.

Dell staggered back, his eyes rising to me, seeing me. Mouth open, eyes so…bewildered.

And rage lit within me.

He rose up fast, the blade glittering in the blue lights behind him.

"And Bella's *mine*." I fired again, the shot ringing.

Dell Gregory paused, looked down at his shirt in the darkness.

Shouts came from behind.

"And no one will take her unless she's good and ready to go."

Dell screamed, his mouth a black pit. He lunged at me.

I fired again. Last round of a five-shot .38. Counted down as Daddy had commanded.

Dell sank to one knee.

Lights exploded around us. Bodies crashed through the cane. Someone grabbed me from behind, threw me to the ground, ripping the gun from my hand as I spun. I landed with a knee in my back, spine popping.

Ribs cracked again. Bella screamed, "Stop! It's Mama! Mama! Stop!"

The weight on top of me was gone with a faint woof of breath. Knocked aside. Bella fell over me, rolled beside me, gathering me up in her arms. "It's my mama. And if you hurt her I'll—I'll—I'll shoot you myself."

"I'm okay, Bella," I grunted. "He was just doing his job."

The man Bella had crashed into stood slowly. "Sorry, ma'am. In the dark and all you looked like..."

I waved away his words. Holding my bruised ribs, freshly damaged, I rocked into a sitting position. Found Dell in the darkness, a faded mound on the pathway.

A beam of light appeared and focused on him. Feet shuffled closer, enclosing us and a puddle of light in a ring of combat boots. Dell was dressed in jeans, boots and a black shirt, open at the neck. His arms were outstretched, legs bent beneath him. A hunting rifle was on the path beside him, a boot securing it to the earth with its wearer's weight. The knife was still clasped in Dell's fist. Blood, blacker than the shirt, gleamed wetly as his chest rose and fell. It trickled up across the pale flesh to pool in the little notch in his collarbone. His fingers slowly relaxed. The knife fell to the path with a soft thump.

"You okay, Mac?" Caleb asked.

I looked into his eyes, bluer than the night sky, flashing with inner fire. "I'm fine." It surprised me to know it was so.

Bella snuggled under my arm, hugging me too tightly. But I didn't push her away; I wrapped my arms around her and hugged back. I looked up at the man who had tackled me. "We are not going back in the helicopter with him."

The SWAT-team cop, who looked American Indian with dark eyes, ruddy skin above and below black grease streaks, jet-black hair, placed the fingertips of his left hand on Dell's neck. "No, ma'am. You aren't."

"Simon, see that the ladies get on the chopper and are taken to the trauma center. Notify the proper authorities we have a DB at the scene."

"DB?" I asked. "Oh, never mind." I understood. DB. Dead body. Got it. Dell Gregory was dead. By my hand.

"There'll be questions, later, ma'am. I hope you understand."

"Yes. I understand." *I had killed a man. There would be questions.*

Simon helped Bella and me to our feet. When Bella swayed, he plucked her from the path and carried her, stepping over Dell, through the cane to the waiting light. I followed, not looking down.

"Mac?"

I turned to Caleb.

"Try to stay out of trouble and not shoot anyone else till I can get there." There was humor in his tone.

"I can't shoot anyone. They took away my gun."

"Good for them." With a flash of a grin he was gone.

45

We arrived at the hospital, setting down on a landing pad, the sound of the rotors thunderous. Bella was placed on a stretcher by three uniformed nursing personnel and strapped in place, while I was given a wheelchair. Microphones were thrust at us, reporters and cameras in a circle behind—media screaming for the Morgans to tell what had happened.

Together, Bella and I were whisked through the open doors of the hospital, warmth and medicinal smells enveloping us. Bella refused to be separated from me, holding tightly to my hand, her eyes on my face, unwavering. I gripped her just as tightly.

They cut away Bella's clothes and mine and swaddled us in warm blankets, started IVs, took blood and X rays, made us both collect urine samples. Two doctors came and went. A surgeon probed Bella's wound with a metal rod while she squeezed her eyes shut and panted with pain. That was the only time she took her eyes off me as she lay on the stretcher, shaking with shock and the release of almost a week of fear. I let her hold me with her gaze, knowing I was the only fixed point in her world. When he snapped off his latex gloves, the surgeon said, "Lucky girl. Missed everything. Nice clean in and out. Couple of stitches and you'll have a dainty little scar to show your friends."

Bella laughed at that, tears leaking down her face.

The only other words I remembered when my own shock began to wear off, was when a young pretty nurse asked Bella if she had been sexually assaulted.

Bella said, "No. He just tried to beat me to death. Sometimes a curse is a good thing."

I squeezed her hand as she said the words, tears dripping off my chin and jaw in relief that she had been spared that one horror and the indignity of a rape exam after. Of course, Bella had to explain her comment and Dell's abhorrence of the curse, but the story made the nurse smile with amusement, and she patted Bella's shoulder in womanly understanding. A moment of near ecstasy in the dreadful night.

Wednesday
2153 hours

The cops wanted us. Not the SWAT team, but men in ill-fitting suits with notebooks and cameras and tape recorders. I refused to allow them to talk to Bella until she had rest and food, and I knew better than to speak with them myself until I had a lawyer at hand. I had killed a man. Each time I thought about it, an electric current of shock zinged through me. I had killed a man. With a gun.

The Tennessee detectives didn't like my refusal—not that I cared—and tried to talk me into giving a statement. About half an hour into the discussion with law enforcement, Caleb appeared in Bella's room, my knapsack in one hand, a lawyer at his side. The main tracker was a miracle. Seemed to know just what was needed at every turn, and was able to provide it.

"Are you always this prepared?" I asked him over the shoulder of the lawyer, who was shooing the cops out of the room.

"I was a Boy Scout. A soldier. Got two degrees, graduated cum laude. Was a park ranger, then a main tracker." His dark blue eyes gleamed in the fluorescent lights. He had cleaned up, shaved and was wearing clean khakis, loafers, a woven shirt over a T-shirt. A leather jacket hung over one shoulder and a brand-new cowboy hat was pushed back on his head. He looked nothing like the rough and ready main tracker who had taken part in a gun battle only hours before. "Prepared is the only way I know how to be, Mac."

"You should marry the man, Mama," Bella said, reviving the old tease. I started to object, but shadows flitted behind her eyes, the taint left by Dell Gregory marring her soul. Bella was trying. Trying so hard to be the carefree teenager she had been. She blinked the darkness away. "Anyone can see he's hot for you."

"You got a good eye, Bella," Caleb said.

"Is she hot for you, too?"

"IsaBella Morgan!" But I was laughing through my first stirrings of discomfort. This was my baby, irrepressible, even after a kidnapping and six days of terror.

Caleb cocked a brow, placing his hat on the counter at his side. "I'm not too sure about the hot part, but I've done my dead-level best to become indispensable to her."

"You kissed her yet?"

"Bella! Stop—"

"Once or twice. Not enough."

"Are you a photographer?"

"Nope. I can point and click enough to get Christmas photos of my nieces and nephews, but that's about it."

Bella rolled her eyes and gave him the you'll-have-to-do-better-than-that look that all teenage girls have mastered.

"But I do know every square inch of the most beautiful land God ever created and I'm willing to show it to her. And you, too. And I got a dazzling little gray mare, provided we can get back to her before she wanders off. Right now, she's in a little valley in a makeshift pasture with a bunch of stolen horses. But she's a beaut. Ask your mom. Mac rode her."

Bella acted as if she didn't hear the suggestion to include me in the conversation. "Is that a bribe to win the affections of the daughter?"

"Absolutely."

"Oh, for pity's sake," I said.

Bella looked at me. "He's a keeper, Mom."

Once, such words from my daughter would have resulted in embarrassment for me and a quick retort to her. Instead, I looked at Caleb and decided to join what I couldn't hope to defeat. Not completely certain I was only joking, I said, "It's true. I might have to marry you. I have a feeling my daughter would frown on us living in sin."

"*Mom*!" Bella made the word three syllables, as if I had taken the game too far.

"I consider myself properly proposed to, ma'am."

My mouth opened. Closed. "Oh. You do," I managed to retort. My world was changing way too fast. It left me feeling a little woozy.

Thursday
0615 hours

As the sun rose on a new day, Caleb filled me in on the standoff at the cabin in the two-tiered valley. In the hotel bathroom, separated only by a door and ten feet of industrial carpeting, Bella was showering off the blood and filth of a week on the run, her wounds protected by bread bags borrowed from the desk clerk, taped in place.

"The SWAT team threw in canisters of tear gas and after a couple minutes there was movement at the door. There was this white cloth being waved in a flashlight beam in the doorway. Lots of coughing and cursing. The woman wanted to come out and give herself up." Caleb looked at me with calm eyes, still as the ocean beneath the high sun. "It was Gianna Smith." His lips quirked once. "Your snow bunny."

"Not my snow bunny. Marlow's."

"The nurse who took care of Rachael Morgan as she died," he compromised, "living on the fancy estate, under a Hollywood idol's roof, sharing three-star meals with the family, sleeping in a deluxe suite set aside for guests, answering the phone to the press when they got through. Living like she had never lived before. And she never wanted it to end. Think you said that to me once."

This conversation could have waited until later, but the press might find us by then. I needed to be prepared. I rubbed a hand over my face, trying to summon a trickle of energy into my body, finding instead new scrapes, a bloodied lump I didn't remember acquiring, a patch of dried blood. I hadn't looked at myself in a mirror in what felt like days. I probably looked like a corpse. I felt like one. "Yeah. I remember." I also remembered my emotional torment, my anger, my bitterness. All that was gone now. At the moment I was just numb.

"She also cared for Dell Gregory in the mental hospital when he was there. Knew his history, or some if it, anyway," Caleb said.

I settled on one of two plaid chairs in the corner, situated to either side of the small circular table, typical, battered, fake wood. The table was cozied up to the nearest double bed, almost touching its plaid spread—uglier than normal even for hotel room furniture. With the exception of cracked plastic seats in the trailer diner, it was the first time I had sat in a padded chair in days. My body didn't want to bend into the shape. It was too soft. My blisters were too sticky and painful to accept the comfort. And I was too dirty, unwashed beneath the clean shirt retrieved from my small pack. "I recall that from Har Har's report."

"Right. Best as the cops can figure, she gave his name to Burgess. Apparently Gianna and Dell had developed a rapport in the hospital while he was there."

"Sweet of her to offer the name of an unstable psychotic patient to him."

Caleb settled into the other chair, seeming entirely at ease. His hat dropped on the table between us. His eyes were steady, as if watching to make sure I was taking the news in a reasonable frame of mind. As if I might somehow be...dangerous.

I recoiled from the image of Dell lying in the dark, the SWAT team leader's fingers at his throat. Closed my eyes against the vision. I guess after a woman shoots a man three times, kills him and leaves him lying in the dirt, it could make another man a bit nervous to provoke her. I looked down at my hands. Filth and blood were still ground beneath my nails, into my cuticles.

Caleb continued. "I don't know who had the idea first, her or Burgess, but they cooked up a plan to get you and Bella out of the way. Take the inheritance for themselves.

"We got all this later, Mac. At the time, all we knew was Gianna wanted to give herself up. Cops told her to put her hands on her head and walk toward them real slow. Musta been fifty guns trained on the cabin, counting Jedidiah and me. But she walked out of the cabin like God himself gave her the power. Burgess crawled out onto the porch after her, screaming, guns in both hands.

He was yelling that she betrayed him." A faint smile flitted across Caleb's face. "He was in shock from the lacerations on his face and a gunshot wound to his shoulder, but he was still making sense." The almost-smile tightened the flesh of his cheeks. "Nice shot, by the way. For a lady who can't and won't use a gun."

When I said nothing to that, Caleb went on, his voice gentle, the same tone he had used to calm the skittish horse after the explosion. "She was shoutin' that Burgess set up the whole thing. Burgess was yelling that she'd set it all up, that it was her idea. Then he called her some names, the most polite being slut. Seems she was doing both brothers."

"That's a lovely turn of phrase."

"Fits. She sure wasn't making love to them both. I don't think love was in there anywhere."

"Good point." I squirmed on the cheap foam of the chair seat. I could smell myself as I moved. I had the next shower. If Bella left any hot water in the entire hotel.

"While they were busy laying blame, two cops rushed in and took control of Gianna. One group began negotiating with Burgess to give up. While they were haggling, Jedidiah and I made a deal with the SWAT team helicopter pilot to drop us off at the horses. We brought them down to the pasture with Dell's animals and made it back to the valley just in time to take off with the SWAT team. Once the cops finished with us, we cleaned up and here I am."

I had forgotten about Jedidiah and Big Bertha. Forgotten about the horses saddled and hobbled on the mountaintop. There were so many things I needed to remember, needed to do. Exhaustion, like a peculiar tremor, tickled at the back of my mind. Fearing I might fall apart if I moved wrong or coughed or sneezed, I pushed it away. "How are Jed and Big B?"

"Being treated to a steak dinner and a six-pack of Bud back at the ICP. Where Marlow just finished a press conference."

"Oh, no. Please tell me he didn't." I closed my eyes again. *Oh, Marlow…*

"He did. A fine portrayal of the outraged, innocent man, the abused father, the husband deceived by a marriage-breaking Jezebel. The brother betrayed by a back-stabbing Cain, who dyed his hair and set up false evidence, including dressing and acting like Marlow for a meeting with the psychotic man he hired. Reformed and penitent. A man who will do anything to get his family back."

"While he takes up the financial reins of the Morgan empire?" I asked, my lids still closing out the world.

"There were hints of something like that. You thinking of taking him back?"

"No way. Never." I smiled tiredly. "Besides, I proposed to this main tracker I've known less than a week, didn't I?"

Caleb pulled my hands apart and touched my chin, trying to get me to open my eyes. When I finally sighed and let him have his way, he said, "I think we'll put that one on the back burner awhile. I'd like to start out by taking you to a movie. One of those silly little love stories that always make women cry. Maybe dinner at a restaurant, a place where we can eat at a table not covered by plastic cloths."

"Just a table and chairs would be a novelty."

Caleb smiled, that special smile that seemed to blaze up from within. His hands were hot on mine, on my chin where one finger still rested. I wondered what it would feel like to curl up around him on a cold winter night. Pushed that thought away quickly, but saw an answering heat in his gaze.

"Dinner would be nice. Tablecloths? Cloth napkins? A place where I could wear a dress and heels? Perfume that has some other scent besides eau de horse, dog and unwashed female?"

He nodded. "Good." And I thought he was speaking about something more than dinner. Moving like a well-oiled machine, limber and lithe, Caleb stood and settled his hat on his head. "I took the room next door. You need anything, or the press comes knocking in the night, just bang on the door."

"Thank you. Thank you for not giving up. Even when Joel told you to come back in." Tears I had repressed for hours spilled over in a torrent, casting the ugly hotel room into bright plaid blurs.

I felt heat on my lips for a moment, only a moment, and he was gone.

Epilogue

August
1600 hours

I climbed from the air-conditioned Bronco into the dripping humidity and ninety-nine degree heat and wandered across the lawn to the four-rail, white-painted fence that enclosed the pasture. I was in jeans, a T-shirt and western boots, a new F4 Nikon slung around my neck like an oversize bauble on a leather cord. Propping one foot on the lowest rail, I rested both arms on the top rail, my chin in my hands.

In the pasture, Bella rode Wicked, a bloodred standardbred stallion with four black socks, black mane and tail. He was a flashy beast, sixteen and a half hands high, with a flowing, easy gait and the ability and desire to jump anything Bella pointed him at. For a stud, he was remarkably good-tempered, wanting to please my daughter almost as much he wanted to cover any female horse within ten miles of our home.

Together, they flew over a three rail jump, followed one stride later by a difficult water hazard. They were a fluid, single organism, muscle, heart and purpose balanced in one elegant moment of flight.

My baby was preparing for a steeplechase event, a

local show put on by the white-glove-and-lace-hat crowd. And Bella was determined to win. Not just place—win. Typical, unbroken Bella. Only she and I— and her therapist—knew of the night terrors from which she woke, screaming. But less often now. Only once a week or so, not every night. The fear of Dell Gregory was fading into dull memory.

I glanced at my watch, the same watch I had worn on the SAR clipped to a belt loop. Along with Bella's water-wrinkled and bloodstained note—which was framed over my bed—the watch was my good luck piece. Photographs of Bella taken before Dell entered our lives, and immediately after I found her, were framed and hanging all over the house, too.

Wicked took another jump, the motion effortless, and Bella laughed as they landed, carefree delight in the tones. Our lives were changed forever. But we were getting back to some semblance of normalcy, and the laugh was evidence of that. Not that the cops were entirely satisfied with everything.

Tennessee law enforcement had wanted to hold me for questioning and possible charges, until a political official running for re-election—and feeling the heat from women's groups and domestic abuse political action groups and lobbyists—pulled a halt to it all. The media attention helped, of course. After all, Bella was Rachael Morgan's granddaughter. And heir. And the clear victim of a mentally unbalanced man, along with her hero mother. The lawyer Marlow had hired to represent the Morgans' interests had pulled all the emotional and legal stops he could find. And for once I hadn't protested.

Back in North Carolina, Har Har had never determined who had riffled through the evidence locker at the sheriff's department and sent me my few belongings, including the .38. I was betting on Rick, the multitalented

EMT who partnered Ruth. But I'd never ask. The .38 had saved my life and Bella's. I owed a debt to the thief.

Adin was well, having recuperated quickly with the resilience of youth. Even with only one kidney and half his liver gone, he was up and riding. He had called several times and had met Bella when we went back for the Tennessee hearing that cleared my name. Both Adin and Yo had been at the party in the SAR headquarters after the hearing. I had brought in steaks and beer for the entire SAR contingent. Yo ate with her left hand now, and depended on the kindness of her friends to cut her meat and butter her bread. She had undergone three surgeries to save the circulatory system in her hand, to repair the tendons damaged by the bullet and insert a new nerve taken from her lower leg. It would be another eight months before we could tell if the nerve implant had worked, but the surgeon had high hopes that she would regain at least partial use of her hand. For now, Yo was contemplating retirement from the park service when she reached her twenty years, and was taking physical therapy while looking for a new career, possibly in teaching.

I rested my chin back in my hands. I had half an hour before I had to go inside, shower, change and primp for my date. Caleb was punctual. If I wanted to be pretty for him, I'd have to be on time, too. I was still trying to replace his memory of me as battered, bruised, bloody and reeking, with the real me—clean, wearing makeup, a dress and heels.

It seemed to be working. He'd proposed. I figured if he could reconcile the Mac he'd known on the SAR with the MacKenzie Morgan I'd shown him since, perhaps he really did love me. Just me. Just as I am.

I was considering saying yes. Bella had already done so for me, of course. They were conspirators. Planning our futures together.

A red dog trotted out of the barn, crossed under the fence and sat by my feet, his tongue lolling from one side of his mouth. "Good afternoon, Rufus," I said. The mutt huffed hello, his eyes amused. I bent and scratched his head.

Marlow? He was out of my life. A beaten animal. Cowed by his time in jail and the reaction of the media to the kidnapping and to his affair. Yet, in many ways, my limp duck was unchanged. He already had a new girl-friend, another blonde, tall and statuesque, with bought-and-paid-for double-D boobs. Nothing new there.

And me? I was changed beyond recognition. Was nothing like the woman I had been before Bella was kidnapped—afraid of my own shadow, terrified of being alone. That had been sliced out of me by the events in the mountains on a search and rescue that had already made the SAR training manuals as an ex-ample of how to deal with a case that goes to hell in a handbasket.

I was cauterized by death and the memory of Dell's face as he fell, my bullets in his chest. There wasn't a pho-tograph. But I'd never forget it. Never.

Bella and Wicked cleared the last jump in a fluid movement so clean and purely athletic that it appeared to be almost slow motion, the horse's black mane and tail rippling out behind, his bloodred coat sliding over mus-cles like velvet over steel. At a slow trot, horse and rider crossed over to me and came to rest at the fence.

"Well?" Bella asked.

"Pure art. Pure perfection. If the judges don't give you first place then they are blind or being paid on the sly," I said promptly.

"Well, of course. But I meant, well, can we have a Christmas wedding, or are you still going to be an ass?"

I dropped my head to my hands on the top rail and

banged it twice. "I'm thinking about it, IsaBella Angeleena Morgan. And *ass* is not a nice word."

"An ass is an equine known for its stubborn attitude, but unflagging energy. If you were an equine, you'd be an ass." Her expression was sublime. And how could I counter? My baby was right.

"I love you, IsaBella," I said, as I did every time I saw her.

"I know you do. I never doubt that. And I love you, too," she replied, her own statements always repeated verbatim. With them, she turned the huge red stallion to the barn and moved away, holding him to a slow walk.

I had a Sunday school teacher once, years ago, when I was young, who told me that for each of us there existed a reason, an event, that could cause us to do violence. To take another life.

I never believed her. Until now.

Now I know.

Deep in the dark heart of each of us lies a primitive soul. A soul dedicated to blood and the taking of life. I killed to protect, to save. And if God is watching, perhaps that is my only absolution.

Author's Note

I had a ball writing this novel! It is a romp, an adventure, and intended to be just plain fun! While the location is set near the tri-state area of North Carolina, Tennessee and Georgia, I borrowed liberally from all across the Appalachian Mountains for features, trails and interesting sites to write about.

There are state and national parks in the area and I used bits and pieces of several and blended methods of Search and Rescue and law enforcement, all of which differ in each state, county, park, etc. I also changed some terminology to make things easier to follow and understand for my city-dwelling readers. If there are errors in the methods used here, the responsibility is mine alone, not the fault of the able SAR volunteers and park service rangers who helped with technical questions.

Horse trails exist in abundance in the mountains and many parks do allow horses to track in. If you haven't been on a horse excursion just ask the National Park Service for places to drop your horses and take off, or search the Web for good dependable private businesses to take you and your family into the near wilderness.

Thanks for reading!

Gwen

If you enjoyed what you just read,
then we've got an offer you can't resist!

Take 2 bestselling novels FREE!
Plus get a FREE surprise gift!

GWEN HUNTER

32006	GRAVE CONCERNS	___ $6.50 U.S.	___ $7.99 CAN.
66916	PRESCRIBED DANGER	___ $6.50 U.S.	___ $7.99 CAN.
66803	DELAYED DIAGNOSIS	___ $5.99 U.S.	___ $6.99 CAN.

(limited quantities available)

TOTAL AMOUNT	$_____
POSTAGE & HANDLING	$_____
($1.00 for one book; 50¢ for each additional)	
APPLICABLE TAXES*	$_____
TOTAL PAYABLE	$_____

(check or money order—please do not send cash)

To order, complete this form and send it, along with a check or money order for the total above, payable to MIRA Books, to: **In the U.S.:** 3010 Walden Avenue, P.O. Box 9077, Buffalo, NY 14269-9077; **In Canada:** P.O. Box 636, Fort Erie, Ontario L2A 5X3.

Name:_____

Address:_____ City:_____

State/Prov.:_____ Zip/Postal Code:_____

Account Number (if applicable):_____

075 CSAS

   *New York residents remit applicable sales taxes.
    Canadian residents remit applicable GST and provincial taxes.

MIRA®

www.MIRABooks.com   MGH0105BL